THE LEGACY OF MARSHALL COUSINS

FOR THE LOVE OF ADVENTURE CHRONICLES BOOK 2

Z.A. ANGELL

CONTENTS

DRAMATIS PERSONAE

Among nobility in France circa the 1700s, the family name differed from the titular name (Francis de Brangelton, Comte de Tournelles). The titular name took precedence over family name. For the clarity of the narration, the family name is omitted when a titular name exists (Comte Francis de Tournelles).

Even among close acquaintances, Monsieur, Madame, and Mademoiselle were commonly used in regular speech, and are abbreviated as M., Mme., *and* Mlle. *in the written text.*

Main Characters

Henri de Brangelton - *nobleman from Ferrand*

Charlotte de Brangelton, a.k.a "Charles" – *Henri's younger sister*

Francis de Brangelton, Comte de Tournelles* – *father of Henri and Charlotte*

Henrietta de Brangelton, Comtesse de Tournelles* – *mother of Henri and Charlotte*

Antoine de la Fleure, Comte de Flancourt* - *nobleman from Lyon*

Raoul de la Fleure – *Antoine's younger brother*

Bertrand de la Norte – *nobleman in Paris*

Maurice de Tavoisier, Marquis de Ternille* - *nobleman in Paris*

Andrew Marshall – *adventurer from New World, cousin to Harold*

Harold Marshall - *adventurer from New World, cousin to Andrew*

Honore de Courbet - *Knight of the Order of St. John*

Rene Prassal – *Head of Household Staff and Confidant to Marquis de Ternille*

Oliver Durrant – *conspirator in league with Rene Prassal*

Mathew Johnson - *Owner/Captain of* Golden Sails

Supporting Characters

Ferrand

Red Jacques – *in Comte de Tournelles' service*

Captain de Molienier – *member of French Calvary*

Lyon

Laurent de la Fleure, Comte de Chatreaux* - *father of Antoine and Raoul*

Marguerite de la Fleure, Comtesse de Chatreaux* - *mother of Antoine and Raoul*

Armand –*Antoine's valet*

Louis de Boucher – *nobleman.*

Guy de Boucher – *Louis' younger brother.*

Orleans

Comte de Chambreau – *nobleman*

Guy de Brault – *nephew to Comte de Chambreau*

Jeanne de Chaudat – *cousin to Guy de Brault*

Vincent Bourzat – *painter*

Paris

Cecilia de la Mareils, Marquise de Fabvre* – *sister of Bertrand de la Norte*

Jean-Paul de la Norte, Marquis de Louiviers* – *father of Bertrand and Cecilia*

De Rousard; de Rameau; d'Signac; de Bonnard - *Royal Musketeers*

Geoffrey de Contraille - *noblemen*

De Chassigneau; de Vergne; Comte de Bearteau; d'Chantal – *noblemen and courtiers*

Anaïs de Cuisse – *noblewoman*

Cybille; Gabrielle; Eloise – *noblewomen of Henri de Brangelton's close personal acquaintance*

France

Duke Collingstone - *peer of England, alias Lord Nelson*

Lord Stevenson - *Head of Duke Collingstone's entourage*

Captain de Varbes; Lieutenant de Clouet; Lieutenant de Lauzon - *of French Army*

Daniel Rabatin - *owner of warehouse in Le Havre*
Marcoux - *Commandant of Marseille Harbor*

D'Arouet – *fencing master in Montpellier*

PROLOGUE

LYON, FRANCE – JULY 1707

Adventure is my mistress;
I am always at her command.

Francis de Brangelton to Henrietta d'Arringnon - 1694

"The Great Mogul Diamond is the largest diamond in existence," Laurent de la Fleure, Comte de Chatreaux read aloud from *The Six Voyages of Jean Baptiste de Tavernier*. "The only Western record of it exists here." He handed the book to Francis de Brangelton, Comte de Tournelles.

His old friend held the diamond to the light. He examined the illustration, glancing back and forth between the fortune in his hand and the page in the book. "This must be it." He tossed the diamond to Laurent and leaned back, absorbed in reading.

Laurent eyed the clear sparkling jewel in the light. It matched the description perfectly: the right size and shape, the surfaces cut in the same way as the one shown in the book, and

1

almost colorless. There could be no mistake. *"Only de Brangelton,"* Laurent marveled. What were the chances of anyone else accidentally discovering and appropriating the Indian Great Mogul Diamond in the New World?! "Is your curiosity satisfied?" he asked over his shoulder.

"Who moved this diamond to the New World? How could he, and why would he? I am certain its sanctuary in the ruins was granted recently, but when exactly?" De Brangelton flipped through the pages of the book. "Keep this sparkler for me till I find out more about its previous ownership, will you?"

Laurent sat down and flattened a sheet of paper. *"I, Laurent de la Fleure, Comte de Chatreaux, solemnly and in sound mind stand witness that the diamond described below and contained within this package is the rightful property of Francis de Brangelton..."* He diligently recorded the deed, signed it, set his seal to the top and bottom of the page, and left the page to dry. He polished the diamond on his sleeve. "You don't mind if I show this jewel to Marguerite, do you?"

"As long as she promises to keep it secret." The sly reply started an unexpected sea of memories for Laurent. A dozen years had passed since Marguerite's arrival to Paris had triggered a chain of events which led him, a Lieutenant of His Royal Musketeers, to quit the regiment, return home to Lyon, and settle into marital bliss. His peaceful civic existence was continuously enhanced by participation in the creative activities hatched by his friends, mostly de Brangelton, whose recent adventure to New World deposited his children, Henri and Charlotte, with Laurent and Marguerite for a year. Henri was a year younger than Antoine, and Charlotte was a year older than Raoul. The quartet always kept Laurent and Marguerite on their toes. Laurent became aware of the children's voices drifting from outside and leaned out of the window, just in time to witness the beginning of a commotion between Raoul and

Charlotte. Even at her tender age of seven, the girl was willful, clever, adventurous, and reckless, and Raoul was mortified by the mere thought of failing to keep up with her. His fears were mercilessly exploited and fueled by Antoine and Henri - these two young miscreants found endless entertainment in no-holds-barred competition between their younger siblings.

Right now, Antoine and Henri were arbitrating a game of tug-of-war between the arguing youngsters. Raoul had a slight advantage of pure strength, and he used it to tug hard on the rope. Charlotte toppled forward, her toe barely touching the dividing line, but her sudden move caused Raoul to struggle for his balance. She took the advantage and jerked the rope back. Raoul stumbled forward and his bare toe landed on the line. The older boys hooted.

"You cheated!" Hands on hips, Raoul glared at Charlotte.

"I did not!" She mirrored his posture.

"You are a weasel!" Raoul articulated his unrefined opinion.

"You are a lout!" Charlotte, unburdened by the concept of nicety, readily retorted.

"Shrew!"

"Dung beetle!"

At that shot, Raoul failed to find a suitable response and unceremoniously shoved the girl backwards. She reciprocated. He pushed her again. Charlotte took a swing at him. In a heart-beat, the two were rolling on the ground. The older brothers half-heartedly commanded them to stop and were duly ignored. They finally separated the fighting parties before either one landed a punch on the other.

"You are..."

Henri's hand over Charlotte's mouth cut off her endeavor to quarrel.

Antoine twisted Raoul's arm behind him and waited till his

younger brother stopped struggling. He released the boy and jostled him away from Charlotte. Raoul stomped away with an air of righteous indignation. Henri nudged Charlotte in the opposite direction. The older boys suspiciously watched Raoul and Charlotte till the combatants reached the opposite sides of the yard.

"Is my girl finished exchanging pleasantries with your son?" de Brangelton asked.

"Add yet another trivial scuffle to their affectionate history. I appreciate your desire to make certain your strong-headed girl is capable of self-defense, but I wish my younger son was less willing to tussle with her." Laurent turned away from the window.

"I stand in awe at how excellently Antoine and Henri have perfected the skill of blaming Charlotte for all their mischief. They experimented with gunpowder because Charlotte wanted to see an explosion. They snuck out to ride at night to prove to Charlotte they are not afraid of the darkness. They lost track of time and thus failed to present themselves to our visitors because Charlotte insisted on tracking a magpie. They stripped Raoul to the breeches and painted him - and his breeches - in war colors like a New World savage and made him run across the wood clearing to the accompaniment of drum beat and these war-yells you taught them. Stop laughing. This performance happened to take place during the formal reception at our neighbors' garden facing the aforementioned wood clearing. Some young heads gathered to give chase, and I felt obligated to advise on strategy. Thus the performers safely reached home. When Marguerite and I arrived, Antoine and Henri were frantically scrubbing the paint off Raoul. Washing the soot out of Raoul's hair took three baths –and yes, his hair was darkened for the occasion. Our fine boys did not miss a single detail. Did I mention that the little savage brandished the spoils of a fake scalping? One of my household horses is missing half a tail. And the reason for this escapade? Charlotte dared Raoul. Upon hearing that explanation, I could barely keep a straight face, and merely sent them all out of my sight without even a lecture on their unacceptable behavior."

Tours, France - May 1710

Under the ominous gray clouds, the fine foggy mist enveloped the streets, and the murky dusk descended much faster than Henrietta de Brangelton had expected. People hurried indoors before the rain fell, and Henrietta cut through the narrow alley behind St. Martin's Basilica to shorten the trip. She and her daughter were halfway down the lane when two seedy-looking men stumbled toward them. The daylight was almost extinguished and the street was deserted. Every building had closed their shutters in anticipation of the rain. Henrietta glanced back. No one behind her, which meant no ambush was likely to be forthcoming, And yet, the relative safety of the busy street, filled with witnesses, was too far.

She put a protective arm around her daughter's shoulders. *"Stay behind me and out of their reach,"* she whispered to Charlotte and steered to the left, keeping her daughter between herself and the wall. If these men meant trouble, they would try to surround them. Henrietta slipped her hand to the slit in her skirts and closed her fingers around the hilt of her small sword.

The men leered at her with bleary eyes and slouched against the wall.

Henrietta tensed in anticipation of confrontation. "If there is a fight, run forward onto the street and head home. I will catch up with you," she instructed her daughter, who fearlessly, even appraisingly, stared at the men. Fortunately, the men ignored the child as they focused on disengaging themselves from the supporting wall. "It's a fine evening, Madame," one of them said with a malicious sneer when only a few paces separated them.

Henrietta steeled herself for action and confidently strode forward.

"Will you join us for the celebration, Madame?" the second man slurred.

Henrietta pretended to tighten her left arm around Charlotte's shoulders, aware she might be forced to make her daughter run. "Move out of my way," she commanded and continued to march forward.

The men startled at the unexpected notes of authority in her voice. They warily looked around, but recovered from surprise at the moment her path aligned with them. "That was unfriendly, Madame. Is your daughter...?" The first man reached for Charlotte.

Henrietta's caution transformed into intense fury. She nudged the girl forward and backhanded the man with her right hand. His feet lost contact with the ground, and Henrietta used that split-second advantage to follow through with a heavy punch into his temple with her left arm, throwing her whole weight into the swing. The second man belatedly attempted to seize her hand, but the crumbled body of his friend collided into him. Henrietta used that moment of confusion to draw her small sword and faced the second adversary who, with an effort and copious obscenities, finally untangled himself from his collapsed friend. He blinked at the sight of the steel and fumbled for his weapon. Henrietta swept her blade in front of his face and advanced. His widened eyes focused on the point of her sword. He recoiled and flattened himself against the wall. Henrietta held the sharp blade against the side of his throat, under his jaw. He still frantically fumbled to untangle his sword. He was not sober enough to comprehend that he was completely on her mercy. With her left hand, Henrietta deployed a solid punch into his jaw, perfectly timed with the removal of the edge of her blade from his neck. His head bounced off the hard wall with a thickening thud as he slumped forward and slid down to his friend on the muddy ground.

The alley remained deserted. Henrietta concealed her weapon and, tightly holding Charlotte's hand, ran onto the main street to blend into a thinning crowd of hurrying citizens. She glanced over her shoulder, both men remained motionless heaps. "*Serves them right,*" Henrietta fumed. "*In fact, the one who reached for Charlotte should be grateful I did not kill him ...*"

"No one witnessed the clash." Charlotte was perfectly calm. "I watched the windows. Nobody peeked. No one was in the street either."

Henrietta's stride faltered for a moment. "Not a word about it outside the family, Charlotte. I just injured two men, and I don't care to justify my actions to the city magistrate."

A reckless grin, just like her father's, spread across the girl's face. "Mother, did you figure these bastards meant trouble before they spoke to you?" Charlotte had inherited her father's expressive dark blue eyes, his slim build, his agility and grace, his disregard for danger, his thirst for adventure, and, thankfully, his quick wit. Unfortunately, she also had a tendency to repeat his vocabulary, although she knew better than to use such language in company.

"We will talk at home." Henrietta held onto a weak hope that she would not have to explain her militant tactics, but she knew her daughter. Charlotte would not abandon the subject until all her questions were answered. They reached their lodgings without any further incidents just as the first rain drops fell. A few minutes later, Francis, Henri and the surrounding fumes of rum and smoke entered the room only few moments ahead of the violent downpour.

"Our son discovered his limits of rum consumption," Francis released his grip of Henri's collar. Their son was as tall as his father, and this fine fourteen-year-old young man swayed and held on to the wall. His smile was a vacant reflection of the rum-induced swirling chaos in his mind. Francis kissed Henrietta on the cheek, kissed Charlotte on the top on her head, and positioned himself by the fireplace. He shook his head when Charlotte headed toward the settee in the middle of the room. She retreated back to the fireplace, and they all watched Henri with unbridled amusement. Henri did not move from the spot Francis had left him.

"Henri, my boy, sleep the rum off," the father advised the son with a wide grin.

Henri slowly and unsteadily wobbled toward the stairs, but collided into the wall. He frowned at the settee, lurched himself towards it, and collapsed face down. He lay still before raising his head and clawing his way to a seated position, leaning forward to pull off his boots. He barely caught himself from falling down on his face and attempted to lie down. He realized that his short sword was between him and the back of the settee. His fingers gripped the backrest of the settee as he worked his way again to a sitting position and then carefully lay down on his other side, his sword dragging on the floor. Upon completing these intricate movements, Henri immediately fell asleep.

"He is a very practical young man." Francis proudly winked at Henrietta and focused his attention to Charlotte. "What news are you bursting to share, my girl?"

To the accompaniment of Henri's soft snoring, Charlotte's

delivered a detailed account of the altercation. The account was complete with unnervingly exact demonstrations of Henrietta's moves.

"Why are you upset tonight?" Francis unerringly read Henrietta's mind when they retired to their sleeping room. "Punching out a couple pisspots, who – mind you, deserved it! - cannot possibly bother your conscience."

"I can hardly believe Charlotte's lack of fear! Did she even comprehend the danger? Or is she unable to obey? Take your choice!" Henrietta shared her exasperation with her husband. "I instructed her to run if there was a scuffle. Did she do that? No! There were no signs of fear, Francis. For a moment there, I was concerned that she would jump in the fray to assist me!..." Henrietta trailed off. "I was terrified to see her exposed to danger."

Her husband was unperturbed. "I assume her account of the skirmish was accurate."

"It was a precise military report!" Henrietta paced back and forth in time to the beat of the heavy rain ranging outside. "But she is only ten years old, Francis."

"She has confidence in you, my dear. Charlotte is wise beyond her years. She has an excellent sense of self-preservation. After all, the girl inherited your determination and de Brangelton blood." He pulled Henrietta into an embrace. "Now hold still while I untie your laces."

"Good morning, father, mother." Charlotte sat at the breakfast table. She had parted her thick, straight black hair in the middle and evenly combed it into the shape of a hood. "And a very fine morning to you, brother. Is your head all clear?" She ignored his incredulous stare.

"What did you do to yourself?!" Henri croaked.

"I look more like mother this way," Charlotte explained. "I will be just like her when I grow up."

Henri rolled his eyes.

Francis smiled indulgently at his girl. "Your mother devoted time and effort to become the extraordinary woman she is today."

"What do I have to do, father?" Charlotte, oblivious to the platter of food in front of her, eagerly asked.

"Learn to pass for a boy."

"I had no choice!" Henrietta interjected. Her husband, the man known as *devil de Brangelton* among the adventurers and cutthroats in all of France and outside its borders as far as the New World, was wrapped around the little finger of their daughter, and he unreservedly encouraged her to do anything she pleased.

Charlotte glanced in her direction. "I can do that," she responded to her father.

"I doubt it." Henri rubbed his temples.

His sister frowned at him. "Being a boy is easy."

Henri dropped his face into his hands. "You have no idea," he raised his head. "Just how will you accomplish that?"

Charlotte waved her arm in a dismissive gesture. "I will behave like you."

"Stop it," Henri moaned. "I have a headache, so do not compound it with your daft whims. Don't even think about it."

"Don't worry, I will never admire girls as you do." Charlotte waved a spoon at him.

"*Just how much does she understand?*" Henrietta wondered again. Henri was at ease in any company. In fact, he lacked any sense of shame or embarrassment, and his amorous behavior among the young women, and even the older ones, had already caused neighbors to have concerns about their own daughters. "*He is on his way to ripen into a distinguished womanizer, maybe even worse than my brother,*" Francis had gloomily predicted.

"I dread the day when you start to admire boys," Henri replied.

Charlotte picked up a slice of buttered bread from her plate. "This will never happen. There is nothing to admire about them," she declared.

Her brother snorted.

"I certainly hope she feels this way for a few more years," Henrietta silently prayed.

St. Domingue, New World – June 1712

Captain Mathew Johnson appraised the pathetic and scrawny carcass of the man in front of him. The gaunt face bore a slight resemblance to the fanatic who had escaped from him years ago, but there was no recognition, no comprehension, and no intelligence in the hollow eyes. The tropical sun mercilessly beamed down on his scrawny body covered with filthy rags, the warm breeze blew his dirty hair into his dark face, and the insects buzzed around his face, but the man did not seem to notice. He stood still as a statue.

"What is this?" Mathew asked the Governor. "I am searching for the Indian warrior, and this is a vagabond."

"When he disembarked on my island, he was dressed like a Maharaja. Jewels on his turban and sword hilt." The Governor fanned himself with a silk handkerchief. "Then he dismantled that cursed house and lost his reason."

"What cursed house?" Mathew moved into the sparse shade of a palm tree. The Governor followed his example, but the vagabond remained standing in the same spot.

"Have you not heard? An evil spirit moved into the abandoned house. The house itself, it stood over...over there," he said as he pointed to the heap of rubble. "The most terrible howls arose from that house day and night. No one dared to approach that ghastly place..." He took off his hat and fanned himself.

Mathew followed his example. The heat was unbearable. "So what happened?"

"One day, the howling just stopped. Some young hot heads decided to investigate. And there he was." The Governor gestured at the vagabond before continuing, "He was scrambling through the remnants of a fireplace with his bare hands and screaming in his savage language."

"Does he speak English?"

"He spoke it well enough before he lost his mind in these ruins." The Governor poked the man in the ribs with his walking stick. "He just repeats a few phrases now."

The vagabond's body twitched, but his eyes remained void. "Mountain of Light," he wailed. "It's God's wrath. My Sacred Oath."

The Governor pushed back his wig. "We threatened him with torture, offered a bribe, filled him with liquor, but nothing worked to loosen his tongue. That's all he says."

This shadow of a man could indeed be bloody Kumaryan; there was a distant resemblance. Was he pretending or had he gone mad indeed? "How long ago did it happen?"

"About a year." The Governor fanned himself with both his hat and stained handkerchief. "He has been searching through the rubble ever since. He moves stones back and forth and digs in the dirt."

Mathew stepped back into the shade. "How does he survive?"

"People here are kind-hearted. They are thankful to him for destroying the house and expelling that spirit." He pointed at an old jug and cracked wooden plate on the ground. "Some bring him food. These howls were frightening..."

"Where did the spirit go?" Mathew watched the vagabond carefully. Why would a warrior pretend to be mad on this forsaken island?

The Governor plopped his hat back on his head. "The priests say that the spirit went away when this infidel destroyed the house, but his madness is the spirit's revenge." He clenched his hands together. "I pray for him to leave my island."

"Buy his passage to England, and I will take him there." Mathew seized his chance.

"Why would anyone want him there?" The Governor forgot his prayer.

"The doctors at Oxford University might be interested in examining him."

The Governor contemplated the prospect. "You should pay me."

"What happened to his jeweled turban and sword?"

"How would I know?" The Governor sounded indignant, but Mathew would wager that the jewels were divided between the curious hot heads and the Governor.

"I might lose him at sea, or the doctors may not bother with his sorry hide, but either way I have to feed him during the voyage," Mathew reasoned.

The Governor shook his head. "You can take him off my island for a case of French Burgundy wine."

"You pay his passage to England, plus give me a barrel of rum," Mathew bargained. "In case this crazy spirit leaves his body and moves to someone else's during the voyage."

Dalmatia - July 1712

· · ·

13

Honore de Courbet had served as a Knight of St. John's order for nearly 20 years. He had begun his career as a young warrior on a ship sailing the Mediterranean Sea to protect the Christians from heretics, to protect Western trade from infidel raids, and to promote himself in the world. He was respected and trusted, his dedication and reputation were beyond doubt and reproach, and he was rewarded with a task to negotiate the acquisition of St. Elias' relics from a dysfunctional monastery of the Byzantine church in Dalmatia. Honore had spent the past two years in that God-forsaken place, had patiently endured long and winding discourses, had watched, waited, and maneuvered his way among the riddles and lies, and was finally in full possession of St. Elias' skull and two rib bones, securely arranged in a small casket with a glass top. He had not taken his eyes from the bundle since the Archdeacon had closed the lid, sealed it, and had it wrapped in a thick cloth and transferred to Honore. To protect it further, Honore hid the casket inside a nondescript cargo trunk, and stored it in his room.

Honore patted the verification papers in his pocket, opened the cargo trunk, and unwrapped the cloth to once again behold the sacred acquisition for the Knights of St. John. He was not certain of his superiors' plans to house St. Elias' relics. The powers from Tours, Rouen, and Reims were willing to pray and pay for the privilege, but Honore had his own agenda: Bourges.

Honore once again admired the craftsmanship of the artisans who made the casket. The construction was solid and surely no one could touch the relics without breaking the seal, but the mosaic of glass windows on the lid afforded one the chance to view the contents inside the casket. The lock and seal would be broken when the relics were delivered, in order to retrieve the authentication papers inside. The papers inside were identical to the ones in his pocket. He prayed for his success. He braced himself to avoid falling under any suspicion by his superiors in the Knights of St. John, to never allow them to suspect that he was forcing their hand to grant these relics to St. Etienne's Cathedral in Bourges. However, he was confident of himself and his allies within the Church.

He lingered in his prayer, in his gratitude to the providence for his formal instructions. His suggestion to conduct the transfer of relics to France in a completely anonymous manner had been accepted. While St. John's elders and Church officials would officially negotiate which city was the most worthy to possess St. Elias' relics, the relics would be delivered to Marseille and would be stored in Montpellier.

That's when the most delicate part of the deal would occur. Upon disembarking French soil, Honore would send a quiet word to his contact in Bourges. The cardinal, on pretense of research at the University, would come to Montpellier, accidentally discover the relics, and claim St. Elias' relics for St. Etienne's Cathedral.

Honore crossed himself and carefully wrapped the cloth around the casket again. He cushioned it with straw on the bottom, and, to protect the casket from shifting inside, he used his personal assets - five rolls of silk, two Persian rugs, and four large bedcovers that had been embroidered in India. He bundled his clothing to protect his other treasures - the small paintings of St. Stephen and St. John inside a double frame of gold, enamel, and pearls; the gilded bowl and salt and pepper set decorated with rubies and sapphires; the silver tray with six matching plates; two porcelain vases from the Orient; a fine Venetian crystal decanter and six glasses; an onyx and ivory chess set in a rosewood box; and five bags of hashish and opium. These herbs helped him to hear God when God spoke to him.

Marseille, France - August 1712

. . .

Rene Prassal had begun his life as an honest man, but he failed to comprehend the subject of his studies for the law, and thus he drifted in his youth, earning his living alternatively the best he could manage. In his checkered youth, he had been a warehouse clerk, a soldier, a courier, a coachman, an armed escort, and even the manager of a boarding house, until finally good luck – and his father's connections - brought him to his current master's employment. This position paid well. At first his duties were straightforward - he was only responsible for the young nobleman's comfort and general provisions for the household. The future seemed promising and secure. When the young Marquis had come into his position and inheritance, Rene's duties had expanded to cleaning up the Marquis' messy love affairs with demanding mistresses and dealing with disgruntled husbands and irate relatives. A lot of money was squandered there, as Rene witnessed again and again. One scandalous affair ended in a duel and forced the young Marquis into exile, and Rene loyally endured years away from France. The Marquis' sins were eventually forgiven and forgotten, and Rene was looking forward to return to their native land, but the Marquis suddenly involved Rene in an affair which had the potential to lead Rene straight to the gallows. This latest assignment entailed acquiring five paintings from the house of a Viennese nobleman without the current owner's permission. The Marquis assured him that the theft was perfectly justified, that these portraits were originally stolen from their rightful owner, and that he, Rene, was compelled to obtain the paintings in order to reunite them with the original owner. Rene cursed the day he was employed by the young Marquis and even thought of quitting the service, but the Marquis promised a large award for risking his neck. He informed Rene when the Viennese nobleman was absent from home, and Rene was lucky enough to break into the house and leave without anyone spotting him and raising an alarm. To Rene's relief, they departed from Vienna within a week. When they arrived in Marseille, the Marquis added six more paintings, each individually wrapped and sealed, for the delivery to the same illustrious personage in England. There was too much secrecy around a pile of canvases for Rene's taste, but if the Marquis and noble Lords generously paid for the paintings and the secrecy...

"So here is the plan," Rene whispered to his brother-in-law, to make certain that not even one drunkard at this dirty tavern could overhear their conversation. "I will arrange for a small escort for the cargo. You put together a small group to attack..."

"Attack?!"His brother-in-law's paunchy figure shook as he crossed himself. Durrant's wit was limited, but Rene needed an accomplice and Durrant knew where and how to contact men willing to do anything for a few coins and to remain silent about it.

"Be quiet!" Rene hissed, but no one paid them any attention. "I will make certain that no fighting will need to take place."

Durrant emptied his mug. "Your Marquis will search for these paintings."

"He will send me," Rene said as he took a swallow of his sour wine.

"How can you be so certain?" His brother-in-law scratched his head.

"I know him and I understand the ways of nobility," Rene replied dismissively. "We hide these pictures now. In half a year, we - I – will tell him that a friend of mine met a Captain from the New World who is selling these paintings, but no questions asked. This is an easy way for us to make money." There was more to his plan, but he did not dare reveal it.

"I... I don't know," Durrant mumbled. "What will we do if the Marquis does not buy them back?"

"You are a fool! He will retrieve his property! The price we will ask – I mean, the Captain from the New World will ask - is nothing to him! Don't you see? My plan is secure! We are about to miss a fortune!" In exasperation, Rene slammed his fist on the table. He swiveled his head to check if they attracted any attention, but no one cared. There were only five portraits appropriated by Rene for his master, and Rene privately wondered if the additional paintings would be of the same content.

"What are these pictures of?" Durrant again exhibited inconvenient curiosity.

"Portraits," Rene answered vaguely. Some portraits, indeed.

TWO YOUNG MEN

LYON, FRANCE - MARCH 1712

A boy becomes a man when he learns to fend for himself among his peers.

Laurent de la Fleure to Henri d'Arringnon - 1694

LAURENT DE LA FLEURE SPENT MANY HOURS IN HIS library room checking the accounts, perusing the news, contemplating civic papers, pondering upon the idiocy of men, debating and plotting the appropriate course of action for both important and trivial issues, reading books, and sipping brandy behind the closed door. He liked the plain white ceiling, the oak cabinet with carved doors, the maps of the world and of France on the wall, and the high bookshelves full of leatherbound volumes, but he did not like to wait for his son. Laurent had summoned Antoine half an hour ago - where was the young reprobate?

Two years ago, Laurent had recognized that Marguerite, bless her heart, most excellent wife and mother, doted on Antoine and spoiled him beyond reason while the young man took shameless advantage of her devotion. *"If he continues to hide behind a skirt, he will never become a self-reliant and judicious man,"* Laurent had explained to his wife. He brutally overruled her loud objections, cut the apron strings, and sent Antoine to military school for a taste of independence and acquisition of life experience. The young ruffian's education in military school had forged his self-reliance and now Antoine's arrogance and disrespect for authority caused disorder in the household. Antoine could do nothing wrong in Marguerite's eyes, but Laurent begged to differ. This difference of opinions caused more and more heated arguments between Laurent and Antoine, between Laurent and Marguerite, and set a bad example for Raoul...

Laurent's annoyance mounted. Just how long does it take for a young man to traverse their residence?! Laurent had lost his temper yesterday, when Marguerite had eloquently expressed her contrary opinion about their son's imminent departure to fencing school. In retrospect, perhaps he should have mentioned his plans to his wife before arranging for Antoine's immediate future...

The door opened and the defiant young man finally marched inside. "Father. You sent for me?"

Laurent silently regarded his seventeen-year-old son, and once again, recognized himself at that age. God only knows if he was just as much of a trial to his own father. He waited till Antoine exhibited signs of impatience.

"I arranged for you to attend the fencing school in Montpellier."

"Why?!" his son yapped. "Pardon me, father, with all respect, but what will I learn there that you have not taught me?"

"You might benefit from extended exposure to different styles of fencing. I trust you will grace the fencing school with your illustrious presence longer than your embarrassingly brief sojourn in military school."

"Yes, father," Antoine answered through clenched teeth, although he managed to maintain a relatively civil tone despite the rather obvious resentment and defiance simmering under the surface. "May I ask, father, when are you planning to ship me out into this, this... glorified exile?"

Laurent slowly exhaled. Any questions phrased in this form inevitably lead to arguments, and each of these arguments was followed by an unpleasant discussion with Marguerite, frequently culminating in a night in the library for Laurent. Definitely, a hundred miles between himself and his beloved son would bring harmony and order to the household.

"We are leaving the day after tomorrow. I trust this is enough time to arrange your important affairs in order?"

"Yes, father." The fury raged in his gray eyes, but his face maintained a mask of indifference.

Montpellier, France - April 1712

Laurent de la Fleure and Francis de Brangelton abandoned their elder sons to the tune of exuberant celebration and retired to Laurent's lodgings for a dignified dinner of roasted lamb to celebrate the occasion of establishing a distant, although probably very temporary, residence for their beloved heirs.

"What happened in military school to the elder son of the famous, respected, legendary, etc, former Lieutenant of His

Majesty's Musketeers?" de Brangelton asked after a second large glass of excellent burgundy wine.

Laurent refilled the glasses. "After four months, my arrogant son was bored stiff and began to question the wisdom and expertise of every military leader until he was advised to refrain from expressing his opinions. He paid no attention to the warning, and it was not long before the headmaster sent me a formal request to remove my precious son from their care... What is so amusing?"

"Were you any different at his age?"

"Imagine my surprise when I met Antoine on the road, three days travel behind him, at his tender age of sixteen." He attempted to smother his pride, but it crept into his voice. "His teachers' forbearance ended sooner than I expected, and they locked him up in his own room. He packed his belongings, climbed out of the window, and saddled his horse in the darkness of the night. Before he escaped, though, he shot the lock on his door off to make his point."

"Commendable," de Brangelton said, lifting his goblet in a toast. "Henri lasted only a couple of weeks in military school."

"You don't say. A de Brangelton in military school? I pity the school officials. How did that absurdity happen?"

"Watch your words. It was Henrietta's idea. I could not stop laughing long enough to object, and so off he went. After a week, Henri compared the tedium of military school routine to a monastery, and announced that a monastery could be more entertaining and useful if the monastery was located close to a nunnery and the monks were teaching him the skills of making liquor. Since he delivered his tirade within the hearing range of the honorable headmaster, feathers ruffled and tempers flared. The headmaster threatened to have Henri whipped, so, in response, Henri took a hostage."

"And you nurture the delusion that your son is reasonable?"

"My son made very reasonable demands, namely, for the headmaster to expel him and, of course, promise that there would be no retribution. The poor excuse for a headmaster had to oblige since the hostage with a knife to his throat fainted. Then my son composed a letter detailing unreasonable actions by the aforementioned headmaster. Henri concluded his epistle by asking if he should head home, or if I would visit and, I quote, '*talk some sense into this buffoon of a headmaster.*' Stop laughing."

"Like father, like son."

"I went to retrieve my son. That enterprise involved forcibly prying him away from the passionate embraces of a well-endowed nymph. I brought him along on a minor business of mine, and assigned him for the lookout one evening. This rooster of mine was distracted by a swaying skirt below a tight corset. He abandoned his post to follow her! So I followed my young buck, restrained him, and choked off the air to his lungs till he passed out. I also nicked his skin with a knife for good measure. When Henri regained his consciousness, I lectured him that, first and foremost, he must pay attention to business and not rely on his father, or mother, or maybe his younger sister to save his life each and every time his groin overrules his mind. When I mentioned his sister, he swore at me. Next time my boy stands guard, he hopefully will not notice a naked Venus sauntering by. I pray he learned the lesson for life."

"And yet, you are wasting money for the fencing school." Laurent left the question hanging.

"Ah, yes. Henri's brazen womanizing did cause mayhem at the de Paulet's household ..."

Montpellier was first populated by Romans. Later on it became an important center of commerce and learning: The University welcomed the scholars from all over the known world since the fourteenth century; the pilgrims on the way to Santiago de Compostela traveled through; and even if the port had dried up, the scholarly reputation would have remained and the legacy of striving commercial and trading glory would linger. The long history, a mix of cultures and influences, prevalence of commerce, a military garrison at the Citadel, and a sizable student population made Montpellier a colorful, clamorous, multi-faceted town, as well as a perfect place for Henri and Antoine to relish their independence. Their fathers, in their infinite wisdom and zealous quest to unburden themselves of their heirs' troublesome presence, allowed Henri and Antoine the freedom to handle their own finances. Certainly not coincidently, the allowances were for the same amount.

In their search for suitable lodgings, Henri and Antoine concluded that there was no reason to stay in a respectable, boring, and outrageously expensive neighborhood populated by Montpellier's noble families and conceited pampered classmates. They had found a boarding house in the University's district, where the other occupants were either students or junior officers, and the atmosphere was boisterous and carefree. Henri and Antoine rented an excellent set of rooms consisting of two separate private rooms with a common sitting room and bath closet. This arrangement also set aside even more funds for entertainment. In a short time, Henri and Antoine were pleasantly surprised to discover that the fencing school prided itself on providing exposure to fighting techniques from other parts of the world – they learned to handle a scimitar and practiced with cutlasses and sabers. Antoine landed himself in an affair with the young wife of a pompous Law Professor at the university while Henri acquainted himself with every good-looking young woman in town. All in all, the two young men happily settled in Montpellier.

Henri arrived at the Promenade de Peyrou with a quarter of hour to spare before Bernadette's appointed time. Due to her scatterbrained disregard for punctuality, it meant he had half an hour to spare. He leaned on the parapet next to Antoine and they contemplated the crooked city streets below and the hazy skies above.

"A music recital!" Antoine voiced a complaint. "She wants me to attend a music recital with her because she thinks all noblemen must patronize music. Yesterday she persisted in asking my opinion on a pair of new gloves because I will have to pull them off. The other day, she wanted me to pick out ribbons for her because that's what lovers do. I am absolutely fed up with her demands."

"And with her bed?" Henri inquired.

Antoine slapped Henri with a hat. "Why do women insist on being so high maintenance after only a month of dalliance?"

"Will you ever figure out how to treat a woman right? Just play along with her little whims."

Antoine shrugged his shoulders. "Why should I dance to her capricious tune? If I cared to march to orders, I might as well be at home, where my father quite delights in instructing me. Or in military school. He insists that I must understand that I am a member of the de la Fleure family." Antoine cleared his throat in preparation for his best impression of his father's lecture. "The name of de la Fleure is one of the oldest and most respected in Lyon. We have the responsibility to promote civic prosperity in our town, as we always have. Your lack of interest and your ignorance appall and mortify me." He switched to his normal voice. "I was happy when my father consigned me to Montpellier and thus removed me from his overbearing presence. Now I find myself an object to other sermons. She complains -"

Fortunately for me, Henri thought as Antoine kept talking, *there are no worthwhile civic activities in Ferrand for my father to involve himself into. He never bothers to discuss his plans and aspirations. No, he drops everyone into situations with only one course of action, such as exiling me to this fencing school. Why not marry Charlotte to Simon de Paulet instead and unload her into that family? Because no reasonable person can deal with the de Brangelton girl, that's why.*

"...she presumes I exist solely for her pleasure," Antoine concluded his monologue.

"Next time my family visits, ask my sister to assist you in your love affairs," Henri said. "No woman will speak to you after such a disaster."

Antoine adjusted his cuff lace. "Would you care to elaborate?"

"Do you remember the de Paulet sisters? Henrietta is a year older than me. Eliza is a year younger. I rather like Henrietta; she has a nice, full figure. To curb the temptation and to avoid suspicion, I paid as much attention to Eliza. She's no hag, by any means. She has pretty eyes..."

Antoine closed his mouth.

"...and neither Henrietta nor Eliza suspected my gallant address to the other, until one fateful day, when Mme. Constance announced that she expected Jean- Louis to marry Charlotte. My sister proposed to marry one of de Paulet sisters to me instead. Both Henrietta and Eliza were excited at that ridiculous idea."

Antoine regained the faculty of speech. "What did happen between you and... both sisters?"

"Nothing more than few kisses with either one," Henri admitted, choosing to withhold that such a situation was not for his lack of efforts or desire. In hindsight, he suspected that Charlotte warned them about his duplicity "I raised hell with Wildcat for landing me in such a predicament, and lo and behold, Charlotte made the sisters aware of my duplicity and rallied both of the de Paulet brothers to blacken my character. My devil sire cast me away till Henrietta and Eliza are married off, and neither one to me."

Antoine slapped him on the back. "Count your blessings!"

2

THE MARSHALL COUSINS IN ACTION

MARSEILLE, FRANCE – SEPTEMBER 1712

The Marshall cousins exhibited an unfortunate error of judgment, idiotic curiosity, appalling lack of common sense, and used excessive amount of black powder.

Antoine de la Fleure to Henri de Brangelton – 1712

UPON THEIR ARRIVAL TO MARSEILLE, HAROLD MARSHALL and his cousin Andrew Marshall conceded that although they were intelligent, sophisticated, and well-educated young men (at least in their own opinions), Marseille had many new experiences to offer. Harold and Andrew diligently explored the cobbled labyrinthine streets snaking around the steep hilltops. They climbed up and prowled around the harbor's impressive fortifications dominated by the imposing austere towers of Fort St. Jean and Fort St. Nicolas. They admired the spirit of Marseille's citizens as well as the wisdom of the Sun King -

massive fort guns pointed toward the town because Louis XIV had never trusted the unruly inhabitants of Marseille. Harold and Andrew quickly became familiar with the vibrant rhythm of marine commerce - ships arrived, unloaded, loaded, and departed; the goods were stored, moved, sold, and resold, and everyone minded their own business. The colorful attires from all corners of the world, the spicy flavors of foods, the exotic drinks and pipes, the dissonant sounds of drums, sitars, lutes, reed pipes, and songs in a hundred languages, all blended together in the streets and markets populated by men from the Orient, from Africa, from Levant, from the New World, and from all the countries in Europe.

Despite the cousins' original intent to stay only a few days, two weeks passed quickly. Their funds were thinning out, but card games in any of the riotous taverns should eliminate that shortcoming. With this noble purpose on their minds, the cousins directed their steps to the neighborhood of Citadel. The dusk deepened into the silky darkness and only the white points of stars adorned the cloudless skies. The ships in the harbor were secured for the night, the sailors on leave were drinking in the streets and the sailors on duty were confined to their ships. In the shadows of St. Nicolas Tower, a group of men were unloading a single nondescript trunk from a barquentine curiously named the *Anne Maria Jane*.

"Isn't it late for laborers?" Harold stared at the disembarking group. Two men carried a large trunk, and four guards with muskets stood at attention.

Andrew slowed down. "That trunk seems oddly light for its size."

The men secured the trunk to the cart. The leader nervously rubbed his hands and his head swiveled from side to side until a fine mare trotted on the dock. The rider dismounted to inspect the trunk. He was a rich nobleman: the yellow glow from lanterns afforded the cousins a clear view of the gilded bridle, stirrups, and sword's hilt, the fine lace on his collar, the overwhelming amount of embroidery on his jacket, and the newness of two huge dyed feathers secured to the fashionable hat with an ornate gold pin.

"Four guards?! You secured only four guards?!" the nobleman reproached the leader of the group. "Do you understand the importance of delivering this cargo safely?!"

"Monsieur, for a single trunk..."

"Follow me." Feathers bounced forward as the commander scrambled out of the way and scuffled after the nobleman.

Harold gestured to Andrew and stealthily glided behind the men.

"Have you lost your mind?" his cousin whispered. Occasionally, Andrew exhibited inconvenient scruples.

"Do you have some feeble objection to eavesdropping?"

Andrew did not. He pointed to the stone wall which wrapped around the building. A narrow yard between the house and the wall was covered with shrubs, and a pale column of light spilled from the window. Harold and Andrew cautiously climbed over the wall and landed on the soft dirt. They noiselessly moved along the path of the feathers bouncing on the other side of the wall. The feathers stopped at the edge of the yard. Harold and Andrew crouched in the shadows. The conversation between the nobleman and the leader was short and one-sided. The nobleman relentlessly chastised the leader for the lack of diligence and ordered him to find more men to guard the cargo.

"Monsieur, I am reluctant to trust strangers," the man whined.

"It's a port. There must be dozens of professional mercenaries for hire." The nobleman's inflections conveyed arrogance and disdain.

"Monsieur, hiring mercenaries may attract unwelcome attention," the leader feebly objected.

"You are not hiring an army - you need just a few more men to guard my personal belongings! Do I have to guide your every step?!"

The Lusty Mermaid Tavern held the well-deserved reputation of fixing the best mussels stew, and the Marquis chose to dine there. Per the Marquis' instructions, Rene Prassal had secured the trunk in the Marquis' room, posted the sentries, and reported to the Marquis.

"Have you hired more guards?" the Marquis persisted.

"I...I am working on it, Monsieur," Rene assured his employer. Once the Marquis had acquired a notion, it was almost impossible to displace it. Besides, the last thing Rene needed was for the Marquis – and his valet, two grooms and additional attendant - to decide to accompany the trunk.

"How?"

"I...I... I have some possibilities in mind." Rene frantically looked around the room. At a far table, a burly middle-aged seafarer was playing cards with a heavily armed and somberly dressed young man. Trouble was brewing between the players. The seafarer blasphemed louder and louder at each turn of cards. "That man over there might be available," Rene speculated in hopes that the aforementioned man would leave soon. "He wears his hat low to cover his face. He does not want to be recognized."

"Are you cheating, landlubber?" the seafarer roared.

"What the hell did you say?" The other man slammed his cards, face down, on the table. His French was oddly accented.

"You heard me," the seafarer sneered.

The other man stood up, casting a large distorted shadow on the wall. "I did not hear an apology from you," he growled.

The hum of conversation faded. Patrons picked up their plates, tankards, bottles, and moved away from the source of brawl. The Marquis backed away and dissolved into the corner furthest from the field of action, but he watched the exchange with vivid interest.

"I will teach you a lesson, scum." The seafarer pushed the table away and bared his cutlass. In a smooth and practiced movement, his opponent drew his sword at the ready. The seafarer charged in a brutal, forceful attack, but the other man steadily blocked the first, the second, and the third thrust. His moves were measured; he knew how to use the advantage of a longer sword against the heavy cutlass.

"To me!" the seafarer bellowed at a group of men. Three sailors with drawn cutlasses moved toward the combatants. One of them collapsed from a blow to his head, deftly delivered with a pommel of the sword by a young man dressed in fine fashionable clothes. The lace on his sleeves did not impede his moves. He expertly wielded the sword in one hand and a dueling dagger in another.

"Call the night watch!" the proprietor yelled. One of the servers rushed out in the night.

The seafarer assaulted his foe again, but no avail. The man in fancy clothes tripped another sailor and parried the thrust from the last one standing. "Behind and left," he said. The card player sidestepped away from a thrust by his burly adversary. The seafarer and his cohort collided. The card player delivered a solid punch to the sailor's jaw and the sailor sprawled unconscious on the floor. The pommel of his sword loudly connected with the burly man's head. In a fluid motion, the man in fancy clothing and the card player positioned themselves back-to-back. They held the swords and daggers ready to keep anyone at bay.

"How much blood shall we spill before law and order shows up?" The card player asked over his shoulder. His breathing was light and steady.

"Anyone for a dance?" His friend was just as unaffected by the brawl as he addressed the crowd.

"No, not at all," the patrons of the Lusty Mermaid murmured. Sailors, merchants and people of business had no desire to embroil themselves in an unprofitable brawl with skilled and experienced mercenaries.

"Excellent." The two men headed toward the door. "Good evening to all."

"What are you waiting for?" The Marquis admonished Rene. "Hire these two cutthroats!"

"Yes, Monsieur." Rene hoped that his sour resignation did not seep through his words. He followed the men outside. A suspicion formed in his mind: Maybe the Marquis' desire for mercenary protection was due to the Marquis' suspicion of him? Did the Marquis intend to add the hired help to keep him honest? Rene crossed himself. No, it was probably sheer coincidence. He did not dare to disobey his employer. "Monsieurs!" Rene called out.

The next morning, the newly hired cutthroats promptly showed up at the appointed time. The card player was named Harold Marshall. In Rene's mind, if his swagger was any indication, Harold was probably raised on a pirate ship. His cousin Andrew Marshall possessed a courtly glitter along with his fighting skills; he might be on a run from the law. They hailed from the New World, but were elusive about their business in France. They spoke English between themselves, but were fluent in French. As seasoned mercenaries, they bargained for the fair amount of pay, and insisted on half up front. Rene disliked them immensely.

The trunk was loaded and secured by Rene's men. The Marshall cousins meticulously checked their saddles, the straps, the hooves of their horses, and the weapons – each carried a small arsenal with him. These young men kept their heads low to shield their faces by the brims of their hats (which were adorned with expensive feathers, no less!). In the daylight, they appeared dismayingly young, they looked nothing alike, and they were far from desperate. Their clothes were made of quality fabric and fashionable style, their weapons were in excellent condition, and the saddle pistols were compact and of the latest design. No, these cousins did not pass for the typical mercenaries who dwelled by the hundreds in the port cities. Rene wiped the sweat off his forehead. He had to keep his force to a small group for the successful defeat in the upcoming staged attack, and his guards were unaware of his plan. If these cutthroats were to rally the men to earn their money, there would be blood. Their group just might fight off the ambush and deliver the cargo as intended. How would he explain that change of plans - and likely casualties - to the Captain of the *Anne Maria Jane?* The Captain had agreed to send only half a dozen men expecting no resistance – and the Captain and his acting troupe were paid for the theatrical display only. The rates for the combat would be significantly higher if blood spilled, and these Marshall cousins seemed alert and eager to protect the cargo.

Rene, judging that the time was ripe for departure, sent one man to ride in the front, two on the left, and two on the right. He climbed up into the cart's seat with the driver and signaled for the cart to move on. "You watch the rear," he told the cousins. They fell in the back, in perfect rhythm. Their timing would make cavalry officers envious; they had obviously seen action together and that was indeed more bad news. Rene could not afford to allow these young men to reach the place of ambush.

Harold and Andrew rode a mile before they judged themselves to be outside of Prassal's hearing distance.

"This makes no sense," Andrew said. "So Prassal forgot his musket at the inn, but is it necessary to send us both on the errand to retrieve it? Not for a moment do I believe his touching concern for our safety."

Harold agreed. The road was well traveled and highway robbery business was unprofitable along this route. Prassal was reluctant to add people to guard the cargo. "Does he intend to pocket the other half of our payment?"

Andrew pulled the reins to a stop. "In this case, there is no musket left at the inn. Indeed, what imbecile forgets his weapon?"

Harold nodded. "Shall we follow him, then?"

Andrew wheeled his horse around. "Yes. I resent cheaters and liars."

Harold and Andrew paused on the top of the hill to watch Prassal's slow progress across the narrow passage. The steep grassy hill stretched ahead to follow the road, which was boxed by the rocky mountain wall on the opposite side. At the far end, the road's sharp turn was encircled by tall trees and dense hedge.

Unexplainably, Prassal's group stopped by the hedge. The men dismounted and clustered around the cart to light the lanterns. The cousins exchanged looks of incomprehension. There was no need for the light yet, and only the most incompetent commander would have all his men turn their back to their surroundings, in close proximity to a thick cluster of trees and bushes, away from horses, and with their hands occupied.

There was a sudden movement behind these very trees and bushes, and a band of men descended on the group. The bandits knocked down half of the guards without a fight and aimed pistols at others. The ambushers' extravagant attire and choice of cutlasses identified them as seafaring men, a supposition supported due to the unmistakable resemblance their speed and actions bore to a swarm of pirates boarding a ship. The whole ambush lasted no longer than a minute. The bandits relieved Prassal and his men of weapons, tied everyone up and loosely tethered them together.

"What? They did not even check the pockets?" Harold whispered when the attackers converged around the cart.

"The incompetence of the modern highwayman is shocking," Andrew snorted. "They have no interest in the saddled horses, either."

On the road, the bandits maneuvered the cart to turn around and headed back to Marseille.

Andrew motioned Harold to retreat deeper into the woods. "These assailants have no horses on their own! Someone brought them here to wait for this cargo, and the retreat was not even considered. Which means...what?"

Harold frowned. "That Prassal expected the attack?"

"Why did he send us away, then?"

The cousins lapsed into a silence while the cart rattled by.

"Shall we follow the trunk and leave Prassal to the mercy of other travelers?" Harold suggested.

An hour later, the sun retired beyond the horizon, and the skies turned deep velvety blue. The assailants had had the foresight to bring along lanterns and torches, and the cart traveled fast. Despite the bright light of the full moon enabling the horses to pick their own footing on the uneven road, Andrew and Harold fell behind. They occasionally stopped to listen and watch for anyone – especially Prassal and his men, - coming behind them. The bells rang ten o'clock when the cousins reached Marseille. The entrance gate was closed for the night, and there was no cart in sight. Andrew and Harold rode around along the walls and crumbling ramparts until they discovered an unguarded back street beyond a pile of rubble. They slipped into the city behind the Fort of St, Jean, housed the horses at the first stable they passed, and hurried back to the harbor on foot. They passed the deserted City Hall and walked around the rectangular harbor toward the *Anne Maria Jane,* contemplating how to interrogate her crew. There were no carts on the dock. The loaded barquentine sat low in the water and all the sails were accounted for. The ship was ready to sail in the morning.

"What the hell?" Harold and Andrew recognized the man on the deck – he had driven the cart earlier in the evening.

In Marseille, the business continued when the night fell - taverns, inns and many shops conducted a brisk and profitable trade till the early hours of the morning. Collecting supplies for pyrotechnics was only a matter of time. Andrew and Harold patronized a dozen shops with purchases of black powder, fuses, ropes, clay storage vessels, and waterproof oiled cloth. The cousins intended to blow a sizable, but repairable, hole in the *Anne Maria Jane's* hull – that should prevent her from sailing away until they figured out what had happened to the trunk.

Andrew and Harold circled the harbor once again, and forced open a window at the City Hall. Once inside, they stripped to their breeches, tightly rolled the clothes around their pistols, and wedged the bundles, along with hats and boots, under the hard benches. They secured the purses, swords, and daggers across their bare chests and eased into the tranquil water of the harbor. Each young man carried a clay vessel lined and covered with waterproof oiled cloth. Each vessel contained black powder in dry sacks, rope, fuses, and kindling lint. The distance across the harbor was less than a quarter of a mile, but the swim took an eternity. Harold and Andrew each paddled with one hand to keep the containers above the water line with the other hand, and they took care to avoid causing even a slightest splash. Both were excellent swimmers, but by the time they grasped the anchor chain, both were exhausted and gratefully hung on to catch their breaths before climbing up on the deck.

Harold wrapped his leg around the chain and pulled himself up with one arm. His other arm was tightly wrapped around the clay vessel, which showed an alarming and pain-inducing tendency to slide down and scratch his side. He could pull himself only a short span at the time, and he could no longer tell if the moisture on his forehead was sweat or water dripping from his hair. When he slid over the railing, he collapsed in the shallow space below the railings. He had barely caught his breath by the time Andrew climbed up, his side bloodied and bruised by the heavy container.

"We should have brought extra rope to haul these pots." Andrew gulped for air.

The cousins secured the black powder sacks together and lowered the parcel outside of the rail just below the deck level. They ignited the ends of the fuses and counted to ten, watching to make certain the fuses remained lit before sliding down the anchor chain. Ignoring the burning sensation in their sides, they hastily swam across the murky water – without any burden, they crossed the harbor in minutes.

The moment Andrew and Harold staggered on shore, the spectacular explosion shook the harbor. The cousins watched in fascination as the flame leapt into the air and the tongues of fire flared toward the sails. The sentry rang the alarm bell and hurried to hack at the wood with the axe. He meant to separate the burning section and to drop it into the harbor, but upon his third swing, a flaming piece launched into the air and landed on the folded sail of the neighboring schooner. The canvas ignited like a giant torch. The men of the ship ran along the deck, shouting and blindly firing musket shots at the hull of the *Anne Maria Jane*.

"*Ship under attack!*" The signal sounded from a Navy corvette moored at the *Anne Maria Jane's* starboard. The boom of a cannon discharge resonated in the air. The ball flew across the harbor, clipped the figurehead of a brigantine, and splashed in the water. A naked man ran out of the captain's cabin. "*Repel the boarders!*" he roared to his crew.

"Damn!" Andrew and Harold recovered from their dumfounded astonishment. They rushed to retrieve their clothes. There was no time to dry and the water dripped from their hair while they struggled to half-button their doublets over their soaked shirts. They wriggled their wet feet into the boots, and hoped that the leather cases protected the pistols from moisture.

The bells of St. Laurent's church and St. Victor Abbey rang and blended with the sounds of whistles from the city night watch and of the horns and bugles from the Navy ships. The cacophony woke up the citizens, and the pandemonium raged on shore as much as on the water. Half of the ships in the harbor declared a war at each other and the men jumped from one ship to other brandishing weapons. Darkness receded as the red and yellow flames increased in size and ferocity.

Andrew and Harold ran around the harbor toward the *Anne Maria Jane*. On their way, they noticed that under the respectable pretense of salvaging the goods from incidental small fires, mostly unauthorized and highly disputed transfers of barrels, sacks, bags, crates, and trunks took place left and right in the chaos.

On the deck of the *Anne Maria Jane*, panic and confusion still reigned, but two men carried the familiar trunk down the ramp. Once they reached the ground they collided with a group of four cutthroats carrying the trunk of the same size and shape. Both groups dropped their cargo, bared cutlasses, and hollered defiantly at each other. Harold and Andrew's further advance was cut off by a gang disembarking from a brigantine named the *Sacred Allegiance,* moored at the *Anne Maria Jane's* portside. These men also carried a similar large trunk, but abandoned it in front of Harold and Andrew to fend off the group of sailors pursuing them. The cousins veered off to the side, but yet another skirmish blocked their way. They circled around it and into the path of a large barrel rolling on its own. The cousins frantically leapt out of its course and detoured into the shadows of the buildings surrounding the harbor. They proceeded on their way toward the *Anne Maria Jane,* and lined up with the barquentine just when five men carried the trunk back onto the ship's plank. The gang from the *Sacred Allegiance* chased after the trunk and succeeded in wrestling it away and carrying it back toward their ship.

On the dock, the isolated brawls merged to create a battlefield where the combatants no longer seemed to know who or why they fought, and the gang from the *Sacred Allegiance* was forced to once again abandon the trunk and to defend themselves. The orders were shouted from the deck of the *Anne Maria Jane.* In the pattern of a tidal wave, more crewmen poured out onto the dock, and the seamen from the Navy corvette entered the fray. Illuminated by the crimson and orange plumes of fire, the men punched each other with bare fists, exchanged blows with sticks, struck with the pommels of their swords and pistols, and tossed rocks at each other. A chorus of curses boomed in the smoke-filled air. The intensity of the battle diminished as the casualties mounted. Some men were knocked unconscious and sank to the ground tripping the others. Some men staggered in disorientation outside of the battlefield, a couple of enterprising souls sneaked away, and those who remained standing paused to regroup.

"Now!" Andrew and Harold took the opportunity to weave their way through the exhausted combatants. The cousins grasped the handles of the trunk and almost fell on their faces upon realizing its weight.

"That one!" Andrew and Harold moved to heave another trunk, picked it up and even carried it a half a dozen paces before the mob of men roared and rushed to attack. Harold and Andrew swung and tossed the trunk forward to trip the assailants, but that did not deter the crewmen from the *Anne Maria Jane*. Neither did it deter the gang from the *Sacred Allegiance*, the sailors from the Navy, nor Prassal himself.

Andrew and Harold wasted no time in retreating. As they had been taught, they swung their swords backwards, in the hopes of preventing anyone from diving down to grab their ankles. The moment Harold placed the blade in position, he heard a yell of pain behind him. He risked a glance at his cousin. Andrew raised his arm, drove the blade backward, and one more pursuer dropped behind. The cousins ran up the hill away from the harbor. The austere shape of St. Victor Abbey loomed ahead, and on their right, they glimpsed the soldiers from the neighborhood of Citadel running toward the harbor.

Andrew and Harold gained a safe distance from Prassal and his men, but their lungs were on fire, their hearts pounded like the hooves of galloping horses, their mouths were parched, and they wobbled on their feet when they reached the long narrow street between the sheer stone walls of St. Victor Abbey and the residential houses across from it. The thin light from the open windows afforded a glimpse of a thick sturdy vine covering the front of a three-story building, the thick branches extending to the roof. Andrew hoisted Harold up to the first balcony. Harold hooked his leg to the iron railing, grasped Andrew's hand to pull his cousin up, and tentatively tugged on the vine. The branches creaked, but underneath the leaves, Harold felt the sturdy rods. The trellis had to be nailed to the wall. He climbed up to the second balcony and motioned for Andrew to scale up to the roof. A flock of birds flapped out from their nests; the branches creaked and swayed but held. The moment Andrew grasped the ledge of the roof, Harold resumed his ascent and, not a moment too soon, the cousins collapsed in exhaustion on the muddy roof.

The band of panting and cursing pursuers spilled into the street and reluctantly halted to helplessly gape into the quiet and gloomy alley.

"Where did they go?" Prassal wheezed.

Harold and Andrew held their ragged breath. They had the advantage of higher ground, and they could take two more men out with their boot knives. Blood had already spilled in this chase, so they had nothing to lose now. On an optimistic hope, if their adversaries were reckless enough to climb up all at the same time, maybe the vine would break. "Did they climb up?" A question drifted from below.

"Up these walls?" another man said with disbelief. "Do you see any rigging up here?"

"Did the monks shelter them?" a third man chimed in.

"Search the street," Prassal ordered. The company below fanned out to cautiously check every shadow, corner, and nook.

"Sooner or later, they will notice the vine." Andrew wiped the sweat off his forehead.

"Can we make them believe we took sanctuary inside the abbey?" Harold said.

The cousins conferred in hushed whispers. They amassed tile pieces, pebbles, shards of wood, and loose clumps of dirt, and squeezed water from their hair to paste the debris together. When the men below finished their futile search and regrouped, Andrew hurled a heavy piece of a broken tile into the lit abbey's window, and followed up with another projectile into the unlit window positioned above the group of men. At the same moment, Harold half-dropped, half-tossed the handful of small hard pieces into the abbey wall under the window. The fragments bounced off the hard stone and rained onto the men's heads.

A man with a musket on his shoulder spun around when the debris hit his bare head, and the musket's barrel banged against the head of another man. The man reciprocated with a blow to the stomach. Two other men attempted to pull the combatants apart, but were assaulted themselves.

"Stop it!" Prassal's scream was overshadowed by the shouts from his men. "Friars are hiding them!"

The diversion worked better than Andrew and Harold hoped. To the accompaniment of the abbey's bells signaling the attack, the rowdy and incensed sailors converged at the abbey's door and pounded on the heavy wood. More windows opened in the residential building, and the unhappy citizens screamed at the sailors to go away. From behind the abbey's walls, the dismayed monks screeched threats of eternal damnation. The frustrated sailors yelled demands to yield the criminals. The earnest night watch marched in and hollered for peace and order. A group of enthusiastic soldiers from Citadel marched in and bellowed the orders for everyone's surrender.

Neither a hurricane nor an earthquake would dislodge Andrew and Harold from the safety of the roof. They remained there long after the monks spilled outside of the convent with raised clubs in their hands, the soldiers pushed the monks back and chased away the residents who ventured into the street, and the night watch arrested the sailors and Prassal for the raid on the abbey. The cousins waited till the skies above the harbor lost their yellow and orange hues and the noises subsided. The residents extinguished the lights and shut the windows, the flock of birds settled back in their nests, and the night darkness and calmness descended once again. Harold and Andrew fought their drowsiness until a thin strip of dawn light shimmered on the horizon. They crawled to the other side of the building and eased from balcony to balcony to the ground. They successfully avoided the groups of patrolmen now scattered on the streets, and found the stable and their horses without any incidents. In the pre-dawn soft light, Harold and Andrew brushed the dirt off their still damp and newly stained clothes, saddled the horses themselves, and blatantly rode out to the city gate.

"No one leaves the city today," the guard said pompously. "Not after the battle last night." He suspiciously eyed the stains on their clothes.

"Battle?" Andrew raised his eyebrows in his most sophisticated courtly manner. "Did this battle cause such insufferable noise last night?"

The man looked at him with contempt. "Where were you?"

"A paradise," Harold winked at the guard. "My friend would never admit his attendance either to his mother or his beloved."

"Ah. Yes. No." Andrew held the most placid expression he could muster. "Every man should enjoy himself." He pulled a coin from his pocket. "Here, I recommend a girl named Anne."

The guard pocketed the money, cracked the gate open, and waved them on.

3

DAWN OF INFAMY

MARSEILLE, FRANCE - OCTOBER 1712

Dear God, forgive me for my lies, but I have no other choice.

Henrietta d'Arringnon - 1693

HONORE DE COURBET, A SENIOR KNIGHT OF THE ORDER of St. John, was furious. There should be neither clemency nor forgiveness for the perpetrators who dared to raid the ship contracted by the Knights of St. John! The audacity of the scum who dared to board the ship must be punished by the sword, and nothing less, but Honore's hands were tied. He was under orders to transfer the precious cargo in utmost secrecy. He had planned to carry St. Elias' relics onto the Knights' own ship, but his superiors had overruled this arrangement – Portugal's Knights of Christ's Order had objected to the acquisition, and the upper-level officials of the Knights of the Order of St. John now waited for the papal response. Honore prayed for forgiveness of his uncharitable thoughts about his superiors' decision and for the delay of response from the Pope. He praised Heaven for guiding him and the untrained crew of the ship to drive away all intruders and to retrieve the trunk. In the misty pre-dawn hour, he strode to the deck. All fires had long been extinguished. Though the bitter scent of smoke still hung in the air, the harbor was, once again, at peace. Honore leaned on the rail and watched the murky water flowing below. The lantern light flickered overhead, and a sudden fear seized him. The men who fought to obtain St Elias' relics– did they know what they were after? Had they been hired by the Portuguese? He wiped the sweat off his forehead, went back to his cabin to pick up a small lantern, and navigated his way down to the cargo bay.

The trunk was positioned at the far wall. After the attack, Honore had wrapped it with iron chains and secured the chains around the support beam. He touched his hand to the smooth top and froze. He did not remember the narrow wooden strip in the center of the lid. He involuntarily hissed a curse, lifted the lantern with shaking hands, and gaped at the crude identification carvings along the decorative strip. There were no identification seals! Cold sweat burned his eyes. He struggled with the key to unlock the chains, raised the lid, and felt as if his soul left his body. The trunk was full of vile tobacco leaves. Honore screamed in rage, but quickly covered his mouth and fell on his knees. His body remained motionless, his mind blank, until the sun rose and the streaks of light shone through the gaps between the planks in the door. Honore staggered back to his cabin, and prayed for hours in hopes of guidance in his search for St. Elias' relics. He knew he had told untruths, and he prayed for forgiveness, knowing he was justified in his cause to restore St Elias' relics to St. Etienne's Cathe-

dral in his native town. He vowed that whoever took St. Elias'
relics would pay the full price for the sacrilege.

Captain Mathew Johnson of the *Golden Sails* was furious. He
did not cherish the prospect of reporting the complete failure in
his search for the Great Mogul Diamond. He was to be paid
upon finding the diamond, and no money was forthcoming
otherwise. He had brought back only Kumaryan, a wretch who
could not remember his name, let alone the location of the
diamond. When the chaos erupted last night, Kumaryan
escaped and with him faded all hope to find the diamond. Or
maybe the infidel had been kidnapped when the raiders
descended on the decks? The facts remained: When the *Anne
Maria Jane* was boarded, Mathew's crew repelled the attackers,
chased them onto the dock, and brought back a large lightweight trunk – they claimed it belonged to the perpetrators.
Then a cannonball hit the deck and the fire broke out. By the
time Mathew restored order on his ship, Kumaryan was
nowhere to be found.

Mathew did not care for the trunk. It was too light to
contain coins or anything of value. Two different imposing
seals could mean trouble, and he was certain the owners would
search for their cargo. Maybe if he played his cards right, he
might be able to have the trunk ransomed? He neatly cut the
seals off and lifted the lid to behold a sealed and oiled leather
bag. He groped at the shapes concealed by the leather. From
the feel of it, the bag contained rolled fabric, maybe even silks?
To his deep disappointment, it was merely canvas. Mathew
cursed aloud before it occurred to him that the fabric felt too
stiff, and why would anyone waste money for the oiled leather
bag to protect canvas rolls from the moisture?

He untied the wide ribbons which held the roll together, and saw that the inside was painted. He unrolled the canvas, spread it on the floor, and whistled in surprise. The painting depicted a violent battle in a desert, the horsemen wearing white tunics with red crosses and battling enemies on camels. Two angels with golden crowns were lifting knights to Heaven, and fire-breathing monsters were dragging three Saracens to purgatory. The poses, the bodies, and the facial features were life-like, the colors were bright, and the angels' halos were gilded.

He carefully rolled up the painting of the battle, re-tied the ribbons, and checked another roll. The painting depicted a man with long hair and a halo, and a winged lion standing next to him. Mathew recognized the Clock Tower of Piazza San Marco in the background.

He rolled up the picture of St. Mark, unrolled another painting, and the air in his cabin felt much warmer. This next picture was a life-size, full-body portrait of a beautiful and completely naked young woman, in a pose which left nothing to the imagination. She was looking directly at him, her black hair spread against the pale blue sheets on the elaborate bed. Mathew was startled to realize that he reached out to touch the nipple, but the feel of a cold flat surface brought him back to his senses. He wiped away the sweat dripping in his eyes, carefully rolled the picture up, and set it aside on his bunk. This picture would bring some money. He took a long sip of rum to calm his nerves before unrolling another painting.

Mathew recoiled from the grotesque image of half-man, half-goat leering at him from the entrance to a majestic temple. He hastily rolled it up and searched for the canvas of the same size as the beautiful portrait.

The canvas of the woman's portrait was newer and of a finer texture, and Mathew easily found another roll. The woman in the portrait had golden hair and reclined in the same pose on the same bed, only the sheets were maroon.

With shaking hands, Mathew unrolled the next painting, purposely avoiding another portrait. The scene was serene. A veiled woman rode a donkey, an old man walked next to her, and three men wearing crowns and bejeweled robes worshipped a bright star in the sky. It was a pleasant Nativity picture, but not as enjoyable as the portraits.

The next portrait depicted a dark-haired beauty reclining, in the same pose, against golden sheets, and another beauty's rich brown hair shone against green sheets.

Mathew's throat was dry and his breeches were tight. He hurried through the rest of the pile. The temperature in his cabin seemed to drop when he unrolled a painting of a galley ship battling a giant sea serpent in a storm. The scene was complete with huge waves and bolts of lightning. His breathing returned to normal when he unrolled another painting and beheld a knight on horseback charging the fire-breathing dragon, the lance poised to pierce the beast's neck.

Mathew slowly unrolled the last portrait: a copper-haired woman against lavender-colored sheets. All these portraits depicted different women. Whose collections was it?

Mathew recognized that such extravagant paintings were worth a lot of money to rich noblemen. So this trunk must have belonged to an art dealer, but the artists and their associates comprised a capricious human lot, and generosity was not in their blood. Even if he could find the rightful owner, the chance of reward was slim. No, Mathew decided, he might as well sell these paintings himself.

He finished his measure of rum, separated the portraits from the other paintings, wrapped the bundles into separate leather bags, and placed everything into the trunk. He secured the trunk with locking chains, climbed to the deck on unsteady feet, issued orders for high alert, and scuttled offshore, straight to the nearest house of ill repute.

After two days of imprisonment in a putrid cell, Rene was unceremoniously kicked out in the street, grateful to the magistrates who listened to his description of the Marshall cousins and, in return, contacted the Marquis. Rene stumbled into fading daylight and squinted at the brightness surrounding him. His mind still reeled from disbelief that someone had aimed to steal the trunk. No one knew what was in it! These pirates had descended from nowhere, they had taken full advantage of the chaos, but who had hired them? Rene recognized one of the Marquis' footmen, who pointed out that he brought the bail letter and money, and reminded Rene that the Marquis expected immediate delivery of the cargo.

Rene hurried to the *Anne Maria Jane*. Her Captain was beyond furious, since the hole in the hull had doomed the ship to stay in the harbor waiting for repairs while other ships were prioritized. Rene hastily departed when he found out that Durrant had transferred the trunk to the inn onshore.

"One of the seals broke off," Durrant greeted him.

Rene froze at the sight of the insignia of the Order of the Knights of St. John. He drew his dagger. "This is not our trunk!"

His brother-in-law scrambled back away from the blade. "It is, I swear! What are you doing? Put the dagger away! I watched it all this time!"

"The seals! Look at the seals!"

Durrant's face remained blank.

Rene's mind was in a fog, and not only due to hunger. He carefully pried the other seals open, lifted the lid, shifted the top package, and poked through the folded clothes and leather pouches with a distinct smell of hashish. He pushed aside a bundle of clothes, and froze when he noticed sparkles and glitter. He moved away the roll of fabric to uncover a casket with glass panels on top, and his heart tightened at the sight of a skull and a bone inside. He slammed the lid closed and sunk to his knees.

"What is the matter?" Durrant opened the trunk and rooted through the contents. His eyes bugged out. With a gulp of air and a high-pitched yelp, he bounced back and crossed himself. "What is it?!"

Rene clenched his jaw to stop his teeth from chattering and slowly raised himself up. He wordlessly handed the roll of silk to Durrant, lifted a set of clothes, and realized there was a heavy object wrapped inside. With shaking hands, he traced the shape; no, it was not a bone. He set the bundle on the table and unwrapped the oil painting of St. Stephan. The gold frame was generously decorated with pearl seeds.

Durrant craned his neck to peek inside the trunk, crossed himself again, and lifted up a brown wool cloak. It was folded to protect a shimmering gold bowl covered in intricate patterns and lavishly adorned with red and blue precious stones.

"We can sell it." Durrant rubbed his hands together, sniffed the air, and held up a leather bag. "This is hashish. It alone is worth a small fortune!"

"There is not enough to hide for the rest of our lives!" Rene shouted, his heart pounding in fear. He picked up another roll of fabric and forced himself to reach down and shift the clothes and bags to reveal the casket. The inside was cushioned with purple and red velvet fabric, the lid was locked and sealed with gold seals, and the matching red and gold seals were visible on papers inside. The cargo belonged to the Vatican and the Knights of St. John. There would be a large price to pay! Rene's knees wobbled and his vision blurred, but the clunk of solid metal in the trunk woke him from his stupor.

Durrant held up a silver tray. "Look at these figures around the edge! You can see a nipple."

"No!" Rene tore the tray from Durrant's hands. "We secure it all – You hear me, you cretin? – *all* of it for now, and wait till the right time to trade these relics for our lives. Do you understand?" He placed the objects back inside the trunk. "Where can we hide it? Where is contraband merchandise usually hidden at ports?"

"These goods are worth more than we planned to ask for your Marquis' paintings." And despite his own fear for his life, Rene was tempted as well by this small fortune. The gold and silver could be melted - less money but safer. Fabric and clothes could be sold one-by-one in different towns. The bones... Under the cover of the night, Rene wanted to leave the casket at the doors of a large cathedral... but he needed time to think it over. "We must store these goods until the owners give up the search. How much will it cost?" He choked at the price. "For a single trunk?"

"You want to keep it safe and secret? Rabatin runs the most trustworthy warehouse in France. And it's in Le Havre. No one, believe me, no one will search that far from Marseille."

Rene reluctantly agreed, even though the amount of money was outrageous. On the other hand, they could – and should – sell the hashish and opium before the potions lost their potency and their value, and that would more than pay for a couple years of storage. They should sell the clothes before the style changes. And if Rene played his hand carefully, the Marquis might even provide more funds for the search for stolen cargo. But first he had to face his employer.

Rene was acutely aware of his torn and filthy clothes, his grungy stubble and the swollen eye, but at least, he had devoured a meal on the way. He entered the room with his heart pounding in fear and with hope for a grain of sympathy and mercy, but the hope shattered against the Marquis' stony expression. The older nobleman sat at the table and he pointedly held a scented handkerchief to his nose.

The Marquis backed to the open window and gestured for Rene to remain at the door. "Where are the paintings?"

"Please forgive me, Monsieur. The bandits stole the trunk-"

"What?!" The Marquis sunk into the chair. The other man stood up and grabbed the edge of the table to steady himself. The blood rushed to his face and his features twisted in a fury. Judging from his pursed lips and the murderous gleam in his eyes, he was the man whose compassion Rene would be very unwilling to gamble on.

"I... I have a suspicion who they are..." Rene faltered under the livid stare of his employer.

"Did you do nothing to prevent the loss?!" the Marquis screeched.

"Monsieur, the trunk was taken from me by force! We were ambushed and - and - I suspect - I am certain - the Marshall cousins were involved..."

"Who?" The older nobleman asked.

"The mercenaries-"

"You hired mercenaries? Only an idiot -" The noblemen placed the handkerchief back to his face. "You God-damned imbecile, what devil possessed you to hire the mercenaries?!"

Rene did not dare to even glance at the Marquis, let alone to admit whose idea it was. "They hail from Port Royal, Monsieur, and they just recently arrived. I could not imagine they would organize a gang overnight."

The Marquis' face slowly regained color. "Explain what happened."

"We made a bargain, and they rode with me halfway, but

then..." Rene kept his eyes on the dry muck covering his boots. "They just... disappeared. I paid only half of the fee. When I stopped to light the lanterns, they attacked." He risked a glance at his employer.

"Who attacked?" The older nobleman sat down.

Rene truthfully described the following events, how they were freed by passing travelers, and how the horses scattered, and how they, exhausted, reached the harbor and the battle broke out. "And then I saw the Marshall cousins on the dock. We gave chase, but they escaped. I beg your forgiveness, Monsieur."

"Did you have enough wits to learn their names?" the Marquis asked.

"Andrew Marshall and Harold Marshall."

"Describe them."

"Both are the same height, this much taller than me. Andrew has shoulder-long brown hair and light eyes. Harold has short black hair and dark eyes."

With a visible effort, the nobleman gained control of his emotions despite the bright color in his face. "What is their age?"

"Neither one could have been a day over twenty." Rene added a few years.

The older nobleman's lips were compressed in a thin line. "Are you certain they are young? Does this Andrew have a scar across his forehead? A broken nose? Anything unusual at all?"

"No, Monsieur, nothing at all," Rene shook his head. "There is nothing remarkable about them."

"Get out of my sight," Rene's employer ordered. "Clean up with soap and burn your clothes."

Andrew Marshall and Harold Marshall were furious, exhausted, sore, hungry, thirsty, still wet and short of funds. Damn it all - Prassal, noble intentions, black powder, pirates, double-dealings, jumpy naval officers, running and swimming all night, riding all day, and the inn, which had no room for them.

"I will kill Prassal if I ever meet him again," Harold fumed.

"I will slam the lid of the nearest trunk upon his head," Andrew sourly stated.

"You are not advocating continuing to search for the trunk?" Harold asked. Andrew's concept of honor sometimes caused him headaches. "We owed services to Prassal, and, if I recall correctly, he dismissed us."

"I don't disagree. But the fact remains that a vicious attempt was made to steal the nobleman's property, and there are no guarantees it will be delivered per his instructions."

"We don't know who he is, or where to search for him. By a miracle, he even might be reunited with his possessions after this little mishap," Harold's mood slightly lifted upon this improbable, but cheerful scenario.

"When Prassal turns into an honest man."

Harold grinned for the first time since the swim in Marseille's harbor. "There is always hope," he consented with equal sarcasm. "For my peace of mind, I will forget this fiasco."

Andrew digested that proposal. "I pledge my life and honor that I will never mention this debacle to anyone."

"So do I." Harold solemnly shook his hand. "I am embarrassed to ever admit to our idiocy."

London, England - November 1712

. . .

Captain Mathew Johnson dropped to his knees on the hard floor in the richly appointed parlor. "Your Grace! I found the Great Mogul Diamond among the abandoned ruins in St. Domingue, but it was stolen from me in Marseille's harbor," Mathew hoped his tone delivered a believable mixture of humbleness and desperation. He had invented and rehearsed his story a hundred times, and yet, his mouth was dry and his heart beat as a fish on a deck.

"What happened?!" His Grace slammed his fist on the desk.

Mathew held out Marseille's newspaper. "When we docked in the harbor, the Marshall cousins swooped onto my ship ..."

His Grace exhaled sharply, rolled up his paper, and pounded it on Mathew's head. "I don't need bloody excuses! Where is my bloody diamond? "He searched for another newspaper on his desk and shoved the print under Mathew's nose. "The city elders are bloody fools. They could not even secure a description of these bastards!" He rolled up London's newspaper and slammed it on Mathew's head again before tossing it on the floor. Mathew craned his neck, seeing that the news of the near-destruction of Marseille Harbor had already officially reached England. His Grace picked up Marseille's newspaper from his desk. "Andrew Marshall and Harold Marshall, twenty years old, above average height. Andrew Marshall has shoulder-long brown hair and light eyes. Harold Marshall has short black hair and dark eyes," he read out loud. "Half of my guards fit this precise piece of intelligence! These bloody cousins own my diamond because you are an incompetent idiot and could not provide security on your own bloody ship! Give me a reason why I should not have your ship impounded." He threw himself into the chair.

"I found the Great Mogul Diamond once, Your Grace, and

I swear I will find it again, and make those insolent Marshall cousins pay!" Mathew begged in terror, the fear of losing his ship adding passion to his pleas.

"The bloody hell you will" His Grace upbraided him. "Why did you sail into Marseille with it?"

"My cargo was scheduled for delivery there."

"My diamond was scheduled for delivery here."

"I beg your forgiveness, Your Grace! I could not possibly imagine..."

"Of course not." The Duke sipped a honey-colored liquid from a gold-and-crystal goblet, and gestured for Mathew to continue.

"I found the diamond in the ruins where the infidel Kumaryan lived. He seemed mad, but I did not trust him. Maybe he was pretending? I brought him along and kept him in the brig. None of my men were aware of the diamond." "How did the Marshall cousins find the diamond on your ship?" His Grace scoffed. " Didn't you hide and secure it?"

Fortunately, Mathew had anticipated the question, and he attempted to appear dejected and embarrassed. "I kept it in a locked box, and the box was chained to the wall. The Marshall cousins chopped the door, and probably used the same axe to cut the chain," he explained.

"You damned fool. How did the Marshall cousins know about Kumaryan?"

Mathew's knees hurt, but he did not dare to stand up. "I... I am not certain," he said. "I might have heard their names in St. Domingue. Maybe they followed me?" He glanced up.

"Bloody imbecile," His Grace muttered as he finally motioned Mathew to rise.

After this audience, Mathew Johnson contemplated retirement in the New World. Once again, while consuming his customary nightly doze of rum, he thought how much money these pictures were worth. Selling the portraits on the continent or England would be too dangerous. Surely, there must be husbands or lovers anxious to find these portraits, but he had no desire to stick his neck in the noose by asking awkward questions. He would have to sell the portraits in the New World, but at what price? Even his untrained eyes recognized the high quality of the paintings. Besides, the demand for religiously themed art was almost non-existent in the New World. He consulted his tankard of ale, and an inspiration struck him. Suppose, just suppose, that the portraits and paintings were originally intended for different clients? And even if that was for the same person... whoever purchased religious ones would not admit to owning the women. Mathew Johnson raised a tankard to his own cleverness.

Montpellier, France - January 1713

"M. Antoine de la Fleure, what a coïncidence." Geoffrey de Contraille's father hailed him.

Geoffrey de Contraille introduced Antoine to his family, and, in particular, to his sister. At first, Antoine was unwilling to cause any hurt feelings for Mlle., but if her family continued their matchmaking attempts, he would have to abandon the inconvenient courtesy and just plainly tell her parents that he had neither the intention nor the desire to marry their daughter. No matter that the de Contraille family was one of the most prominent in Montpellier.

"Beautiful day, isn't it?" De Contraille's father fell in step with him, and his friendly chatter presaged a feeling of doom onto Antoine. "And what your plans might be for tonight, young man?"

"Carousing with Henri de Brangelton," Antoine repeated the answer he had provided to Mme. and Mlle. de Contraille a week earlier when they cornered him, and since that day he had enjoyed peace and quiet from their tacit disapproval.

"Ah, youth!" Monsieur was not as easily offended. "And tomorrow night?"

"My lips are sealed," Antoine bluffed. He had no intention to join the de Contraille family for dinner. Once was enough to give a man nightmares for a year. Antoine shamelessly watched the female shape crossing the street in front of them.

The man followed his line of vision and slapped him on the shoulder. "Of course, of course, I understand, I was young once..."

It took Antoine another half an hour to extricate himself from the eager father of Mlle. de Contraille.

Antoine's gloomy mood did not improve by the time he arrived home and found Henri reclining in a chair with a bottle of rum in his hand.

"I wish to heaven and hell that none of my friends, or even acquaintances, had any unmarried sisters. Give me that." Antoine confiscated the bottle and took a swig from it. "All fathers and mothers of all unmarried young women hide their daughters away from you when you introduce yourself. Why am I being hounded?"

Henri snatched the bottle back. "You seem trustworthy and responsible." He swirled the contents in the bottle and watched the liquid's motion. "Your family is one of the oldest in France and holds prominence in Lyon, whereas I..." he spread his hands in a theatrical gesture and grinned. "...am an irresponsible womanizer, and my father is an infamous adventurer known as devil de Brangelton. Need I say more?"

"Fortunate you," Antoine said feelingly as he pried the

bottle from Henri's hands before noticing a mix of anger, amusement and disbelief in Henri's face. "What is wrong?"

"The honorable fencing master just expelled me." Henri sounded resigned to his fate.

"Why?" In a single gulp, Antoine finished the rum and regretfully shook the empty bottle.

"He caught his daughter - Marielle, the brown-haired one - kissing me, so he insisted that I leave town immediately, or he threatened to kill me," Henri explained.

Antoine sat back and shook his head in amazement. Henri's love affairs - was he still sleeping with Bernadette or had he moved on to Nicole's bed? - were a subject of speculation, admiration, and wagers by their classmates in the fencing school and beyond.

"You already have a mistress. Or is it two now? What were you thinking?!"

"I was not thinking," Henri admitted. "Let me have that." He shook the empty bottle upside down to make certain no drop of precious liquid was wasted.

"What is the official rationale for expelling you?" Antoine asked.

"He will not tolerate my extended absences from his school. Within the past month or two, I missed more than half of my fencing sessions."

"Did I miss as sessions many as you?" An excellent idea formed in Antoine's mind.

"You are not being expelled," Henri said defensively.

"But it is an outrage that you are expelled and I am not when we are both guilty of the same offense."

Henri chuckled. "Are you looking for an excuse to run away from Mlle. de Contraille?"

"Maybe," Antoine conceded. "Besides, if you leave, who will be my challenge at the fencing competition?"

They stopped at the Singing Monkey tavern to fortify themselves with dinner, and afterwards barged into the honorable fencing master's office to dispute the unfairness of Henri de Brangelton's treatment. The fencing master wasted no time in expelling Antoine de la Fleure as well, and he added drunkenness as another cause for their dismissal.

A tad unsteady on their feet, the friends climbed up the stairs to their lodgings. "I suppose we are leaving tomorrow." Antoine kicked off his boots.

Henri paused in the process of untangling the sword belt. "No. I promised to see my love before I leave."

"Have you lost your mind? Her father will force you to marry her!"

"I doubt it."

Antoine reached for his saddlebags. "We are leaving tomorrow, or I am heading to Ferrand and begging your father to save you from the misfortune about to be brought by your womanizing. Your choice."

"Why are you in such a rush to leave? Are you afraid Mlle. de Contraille will bid you a proper adieu?"

"You can have Mlle. de Contraille and her adieu!" Antoine slammed the door to the wardrobe. "Why don't you roll the dice? Even number - we stay another day, odd number - we leave early tomorrow."

Henri shook the dice and tossed, uttered elaborate profanities upon the numbers two and three, but he did not have a choice.

4

BROTHERS AND SISTER
LYON, FRANCE – MAY 1713

Charlotte is the daughter of my and your mother's closest friends. They handed her over to our family's custody. Our family. That includes you. I trust you and Henri will make certain she does entangle herself or Raoul in any trouble.

Laurent de la Fleure to Antoine de la Fleure - 1713

THE SUN SHONE BRIGHTLY IN THE CLOUDLESS SKY. RAOUL and Charlotte were nowhere in sight, father was occupied with sorting through the business ledgers, and mother attended to her correspondence. Peace and quiet reigned in the de la Fleure household, and Antoine and Henri were bored to oblivion. By mid-day, they had swum in the river (before their siblings woke up), shot at the rats (their siblings bet and watched), finished a fencing round (their siblings watched and bet), ate omelettes (so did their siblings), and read the newspapers (their siblings inexplicably disappeared during this activity). The two young men roamed aimlessly around the chateau, retreated from the sight of their siblings (who occupied themselves by tossing what appeared to be a tankard -?!- back and forth), and headed to the stables.

"It is frayed," Henri inspected the bridle. "I should probably buy a new one."

"That means a trip to Lyon," Antoine proposed. The bridle was indeed slightly frayed, and Henri did need a new one. "We might as well stay there overnight." His father kept a small townhouse in the center of the city for the family's convenience and comfort.

Antoine and Henri left instructions to saddle the horses, said farewell to mother, carefully avoided father in case he decided to assign some civic duty to them, and returned to the stables only to discover that Charlotte and Raoul had supervised the saddling of not two, but four horses.

"Where are you going?" Antoine asked Raoul.

"Aren't you going to Lyon to fix the bridle?"

"Yes, we are, but you are not."

"She is going, so why shouldn't I?" his brother argued.

"No, she is not." Antoine turned his attention to Charlotte.

She blankly stared at him, put her foot in a stirrup, and swung herself into the saddle.

Antoine held onto the reins. "Get off."

"Why?" Her dark blue eyes were wide set and slightly slanted. At her age, most girls blossomed had into young women and flirted with him, but Charlotte de Brangelton could easily be mistaken for a boy - on this day, she wore breeches and a doublet over a linen shirt, and her thick black hair, only shoulder long, framed and shadowed her face.

"Neither I nor Henri recall inviting you and Raoul along." Antoine's severe tone should have precluded any arguments.

"Get off the horse. Now. Do not make me pull you off," Henri threatened.

Charlotte unblinkingly regarded her brother till his patience reached its limit and he moved toward her. Only then she slowly dismounted and stomped away, swearing under her breath with every step.

Antoine was checking the saddle on his horse when he heard the sound of hooves coming toward him. Across the stall, Henri raised his head from inspecting his stirrup, and hollered for his sister to stop. Antoine reached for the reins of her horse, but she jerked the reins high above her head and out of his reach, and kicked out with her foot. Antoine hurriedly retreated in fear that she would lose her balance. He should have known better. Her confident posture taunted him as she flew past him and outside.

"Stop, you...!!" Henri yelled. He vaulted onto his horse, and followed his sister.

Charlotte leaned forward and urged her horse into a full gallop.

"I must see this." Antoine followed Henri.

In a mad dash, Charlotte crossed the gully before they even started the chase. By the time they were half-way, she disappeared behind the trees. Once they cleared the turn, they almost missed her – Charlotte managed to stop and guide her horse off the road. The mare pranced in the tall grass of the flower-speckled meadow, and Charlotte idly practiced standing up in the stirrups.

Henri plunged into the meadow, caught up with her, and took a swing to slap her on the back of her head. Charlotte lurched her body sideways and disappeared behind the horse. Antoine heard Raoul's loud hiss, and both involuntarily stood up in the stirrups to check if she had fallen - which was unlikely - or jumped from the horse. Henri grabbed the reins and brought her horse around. In a feat worthy of an acrobat, Charlotte was balancing herself along the side of the animal, her body parallel to the ground, right foot in the stirrup and the left knee thrown across the horse's neck for balance. Her left hand gripped the saddle and the right hand held the reins.

"What?" She did not move.

"What are you doing?" Henri inquired.

"Practicing my riding skills." Charlotte glowed with innocence, pulled herself back up into the saddle, and gave her brother the same blank stare she had given Antoine in the stables.

"You are not coming to Lyon with us," Henri insisted.

She clicked the reins, riding deeper into the meadow. "I don't want to go to Lyon with you."

"Glad to hear that," her brother said to her back and steered his horse back to the road.

"Why did you take off after her?" Antoine asked.

Henri stroked the neck of his horse. "I thought she was riding to town ahead of us," he grudgingly admitted.

"By herself?" Raoul uttered in disbelief.

"She would have ridden halfway and waited for us to catch up."

"Would she do that?"

"Yes. I cannot send her back by herself, and I will not waste time backtracking with her," Henri explained in exasperation. "She has done it before."

"And you don't mind?" Raoul wondered.

Henri ignored the question. He probably regretted sharing his experiences dealing with his sister.

"Did you ever try to slap some sense into her head?" Antoine prompted.

Henri rolled his sleeve up. The scar was small. It seemed inflicted with a knife. "Reminder from the last time I hit my sister. She went after me with a boot knife. Keep that in mind, you reprobate." The last sentence was intended for Raoul, who exchanged horrified glances with Antoine.

"She was severely punished for that," Henri clarified. "In truth, Antoine, it served me extremely well," Henri leaned over to shove Raoul outside of hearing distance. "There was a very fine woman in town. She believed it was a wound on her account. I did not disillusion her. She took care of me, in more ways than one... I will tell you on the way to town."

Raoul had eagerly edged closer.

"What are you doing?" Antoine asked his brother.

"Can I come with you? I promise, I won't cause any problems."

"No," both young men answered at the same time. They did not need the company of children in town.

Raoul swore, repeating Charlotte's phrases and mimicking her manner, and let his horse fall behind. Antoine made a mental note to mention this incident to his father. Raoul's behavior was drastically deteriorating with the increasing duration of Charlotte's visit. The boy's attitude had become confrontational and argumentative in her company.

Antoine and Henri abandoned their siblings to frolic in the meadow, and peacefully proceeded on their way.

Antoine and Henri left the horses with the keeper of the townhouse and looked for a new perfect bridle. After the dinner of partridge pie was consumed, Henri introduced himself to a bright-eyed Mme. Emilie and his conduct brought a blush to a merchant's young daughter till her father glowered. The crowd promenading in Place Louis-le-Grand Square was diverse on this late afternoon. Antoine and Henri strolled around and entertained themselves by guessing the origins of the men. There were braids and brass from Austria, gold and furs from

Poland, elaborate costumes from Venice and Savoy, somber fashion from the Swiss, and even turbans from the Ottoman Empire and long dresses of African countries, along with distinctive outlines of hats and gowns from the Orient. Lyon, the town at the juncture of the Rhone and Saone rivers, was a thriving city of commerce and a port - a sophisticated, expanded, orderly port, but still a port. The afternoon's long shadows foreshadowed the approaching dusk. From behind the equestrian statue of the Sun King, a familiar voice floated above the din of the crowd and stopped Antoine and Henri in mid-step.

"I was not cheating!"

Antoine and Henri cautiously eased their way around the base of the statue and peeked around, in time to witness Hugh de Boucher swinging his fist at Charlotte. He was the same age as Raoul, but slightly built, and shorter than Charlotte. She evaded his punch and countered with an accurate blow to his chin. He fell back and screamed. The noise emitted by his vocal cords interrupted his older brother's conversation with a young woman and the irate older brother approached the group of youngsters with a severe frown. "What happened here?" de Boucher asked.

Hugh stood up, gingerly rubbed his chin, and pointed at Charlotte. "He was cheating at marbles."

"I was not cheating," Charlotte said. "You have no skills."

"He was not cheating," Raoul defended Charlotte. Antoine and Henri exchanged looks of pure amazement and waited to see what will happen next.

"I did not ask you," the older de Boucher snapped at Raoul and grabbed Charlotte by the hair. "You owe my brother an apology, you little...."

"Get your hands off me!" Charlotte screamed in a high-pitched voice.

De Boucher shifted his grip on her hair to better see her face.

"Let her go." Raoul grabbed de Boucher's arm. "My father will kill you if you touch her."

"Her?" He pushed Raoul away and pulled Charlotte closer, lifting her chin up with his other hand.

Charlotte arched her back and dropped her hand to her boot.

Henri lunged forward and closed his hand around her wrist. He barely acted in time to prevent her from puncturing de Boucher's shoulder with her boot knife.

"Get your hands off my sister," Henri demanded.

De Boucher's eyes crossed when he fixed them on the blade aimed at his collarbone. He released Charlotte and jumped back. Raoul stood frozen with utter bewilderment, and Antoine realized he was probably doing the same. Henri's other hand grasped Charlotte's shoulder, and he pulled her away.

"Your sister." De Boucher thoughtfully regarded Charlotte. "She was cheating in a game with my brother."

"...was not cheating," Raoul and Charlotte objected in chorus.

"Maybe your sister can play with me." De Boucher's eyes remained locked on Charlotte.

"Go to hell," she said before Henri had a chance to open his mouth.

"Is she always so ill tempered?" De Boucher finally looked at her brother.

"Are you always so bad mannered?" Henri responded.

"Are you always so brave?" De Boucher's fingers curled around the hilt of his sword.

"Hold her." Henri handed Charlotte to Antoine.

Antoine secured her upper arms. Restraining her was a prudent action, as she still held the knife in her hand.

Predictably, she pulled forward and tossed her head back, nearly hitting his jaw. Antoine tightened his grip. "Stay out of it, or I will knock you out," he warned the wriggling Charlotte. "Your brother will deal with de Boucher without your help. Put the knife away."

"Get your hands off me."

"Put the knife away."

"Get your hands off me."

"Do I have to knock you out?" Antoine threatened.

The knife disappeared into her boot.

Henri's face settled in a stone mask, his hand resting on the hilt of his sword. "I am warning you, de Boucher: stay away from my sister."

De Boucher thoughtfully regarded Charlotte, shifted his gaze to Antoine's hands on her upper arms, and held Antoine's look with disdain. "Mlle," he tipped his hat to her and left.

"What are you doing here?" Henri inquired of Wildcat. "Where are your horses?" he added with more passion. "You said you did not want to go to Lyon!" He took a half-hearted swing at her.

"I did not want to ride with you." Charlotte kicked a pebble into a wall. "But I am glad you are here." She squeezed his hand.

Henri put his arm around her shoulders. "What shall we do about you, Charlotte de Brangelton?" he asked rhetorically.

Antoine had no desire to explain to his father why and how Charlotte ended up in town without Henri and himself. "What are you doing here, Raoul?"

"I... Please don't tell father, Antoine! I could not stop her!" his brother begged with desperation. "Wildcat claimed I was afraid to ride to town by myself. I had no choice. Don't you understand? She accused me of cowardice! Did you know that she carried a knife?"

A boot knife for a child's twelfth birthday was a de Brangelton family tradition, but Antoine had not expected this tradition to carry over to a girl. "When were you planning to return home, you dimwit? Didn't you notice the time? The sun will set in an hour."

Raoul kicked a pebble from under his foot. "We... we stopped at the townhouse. We expected you and Henri to stay overnight, so we – she - figured that we would ride back home with you. Charlotte said everyone will think we rode here with you."

"Has it occurred to you that we might bring loose women to the townhouse?" Henri shamelessly speculated. "There are reasons why men need to leave the children behind."

His sister wriggled her nose in distaste. "Monsieur Laurent will kill you both if you convert his residence into a brothel."

Hours later, after feeding the siblings at the Lucky Rabbit tavern and staying to watch the tricks of a trained monkey, Henri and Antoine finally ushered their siblings inside the townhouse.

Henri lingered at the entrance. "Why did de Boucher back off so readily?" he pondered.

"Did not dare to risk a duel with my friend," Antoine guessed.

Henri shook his head. "She is no beauty, but to each his own. I had an impression that he might have liked her."

"You are not serious," Antoine dismissed the notion. "You have passionate feelings about most women, but, with all respect for your family... who in his right mind would desire a girl with a knife in her hand?"

Inside the house, Charlotte and Raoul finished lighting the candles. She pulled her knife out and handed it to Raoul. They leaned their heads close for inspection.

"She likes Raoul," Henri commented.

"What?" The image of Charlotte and Raoul bound by matrimonial chains sent a shiver through Antoine's spine. His younger brother deserved a better fate than commitment to the insane Charlotte. "Do you recall a single day without an argument?"

"Not even half a day, but they reconcile quickly. She does not speak to either de Paulet brother for days."

Raoul waved at them. "Why are you outside? Antoine, look at her knife!"

Antoine had no desire to listen to Henri's far-fetched conjectures. He checked the sharp knife and reluctantly handed it back to her. "If you had stabbed de Boucher, what do you think he would have done? How would he have reacted?" he asked.

"I don't care. I would have been on the opposite side of the square by the time he recovered enough to do anything."

"Allow me to explain to you the most likely outcome," Antoine felt obligated to point out. "He would have chased you down and killed you on the spot."

"He would not have chased me when his shoulder was bleeding," Charlotte countered.

"Yes, he would," Antoine disputed. "Men tend to lose their temper when stabbed, and most men turn violent upon such an occasion."

The candlelight reflected in her opaque eyes. "What is your advice, then? Should I have grabbed his sword and hit him with the hilt?"

Antoine could find no intelligent answer. "You explain to your sister, Henri."

Henri shook his head. "Don't you understand that common sense has no place in arguments with my sister?"

Later in the week, after Sunday service at St. Jean's Cathedral, Antoine only wanted to wander around Lyon and to watch the new and the usual street entertainers. He could not revel in carefree existence on a pleasant afternoon, he thought sourly as he exercised his self-control to appear unconcerned and oblivious to the smoldering glances from Mlle. Anne and her mother. No matter how fervently his mother wished for him to behave politely, he refused to corner himself into any situation which could be interpreted as any hint of remote interest in Mlle. Anne. Better rudeness now, than confrontation later, he decided as he justified his inaction to himself.

Henri joyfully entertained the audience of half a dozen young women, thus helpfully emphasizing Antoine's indifference, and Antoine dwelled upon the unfairness of life. Anywhere in France, Henri was free to act as he pleased. No one expected a de Brangelton to follow any conventions, but Antoine de la Fleure was the son and heir of Laurent de la Fleure, Comte of Chateaux. Their family was one of the most prominent in Lyon, and to add to Antoine's misery, Raoul and Charlotte were absorbed in a heated argument and approaching him.

"What now?" he asked when they stopped in sullen silence.

"We are heading to Place Louis-le-Grand," they blurted out at the same time.

"Last week, there was a puppet show. We're hoping maybe they will perform another play today," Charlotte added.

"Didn't Henri make it explicitly clear that you must stay within his sight all the time?" Antoine reminded her.

Charlotte's dirty look at Raoul was accompanied with an elbow into his side. "My brother is pre-occupied now. He will be vexed by any interruption, so we are telling you," she explained. "In case he recalls my existence, tell him, will you?" she added over her shoulder as they walked away.

An excellent idea occurred to Antoine. "I will join you."

"You will?" Raoul and Charlotte exclaimed in happy relief.

"Lead the way," Antoine waved to his mother and happily followed, privately speculating on how she would explain his disappearance to Mlle. Anne and her mother. And he would be spared a lecture about the obligations of a de la Fleure, since he was only following father's instructions to keep an eye on Charlotte. Her brother was obviously not up to the task.

A group of dancers provided the entertainment at Place Louis-le-Grand. Charlotte, glowing with innocence, headed toward City Hall and away from the bridge across the Saone. Raoul stayed at her side, and Antoine, having no particular desire to find himself within Mlle. Anne's line of vision again, followed in their footsteps. At the City Market, he bought beef-filled pies and a jug of watered wine. They lunched at the riverbank to watch the boats and barges gliding back and forth. After a while, they strolled to Place des Terraux and watched a juggler there. Their peaceful pursuits were shuttered when a group consisting of Henri de Brangelton, a couple other young men, and half a dozen young women, appeared at the end of the street and Mlle. Anne enthusiastically waved at them. Antoine shuddered. His disappointment reflected in his cohorts' faces.

Charlotte pulled onto his sleeve. "Antoine, I don't want to deal with them."

"Neither do I," he concurred. In fact, there was a way to avoid this unpleasantness. "When I look away, you two run to the left and around that building. Take the second traboule on the right. At the end of the alley, wait for me by the wall," he instructed and turned to greet the approaching group with a formal bow. With perfect timing, Charlotte bolted at top speed and Raoul followed her a moment later. Antoine stopped in mid-bow and contracted his face into a murderous frown. He pretended momentary hesitation and headed after his brother and Charlotte. As soon as he disappeared from the company's sight, he raced toward the old wall to regroup with his charges. Antoine climbed up first, pulled up Charlotte, and then made certain that Raoul had made it as well. The wall was slightly higher on another side, so Antoine climbed down half-way and jumped off. Raoul followed his example but Charlotte apprehensively eyed the height.

"Jump. I will catch you." Antoine held out his arms and Charlotte fearlessly leapt down.

A quarter of an hour later, Henri caught up with them. "You are using my sister as an excuse to escape from Mlle. Anne."

"Yes, if such desperate action discourages Mlle. Anne. Why are you here?"

"After you and your juvenile conspirators hurried across the Saone, the distraught Mlle. Anne insisted we search for you." Henri ignored Charlotte and Raoul making faces upon hearing Mlle. Anne's name. "She was adamant about assisting you with overseeing these brats. I led the expedition to the best of my ability , but eventually your luck ran out and Mlle. Mariette noticed you. Luckily, Mlle. Anne's fastest pace compares to Wildcat's speed like a jackass' trot to an Arabian's full gallop. By the time we rounded the corner, you were nowhere to be found. I left the search party to figure out the escape route and challenged myself to guess correctly. Mlle. Anne was quite aghast at my sister's pace... Stop it, you two," the last words were addressed to Charlotte and Raoul. "What are your plans now?"

"Roman amphitheater?" Antoine suggested.

Charlotte perked up.

"We have to cross the Saone and trudge up the hill to the amphitheater, don't we? That excursion will take a couple hours," Henri objected. "My beloved Mlle. Mariette will desperately miss me."

"And Mlle. Anne will pine after Antoine," Charlotte snickered. So did Raoul.

"It might work to your advantage, Henri," Antoine said. "Isn't there some nonsense that absence makes the heart grow warmer?"

Henri whistled. "An interesting theory."

"And, even better for you, Antoine, it might possibly break ... ah, what is the word? - love struck? - Mlle. Anne's heart," Raoul was blessed with inspiration.

"Mlle. Anne is marriage-struck. Mlle. Mariette is silly. She might even worry about Henri." Charlotte placed her hand in the proximity of her heart and pretended to swoon. Raoul crossed his eyes and panted.

"Quit that mockery," Henri admonished his sister and Raoul.

The deep shadows on the evening created lacy patterns on the road, the air was pleasantly fragrant with the smell of blooming flowers, the breeze rustled the leaves, and the birds had organized a choir. Father and mother rode ahead as Raoul and Charlotte peacefully and excitedly chatted about their experiences of the day and Antoine and Henri fell back from the little cavalcade.

"I am amazed that you were right," Henri mused. "Mlle. Mariette was ecstatic when I came back."

"And?" Antoine prompted after an uncharacteristic pause in narration.

"I... I needed an excuse why I was absent so long... so I claimed that I felt obligated to stay with my sister... and that was fine, and admirable, until ... until the time for explanation why you did not return with me," Henri said guiltily.

"I cannot wait to hear what extravagant excuse you invented."

"I could find no better explanation that my sister was hungry and insisted that we stayed to eat. Then I claimed that I was starved for Mlle. Mariette's company and thus deflected the inquiries about my extended long absence." Henri sighed. "I am sorry, Antoine, but other fine young men promptly pointed out that you..." Henri dramatically paused, "might prefer my sister's company."

"This is preposterous!" Antoine exclaimed, but the absurdity of the concept overcame his indignation and they roared in laughter. He could not care less about a wild horde of marriage-minded females, and maybe his non-cavalier actions would discourage any opportunistic notions. He had had a very pleasant day. Raoul and Charlotte, enthralled with sightseeing, had not quarreled even once, and he would have chosen their company again over Mlle. Anne.

CHOICES

LYON, FRANCE – JULY 1713

Or the freedom on the road,
I can only be at peace
When across the world I roam!

From a popular song, - c.1712

THE DELIBERATIONS BETWEEN THE CITY ELDERS AND
magistrates about one or another city ordinance seemed to last
an eternity. Afterwards, Antoine and his father rode home in
the scorching afternoon heat. The last stretch of the road
circled around the gorge until the post with the de la Fleure
coat of arms marked a narrow path which snaked through the
sparse trees and rocks and led toward the chateau. A mile
further around the bend, Antoine and his father paused to
enjoy the view of the stately building. Antoine's grandfather
had demolished the medieval heap and constructed the new
home during the Sun King's reign. In line with the fashion of

those glory days, the chateau was three stories high and symmetrical, with a steep roof and a raised round turret in the middle.

For another mile, the road gently sloped down and across a small gully. Centuries ago, the moat had protected the dwelling, but now shrubs and tall grass had successfully claimed the land. Beyond the gulch, the path widened into an alley guarded by the evenly spaced maple trees and guided the visitors toward the formal entrance in the center of the chateau. On the right, the old-fashioned herb and flower garden was punctuated by trellises, classical statues of Roman gods, bird baths, and a raised sundial. On the left lay the paved yard and, beyond it, the pathway around and behind the chateau toward the stables and the storage and service buildings. Above the formal front entrance of the residence, the de la Fleure family Coat of Arms was prominently chiseled in stone and brightly painted. The centuries-old escutcheon-shaped shield had a gold turreted stripe on top, a black stripe below, and a red narrow stripe which defined the border of the quarters. A golden horse pranced in the dark green pasture on the upper right, and a golden turret stood against the dark green on bottom left. The white fields boasted the sun on the upper left and three gold fleurs-de-lis on the bottom right.

"Antoine. Do you recall a single word from this morning?" Father asked after they collapsed in the library to consume cold lentil soup.

"No," Antoine answered truthfully. His mind had meandered after half an hour of deliberations.

"You are a grown man, but you have no inclination to recognize your civic duties and responsibilities."

Antoine braced himself for a familiar lecture about the de la Fleure obligations.

"Thus, it is military service for you," father announced. "You shall enlist with the Musketeers."

Antoine had expected that, and he was ready for the imminent confrontation. "With all respect, father, I would rather not enlist with the Musketeers."

"You. Don't. Say." Father was barely able to speak in response to this heresy. "Have you conjured a better occupation for yourself?"

Antoine was unprepared for this question. "I have no inclination or desire to serve in the military, father," he repeated.

The conversation took a turn for the worse after that, and concluded when father threatened to drag him out to Paris by his ears. Antoine left the room in ominous silence, collected all the money he had on hand, which, he calculated, should last him for a couple of months, packed his saddle bags, and left home. As he left, he heard a shouting match between mother and father. Mother was defending him, and, most likely, she would prevail, but now hell would freeze over before his father would relent and loan him money. Antoine needed to survive. Enlisting with the Musketeers would be one option, unacceptable as it was. Another option was to hire out his blade, and this concept led him on the road to Ferrand. He would discuss his predicament with Henri, and maybe Henri's father would give him much-needed recommendations.

Ferrand, France – July 1713

M. Francis sat through Antoine's narration with a serene expression. Toward the end of his recitation, Antoine began to ponder if the man had even heard a word he said. "M. Francis, if you would provide any recommendations for me?" Antoine asked at the conclusion of his monologue.

M. Francis regarded him with opaque, unreadable eyes. "You dim-witted young rooster," he pronounced, "has it occurred to you to think before acting on impulse?"

"Yes, it occurred to me." This interview was no better than the exchange with his own father. "But I will be damned if I blindly follow my father's whims."

The Comte de Tournelles pig-headedly continued his previous line of thought.

Antoine stood up to finish this interview in the same manner he had finished the discourse with his father.

"After your unacceptable stand-off with your father, Captain d'Ornille will not even allow you within a mile of the Musketeers' Headquarters," M. Francis continued as Antoine walked toward the door. "I, on the other hand, am soft-hearted and just might bring you along on my next business."

Antoine stopped in his tracks.

"Provided that you first reconcile with your father," M. Francis casually added.

"I doubt my father will speak to me any time soon," Antoine said before his mind caught up with the conversation.

"He just might, if you apologize."

"No, I will not." Antoine sputtered.

"Do you wish to drive your parents apart because of your stubborn refusal to recognize the error of your ways?"

"What?!" To the best of Antoine's recollection, he had mentioned nothing of hearing their argument.

"Your mother is a woman of impressive diplomatic skills," M. Francis reminded him. "Do you have any idea, you hasty idiot, how much effort she has exerted over the years, to keep the peace between you and your father? No? Have you ever questioned, young ass, why your father and mother ever quarreled? Yes, over your irrational conduct. Stop glaring at me and thank your mother who always defended you! Marguerite is probably still advocating on your behalf right now, that is, if she and your father are still on civil terms!"

A belated realization occurred to Antoine that indeed, his mother must be worried. He should have left her a message, but in his own defense, he had not known his destination when he left.

"Do you wish to be the cause of estrangement between your parents?" M. Francis repeated.

"No," Antoine answered.

Antoine emerged from his interview with the elder de Brangelton in a state of dazed agitation. Conflicting emotions danced in his mind, not least of which was guilt and embarrassment for his behavior.

"What did my father say?" Henri anxiously inquired.

"He bestowed many colorful epithets on me," Antoine provided a shortened version of his interview with M. Francis. "I and my father must reconcile before your father allows me to accompany him on his next trip."

Henri nodded sympathetically, although without any surprise. "My condolences. Travels with my father on business exhaust body and mind."

"Your father does not understand. It will take my father years to calm down."

"Don't underestimate my devil of a father. But why don't you enlist with the Musketeers? Women love the uniform."

"I don't see you joining the troops".

Henri emitted a regretful sigh. "Captain d'Ornille refused any de Brangelton's presence in the Musketeers because my sister expressed her ambition to enlist in the regiment. Besides, I don't need the uniform to impress women. You, on the other hand…"

"Why am I listening to you?" Antoine asked.

The next day, despite the oppressive summer heat, Antoine, Henri, and Charlotte rode to Clermont. She dressed in boy's clothes, and completed her outfit with a dagger strapped onto her belt.

"I see you moved a weapon within an easy reach," Antoine commented. "How frequently do you feel the inclination to stab a man?"

She narrowed her eyes. "Only when some jackass provokes me."

At the Town Hall square, a group of boys had set up a straw bale for a target in their knife throw competition. Charlotte dismounted, tied her pony to the rail, flung the phrase *"I will stay around here"* in her brother's general direction, and hurried toward the players. She stepped forward to the marker, retrieved her boot knife, and neatly tossed it into the center of the target. The boys emitted a uniform groan, loud enough to be heard across the square.

"The de Paulet brothers are there. They will find me if she causes any trouble." Henri dismissed Antoine's questioning look.

"Aren't you worried about her?" Antoine regretted his impulse as soon as the words escaped his mouth. Charlotte's activities were none of his business.

"Why?" Henri gave him a curious look. "How much do you worry about Raoul?"

"Charlotte is a girl. I think," Antoine reminded him.

Henri remained unconcerned. "I am just her brother, Antoine; what can I do? Father challenges her to pass for a boy, and she succeeds very well. What a pleasant surprise to see you, my beautiful Mlle...."

Antoine finished securing all three horses and exchanged polite pleasantries upon a perfunctory introduction with yet another one of Henri's admiring female acquaintances. He realized that his presence was unwelcome for the arduous journey to the Cathedral de Notre-Dame-de-l'Assomption located two blocks away and he strolled back to check on Charlotte and her friends. She won another game, the money transferred to her purse, and a loud argument commenced. The boy insisted on a re-match, but she refused to play against his empty pockets.

"Where is Henri?" she asked Antoine.

"He was...ah...detained."

"Ah. Detained." she mocked. "In other words, he will be occupied for a while. Shall we visit the armory?"

"You are not allowed to go in there," Simon de Paulet sulkily reminded her.

"I am not allowed to go there by myself," she amended. "Just tell my brothers if he happens to stroll this way, will you?" She waited for his almost imperceptible nod before she sharply turned around. "Are you planning to stand here all day?" she asked Antoine over her shoulder and sauntered away without bothering to wait if he followed.

Both de Paulet brothers breathed a sigh of relief at her departure.

"... a weapon from the Orient," Charlotte was saying when Antoine caught up with her.

Charlotte led him toward the no man's land between Clermont and Ferrand. A good half an hour later, they crossed the empty glade that seemingly divided the two formerly separate towns. No wonder she was not allowed to visit the armory by herself: The thoroughfare boasted a tavern, a fencing room, a brothel, another tavern, and a farrier, and it led directly to a military garrison. An ideal place for the weapons shop, but obviously not the place even M. Francis would allow his young daughter to casually visit. Charlotte speedily crossed the street and slid inside the armory.

"What are you doing here?!" The gruff voice belonged to an older, grizzled man with the demeanor of an old soldier.

Charlotte saluted. "Good day, Monsieur. I am with him. He is a guest of my father."

The man cussed under his breath, sighed, nodded to Antoine, and resumed his conversation with an Army Lieutenant.

A young man entered the shop. "Good day, Charlotte," he called softly. "What a pleasant surprise to meet you here." He approached her. "But of course. The armory. Shall we meet at the garrison next time? Or two doors down."

"Go to hell." Without any hesitation, Charlotte dropped her hand toward her dagger.

The conversation between the two other men faltered. "M. Guest of Charlotte's father. If your charge spills Monsieur's blood here, you will pay for the cleanup," the grizzled man warned him.

"Leave her alone." Antoine addressed the recipient of Charlotte' wrath.

"Who are you?" he asked, and not without reason.

Antoine took a moment to determine if he should just repeat Charlotte's favorite phrase, or to keep the dialogue as civil as circumstances allowed. That was a strategic mistake.

"None of your business," Charlotte forestalled him.

"You possess such a fiery disposition, Charlotte. Does your father know him?"

"Go to -" She spattered in indignation when Antoine clapped his hand over her mouth. She obviously was very accustomed to the frequent use of this statement.

"Do not make me quote her." Antoine recognized the man.

"What have I done?" He spread his arms.

"You spoke to her. Don't repeat the same mistake." Antoine recalled the circumstances of their acquaintance from years ago. The name escaped him, but the memory of a brawl in the town square arose with a vengeance. "I will trash you at the slightest provocation."

The object of the discussion sunk her teeth into Antoine's hand and he promptly released her. "You will have to roll the dice with Henri for this pleasure," she said.

The man regarded him with distaste before his eye twitched in recognition. He left without another word. The grizzled man and the Lieutenant resumed their conversation.

Lyon, France – August 1713

"De Brangelton," Laurent de la Fleure glanced over the rim of his wine cup. "My oldest son must learn discipline. Yes, I am aware that you do not understand that concept. I have no doubts that Antoine purposely provoked his teachers in military school in order to be expelled. I have not detected any inclinations for drunkenness, and we can very successfully surmise the real reasons for his expulsion, along with your son, from fencing school. Last year, Antoine did not hesitate to challenge a neighbor to a duel over a card game. My son left home in a fit of temper. Didn't he realize that his mother was beyond herself with worry about him? Antoine has no notion of obligation nor duty nor respect..."

"Where you any different at his age? I suspect that you were just as pleasant to deal with," Francis goaded his friend.

Laurent wisely refrained from answering the rhetorical question. "At his age, I considered myself only just as smart as my father. My son believes he is more intelligent than I."

"At least, he is not single-mindedly intent on sleeping with every willing woman of decent appearance, which seems to be life's purpose for my son."

"Ah, yes, and my elder son explained to a Marquise with four daughters that he did not intend to allow a silly woman to chain him down in domestic purgatory. His words. Stop laughing, de Brangelton. I had to apologize for his crass eloquence!"

"Back to the current matter. At least, Antoine asked my advice," Francis reminded him.

"No one with common sense ever asks your advice." He smirked at that consolation. "Allow me to guess. You encouraged him to do anything he damn pleases, didn't you?"

"Not at all. I only invited him to join Henrietta and me on a trip."

"You. Don't..." Laurent sputtered.

"... on the condition that he reconciles with you first."

Laurent took a deep breath. "And how will you achieve such a miracle?" he asked with forced patience.

"You are wiser than your elder son and heir. I expect you will forgive his impetuous action when he apologizes for it."

He contemplated the luster of his goblet. "Did my elder son and heir express any remorse for his behavior?"

"Bet you a bottle of brandy that he will apologize." Francis offered.

"Accepted. And then will you please relieve me of his immediate presence?"

"Temporarily. I suspect that after a couple of months in my company, your son might beg you to send him off under Captain d'Ornille's command."

The former Lieutenant of the Musketeers grunted. "I doubt it. He is too stubborn and conceited to admit defeat. I am happy to accept your kind and generous offer."

Antoine took a deep breath and slowly exhaled before turning the door handle and entering the library. "Father."

"Guilty as charged."

"I apologize for walking out," Antoine forced himself to say. "But I am not enlisting with the Musketeers."

"You informed me of that," father reminded him. "Explicitly."

"Yes, father."

"Be thankful that I have chosen to overlook your unacceptable behavior. Again."

Antoine inclined his head.

Father gritted his teeth. "I would be significantly less lenient if your mother had not interceded on your behalf. Again. I trust you have had the decency to thank her for that."

"Yes, father." Antoine kept his temper in check. "I profusely apologized to mother for causing her worry," he added. She had been distressed enough to greet him with a slap across his head, and he endured an hour long lecture after that.

"I am pleasantly surprised at that." Father critically looked him over. "I changed my mind about recommending you for service in the Musketeers. Why would I saddle my friend d'Ornille with a disobedient headache like you?"

"Yes, indeed, why?" Antoine seconded.

Father chose to ignore his comment. "I expected the Comte de Tournelles to withdraw his invitation, but, unfortunately for you, he is willing to deal with you."

"Don't you mean, fortunately for me?" Antoine clarified.

Father shook his head. "No. You have no idea of what you volunteered yourself into." He stood up. "Listen carefully, Antoine, and heed my warning. I expect you to make yourself useful to the Comte de Tournelles, or I will disown you and no appeals to your mother will save you. Is that understood?"

"Yes, father."

His father seemed to smirk. "Good luck, my boy. You will need it."

Marseille, France – December 1713

Commandant Marcoux of Marseille had seen plenty of cutthroats in his life, on land and at sea. He had been a soldier for ten years, he had sailed on a privateer boat just as long, and there were days which he would never care to remember and days he could not remember no matter how much he cared to.

The man who entered his office was a fine example of an elite cutthroat. The stylish expensive clothing and the wig of a government official could not conceal the truth put forth by his confident swagger and the ruthlessness in his eyes. The Commandant did not even see the Musketeer until the Musketeer slammed the door into the face of Marcoux' officer on duty, and stayed by the entrance, a sinister figure with a hat pulled low over his face. The fine-dressed cutthroat stood in front of his desk, wordlessly and unblinkingly staring at him, and Marcoux found himself raising up from his chair.

"May I help you, Monsieur?" he said and realized that their admission into his office was neither requested nor announced. These unwelcome visitors, in their assumed authority, had forced their way.

"Here are my papers from the Navy." The man lay his assignment papers on the table. Marcoux recognized the seals and signatures and reached to read the documents, but the man slapped another paper on top, in Marcoux's own handwriting. "And here is your confession of fostering a nest of pirates in this harbor," the man added in the same casual tone.

Marcoux froze, hypnotized by the menace in the man's

blue eyes. "Monsieur! I beg your pardon. I am a faithful servant of His Majesty...."

"This report," the man said, sitting sideways on the desk, "clearly indicates that twenty-three ships were raided in one night, and the explanation is that two young men from the New World are responsible for it." He picked up the papers and brandished them under Marcoux' nose. With his other hand, the man clenched the front of Marcoux' doublet and pulled him forward and across the desk. The visitor was surprisingly strong for his lean build. "How dare you make a joke out of the Navy's intelligence? Are you sharing in the take here?"

"No!" Marcoux screamed and pulled back, but he was unable to free himself from the man's grip. The visitor held tight, and Marcoux did not dare to resist. The accusations against him could lead him to the gallows already without the added offense of assaulting the representative from the Navy in the presence of His Royal Majesty's Musketeer, who motionlessly witnessed their exchange. "No! If a pirate were to be caught here, under my authority, I guarantee he would hang," he gasped as the man shoved him back into his chair, which toppled over and bounced Marcoux' shoulder off the floor.

"Indeed, Commandant ," the man mocked. "Explain to me, how could two young men successfully raid twenty-three ships in a matter of hours?"

Lyon, France – June 1715

Raoul carefully timed his arrival home, and was pleased to see that he succeeded. The skies had barely darkened to deep blue, and the first course of formal dinner was served. He had successfully missed the hustle of dressing up for pre-dinner socializing and he was spared the suffering of listening to the chatter (of no interest to him) between his parents and their guests. He rode to the stables behind the chateau, handed the horse to the grooms, circled around, and headed to the kitchen.

"You have grown taller," his brother said behind him.

Raoul swerved to avoid a slap to his head, twisted his body to trip Antoine, and would have succeeded if Antoine did not grab his wrist and twist his arm. Raoul threw his weight back to pin Antoine to the wall. After a brief struggle, Raoul had to concede defeat.

His brother released the grip on his wrist. "Not bad. You are learning."

"Does mother know you are home? And she did not drag you to entertain the guests?"

"I wore myself out to reach home. Don't you know, I am exhausted from the arduous travel, and thus in no shape to co-host a formal dinner. Mother was kind enough to pretend she believed my claims of fatigue."

"Where have you been?" Raoul asked. "Did you acquire a mistress?"

"Pardon?"

Raoul gulped. Charlotte de Brangelton had recently stayed at Lyon, and she narrated interesting stories about Henri's exploits. "Don't you indulge in love affairs?"

Antoine's elbow connected with his side. "I never court a woman longer than two weeks, and never dally longer than a month. Did you discuss love affairs with Wildcat?"

"I did not!" Raoul protested. His brother would not tell him about his love affairs, so why should he tell Antoine about his discourses with Charlotte?

Antoine talked about his trip until they entered the bustling kitchen and left with instructions to bring their platters to a small sitting room located farthest from the formal dining room. Antoine picked up a bottle of wine and continued his narration as they retreated to the sanctuary and Antoine generously filled Raoul's goblet.

"What trouble did she cause for you?"

"None..." Raoul paused to allow disbelief to manifest itself. "...For the first two days. Or maybe even three," he amended.

"And then the joy of reunion wore out?" Antoine persisted.

Raoul savored his wine. "I don't even know where to start."

"I suggest chronologically."

"We bickered, we argued, we quarreled, we shouted insults at each other, she claimed that my manners were unfit even for a stable hand, I observed that she had the looks and temperament of a stable cat. She took a swing at me. She left me no choice but to slap her to put her in her place. I ended up with a black eye. Father pulled us apart and threatened to send Charlotte to a convent and to send me to a monastery if we ever start a fight again."

His brother's jaw momentarily fell open in surprise. "You had a black eye, compliments of Charlotte de Brangelton?"

"The sun was shining into my eyes," Raoul explained through clenched teeth. "I challenged her to a fencing round. She had this magnificent idea to treat it as if it were a real duel. We rode out to the woods, found a nice clearing, started fencing, and did not see a bear that charged at us. We only brought practice swords, so we ended up in the nearest trees. We had to stay there for an hour because the bear would not leave! Our horses galloped off. Took us a long time to find them, and it started to rain. We lost our way in the darkness till we saw the Rose and Arrow. She pleaded to stop there and wait till the rain subsided."

"Did you?" Antoine forgot about his food.

Raoul shifted in his seat. "Father discovered us at the Rose and Arrow. He had been searching for us all over for hours."

"I bet his passion over the fistfight paled in comparison to his fury upon this adventure," Antoine accurately guessed. "And there was no help from mother, either."

"Hell broke loose when we reached home. Father swore without restrain. Mother yelled till my ears rang. Father whacked me a couple times. It was not too bad," Raoul answered Antoine's sympathetic glance. "I forgot about it as soon as he slapped Wildcat. Mother had no objections."

Antoine sputtered his wine in surprise. "They allotted the blame on her? I thought Charlotte could do nothing wrong in their eyes."

"I was just as astonished. She argued when father forbade us to leave the house after sunset, but he would not hear of it."

Antoine shook his head. "What were you thinking, my daft brother, to go riding in the woods with a girl alone? Was it where you discussed love affairs?"

"No!"

"Rejoice that she did not lay any claims on you! Can you imagine yourself married to her?"

"God forbid!" Raoul shuddered and crossed himself. "Officers at the garrison are convinced Charles d'Arringnon has a promising career as a Musketeer."

"Garrison? Charles?!" His brother took the empty glass from him.

"That was her idea."

"What was her idea? Another one?"

"We were only planning to watch the officers' fencing practice!" Raoul felt the warmth spreading from his stomach outwards. "And what do you know? – the Commander greeted us, and she – he, I mean, Charles, - saluted, introduced himself, pronounced his ambition for the Musketeer's uniform, and offered to be of service! The Commander ordered us to conduct a fencing demonstration to entertain his officers, and..." Raoul gulped at the memory. "...and Charles asked if the Commander would allow him to shoot a pistol when he won the fencing round." Raoul eyed the wine.

Antoine, rendered speechless, poured some in the glass, and handed it back to him. Their platters of roasted duck and glazed carrots, pies with smoked ham, and bread finally arrived. To Raoul's joy, Antoine sent for another bottle of wine and, to Raoul's chagrin, Antoine found his voice. "You are an undisputed idiot to bring a disguised girl to a military garrison. Next time she has any outrageous ideas, knock her out," he advised when the pangs of hunger were satisfied.

"I suppose." Raoul reluctantly nodded, and the room swayed. "Wildcat avows that if anyone dares to touch her, she will stab him. I believe that, don't you?"

He was awarded with another spell of incredulous silence from Antoine. "Ah, yes, that is an excellent strategy, allow a girl in your charge to stab an officer. You would be whipped along with her."

"Yes," Raoul squinted. The food on his plate seemed to move. "I mean, no. I had to go back to the garrison."

Antoine took away his glass and put away his own. "You went back, you dim-witted jackass?"

"I lost that first round. The Commander taunted me. He thinks Charles is younger. The Commander set a rematch. I complained to father."

"And?"

"Father escorted us to the garrison."

Antoine froze with a piece of smoked ham pie in his hand. "Father condoned this escapade? Has he lost his mind along with you?"

6

ABOUT LOST CARGO
ATLANTIC OCEAN - JANUARY 1716

I appreciate art for its monetary value.

Francis de Brangelton to Jerome de la Norte – 1713

CAPTAIN MATHEW JOHNSON OF THE *GOLDEN SAILS* finished checking the coordinates, completed the inspection of the decks and below decks, issued the orders for the day, and gazed at the endless blue-gray horizon. If this calm weather continued, the crossing would take at least another week, but even at this speed, the food and water would last till their arrival in St. Malo. Most of his men were experienced sailors and an additional week of voyage made no difference to them, but Mathew had made the mistake of taking on a passenger, and Bourzat was very apprehensive about the time to cross the ocean. *Landlubber*, Mathew thought with contempt, and turned away from the approaching short man with a curled moustache.

"Are you certain we are on the right course, Captain?" Bourzat asked yet again.

Mathew gave him a scathing look. "Yes, we are. I have experience in navigation. Do you have any doubts of my skills?" This exchange happened every day.

"Captain! I paid a large amount of money for the privilege of delivering my precious cargo by your ship in the shortest time possible."

"What is your cargo?" Mathew asked idly.

"A year worth of commissioned paintings."

"Paintings?" Mathew echoed.

"Yes. If this perpetual dampness seeps through, my paintings will mold, and a year's worth of painstaking labor and suffering of the barbarity of the New World will be wasted!" the man complained. "This work was commissioned by the honorable Comte de Chambreau of Orleans himself!"

The Comte's name meant nothing to Mathew, but the information was beneficial. "You are a painter, then?"

"Yes, I am an artist, yes, and I am very respected in my trade," Bourzat puffed out his chest and stroked his moustache. "The Comte trusted me to reproduce the landscapes of the New World. I suffered through foul weather, uncivilized company, crude lodgings, awful food, and unacceptable wine to complete this commission! My paintings must arrive in Orleans in pristine condition!"

"I am sorry to hear about your sufferings." Mathew made an insincere apology to this windbag. "I understand your impatience now. Does the Comte pay well?"

Bourzat gave him a suspicious look. "Why? Are you an artist yourself?"

"No, not at all," Mathew reassured him. "By any chance, do you know anyone interested in purchasing very fine religious paintings?"

"Who painted them?"

"I don't know. One of the paintings is of St.Mark. When you look at him, you expect him to speak to you and his winged lion to roar. On another painting, the armor of St. George practically shines, and you can count the scales on the dragon's back."

Bourzat's eyes lit up and he thoughtfully scratched his head. "How did you acquire them?"

Mathew tugged on the ropes, checked a rigging, and carefully rehearsed the story in his mind for the thousandth time. "Some time ago, my ship was careened for repairs in Martinique." He casually turned to the expectant Bourzat. "I met two cousins there - Marshall is the name, I think. We played cards, drank rum, luck favored me, and they gambled the paintings to redeem their loses. They assured me that these precious masterpieces were by old masters, and worth a fortune in Europe. I was drunk enough to take the bet, since I was on a winning streak."

"Yes, yes," the painter panted. "What are the other pictures?"

"That Greek creature, half-man half-goat - Centaur, I think?"

"Satyr."

"Yes, him. You expect to hear the pipes it plays!"

The edges of Bourzat's moustache jiggled as he bounced back and forth on his feet.

"Are the colors bright? Are these pictures large? May I see them?" he panted. "How many paintings do you have? Where do you keep these pictures? The paintings must be kept dry and cool- this is very, very important, because nothing can damage a painting like moisture..."

"All the paintings are stored at a warehouse in France,"

Mathew said. "You may see them, if you vow to honestly tell me what they are worth, will you?"

London, England - March 1716

Three years had passed since that fateful day when Antoine had first left home on the trip with the Comte de Tournelles, and these years were packed with a lifetime's worth of adventures. Antoine lazily contemplated his embarrassingly wrong first impression of the day he came along with his father's friend. In all fairness, Henri de Brangelton had warned him what to expect. Only pride and stubbornness had made Antoine persevere, and after the first months – which seemed years long – of apprenticeship, he became quite accustomed to the hectic pace and the Comte's mid-boggling schemes and activities. After participating in a year-long blur of events, Antoine was quite content to relax in Paris under Captain d'Ornille's tender care. That peaceful existence lasted for a couple of weeks, until the Captain unceremoniously assigned Antoine on a mission with a Musketeer named de Rousard. Antoine had barely recovered from that adventure when the Comte de Tournelles dragged him along again on yet another one of his enterprises. After that, there was a quick trip to Genoa with Captain Brandon, more errands for Captain d'Ornille, a trip for Cardinal de la Fleure, then off again with the Comte de Tournelles, and this trip to England with M. Jerome de la Norte. They had landed at Dover a week ago and rode to London. M. de la Norte departed back to France, but Antoine chose to remain in England. He was fascinated with the concept of the monarch's limited power, where the nobles like himself had rights and the vote. In France, the legacy of the Sun King had left the noblemen idle and powerless, prone to intrigues, pointlessly proud, peevish, and highly taxed. Years ago, Antoine's father had wisely abandoned the filthy corridors of Versailles for the Musketeer's barracks and the mercantile air of Lyon. The Comte de Tournelles managed to remain a free-spirited mercenary. Captain d'Ornille was happy in military barracks. Jerome de la Norte happily resided in the New World. And speaking of the New World... Antoine had overheard curious comments about investments in the New World and decided to search for more information. Both his father and Comte de Tournelles were interested in this scheme, strangely. Since he left home, Antoine was gradually comprehending that his father was not just a meddling autocrat, but an intelligent man, deeply involved in multiple business ventures and current political matters. More like English peer... Antoine promised himself that when he returned to Lyon, it would be with the honest intention to stay at peace with his father. For now, London called.

Antoine took residence at the White Stag Inn on the outskirts of London, and he planned to stay there till he made respectable acquaintances and connections in society. He rode into London every day, made his name and presence known, and expected to be acknowledged soon. On this day, the weather turned atrocious, the rain pounded all night, and Antoine resigned himself to spend the morning – and probably the whole day - at the inn. Venturing out and drenching himself in the downpour was an unpleasant prospect. He listened to the sound of water falling outside, dressed, and considered his options for a meal when the agitated Armand burst back into the room. M. Antoine might need to know that three English gentlemen stopped at the inn last night, and one of them ordered a groom – he dared to order the head groom! – to remove M. Antoine's horse to the common stables, because the

English gentleman regarded his English horse to be superior to a French horse!

Armand had picked up the language impressively well, but Antoine was skeptical – a horse is a horse, but to move another noblemen's horse would either mean a much higher social standing, or unforgivable breach of etiquette.

"What is the gentleman's name, Armand?"

Armand was worth his weight in gold. The name of the insolent gentleman was Lord Brickton who carried the sword with the pearl-encrusted grip. His friends were Mr. Smythe and a well-nourished Mr. Simmons. The three of them were currently waiting for their meal in the dining hall, occupying the table by the large window. Antoine checked his sword, tucked the dagger into the holster in the small of his back, slipped a copper knuckle clip under his glove, and went downstairs.

"Pardon me, gentlemen. Lord Brickton?" he addressed them in English. "I believe there was a misunderstanding about the placement of the horses last night?"

No one at the table acknowledged him. Brickton's decorative sword was impractical for combat. Simmons would have difficulty reaching for his sword across his round belly. Smythe was the first to look away.

Antoine made a sharp turn-about and exited to the accompaniment of jeers and snickers.

"Armand, pack and saddle the horses – quickly. I will bring my saddlebags to the stables. We are leaving. As soon as I take care of a final detail."

A quarter of an hour later, Antoine opened the door to the stall of Brickton's horse. The well-behaved Arabian mare did not mind a rider without a saddle, and he encouraged the animal toward the door. It bucked at stepping out in the rain, but understood that Antoine meant business and obeyed. The dining area of the White Stag Inn had high ceilings, and the entrance was tall enough to admit the horse and the rider. The mare was pleased to escape from the rain and high-stepped inside.

Brickton and his friends jumped up.

Antoine urged the horse forward. "Lord Brickton, since you value your mare so much, you should enjoy your meal in her fine company." He vaulted down and slapped the horse's flank. The mare reared, and Simmons dropped on his hands and knees in a frantic attempt to scramble under the tables toward the door, Smythe followed him on foot, but Brickton flashed the small sword. The horse kicked and neighed while the grooms coaxed her outside.

"You bloody Frenchman," Brickton screeched and charged. Antoine parried the first thrust and merely twisted out of the way when Brickton repeated his first move. At the third reprise, Antoine kept the blades crossed and lunged forward, bringing them face-to-face. With the help of the knuckles clip, Antoine knocked the Lord out.

The grooms coaxed Brickton's mare to the door, but chaos reigned in the room. Simmons and Smythe, witnesses to their friend's defeat were compelled to act. Simmons succeeded upon his second attempt to unsheath the sword. Antoine leapt over a table and knocked the sword out of the man's hand before Simmons could even position himself in a proper fencing pose. Simmons, being a very non-enthusiastic oppo-nent, deemed the conditions favorable for his escape, and puffed away.

Smythe picked up a chair, swung it at Antoine from a safe distance, and screamed "At arms! At arms! Murder!"

Antoine lunged to trip him. Smythe crushed down and, spitting profanities, spread on the floor face down. Half a dozen men still remained in the room, and they were undecided as to their next action. Antoine pulled a cocked pistol from his belt to help them conclude that inaction was their best choice. He backed out to the door. Armand was firmly planted in his saddle and holding Antoine's horse for him. Antoine mounted, and they rode off through the curtain of cold water falling from the sky. As he and Armand galloped down the road leading to Portsmouth, Antoine reflected that it was probably a shame that his stay in London was cut short by a brawl in a tavern. Over a horse. Was it a step up or down from an argument about cards?

Marseille, France – June 1716

In the aftermath of the catastrophe in Marseille's harbor on 20 September 1712, the Knight of the Order of St. John, Honore de Courbet, prayed daily for the guidance in the retrieval of St. Elias' relics. For a week after the chaotic battle, the newspapers had published nothing but conflicting accounts on how the infamous event had started, progressed, and ended. The only constant feature was the mentioning of the Marshall cousins, Andrew and Harold.

Honore made inquiries, but no one was certain how their names became known. The common speculation was they were denizens from the New World.

Honore could not admit the loss of the relics to his superiors, or to his contacts in Bourges. He postponed his trip to Montpellier, deciding to blame the delay on the situation in Marseille's harbor. For a month, he alternated between praying and prowling the streets in search of men fitting the Marshall cousins' descriptions, to no avail. Award notices for the Marshall cousins' capture were posted – the city accused them of piracy, a private party accused them of theft, and the Navy accused them of sabotage.

Honore realized the far-fetchedness of the allegations, indeed, could it be that two men were responsible for all the crimes of the evening? His hope dimmed and the dread settled in. Then deliverance descended, gloriously and surprisingly, from the Knights of Christ in Portugal.

Honore found out that while he was sailing into Marseille's harbor, the purchase of St. Elias' relics had come to light, and the pride of the Portuguese order suffered upon the insult to their prestige and influence. They escalated their arguments, loudly and publicly challenged the authority of the Byzantine church to determine the ownership of St. Elias' relics without consulting Rome, and appealed to the Pope.

Honore received instructions to quietly store the trunk at the warehouse in Montpellier. He praised the Lord, and cried tears of joy and relief. He was unaccustomed to acting on his own, he was unaccustomed to intrigue, he was unaccustomed to caution – he and his brethren were always in the right, and they had nothing to hide. They acted on behalf of the order and for the glory of God. Even the clandestine negotiations in Dalmatia were carried out as per his superior's instructions, but now Honore had no choice; he was on his own, in an uncomfortable position of masterminding a secret search for relics!

He sold the tobacco, retrieved the old set of armor from his private lodgings, packed the armor inside the trunk for the weight, carefully sealed the lid of the trunk, carved the word "*Faith*" on the side for identification, and left the trunk at the warehouse in Montpellier.

He returned to Malta and requested permission to undertake the holy mission of finding and punishing the insolent assailants responsible for the incident in Marseille's harbor. He fostered a suspicion that the Marshall cousins might have been hired by the Knights of Christ to steal the relics from the Knights of St. John. Honore was authorized to confidentially conduct the search, and he vowed to himself to restore St. Elias' relics to the trunk at Montpellier, at any cost to himself. The retrieval of St. Elias' relics became his personal crusade.

The political turmoil swept like water through a breeched dam. Rome announced the intent to review the case of legal ownership. Honore's conspirators in Bourges conveniently forgot the existence of St. Elias' relics altogether. Honore's superiors in the Order of the Knights of St. John suspected that Pope Clement XI had designs to appropriate St Elias' relics for himself. They implied that the Knights of Christ illegally possessed St. Elias' relics. The Knights of Christ claimed that St. Elias' relics were stolen from the monastery in Dalmatia, and posted a reward for information about the hiding place of the relics. Rome answered with demands for investigation and sent representatives to the Byzantium church. Byzantium church officials politely dismissed all inquiries regarding the excommunicated monastery in Dalmatia.

At that stalemate between the Knights of St John and the Knights of Christ, Honore was free to act as he pleased.

For two years, he traveled along the coast of France, occasionally visiting his humble private lodgings in Montpellier, fatigued and battered by his endeavors to secure a reprieve from the aftereffects of the disaster in Marseille. He abandoned his search for the phantom cousins, and privately offered a generous reward for the retrieval of the family heirlooms lost in the chaos: the silver serving set and the chess set. But no one brought him either of these items, not even counterfeit articles.

In a flash of inspiration, an ingenious idea occurred to him on the glorious Easter morning in 1714. Within a week, he bought a list of ships that were in Marseille's harbor that night. Since then, Honore spent his life at busy harbors and disreputable ports, at the seashore and by the rivers, waiting, watching, and seeking out the captains of these ships. He was diligent and relentless in his quest, but no one provided him with any clues.

The argument over the possession of St. Elias' relics was slowly losing its heat, and sooner or later, either Honore's superiors at St. John or his conspirators in Bourges would expect to take possession of St. Elias' relics – and Honore desperately desired to find St. Elias' relics before he had to deliver them. He sailed back to Marseille.

Honore finished his prayers at the St. Victor Monastery, descended the hill toward the harbor, and strolled around the docks to the base of the formidable St. Jean Fortress. He stopped and broodily stared across the water at the bleak Chateau d'If.

"A fine day, isn't it, Monsignor?" A rotund man approached Honore. The ominous clouds loomed on the horizon and the salty wind was picking up, but the man was in no rush to seek shelter. His eyes were fixed on his Knights of St. John cross. "Are you the man who lost an ivory and onyx chess set?"

Dijon, France – August 1716

Rene Prassal was not a seafaring man, and yet, twice a year, he crossed the murky waters between England and France, not by his own choice, but upon the Marquis' instructions. "*Sail to St. Malo, inquire about the Marshall cousins there,*" the Marquis instructed. It was Dieppe last time, and Le Havre before that. Rene always was violently seasick on the shortest crossing from Dover to Calais. The orders this time included riding to Dijon to check on the Marquis' estate, and Rene figured, sailing to Calais and riding to Le Havre, or Dieppe, or St. Malo. What would it be next time, La Rochelle? Rene missed the sunshine, the wine, the songs, and the comfort of his native land. He understood the confounded English language, but did not speak it, and he prayed for the Marquis to return to France. It was never far from Rene's mind that the Marshall cousins were less likely to appear in France.

Rene stepped outside in the stifling summer heat. It figured that, this time of the year, he might prefer to be in the English countryside, where the Marquis rented a cottage. Rene swatted at the flies, and thought of taking the carriage to town – to check if the conveyance had been properly maintained. He decided against it, the heat inside will be unbearable. He retreated into the empty hall. How much longer could he wait for Durrant to show up?

"I have news!" Durrant panted in excitement. "A holy man is looking for the chess set and silver!"

"Hmmm?"

"He is a man of the church. He lost a silver set and chess set with onyx and ivory figures in a rosewood box. He offers a generous reward." Durrant rubbed his hands.

A feeling of dread gripped Rene. "Did he explain how his treasure got tangled with bones?"

His brother-in-law averted his eyes. "Yes, about that. He thinks these bones might be holy relics."

The ground shook and roiled under Rene's feet. "He... he... you already spoke to him? You blubbered about the bones?"

"He is a man of the church!" Durrant crossed himself. "He promised to pay another generous reward if these relics are real."

"What position does he hold in the church?" Rene asked.

"Monsignor is not clergy. He says he will help us sell the rest of cargo."

Rene gaped in terror. "How does your man know how to sell suspicious goods?"

Durrant chewed his fingernail. "No one will question a Knight of St. John."

Hair stood up at the back of Rene's neck. "What? You lying bastard, you vowed to keep your tongue behind your teeth!" He approached his cheating brother-in-law with a drawn dagger.

Durrant thrust a chair between himself and Rene. "You promised to sell the goods, too!" He whined.

"You cretin!" Rene tossed away the dagger, tore the chair from Durrant's hands, and swung it over Durrant's head.

Durrant dropped on his knees and dove under the table. "I am not a fool! You are!" he yelped. "We have a fortune stored in a warehouse! Why don't we sell it?"

Rene kicked under the table, missed the worthless flesh, and instead jabbed his own knee on hard wood. A Knight of St. John! The original seals clearly indicated that the order was the rightful owner of the relics. "He will kill us both when he gets his hands on these relics!"

Durrant peeked out. "He pledged a holy oath that no harm will come to us!"

Rene's head swam. "Us?"

"No, no, he will only deal with me." Durrant crawled out. "I did not tell him about you. Monsignor promised to secure a position for me when he becomes a Bishop."

Rene consoled himself that matters could be worse. He now regretted his caution; they had only sold the hashish and opium, the clothes, the silver set, two rolls of silk, and one bedcover. He had coerced Durrant to share the rewards when received, and Durrant took the risk of dealing with his Monsignor – the cretin did not even bother to find out the Knight of St. John's name. Rene handed the warehouse claim papers to his brother-in-law and sailed to England. He now prayed that the Marquis would be in no hurry to return to France.

Lyon, France – October 1716

At the yard of the Rose and Arrow tavern, the hens and geese scatted upon the arrival of a creaking cart loaded with a single large trunk. In the late afternoon, the place was almost deserted, and only a huge pig stretched in the middle and blocked the path.

Charlotte – as Charles- and Raoul stopped by the fence to idly watch the activities.

"Innkeeper!" a rotund man shouted. "Move this pig out of the way!" Upon receiving no response, he clumsily climbed down and poked the animal with his foot. The pig did not bulge. He tried again. "Innkeeper!"

A man appeared in the front door and spat. "I am no innkeeper. This is a tavern," he clarified before descending the stairs and kicking the pig. "Away with you!"

The animal snorted but refused to move.

Charlotte's stomach growled in hunger, but the scene was amusing. "Bet you the usual the swine will cause havoc."

"Accepted. It seems too lazy to even squeal."

The rotund man pushed the pig with a broom. "Away with you, damn beast! Move! I will no longer wait for you!"

The tavern owner wrestled the broom from other man's hands and swatted the pig on the rump. The animal squealed, shook its head, and rolled over. He continued the exercise and the pig continued its concert until it relocated to the side of the yard and the tavern owner left it alone.

"You lose," Raoul claimed.

"You said the pig would not squeal, but it did."

"You weasel." He reined in his horse. "Fine, it's no-win. Shall we go home now?"

Charlotte watched the rotund man hustling his hired help to unload the trunk and to carry it to the entrance. "There is something odd about that trunk."

"Yes. I am hungry. The trunk does not seem to contain a meal," her little-brother-in-spirit complained.

"Why would anyone bring a trunk to a tavern? And the trunk is lightweight for its size. Is it half empty?"

"My stomach, I shall have you know, is painfully and completely empty."

"Stop thinking with your guts," she admonished him. "Are there private dining rooms here?" She rode around the building.

Raoul reluctantly followed her. "Two or three on the upper floor ...and no, don't even think about climbing up to the windows."

The windows of two private dining rooms faced the woods. The building stood on the slope, so the windows were high and there were no vines, ledges, or decorations to climb up or down without a ladder. But a twisted pine tree was growing in a convenient location. "This will serve," she pointed.

"I want a meal, not pinecones," Raoul grumbled.

Charlotte tossed the reins onto the fence post and ran toward the tree. He swore and followed. Being the taller and faster, he reached the tree first and, pushing her out of the way, climbed up ahead of her. Charlotte had to settle on the lower branch. "It was my idea. You did not even care," she hissed.

A lone occupant with a military bearing waited in the room with his back to the open windows. When the trunk was brought in, he locked the door and dropped to his knees. So did the rotund man who was the only other person left in the room.

"Are they praying to the trunk?" Raoul asked some minutes later. "Will it procure a plate of a roasted duck for me?"

"Stop whining or go home."

"You are in my way."

"I am not moving," Charlotte declared. "You should have allowed me to climb first..."

The military man finally raised his head. He stood up to reach for a knife and carefully cut the seals. When he raised the lid, he froze with his arm up and stared. He abruptly threw the lid wide open and frantically shuffled the contents. He recoiled with a violent shiver.

"Monsignor?" The rotund man clumsily raised himself. " Are you unwell?"

Without a word and with shaking hands, the military man aimed a pistol at his accomplice.

"Monsignor! What is wrong? I delivered it as promised!" The other man wailed. He scuttled around the trunk and halted. "What...There is a devil at work!" He fervently crossed himself. "No, no, Monsignor!" He pleaded when the other man turned the pistol to his own head.

Raoul crawled forward in hopes of glimpsing the contents of the trunk when, with a loud snap, the branch broke under his weight. He flailed his arms in a fruitless effort to find another hold, and Charlotte grasped his arm to slow his fall. Her branch could not support the added weight and yielded. They tumbled down on the ground in a tangle of arms and legs, and the startled pheasants screeched in protest. Charlotte and Raoul raced back to their horses and galloped away without a glance.

May 1717 - Le Havre

. . .

Daniel Rabatin's main warehouse in Le Havre and the second one further inland were reputed to be the most secure in France, and the owner held the reputation of efficiently conducting all his business with complete secrecy and security. Even the Knights of St. John, when dealing with a marginally legal cargo, distributed it through Rabatin. He would neither risk his fortune for a trifle, nor yield to a threat – Rabatin's clients included cutthroats in the New World and the royalty of France. And yet, the contents of the trunk were raided in the inland warehouse – or in transport. Although... when, where, how? There were no admissions forthcoming from the Knights of Christ, and Honore de Courbet was at loss as to who would conduct such a brazen heist for seemingly no profit and for what reason.

"Two of you?" the guard asked when Honore and Durrant arrived for the appointed audience. "Is M. Rabatin expecting both of you?"

"He... he is my ...ah... partner," Durrant stammered.

"Hmm. Wait here." The guard returned half an hour later and motioned for them to enter. The effectiveness of this storage enterprise was impressive; the discipline was solid, and the guards were loyal and alert. Their posture indicated that every man was either a former soldier or had sailed – dishonestly, no doubt. Honore had met enough privateers in the Mediterranean to recognize one even in a respectable disguise. The wide hallway was empty except for a landscape painting on the wall and two narrow benches with plain cushions. Rabatin's office was sparsely furnished with four sturdy visitor's chairs, and Rabatin's own unadorned writing desk and chair were positioned next to the window. The only decorations were the colored detailed maps on the walls.

"What can I do for you?" Rabatin rose to greet them.

"I stored a large trunk here," Durrant recited. "You replaced the contents."

"What the hell was that?" Rabatin stepped around his desk toward the window, which was located above the entrance to the building, in the plain view of the two guards posted across the courtyard at the entry gate. Rabatin could raise the alarm with a single exclamation, and now Honore had no doubts that such a possibility had already been considered and rehearsed.

"The contents were replaced," Durrant continued as per his instructions. "I want my property restored to me immediately."

"You inspected the seals upon retrieval of his trunk, didn't you?" Rabatin was not concerned or intimidated, but he turned slightly, and his hand rested on the hilt of his sword.

"Yes, I did. You must have replaced them."

"Now, why the hell would I do that?" Rabatin sat on the window sill and casually glanced outside.

Honore expected denial and indignation, and he had not prepared Durrant for cold-blooded discussion.

"M. Rabatin," Honore interjected. "I suggest you will be honest with us." He knew he had blundered by disclosing his interest in the transaction, and there was no turning back.

Rabatin waved his arm in a deliberate gesture – Honore did not notice it before, but Rabatin held a quill pen in his hand, and Honore belatedly recognized it as a signal. Rabatin turned around to face Honore. He was no longer fooled, if he had ever been. "You are accusing me of tampering with your cargo. Very well, I am willing to help you clear up this misunderstanding. What did your trunk contain?"

It was a master stroke on Rabatin's part, and Honore involuntarily gasped. "The contents are immaterial."

"In this case, I suggest you file an official complaint." Rabatin knew his clientele.

111

"You will not leave this room alive unless–" Honore never finished the sentence. Rabatin whistled and Honore twisted around as the door behind him opened. Two men immediately seized him, and a third held a cutlass to Durrant's neck.

"Let's reach an understanding, Monsieurs." Rabatin sat down at his desk. "Either you will be honest with me, or take up your business with authorities, or you quit your outrageous scheme."

7

CURIOSITY IS A VIRTUE

FERRAND, FRANCE – FEBRUARY 1717

*Curiosity is a powerful force which leads to knowledge,
and, consequently, to wisdom.*

Francis de Brangelton to Batiste de Brangelton – 1688

MARGUERITE'S LATEST LETTER WAS COMPRISED OF THE usual complaints about Antoine - he traveled as far as he could contrive, and she suspected that he did so on purpose. *"I asked my prodigal son - thrice - when he was planning to recall that he had a home? I received the obligatory brief sentences of assurance that he thought about me often, but he neglected to mention if he intended to allow me to embrace him any time this century,"* Marguerite wrote. *"If you happen to encounter my beloved son, will you please truss him and deliver him to Lyon?"* The second part of the letter was less acerbic, although Henrietta surmised that Raoul's departure for military school had affected his mother more than she admitted.

Henrietta read aloud selected paragraphs of news from the de la Fleures.

Charlotte listened with dangerous eagerness to the news of Raoul's departure to military school. "Father, when will I attend fencing school?"

Henrietta almost dropped the letter. "What do you mean, Charlotte?" she managed.

"I will follow your path, mother," her daughter innocently continued. "I have been practicing my swordsmanship as much as Henri. I should have the same opportunity to improve and gain outside experience."

"I shall not allow you to leave home by yourself," Henrietta thought. *"God only knows what trouble you might bring upon yourself."*

"Father," their daughter asked, turning her attention to him. "Do you believe I am ready now?"

"Yes." Francis' eyes sparkled with gentle humor. "Why not, Henrietta?"

"Why not, Francis?" Henrietta glared at her husband. "Don't you understand?" *"Don't you remember the mistakes I made on my own? - of course you know, I will not bring that up in Charlotte's presence!"*

"No." He read her thoughts. "I never meant to send her off by herself."

"Will you chaperone your daughter for a year?" Henrietta paced around the room. At Charlotte's age, Henrietta's naiveté and lack of worldly knowledge had led her onto an embarrassing path. Her daughter's upbringing made her just the opposite - the girl's worldly knowledge left no room for naiveté, but still, Charlotte was very young and impulsive.

"No," Francis said. "Neither will Henri. After all, he is bound to find distractions."

"That leaves me." Henrietta noticed the gleam in his eyes. "What scheme have you concocted?"

"Would Henri d'Arringnon like to attend lectures at the Montpellier University of High Learning while his young cousin Charles improves his skills at fencing school?" Francis laid out the whole plan in one sentence.

Henrietta's heart leapt in excitement. Indeed, she would like to attend lectures on classical studies and philosophy, but donning a student's image had never seemed an option – until this moment. *"How does he conjure his plans?"* she marveled for the millionth time. "How will I explain my sudden desire, at my age, to pursue high learning?" she asked carefully.

"You, my dear, are a minor nobleman who recently received a small inheritance. You quit the military, and you desire to better yourself intellectually. What are you inclined to suffer through? – Law? Theology?" Francis mused. "I will procure for you a letter of reference to one of the instructors." He had anticipated Charlotte's intent to cajole her way into a fencing school and, as usual, found ways to accommodate his girl's desires. Along with Henrietta's interests.

"Yes, mother! Cousin Henri!" Charlotte jumped up and down. "When can we leave?" Henrietta folded Marguerite's letter. "Your father will make all the necessary arrangements," she deferred.

Montpellier, France – April 1717

In Montpellier, Henrietta rented modest lodgings – the sitting room was spacious and faced the street, two narrow beds in the sleeping room boasted clean linen, and a private water closet snuggled in a separate nook. More importantly, the location was excellent, halfway between the fencing school and the University in the respectable part of the town; the population around their quarters consisted mostly of merchants, students of Medicine, Law and Theology, and the houses of minor nobility. The citadel and the officers' housings were located blocks away. The port was backwater and the lack of marine activity did not encourage any extensive congregations of adventurous elements usually found in busy commerce cities. Henrietta deemed Montpellier a reasonably safe locality for 'Charles.'

Monsieur d'Arouet, the master and owner of the fencing school, was no more than forty years of age, slim and agile as was fit for his occupation. He received them politely and his eyes critically evaluated the small frame of his future student.

"The boy is very young for the elite classes I teach, Monsieur," he sounded skeptical. "It might seem to you that he is quite mature, but pardon me, he seems rather... ah...delicate."

"I trained Charles myself." Henrietta laced her tone with arrogance, which seldom failed to provoke a fencing challenge. "I assure you, M. d'Arouet, Charles is ready for exposure to different styles of fencing."

The man stroked his moustache. "How did you acquire your own skills, M. d'Arringnon?"

"I was first taught by my Musketeer father and later received formal instruction at the fencing school at Rennes. Of course, I truly honed my practical skills during my military career."

"*Among the best representatives of cutthroat societies here and in the New World,*" she added silently. This conference bore only a distant, vague resemblance to her own interview with the fencing master at Rennes, more than twenty years ago, back when her throat was tight with apprehension that he would see through her masquerade of claiming to be a young man. "Would you have a round with me?" she flung the usual bait.

"I will take you up on that later, Monsieur." D'Arouet pushed his chair back. "First, allow me to see what your cousin can do."

"*More than you can imagine,*" Henrietta thought dryly.

Within a week, Charles comfortably settled into the school routine. He played cards and attended plays at a theater, and developed an unyielding, competitive rivalry with a young man named Guy de Brault. Charles and Guy became fanatical adversaries on the fencing floor, all their matches unfailingly followed by a heated, but thankfully relatively civil verbal sparring which d'Arouet usually broke off after a few sentences. De Brault belonged to a powerful family in Orleans. He had good connections and - aside from the moments when he was dealing with Charles - fine manners. "*Does Charlotte like Guy de Brault but refuses to admit it to herself? Or does she value fencing skills above a natural attraction? Or is her distrust in men ingrained beyond redemption?*" Henrietta pondered. "*Regardless of the answer, should I be thankful or worried?*"

Aside from the usual concerns for the well-being of her daughter, Henrietta enjoyed herself immensely. Her request to attend lectures at the University was granted, her genuine interest and mature age appealed to the professors, and they generously invited M. d'Arringnon to participate in the occasional scholarly debates and meetings outside of school walls. Henri d'Arringnon also devoted time to comprehensive fencing rounds with d'Arouet, who introduced d'Arringnon to military officers, and, on frequent occasions, invited him to act as an honorable assistant-guest during fencing lessons. Henrietta was glad of that, as she could keep a watch over her daughter. In a month's time, Henrietta's daily routine became vaguely reminiscent of her own time at fencing school many years ago, but she no longer was a lonely and frightened young girl, afraid of discovery and consequences, short of funds and worried about her reputation. Three months flew by in peace and contention.

"No, I have more important affairs to attend to." Charlotte declined her friends' invitation for *"an evening of earthly pleasures."*

"Oh, indeed? What could be more important than entertainment?" de Brault taunted her. He and his friends were working up the courage to spend their money on nocturnal activities she had no desire, - or, for that matter, ability - to engage in, and she claimed a previous engagement with her cousin Henri.

"De Brault. Everyone can drop a coin and their breeches in a brothel, but I know better than to disclose important business affairs to the likes of you."

"You are a silly, intimidated boy," de Brault sneered.

"When Mlle. Diane dropped her fan, you blushed and stammered while I picked up and handed it back to her," Charlotte reminded him.

"I was not stammering!" He clenched his fists.

Charlotte judged that it was the perfect time to depart. "Give my regards to the whores!" she marched away, waving off the jeers addressed to her back. How did her mother manage to command everyone's respect? Henri d'Arringnon did not swear, did not drink, and did not play cards, yet very few ever challenged him. Of course it helped that her mother was not the smallest or youngest in a group. In contrast, due to her light build, Charlotte claimed to be two years younger than she was. But none of this could be altered. She strolled around Promenade du Peyrou, tipped her hat to the dark-haired and petite

Diane – on whose account de Brault had blushed and stammered - and lingered at the southern balustrade. A cat stalked a squirrel and chased it up the tree. The birds erupted from the branches and circled around. The squirrel jumped to the high branches, and the cat gave up the chase and gingerly descended to the ground. At the Temple of Water, Charlotte sat down on the stairs leading inside the rotunda, leaned her head against the balusters, and watched the white-capped ripples of water dancing below. She raised her eyes to the view of a man wrapping his cloak with the clandestine purpose of hiding the eight-pointed cross of the Knights of St. John. He passed her to go up the stairs, and she slowly rotated her head to watch his shadow. He entered the rotunda and remained there. Within minutes, a city clerk huffed up past her and up the stairs.

"Good day, Monsignor," he breathed, his hushed voice bearing traces of reverence.

Without raising her posterior off the stairs, Charlotte stealthily slid half a dozen stairs up. Inside the rotunda, the sound magnified and bounced off the stone walls, allowing her to easily overhear the conversation.

"...did anyone follow you?" a confident, sharp voice asked.

"The Knight pays this Pierre to copy the shipping records between Marseille and Montpellier between July and November of 1712. He needs the names of ships, captains, owners, passengers, and declared cargo," Charlotte concluded her narration. "Don't you think it's odd?"

"I don't think about it at all. Meddling into the business of any religious military order is unwise and there is no profit in it," Henrietta said flatly, though an alarm sounded in the back of her mind. "What possessed you to eavesdrop?"

"I don't know. Boredom, I suppose." Her daughter shrugged her shoulders. "Mother, have you heard the story of the Marshall cousins? They caused the chaos in Marseille's harbor in September of 1712."

"Their great deeds are greatly exaggerated." Now Henrietta was alarmed. Wasn't there a legal or a religious dispute between the Knights of St. John and the Portuguese Knights of Christ? And it was no surprise that the high tales of the Marshall cousins' deeds had caught Charlotte's fancy... and yet, indeed, why would a Knight of St. John be interested in the time and place of the Marshall cousins' actions?

"Mother, what possible connection may exist between the Knights of St. John and the Marshall cousins?" Her daughter was undeterred.

Henrietta pondered the question. She doubted that even the hare-brained Marshall cousins would have entangled themselves in the affairs of a religious order, but it was possible that yet another deed was attributed to them. What could it be?

Charlotte watched her with a suspiciously innocent expression. "The Knight and Pierre will meet next week at the Happy Goat tavern, six o'clock in the evening." She had no intention to give up her intent of investigation. Her children, true to the de Brangelton blood, often surprised Henrietta, and Charlotte possessed an unerring intuition for any items of interest.

"Like father, like daughter," Henrietta thought uneasily, apprehension taking a firm grip on her mind. "What else?"

Charlotte paced back and forth, absorbed in contemplation on how to implement her – no doubt, already detailed - plans. "I could not follow the Knight along the open space of the Promenade, but Pierre is less intelligent. He hurried to meet his friends at the Happy Goat..." She talked fast, glossing over the fact that yes, she did stop at that seedy tavern. "That pigsty is poorly lit and the ceilings are low. If I hide in the rafters, I might be able to hear them."

Henrietta mulled it over. At the Happy Goat, patrons usually fell face down into their cups, and very seldom did anyone bother to look up to the rafters. There was room for a backup plan, namely that Henrietta could set up a cover for the retreat.

"Off to the Happy Goat tavern we go," she decided. "On one condition." She paused to make certain her daughter understood she meant it. "You will follow all my instructions, and no improvisations. Understood?"

"Yes, mother."

A week later, Henrietta sat at the edge of a bench by the door of the Happy Goat tavern. The room was not merely poorly, but barely, illuminated, the smoke from the fire and tobacco pipes adding to the gloom but not covering the smell of cheap drink and the burned lard which passed for food here. She could not see Charlotte, but she was confident that her daughter had already crawled along the wide beam and positioned herself above the table where Pierre was handing a stack of papers to a middle-aged man of military bearing. The man shuffled through the bundle. In a blur of movement, a fat rat slipped off the ceiling beam and plopped in the middle of their table, barely missing the Knight's head and knocking the papers out of his hands. He was startled and frantically clutched at the papers while the rat twisted upright and clawed at the wood, skidded to the edge, and scurried to the floor. Belatedly, the Knight raised his head toward the ceiling, and, in an instant, he jumped to his feet, pushed away his cloak, and drew his sword. The men around him staggered back. Henrietta kicked her table over. The commotion caused the Knight to momentarily spin around, and the distraction allowed Charlotte the chance to jump down on the table. He faced the wrong direction, and Charlotte, in the middle of her leap to the floor, had the presence of mind to throw a punch into his direction. The impact of her fist against his shoulder, enhanced by the element of surprise and the momentum of her movement, made him reel back. Charlotte sprinted across the tavern and ran to the safety of outside before anyone grasped what had happened.

"Get the papers!" the Knight shouted to Pierre, shoving the throng of confused drunkards out of his way as he rushed after Charlotte with a pistol in his hand. Henrietta collided into him to knock the weapon out of his grip. He lost precious moments retrieving it. In his panic to catch up with the intruder on his conversation, he stumbled into the long street, only to see Charlotte a block away. Henrietta followed him, running noiselessly in her soft-soled boots. In his desperation, he pressed hard but lost the sight of his quarry. His breath came in labored gasps, he wiped the sweat off his eyes, and the tip of his weapon wavered. He slowly turned around, and Henrietta flattened herself against the wall. The Knight headed to the Arc du Triomphe and Henrietta's sense of danger tingled. She picked up a pebble and cautiously approached the structure. She tossed the pebble forward, and from the shadows of the arch, the man lunged at her. She had her weapon ready, but he underestimated the distance between them, and his blade pierced through the empty air. He stumbled forward to regain his balance, affording her a moment to knock him unconscious.

The disposition of the older students in the fencing class bordered on riotous. Henrietta exchanged grim glances with d'Arouet. Guy de Brault and his friends had been bleary-eyed and distracted since the start. Predictably, Charles mercilessly defeated all of them. The young men venomously glared at him, the youngest and the best. *"We will leave as soon as I am finished with this lesson,"* Henrietta resolved while she adjusted the lunge angle of a younger student.

"I don't own you any explanations!" Charles' exclamation cut through the hum of steps, taps, and clinks. He and Guy de Brault stood his-red-face-to-her-pale-face. Their postures indicated that their argument had reached its summit.

"Yes, you do!" he demanded.

"Go to hell." Charlotte replied.

Henrietta pushed Charles and de Brault apart with the palms of her hands. She applied enough force to send the young man stumbling backwards. Charlotte anticipated the impact and stepped back to lessen it, - unlike de Brault, she did not flounder to find her footing, which infuriated the young man even more.

"Silence!" Henrietta commanded in the manner of the commanding officer. Guy de Brault was brought up to listen to his elders, especially immediately after a demonstration that the elder could easily trash him, and Charlotte knew better than to disobey.

"M. Charles d'Arringnon. M. Guy de Brault. You shall sit on the opposite ends of this bench till the end of this lesson. Do not utter a single word," d'Arouet ordered. Henrietta preferred to extract Charles from the room under the pretense of unacceptable behavior, but she could not undermine the fencing master's instructions at his own school. Only a quarter of an hour was left till the end of the session.

"Everyone is dismissed, except M. Charles d'Arringnon and M. Guy de Brault." D'Arouet, with exaggerated civility. He closed the heavy double door after the last student and regarded the two miscreants with a stern frown. "I shall not tolerate brawls in my school. I am waiting for you to apologize to each other."

"He threatened to kill me!" Guy de Brault claimed, probably truthfully.

"I shall tolerate no violence in my school." D'Arouet stomped his foot for emphasis. "Only out of my friendship with your cousin, M. d'Arringnon, I will allow you a chance to defend yourself against this accusation."

"This imbecile accused me of being a girl," Charles said defiantly.

Henrietta involuntary profanity was lost in Guy de Brault's indignant exclamation. "What did you call me, you little bastard?"

D'Arouet restrained him. "This is ridiculous," the fencing master stated.

"Yes." Henrietta closed her hand around Charlotte's wrist.

"M. Guy de Brault, you will owe M. Charles d'Arringnon an apology after he proves you wrong." D'Arouet's solution would have been very reasonable under other circumstances.

"What was that?" Charlotte growled.

Henrietta applied enough pressure to make her daughter abandon the idea of utilizing any other of her weapons.

"I don't own him any proof!" Charlotte shouted.

"Either you explain yourself and apologize, M. Charles d'Arringnon, or you are expelled from my school." D'Arouet raised his voice.

"Go to hell," she answered.

There was nothing else left but to twist her daughter's arm back and escort her toward the door.

"M. d'Arouet, please accept my apologies on Charles' behalf. I understand and respect your decision to expel him from your school." Henrietta bowed and nearly lost her balance when Charlotte tugged her toward the door.

Charlotte's stream of profanities about the generations of ancestors and the future descendants of d'Arouet, de Brault, and all the other young men lasted for a few blocks of fast walking until Henrietta released her. "What happened there?" she asked.

"These reprobates spent another night in a brothel. They were gloating about it! Imbecile de Brault meant to recount all the details to me!" She exploded in more profanities before continuing the narration. "He expected I would regret what I missed! I tried to evade their company, but they taunted me that I was shy as a girl, and I..." Charlotte kicked up a rock and a cloud of dust arose from its impact on the plastered wall. "I just wanted them to leave me alone! ... They were so... so... obscene! I did not mean to blurt out, *Maybe I am!*'" Charlotte kicked another rock against a wood fence and a flock of pigeons took flight.

Henrietta doubled in laughter.

"Then I had no choice but to threaten that I would run my sword through anyone who dares to tease me so," her daughter continued.

Henrietta sobered up.

8

YOUNG AND FOOLISH

LYON, FRANCE – SEPTEMBER 1717

Never dwell on the mistakes of the past. Learn from them.

Francis de Brangelton to Henrietta d'Arringnon – 1694

BY THE SULTRY SUMMER MONTHS, FEMININE CURVES rounded off Charlotte's body and heralded the beginning of her difficulties with men. Now her childhood friends avoided Charles, although the young men, plus a stray officer or two from the garrison, sought out Charlotte at all social functions. Even Simon and Renaud de Paulet treated her with a certain reserve. She was happy to escape from all that nonsense to Lyon.

"I must admit, Wildcat, you are pretty," Raoul commented with his usual candor.

"That causes no end of hassle for me," Charlotte

complained with a premonition of disaster. "Don't you acquire any amorous notions."

"I? About you?" her little brother exclaimed with a satisfactory mixture of horror and disgust. "If I ever acquire any amorous inklings about you, I will beg Antoine or Henri to pound my skull with a rock to bring me back to my senses!"

The reprieve was short-lived. The Sunday service at St. John Cathedral was marred by two gawking young officers, and the day deteriorated upon their arrival to the picnic on the banks of the Rhone. The stream of suddenly close friends of Raoul de la Fleure produced a newly acquired crop of objectionable admirers, Charlotte counted four sources of annoyance. Even Hugh de Boucher - the one who engaged her in a fistfight once - actually stammered a compliment until Raoul kicked him into coherence. The true disaster struck when Hugh's older brother Louis paid her unwelcome attention and laughed off her threats.

Raoul intervened. "You have a dilemma here, de Boucher. She is like a sister to me, but Antoine likes her. A lot. Her father is well received at Court. He and my father are old friends. Figure it out." All Raoul's teeth showed in a nasty wide sneer.

De Boucher abandoned his pursuit, but Raoul's ingenious claim turned into calamitous rumors of her and Antoine's betrothal.

Raoul panicked. "Antoine and you... you, of all women! I cannot imagine him falling in love with anyone praiseworthy, never mind with insane you! He is a hard-headed ass. Don't you ever admit the source of this folly! This is a matter of my life, Wildcat. He will kill me."

"I will keep it a secret, but maybe Antoine will appreciate that fewer marriageable women will be pitchforked at him," Charlotte soothed her little brother's fears.

Raoul pondered. "Or maybe you will like Louis de Boucher someday."

"Have you lost your mind?!"

"You are the opposite of desirable. No amount of lace can hide your wild nature and outrageous ways," he informed her. "What will you do if no one dares to marry you?"

"You dim-witted lout, listen to me! I will never like de Boucher."

"Don't women value men's attention?" Raoul overlooked the insult. "Granted, it's you, but still... don't you want someone to ... you know ?"

"No, I don't know and don't want to," Charlotte snapped.

He was absorbed in weighty thoughts. "Aren't you, you know, curious?"

"About what?" She feigned ignorance.

His stare was incredulous. "About men. I mean, about men and women, about what lovers do," Raoul said frankly.

"No, not at all." Charlotte shook her head in vigorous denial. Deep down in her mind and her heart, she might be wondering, but she would never admit that to Raoul, or anyone else.

He rolled his eyes. "Everyone in their right mind desires a lover."

"Every man does. Very few women do," Charlotte prevaricated.

"Indeed?" Raoul frowned. "Then how do you explain Henri's – and even Antoine's – love affairs?"

His intelligence posed a problem. "Many women are silly. They even like you," she replied.

"Who likes me?" He was eager to know.

Charlotte regretted her treacherous slip of the tongue. Raoul might be skinny, but he was tall, his gray eyes held a deceptively gullible expression, his golden wavy hair angelically fell below his shoulders, and he was aware of young women's flirtations with him. "Mlle. Aline gushed that you have a pleasant voice, but she complained that your conversation is atrocious."

"What does that mean?" he puzzled.

"You, little brother, should talk less and sing more."

Paris, France – February 1718

Henri was not inclined to introspection, but occasionally inconvenient scruples found their way into his mind. He gloomily surveyed the spacious paths of Tuileries Garden where Bertrand de la Norte accompanied two beautiful, shapely young women, his sister and his cousin. Henri stayed away from them, as much as he would have liked to judge for himself if de la Norte's cousin had recovered from her latest absurd attachment or if she was indeed overwhelmed with grief upon the forced – accidentally, by Henri – departure of her worthless admirer.

"Please accept my deepest gratitude for extricating me from a mangled family quarrel," de la Norte had blathered till Henri threatened to introduce himself to Mlle. Rosalynd and to console her. *"I would be happy to explain that she owes me a favor for saving her from an unscrupulous jackass,"* he offered. De la Norte wisely declined. Henri cast a final glance in de la Norte's direction and firmly shoved Mlle. Rosalynd out of his mind.

He had more pressing business to attend to –that of acquiring a new mistress. Henri's affair with statuesque Cybille had commenced in September, when father pointed her out - *"Womanizing son of mine, find out why that young siren is fluttering her eyelashes at me."* Henri was elated to indulge at the time - until he realized that Cybille was acutely interested in his father's involvement in the Company of the West business. *"No surprises here. John Law is a relative of hers,"* father had informed him, then proceeding to supply him with bits of information to feed to Cybille. Henri dutifully shuttled back and forth until he realized that mixing business and pleasure caused him headaches. He communicated his confidence that father was perfectly capable to find another source of obtaining the meager information Cybille provided, and to spread the misinformation Henri dispersed. Father assented, and Henri was poised to regretfully inform Cybille of his brotherly duty to chaperone his sister at Ferrand, but Cybille forestalled him by announcing her imminent departure to Scotland and her carriage had rattled away that very morning.

"No, I have not seen your Marie." Henri greeted his friend and frequent rival, Andre de Rameau of His Majesty's Musketeers.

"She was jealous of my duty to my regiment. Captain d'Ornille was unsympathetic to my plight and threatened to dismiss me. I made a heartbreaking choice." De Rameau adjusted his hat to a jaunty angle and assessed a petite female figure whose face was hidden by a shimmering silver veil.

"So you must find a mistress who adores the commitment along with the uniform." Henri was not intrigued by the mysterious figure; he knew from experience that masks usually preceded silliness or brought trouble. "On the left by the fountain – the russet-colored outfit, golden locks, and nice figure."

De Rameau's eyes gleamed with excitement. "For you or me?"

"Shall we make it her choice?"

"You have forgotten my divine Paulette."

"She was overwhelmed by your uniform. Have you forgotten my beautiful Muriel?"

De Rameau did not. "She has unsavory taste in men." He watched the officer approach the golden-haired woman. "I would wager to teach you a lesson, but fortunately for you, this Aphrodite has a lover."

"I would insist on the wager to teach you a lesson, but Captain D'Ornille will dislike a duel even worse than dereliction of duty, and my devil sire will support him," Henry replied. "Fortunately for you, I like my women taller and better endowed."

A sharp inhale interrupted his discourse. De Rameau froze, and his face turned ashen. "*Arnelle,*" he whispered and Henri spun around. She was as beautiful as he remembered, and Henri felt a pang of despair and betrayal. She had never told him her family name and had left Ferrand without farewell or warning to his fourteen-year-old self. She was his first consummated love, an older woman amusing herself for a week during a tedious trip across the province.

Arnelle's eyes met his. She acknowledged his gaping attention with a fleeting condescending curl of her lips, but there was no recognition on her part. She shifted her attention to de Rameau, and her face became the mirror image of his. "*Andre,*" she mouthed before gaining self-control and averting her eyes.

Henri wished she would have stayed an elusive, sacred, dream-like memory.

Clermont, France – May 1718

From the day Fontaine d'Amboise was built, the square around it had been a popular place for inhabitants of Clermont to meet and socialize. On this breezy sunny afternoon, officers and their companions, merchants and their wives, clerics, soldiers, maids, and students strolled back and forth to exchange greetings, glances, whispers and gossip. Henri peacefully conversed with the Commander of the garrison and kept a close eye on Charlotte. She was besieged by Lieutenant de Lauzon and two of his friends. The officers desperately endeavored to steer her away from Henri's line of vision, that is, to the opposite side of the fountain. Charlotte refused to cooperate and her militant posture signified readiness for action. De Lauzon's grimace revealed that her chat with him has deteriorated to the point of no return to polite convention. Her brief comment elicited loud laughter from his friends and a dozen spectators within hearing distance, and brought a twisted snarl to his face. Henri excused himself and hurried to extricate his weapon-carrying sister from her obstinate admirer, but pandemonium broke loose before his eyes. The Lieutenant reached out to place his hands on her shoulders. Did the lout imagine he could embrace her in public view? Charlotte kicked him in the shin. He recoiled, lurched forward, and swayed as he changed direction to frantically scramble back in sheer panic due to a sweep of steel in front of his face. *Nice work, dear sister, no wonder she did not back off*, Henri approved. In a single action, she disarmed him and armed herself. De Lauzon's hand grasped where the hilt of his sword should have been, and his features twisted upon the realization that his weapon was firmly pressed into his chest. Henri evaluated the situation and found no cause for alarm. No one seemed inclined to assist the hapless Lieutenant pinioned to the fountain wall. All the men and women in the square gaped in disbelief, amazement, and even approval. The water splashing into the basin of the fountain was the only sound in the square.

"You owe me an apology, bastard." Charlotte's barely

controlled voice broke the silence. Henri glanced over his shoulder in time to behold the sight of the Lieutenant launching himself forward to retrieve his sword. The distance between Henri and the combatants prevented him from interfering, but he didn't need to. Charlotte drove the blade with a controlled, deliberate, shallow thrust into de Lauzon's shoulder. Father would be proud of his girl. The Lieutenant produced a muffled groan and fell silent. Henri glanced over his shoulder again – yes, as he suspected, the sword was firmly pressed under the man's jaw, and droplets of blood were trickling down to blend with the stain spreading on his shoulder.

"Mlle. de Brangelton! I will relieve you of the Lieutenant's sword, if you please." The Commander of the garrison recovered from his stupefied astonishment and approached her.

Charlotte did not move. "Shall I trust your Lieutenant to keep his hands off me? Or should I render him incapable of ever touching me?"

The Captain halted and solemnly bowed. "On my honor, I shall stop him, Mlle. de Brangelton, if he disturbs you in any way. At the threat of military disciplinary actions, the Lieutenant shall not, under any circumstances, ever speak to you again, or approach you within a dozen paces. Lieutenant de Lauzon, you are dismissed to take care of the wound on your shoulder. Will you be kind enough to release him now, Mlle. de Brangelton? Please?"

"The bastard had the nerve to threaten me!" Charlotte half-screamed during their ride back home.

"Charlotte, you probably destroyed his career." Henri attempted to calm her down. "I would say, that was quite a severe lesson in manners. Granted, he is a boor."

"The devil take him!" She sounded hysterical. "He... he almost kissed me! The imbecile touched my...my..." She waved her hand over her breast. "I should have killed him!"

That was quite an exaggeration. She never allowed him close enough to touch her, let alone to kiss, but Henri did not bother to contest this point. "Any sensible young woman would have returned to her older brother's side to seek protection from a persistent and unwanted admirer. Did such a reasonable solution ever occur to you?"

"I am finished with genteel behavior! See what tribulations it causes for me? I will never wear dresses again! And I will never give up my sword!"

For the rest of the ride, Henri limited his contributions to reticent nods. Any logical argument would be wasted on his sister.

9

FATEFUL DECISIONS

FERRAND, FRANCE – JULY 1718

- Man of travel, man of sea,
What is your reason?
- I sail across the ocean
To stay out of prison.

From a popular sing, - c.1712

THE TRANQUILITY AT FERRAND LASTED FOR A MONTH, TILL Captain de Molienier was appointed to administer the garrison. The Captain promptly lost his heart – or, rather his mind, to Charlotte. De Molienier came from a noble and well-to-do family, he was only twenty-eight years old, he had excellent connections and therefore career prospects, and he was made even more attractive by his *"dashing appearance"*, as the now-married de Paulet sisters explained to Charlotte. *"He is a man of honor and character,"* they said in praise, to which Charlotte carelessly responded, *"Most men look good in uniform...It is unfortunate that he is unmarried."* The sisters squealed in exasperation, and the same dialogue resumed many times again, with the same success, while de Molienier's goal in life became to win over Charlotte's heart and hand. When Charlotte took apart one of his junior Lieutenants on the fencing floor, the Captain sank in a thoughtful mood. Henri despaired that a chance to marry his sister off was lost, but he underestimated de Molienier's passion, or foolishness, depending how you look at it.

"Captain de Molienier formally asked Mlle. de Brangelton's hand in marriage," father announced. "He is a fine officer, Charlotte."

"Oh, no! No!" Charlotte regained her ability to speak. "Father. You are not considering…" She choked on her words.

"Why not?" Henri reasoned, mostly for father's benefit. "You might as well consider his proposal before he regains his senses." He moved aside from a bowl she hurled at him.

"Charlotte, calm down, no one will force you to marry," father said. "I certainly will not dare."

"Why don't you marry de Molienier?" Henri asked. "The man is a saint –even your performance on the fencing floor has not scared him."

Charlotte punched a pillow. "De Molienier holds on his inexcusable delusion that he knows better than I what is right for me. He expect me, - and it's a quote, *to grow out of my wild ways.* I refuse to spend my life in arguments with a husband."

"Women have the means and ways to make men see the errors of their ways."

"I don't want him to touch me!" Charlotte screamed and Henri dropped his head into his hands.

Henri gained new respect for de Molienier. The man was not intimidated by Charlotte's unconventional conduct, yet he possessed enough self-confidence, stubbornness, patience, and experience to pursue her. Upon hearing, from her own lips, that she would marry him when the sun rises in the west, the Captain smiled and kissed her hand.

"Mlle. Charlotte is young." He later reflected on his distant matrimonial prospects. "My assignment here is for two years. It is plenty of time to lay a siege of passion."

After that, Henri dutifully played both sides, neither encouraging nor discouraging either his sister or de Molienier, but the Captain's desire was the least of his concern. Henri carefully folded the flowery, both in style and handwriting, letter from Cybille. She claimed she wished reconciliation. Why? The woman had put an immense effort into this epistle. Henri puzzled over until he realized that the proposed timing of their passionate reunion would perfectly clash with Jerome de la Norte's departure from France. Henri re-folded the letter as he concocted a plan of action.

"I will passionately reunite with her to prove my love and loyalty, diffuse any doubts and suspicions to the best of my lying abilities, and then pay obvious attention to some another woman. Cybille is bound to make a scene, and her unjust accusations of my unfaithfulness will incense me to leave Paris with you and mother." Henri presented both the perfumed letter and his scheme to father.

"It pains me to acknowledge that your horrendous womanizing occasionally has certain merits. My son, you are devious," father complimented him. "Upon your return to Paris, will you pretend to still desire her?"

"If it benefits your interests in the Company of the West business, I will humbly beg her forgiveness." Henri amended his plan. "What about Charlotte? She will be left alone to deal with de Molienier."

"I am certain he will do her no violence."

"I am concerned about the Captain's well-being if your

daughter runs out of patience with his passion," Henri retorted. "Does she comprehend that running a sword through a military officer will land her in prison?"

Marseille, France – August 1718

Antoine de la Fleure, Comte de Flancourt, happened to be in Marseille. He was now a Comte and a prominent noble citizen of Lyon, from where a significant trade was conducted through Marseille. That definitely was a reasonable explanation as to why he would be interested in experiencing the daily life surrounding the harbor, and who would be a better man to satisfy his curiosity than the Harbor Commandant, Monsieur Marcoux?

"It is a pleasure to receive you, Comte," Marcoux, a man in his forties, said. A couple of his fingers and teeth were missing, and his face was lined with deep wrinkles around the eyes. He must have been a former sailor. "What can I do for you?"

"I have always valued the seagoing community, Commandant, but from afar. Would you be kind enough to guide me through the harbor, Monsieur, explain its workings, and maybe do me the honor of joining me for dinner? Do you fancy rum?"

The man brightened upon this proposition. As Antoine had calculated, he seemed delighted to be seen in noble company and have an elaborate dinner with an unlimited rum supply.

"Very, very impressive." Antoine himself poured more rum into the Commandant's goblet and pretended to fill up his own. "With a man of your stature in charge, I am certain there has never been any trouble in Marseille."

Marcoux winced. "There was. Um, five years ago," he

confided sooner than Antoine expected. "Two cutthroats from the New World... it was in the newspapers all over the world, I heard."

"Ah, yes, I vaguely recall my father mentioning something of this nature when I was, unfortunately, too young to grasp the significance of this event."

"These damned pirates burned half of the harbor. Twenty-three claims of losses, stolen cargo, and damages were filed," the Commandant complained, his tongue loosed by rum. "I had to file a report with the Navy. I have orders to report anything out of ordinary, and that was a full-blown battle!" he said defensively.

Antoine ignored the hollow feeling in his stomach. He was aware that city elders had posted a reward upon the cousins' heads for causing civic disturbance, but the amount would not justify a dedicated search. Instigating a battle would be a significantly more serious offence, on top of the accusation of piracy.

"I am certain the Navy took action to find and punish these perpetrators. Who were they?"

Commandant's expression turned sour. "Yes. The Navy sent a man to investigate."

"What was he investigating, Monsieur?"

Fear shone in Marcoux' eyes. He must have lied somewhere along his narration. "I did state in my report that I suspected that the claims of lost cargo were false!"

"Of course." Antoine was undecided if he should be worried or relieved. He added more rum to the Commandant's cup. "I am certain there was nothing to discover apart from what you knew and reported. Twenty-three ships were affected?"

"False claims, mostly. And the damages were exaggerated. There were no causes for the Navy's concerns!" The Commandant's aggressive denial betrayed a high level of deceit.

"I am confident the man from the Navy found no fault with your report. What was his name?"

Marcoux frowned. "A difficult man to deal with."

"Was his name Devereaux, by any chance? A man about your age, with dark hair and a moustache?"

"No... he was at least a decade younger, and clean shaven." The Commandant gulped the rest of rum in his cup. "I do not recall his name."

"But he must have presented his papers?"

"He left no cursed papers," Marcoux viciously cursed and tried to quench his thirst from his empty cup. His hands had started to shake. "Tell you what, you find out his name and ask him questions, if he allows you to speak to him!"

Antoine hid his disappointment. Either the Commandant was shamelessly lying, or the man from the Navy, or maybe not from the Navy, had imprinted an unshakeable fear onto the Commandant's soul and he would not yield the name unless it was forced out of him.

"I am appalled, Monsieur, that twenty-three Captains would file false claims." Antoine changed the subject. "I would be profoundly disturbed if any of the merchants from my city were to fall into the trap of dealing with such shady characters."

The Commandant gave a sideways look at the empty bottle of rum. "I suppose I could allow you to copy these records. For a fee. Of course, a clerk's payment is not on my expenses."

Antoine signaled for another bottle to be brought in. "How many ships were in the harbor that day?"

"Will you take that list, too?" Marcoux' smirk became permanent. "There will be another fee for that."

"Why not?" Antoine motioned to pour more rum for the Commandant. "I am fascinated with the manner of naming the ships. In fact, I am conducting a study if there was a certain pattern by nationality."

"Tell you what, just come to the office tomorrow. Bring money and a clerk with you, and you can have any record you want."

Antoine was now in possession of long lists which included the names of all three-masted ships, their Captains, the ports they hailed from, their businesses, and their bases. The *Golden Sails* under the command of Mathew Johnson had arrived from Port Royal in the New World; The *Anne Maria Jane,* under Captain Pierro Capone, had arrived from Venice. He did not recognize the names of any other claimants, but maybe Henri de Brangelton would remember. Their paths had not crossed for years. He had not seen M. Francis and Mme. Henrietta for a long time either. Antoine remembered Charlotte de Brangelton and wondered if Wildcat's behavior has improved since Raoul's last report. He unfolded the map to plan his route to Ferrand.

Ferrand, France – September 1718

Charlotte's deep resentment for the current state of affairs was equally divided between sheer boredom and being the subject of unsolicited attention by the gallant Captain de Molienier. She had expected her brother to stay home and she had counted on cajoling him to ride south toward the Mediterranean Sea, but Henri had abruptly left for Paris for a feeble excuse named Cybille. Did her brother, in his rash desire to marry her off, intentionally leave her alone to deal with de Molienier? The Captain admitted that Henri had asked him to keep an eye on her. The Captain assured her that he was happy to oblige. Charlotte expressed her opinion of both de Molienier and her brother, and the contents of her tirade almost - almost! - offended de Molienier and he left with a display of wounded pride. She fervently hoped de Molienier would stay away for a few days, but no such luck. She was not in the mood to deal with him, but she saw him riding up in a meticulously cleaned and freshly pressed uniform.

"I will see you tomorrow, Mlle. Charlotte," de Molienier stated after an hour's visit, which was about an hour longer than she would liked.

"I neither expect nor wish to see you before a week passes." Charlotte would have loved to offer a year, but he was more likely to accept a week.

"Mlle. Charlotte, I will ride over to see you as often as my garrison duties allow."

Charlotte clenched her fists. His garrison duties could allow him to be a daily nuisance. "For the glory of France, do not jeopardize your duties, Captain," she begged. "Properly running a military establishment must be very challenging."

"It is my duty and my pleasure to keep you safe," he answered.

"We already had this discussion," she reminded him. "Can I trust you, Captain, to respect my request to refrain from visiting me?"

"I will see you soon, Mlle. Charlotte." He kissed her hand, made a precise turn around and left.

"Don't bother to visit for a month!" Charlotte said loudly to his broad back.

He momentarily stumbled, but pretended not to have heard her. She waited till de Molienier and his horse disappeared from view, lifted an empty bucket off the ground, banged it against the fence, threw her boot knife in the center of the fence post, picked up a stone and flung it to bounce off the bucket, and paced around, dissipating her anger by swearing aloud. De Molienier posed a complicated problem.

Charlotte did not dislike him enough to run her sword through him, but she would never marry him, a fact that the smitten Captain stubbornly refused to accept. Charlotte retrieved her knife and sat down to think. She needed a plan.

It did not take long to conclude that her very presence at home caused high hopes for de Molienier. The logical solution was to disappear from Ferrand. Where could she spent the next month or two?

Lyon was her first choice, but this plan crashed upon a possibility that Antoine might be home. Her presence would place Mme. Marguerite and M. Laurent in a very awkward position, not to mention that Charlotte had no desire to deal with explaining the imaginary betrothal to Antoine. Charlotte's own memory of him, reinforced by the unflattering second-hand knowledge of his character (the young women of Lyon described him as a heartless, callous, supercilious, uncaring man), indicated that he would be far from delighted at those disgraceful rumors. And rightfully so; she was not happy about it either. What had Raoul been thinking?

Her next viable destination was Troyes. Raoul would be attending the fencing school till December, unless he got expelled, so she could comfortably wait in town till either her parents or Henri came for her. Then again, if she were to travel across the country, why not straight to Paris? Charlotte's spirits soared. She would ride Hera, which meant she'd need a suitable attendant for the mare. Stout, barrel-chested, Red Jacques looked like a brigand, but he was obedient, loyal, and proficient in the use of a hatchet and a musket.

"Prepare Hera and Dawnstar for a trip of two weeks," Charlotte instructed the Elder Jacques. "I will travel light. Red Jacques will come with me. We are leaving tomorrow."

His jaw fell open and his mouth moved but no sound came

out at first. " Mlle. Charlotte?" he finally croaked. "Where are you going?"

"Paris. Not a word to anyone." Charlotte gave him a stern look to emphasize the point. "I do not want anyone - not even the de Paulet family, and especially not Captain de Molienier, to know my plans and destination. Hold your tongue!"

Jacques, who has been in her father's service since before Henri was born, was quite capable and willing to argue with her when it suited him. "Mlle. Charlotte! Will you think it over?" he protested.

"No." There still was a chance for her to catch up with her parents before they headed out to escort their associate out of France - and it meant a trip to the shore! That was about the Company of the West business. She should more actively participate in any New World business. She was already eighteen years of age.

A day and a half later, Charlotte still had not left home. Short on patience, she punched Pierre when he continued to lie about the loss of the horseshoe. A new excuse only made matters worse.

"What do you mean, you cannot find the stirrup?!" Charlotte could not afford any more delays. "Did it hid itself up your arse? Find it!"

"Mlle. Charlotte!" Red Jacques called. "Visitors, two men."

She did not need any more distractions. She had already wasted an hour on de Molienier. She peeked at the men confidently riding up the road. Charlotte moved into the afternoon shadows of the large chestnut tree. "Find out what is their business," she instructed Elder Jacques.

The nobleman in the lead rode a strong blue roan stallion with black mane and tail. His valet followed on a horse of unusual coloring, a mix of brown and gray patches, but the animal's chest was white, and the mane and tail were a solid brownish-gray color. The riders slowed at the entrance. The young nobleman was the image of elegance. A sparse amount of white and gold ribbon trimmed the collar and sleeve cuffs of his perfectly fitting dark green doublet. His matching hat bore two expensive feathers - golden and white. Brown breeches, gloves, and sturdy high boots completed his ensemble. The sword hilt and scabbard were a simple and practical design, and he carried a set of matching pistols in the saddle holsters. His features were familiar. When his astute eyes briefly met hers before he switched his attention to Jacques' greeting, Charlotte recognized him.

10

CLASH OF WILLS

FERRAND, FRANCE – SEPTEMBER 1718

*You try to win an argument with Charlotte de
Brangelton. You might as well reason with a tree.*

Raoul de la Fleure to Antoine de la Fleure – 1716

FIVE YEARS HAD PASSED SINCE ANTOINE'S LAST VISIT TO
Ferrand. This time, he did not miss the inconspicuous half-
hidden pathway twisting up, and he paused to regard the
deceptively derelict appearance of the dwelling. A castle had
been built on the hill centuries ago, but now only charred and
gloomy ruins of the old structure remained to overlook the
valley below. Two glum and forbearing walls of black stone
jotted out at a wide angle from the half-crumbled entry tower,
but behind those dilapidated walls, the residence was well-
maintained and comfortable. The roofless space inside the
tower still boasted the familiar marine cables and rope ladders
where Antoine and Henri, later joined by Raoul and Charlotte,

had spent many happy hours climbing up and down or scaling the walls.

Antoine solemnly regarded the Coat of Arms banner suspended from the top of the portcullis gate. The design caused a sensation when Francis de Brangelton, first Comte of Tournelles, had it recorded. A kite-shaped shield was vertically halved into burgundy and black sections, the golden head of a snarling leopard adorned the center, and the broadsword and the olive branches crossed below it. *"This motif was inspired by illicit oceanic commerce,"* Henri had proudly explained. *"I suppose that the flying Jolly Roger at the Royal Court would indeed be a disgrace even by my sire's standards."* Beyond the gate in the courtyard, the old building nested against the massive stone remains of the wall; the stables, the armory, lodgings for the servants, and a de facto storage place were located there. The new family residence on the right was constructed from the same stone, but it boasted large windows, sloped roofs, iron balconies and wide and high doors. The upper floor was designated for the family bedchambers and the guest rooms. On the ground level, the spacious main hall next to sitting-reception-dining room was located on the first floor, and the large kitchen jutted out to the side of the building.

Antoine rode between two giant pine trees which stood guard at the entrance. Dogs of undeterminable breeds barked to alert the residents of his approach. In the center of the yard, a young man stood motionlessly in the shade of the massive chestnut tree. He was much shorter than Henri, but his posture - left toe out, head inclined to the side - was familiar. His plain clothes - a loosely-fitting sleeveless doublet of stiff brown leather, a shirt of unbleached linen, and black wide-legged breeches - were of quality fabric but devoid of any decorations. A wide shoulder belt supported a full-size sword with a practical leather-bound grip, and tall riding boots completed the outfit. His face was hidden by a wide-brimmed brown hat decorated with a large, expensive, cornflower-blue feather.

Elder Jacques held off the dogs. "Good day, Monsieur," he greeted Antoine. "May I ask ..."

"Antoine de la Fleure!" A boyish voice, still a little high, belonged to the young man in the shadows.

Antoine slowly dismounted. It could not be, he decided at first, but the figure walked toward him with unmistakable de Brangelton swagger and a reckless grin visible under the hat. "I see you did not recognize me."

"Mlle. Charlotte." Antoine's doubts evaporated. He casually bowed. A little formality might be prudent to keep some distance, even if she addressed him informally. The girl was only a year older than Raoul. "You are taller than I remember."

"You are less formidable than I remember," she countered in good humor, raised her head, and looked up at him. Her strangely dark blue eyes conveyed an odd combination of wariness and amusement. "What brings you to Ferrand this time?" She dropped the boy's voice and changed her address to formal.

Antoine did not cherish the memory of the circumstances which had prompted his last visit. "Much to my mother's happiness and everyone else's relief, my father and I are friends now." Since his return from London, his father had wisely abandoned his endeavors to guide Antoine's life. Antoine reciprocated by participation in civic life in Lyon – purely to alleviate his tranquil boredom, but everyone benefited from it. Within the last year, the strained truce between father and Antoine had indeed progressed to amiable comradeship. "Are your parents and your brother well?"

"My parents and my irresponsible oaf of a brother are in Paris. You will have to stay in Henri's room, all the guest rooms are locked up. Tell Elder Jacques if you need anything."

"Thank you." Antoine bit his upper lip as soon as the

words were out. Staying in the house alone with an unmarried female was a daft idea, but she had caught him off-guard, and he did not care to discuss his reasons. He held out his hand to the dogs who, upon Red Jacques' commands, came to acquaint themselves with a newly accepted resident of the household.

Antoine followed Charlotte across the yard, half-expecting her to stumble. Could she see the way from under her hat? She marched fast, in long strides, and Antoine mentally apologized to Raoul for doubting that the men in the garrison never suspected that Charles was a girl. The grip of the sword showed signs of extensive use.

"How long will you visit?" Charlotte asked over her shoulder.

Antoine recognized an unsubtle hint. "I will leave tomorrow morning."

"May I ask where are you heading?"

"Home, Mlle."

"Have you been away for long?"

"Only four months this time," Antoine said to her back.

She kept on walking. "My parents intend to spend Christmas in Lyon," she spoke without a glance back. "We will ride straight from Paris."

"We?" Antoine repeated. What was that about locking the place up now?

"Yes."

Why would her parents go to Paris after picking her up at Ferrand, only to backtrack to Lyon from there? "Who is we?" he rephrased his question.

"My parents and I. I expect Henri as well."

"May I ask when will your parents or Henri return home?"

"Probably next spring. I will join them in Paris soon."

"I beg your pardon?" Antoine stopped for a moment in

surprise, but she marched ahead and he had to catch up with her. "May I ask how will you accomplish that?"

"On horseback."

Antoine made an effort to hide his annoyance. "And may I ask when is your journey commencing?"

"Tomorrow."

"Are you riding out by yourself?" He did not succeed in hiding his doubt.

"I intended to leave two days ago, but the second horse lost a shoe," she replied.

That was a non-answer, and the use of singular "I" was still there. "May I explicitly ask who is escorting you to Paris?"

Charlotte stopped and turned around. "I am quite capable to find my way to Paris by myself."

"I beg your pardon?" Antoine's mouth fell open in bewilderment.

She held his stare. "I said..."

"I have heard what you said! Are you insane?"

"I am Charlotte de Brangelton," she expostulated with familiar defiance and challenge in her stance and her voice.

"Do you comprehend the dangers of traveling alone?"

"You travel by yourself all the time, don't you?"

"I am a man," he reminded her.

"I am Charles d'Arringnon," Charlotte reverted to the same boyish voice she greeted him.

Antoine was at a loss for words. "You are not serious!"

"I am damn serious. Who, and why, would suspect Charles of being a girl?"

Antoine hated to concede that he had no argument against that. "It's a ten-day trip."

"I have survived longer trips than that," she interrupted him.

"With your family, I suppose?" He was at the verge of losing his patience.

"Do you think I have not learned anything from my family?" Her tone matched his.

Antoine deeply resented the turn this bizarre dialogue had taken. Charlotte was extremely skillful at twisting the conversation into the direction she preferred, and at providing non-answers which left no room for any intelligent response.

"I suppose, Mlle, you have been practicing your swordsmanship? In case there is a difficulty during your ill-conceived journey?"

Charlotte suddenly flashed a happy grin. "Are you suggesting a fencing round?"

"At your service," Antoine responded without thinking, then silently berated himself for his decision to come to Ferrand.

Antoine had correctly assumed Charlotte's swordsmanship to be as accomplished as Raoul's. Her reach was shorter, but she compensated with agility and speed, and she was aware of her limitations in the realm of physical strength. She promptly retreated when there was a chance of blades crossing at the handle and forcing brutal force in a hand-to-hand stand-off, and found ways to reverse the line from a different angle of attack. As Antoine expected, she was more experienced at defense than offense - her practical skills had been acquired during fencing rounds with better swordsmen, but she possessed a very mature precision and, surprisingly, cool-headed control. She was a serious opponent, better than many men he had crossed swords with, and this unexpected round required a fair amount of effort and concentration on his part, as well as endurance - for Charlotte was physically and mentally prepared for a long exercise; she must have spent as much time as he did in practicing her fencing skills. She did not bother to remove her hat, so Antoine focused on knocking it off. He finally succeeded in his endeavor, but her focus did not waver. Both of them were out of breath when he finally pressed his sword against her upper arm.

Charlotte picked up her hat and dusted it off. "Now, admit it, I can hold my ground."

"Don't allow it to cloud your judgment, " Antoine grudgingly acknowledged before he remembered what led to this fencing session. "Traveling by yourself is–"

"You are even more annoying than Raoul. I did not think that was even possible," Charlotte complimented him. "I will have dinner prepared at six o'clock in the main hall. Pardon me for now. I must kick the lazy carcasses dawdling in the stables." She pulled her hat low over her face and sauntered away.

Elder Jacques escorted Antoine to his room. "Monsieur, will you please explain to Mlle. Charlotte the dangers of the trip across France with only one slow-witted groom?"

"How serious is she about the trip?" Antoine asked absentmindedly, even though he knew what the answer would be. Even when she was very young, Charlotte de Brangelton would succinctly demonstrate how little she listened to reasons, threats, and instructions.

Jacques sighed. "She will do anything she wants, Monsieur. Her father allows it."

Antoine leaned against the window frame to weigh his options. M. Francis and Mme. Henrietta must have left their daughter behind for a good reason. Even jaded Parisian society would be shocked by Wildcat's behavior and lack of manners. The concept of Charlotte traveling by herself would be ridiculous if it was not so dangerous. He could deliver her into the custody of his parents in Lyon, but he shuddered at the thought of first traveling with her, then justifying their arrival together to the tune of all those rumors. He felt pain in his upper lip when he imagined the chaos his arrival with Mlle. would bring. He could not possibly escort her to Paris either - he was not her relative, her parents would probably be displeased with him, and, most of all, he had no desire to spend two weeks with a young woman - at least, she was supposed to be. As a habit, Antoine avoided, at all means, the company of unmarried young women. He religiously followed Captain de Varbes' advise, which he cherished as the most valuable lesson he had learned in military school. One evening, the drunk and still-drinking Captain had staggered to their housing building. *"My boys,"* he slurred his words. *"If you are a man of honor, avoid, at all costs, being alone with a young unmarried woman. You will be trapped into marrying her. And before you know it, you must draw the blood of a cowardly hapless bastard because it is a matter of honor, when you wish him no harm and when you dream that you could unload your wife into his embrace forever. And that will be the end of your glorious military career."* The Captain had paused to consume a quarter of a bottle in one gulp. *"I have never so much as raised my hand at her, either, until today, but, devil take it, I am not a saint."* He finished the rest of the bottle. *"Do not ever trust young unmarried women, boys,"* he had repeated, and with those words of wisdom, he had slowly crumpled onto the floor.

The main hall of the residence was a casual open room with the feel of a friendly neighborhood tavern. Servants' voices, accompanied by the clinking of pots and pans, drifted from the adjacent kitchen, and Antoine was pleased that there was no formal separate room to eat, and that the dinner was not a private and intimate affair. Charlotte sat across the table from him. She did take the hat off, but her face remained concealed by her black, shoulder-long hair which she styled as a hood.

"Thank you for the hospitality." Antoine took a bite of

freshly baked bread. "May I ask how will you proceed on your trip?" he asked.

"Red Jacques is a burly man with a red beard and he usually carries a hatchet. His looks alone will scare most of the rubble." She liberally watered her wine. "I will send the luggage by post. We will ride light and keep an easy pace to outrun any trouble if needed."

"Is there anything I can do to stop you, Mlle?"

Charlotte shook her head. "Nothing at all."

Antoine's expected her to avert her eyes, but his best resolute scowl had no effect on Charlotte. "Mlle. Why did your family leave you at home?"

She studied the contents of her plate. "I did not insist on coming along." She again avoided answering the pointed question.

"Does anyone in your family expect you?" he pressed.

"No one would be surprised."

Biting his upper lip was a too common occurrence this afternoon. Antoine usually only did that under severe duress, and that normally happened no more than once or twice a month. Dealing with Wildcat had caused him a headache. He felt an obligation to her family to stop her reckless enterprise, but he had no idea how to accomplish that. Maybe a scare tactic would work. "Mlle, I would hate to see you injured."

Charlotte's eyes were cold and challenging. "Listen carefully." She enunciated every word. "I do not give a damn about your useless speculations! I will not abandon my plans. You will not dissuade me from my upcoming journey." Her knuckles were white from gripping the knife and the fork. "Am I making myself clear?"

Antoine was tempted to reach across the table and slap her for this little speech, but held his temper. He gave her an ironic smile. "Very clear, Mlle. Damn clear."

"Good." She stabbed the slice of sausage on her plate and stiff silence settled in.

Charlotte barely restrained herself from throwing a punch at Antoine's condescending replies to her explanations of her journey, but he no longer griped about the dangers lurking on the road. She had to be hospitable no matter what headache it caused her and how much his persistent effort to dissuade her from her trip grated on her nerves. She understood the dangers and she did not need more reminders and explanations. *"If I did not reveal my plans, he would have been out of my way bright and early tomorrow,"* she thought, clenching her fists. *"What was I thinking?"* His superficially formal manners were aimed to define a distance between him and her. Charlotte was thankful for that. Raoul or Henri would roll on the floor in hysterical laughter if they heard him addressing her as *"Mlle"*.

"Raoul wrote that he likes his fencing school," Charlotte said. "Does he truly need to improve his fencing?"

"Yes." Antoine was startled at the unexpected civility, but recovered quickly. "I do not encourage your enthusiasm for the journey to Paris, but I believe you and he are still evenly matched. I would bet Henri on a fencing round between you two."

"Henri would win," Charlotte asserted, but inwardly she cringed upon remembering the wager she and Raoul had made. "Have you ever been in Troyes?"

"Yes. It is a pleasantly quaint town."

Did he stay there for a month? Charlotte wondered to herself, hoping he would have the decency to refrain from boasting of his affairs. "What did you like the most?"

He drunk the wine sparingly. "The stained glass in all the cathedrals brightened my visit."

"Cathedrals?" Charlotte repeated incredulously. "Have you acquired a desire to join the priesthood?"

"No!" Antoine responded. "I am interested only in the architecture aspect."

"I was afraid you would start speaking Latin."

"You greatly contributed to the interruption of my classical education," Antoine reminded her, and the wall between them crumbled upon the memories of their – along with Henri's and Raoul's – elaborate schemes to avoid Latin lessons and M. Laurent's replacement of Latin lessons with Spanish language lessons. By the time the gooseberry tart was served for dessert, they slipped back to informal address, and the conversation drifted to the changes at the de la Fleure estate. Charlotte accepted Antoine's challenge to draw the map of the grounds, and she sketched the paths across the woods, the bend in the river, the garden hedges. She added the changes he described, and they comfortably remained at the table long after the outside daylight faded and the candles were lit.

"Your cartographical skills are very impressive," Antoine complimented her. "May I keep this map?"

"Yes." The activities and sounds in the adjacent room subsided, and suddenly Charlotte was very aware of the lateness of the hour and the silence which suddenly hung between Antoine and herself. "What time will you leave tomorrow?" She returned to the business at hand.

A guarded expression settled on Antoine's face. "If you do not travel to Paris, I will leave at sunrise."

"My actions are none of your business." Charlotte stood up. "It is late. Good night. If you don't leave at sunrise, I expect a fencing round," she added on her way to the door.

"Of course. You need all the practice you can manage.

Good night, Mlle." she heard him sit down and pick up the bottle of wine.

Charlotte locked the door of her bedroom, slammed her pillow against the bedpost, and sat in front of the mirror. She tossed her hair back and studied her reflection. She looked like her father, and no one had ever accused her father of being a handsome man. What did her admirers see in her? Her nose was sharp, her bosom was small - no place in either corset or bodice to hide a knife. And yet, if she were to believe the compliments, she was beautiful. On the other hand, Henri and Raoul de la Fleure had pointed out separately and in chorus, *"No man in his right mind will accept Charles."* M. Patrice de Seveigney certainly had not. At any rate, she faced a different predicament now.

She had held the delusion that dealing with Antoine would be just as simple as dealing with his younger brother, but she had underestimated Antoine. She admitted that despite his faults of arrogance and deviousness, Antoine was a very hand-some and attractive man. He was tall and slender, and he wore his light brown hair neatly tied in the back. His face was square with a dimpled chin, and his gray eyes warmed up nicely when he smiled. Would Antoine treat her differently if she were presented in a dress?

Charlotte frowned at her odd and absurd thoughts. Distrac-tion from the planning of her journey was dangerous. She combed her hair and thought about tomorrow: rise before dawn and search the stable herself, before anyone wakes up. The stirrup could not have disappeared, so it must have been hidden, probably with Elder Jacques' encouragement. She must leave before de Molienier visited again. He was a simple and single-minded man, and if he were to encounter her undesir-able guest, he would challenge Antoine to a duel. She could not possibly explain Antoine to de Molienier or other way around.

Antoine woke up as soon as the first rays of sunshine spilled into the room. He rushed through the morning toilette, dressed, and headed toward the stables in his search for Armand.

"Do you hen-brained rats think I lost my mind? Is this a devil's hoof or the lost stirrup? Or can't you sons of goats tell the difference? Did the stirrup crawl under a bucket, you bastards?!" Charlotte's raised voice rang from the stables, followed by the sound of buckets and a heavier object hitting the wall before the doors swung wide open and two men ran out. Charlotte kept close on their heels. She was securing her hat with one hand and swinging a broom in another, and neither the sword bouncing on her hip nor the hens scattering out of the way impeded her progress. Antoine quickly moved aside. The younger man was a fast runner and he took off in an instance. Another one, with a purple bruise over his eye, demonstrated an amazing agility to climb up the nearest tree.

Charlotte stopped and raised her head. "Climb down, fleabag!"

"I cannot."

Charlotte kicked a small stone off the path into the air, caught it with one hand, and hurled it hard at the man. In a fruitless effort to protect himself from the very accurate projectile, he jerked his body, his hand slipped off the branch, and he almost tumbled down when the pebble hit his shoulder.

"If the horses are not ready within an hour, I will beat you black and blue!" she threatened.

A horse neighed. Charlotte leaned her head toward the sound, sharply spun on her heels, and hurried back in the stable.

Antoine followed her. "You are not having a good morning, Mlle, are you?"

She obviously hadn't noticed him before. "No. They are stalling." She approached the agitated chestnut-colored mare with a black mane and tail. "Calm down, Hera. Onward to Paris we will go!" Charlotte affectionately patted the mare's neck and gently caressed the muzzle.

Antoine marveled at the absurdity of the scene. He has seen women dispersing tender care to small yapping lapdogs and occasional monkeys, but Charlotte's pet was a powerful animal, large in size and strong in body, with an elegant arched neck, a horse well suited for a cavalry officer.

"Beautiful mare," Antoine reached out, but the horse twitched her ears and snapped at him. "Bad attitude. She must be yours."

Charlotte ran her hand through the mane. "She does not trust strangers. Yes, Hera is mine, thank you, and I picked her out myself."

"And you named after the malicious Greek goddess. How suitable."

"Hera is the most powerful Greek goddess," Charlotte corrected him and marched toward the door. "Since you managed to bring your flea-bitten lazy carcass off the tree, make yourself useful and clean the stables!" she screamed at the man with a black eye.

Antoine had acquired Armand's services two years ago, when he paid Armand to obtain information. Armand was assaulted and beaten, but luckily for him, Antoine had saved Armand's hide and paid to cure the wounds. Armand begged him for employment. He had a remarkable talent for gathering information quickly, an incredible memory and an eye for details, and he was delighted at the privilege to serve the Comte de Flancourt. Armand learned to take excellent care of horses, and he progressed into a relatively tolerable valet. However, Mlle. Charlotte was too much for him. Antoine found Armand sitting on the rafters in a horrified stupor. Armand climbed down to explain that he was escaping from the harrowing scene earlier when Mlle. found out that the missing stirrup was actually hidden and flew into a rage - he seldom heard the profanities Mlle. used! He had learned some new ones, but, in any case, he had a report. Despite Mlle's age - she was only eighteen, you know - she run the household with an iron will when her parents and brother were away, as she had established last year. Mlle. was very short tempered when things were not to her liking, as he had witnessed. The head groom had acquired a black eye from Mlle.'s own fist when she suspected they pulled a horse shoe off the horse destined to carry Red Jacques to Paris – that was the man who looked like a brigand! - thank God it was not off Hera's hoof, since that demon of a horse was a special pet of Mlle! Mlle. was very fond of this horse. In all truth, yes, the shoe might have been pulled off. Mlle. forbade anyone from spreading a single word of her plans, and no one in the household would dare to blatantly disobey Mlle. She had taken a fancy to carry her sword all the time. And she was determined to leave today.

A red-headed brigand – he must be Red Jacques - poked his head into the stables and inquired if Monsieur would care for an omelette? - Mlle. Charlotte ordered one to be prepared for her immediately. Where was she? - She was personally packing her saddlebags, and she was in a hurry to set out on her journey. Antoine strolled to the entrance tower, and, to occupy himself, idly estimated the width of the base. Charlotte emerged from the main entrance and headed back to the stables.

Antoine intercepted her. "Is your horse even trained?"

Charlotte grimaced in annoyance. "Do you think my mother would tolerate an uncontrollable horse in the household?"

"Are you certain you want to take you beloved horse on an arduous journey across France?"

"She likes to travel."

"I bet she has enough sense to stay in Ferrand."

"She is intelligent enough to disagree with you," she retorted.

"That is foolhardiness, not intelligence."

Charlotte narrowed her eyes. "We agreed to no longer talk about my travel plans."

When did that agreement happen? Antoine was a patient man, but Charlotte seemed to provoke him in no time. "How long will it take you to reach Moulins?"

"What would I do in Moulins?"

"It is on the way to Paris, isn't it?"

Charlotte rolled her eyes in a theatrical display of exasperation. "The route through Moulins and Nevers is shorter, but the roads are less traveled. I prefer to stay on major thoroughfares, which lead through Bourges and Orleans. Do you have any valid arguments against this route?"

Judging from her aptitude for cartography, she must have consulted, or, more likely, memorized the whole map of France. Charlotte was, after all, a de Brangelton. Maybe she could safely travel to Paris by herself.

"Why such urgency to leave?"

"I crave a taste of coffee at the Song and Spice." The warning notes in her tone forestalled any further questions.

Antoine had no doubt that if he pressed for the real answer, she would inform him that her reasons are none of his business. "Will a broken arm stop you?" he asked thoughtfully.

Charlotte did not miss his meaning, her eyes turned to dark ice. To Antoine's astonishment, her hand moved toward her sword. "My parents will not condone that, de la Fleure."

"They might, if that stops you from this perilous journey by yourself," he pondered.

He was awarded with a glare cold enough to freeze a horse into a statue. "Don't even think about it, " Charlotte said with an impressively steely manner. Antoine had witnessed men scattering back from the same threat in her father's eyes. "I will repay the favor later."

Antoine gritted his teeth. She challenged him to do what he could not, and this situation was completely out of his control. Plenty of women had glowered at him in anger, even screamed, but never in his life, had he even remotely felt on the defensive and about to lose his temper and slap her. However, this morning, he was engaged in a dispute with a woman whose fingers flexed in readiness to either curve around a sword hanging at her hip, or to roll into a fist and throw a punch. It was an unfamiliar situation.

"You are staying home." He stepped closer with the intent of squeezing her shoulder to emphasize the point, but she managed to twist out of the way.

"Do not ever presume to command me. I will do anything I damn well please!" She wheeled around and stomped away, thus effectively finishing the argument on her terms. Antoine caught up with her in a few quick strides and seized her arm above the left elbow.

"Don't you ever dare..." he began.

Charlotte spun around and threw a punch with her right hand. He barely moved his head out of harm's way, her fist knocked off his hat, and he felt the rush of air through his hair. He caught Charlotte's arm and twisted it back, but her left elbow delivered a painful sharp stab to his ribcage. Antoine barely managed to escape the back kick of her foot. Charlotte's hand reached for her sword, and he firmly grasped her left wrist. She sharply threw her head back, aiming for his chin. He floundered at the sudden maneuver and struggled to maintain his balance. Handling Charlotte was deteriorating into combat. She was amazingly strong and agile, living up to her nickname, and he could not hold her much longer without hurting her. "What are you doing?" he hissed, hiding the strain in his voice. "If I wished you harm, I could just allow you to proceed on your happy journey."

To his surprise and relief, Charlotte stopped struggling and twisted to look at him. There was no fear in her glinting eyes. "You have no right to tell me what to do."

There was no good response. The situation would have been ridiculous if it was not completely out of his control. "I owe your father and mother a big debt of gratitude, Mlle. Your brother is my friend. Otherwise, I would not care less what happens to you."

"This is a family affair," Charlotte interrupted him, "Stay out of it."

"May I point out that this is a matter of life. Your life." Antoine reminded her.

"May I point out that I am perfectly capable to manage my life without your interference!" she mocked him. They could stay and argue there till the end of time, while Charlotte utilized her talent in making a bad situation worse. Antoine could either release her, admitting defeat, or knock her out, admitting his helplessness and inviting the wrath of the whole household.

"May I remind you that your life and your well-being is a concern to your parents."

"They trust me to make my own decisions." She struggled to pull her arms free. "This is none of your business. Get your hands off me!"

"I have a proposition for you," Antoine heard himself say. He released her, although he kept his hand on the hilt of his sword, just in case she was to attack him. "I will ride with you."

Charlotte glared at him. "No! I don't want your company."

"I am not delighted at the prospect of your company either, but I am not convinced that you can safely make it on your own."

Charlotte's eyes flashed murderously. "If you worry about my hide, why don't you follow me for a dozen miles, just to make certain your concerns have no justification?"

"I am not following you anywhere," he stated, watching a smug, happy smile spread on her face. "I will ride with you as long as I deem it necessary." he stipulated. Her smile disappeared. "And if I deem you unfit to continue your journey, I will bring you back home." Antoine braced himself for a violent outburst if the inferno in her eyes were any indication of her feelings about this truly idiotic suggestion of his.

"You shall not ride with me further than Montlucon," she countered. "No matter what you deem, I will continue on my way to Paris. You can go to Lyon or go to hell."

Antoine regretted his preposterous impulse, but backing out was no longer an option. "Very well," he growled, disgusted at the elation he felt upon the conclusion of their argument.

"Give me your word we shall have no more debates about my business," Charlotte insisted.

"You have my word!" Antoine picked up his hat, and they stood still, regaining their composure to the accompaniment of the soft sounds of the wind and the lazy rustle of falling leaves.

"Montlucon is about fifty miles from here. There is a road leading straight to Lyon through St. Pourcain-sur-Sioule," she informed him.

Antoine made a mental note to check the map, but the confidence in her tone indicated that yes, she had memorized the map of all of France.

"We will leave right after the meal," Charlotte said.

"Why such haste?"

"A strong desire to part ways with you as soon as possible." Charlotte delivered yet another non-answer.

"The feeling is mutual. I will be ready if you are."

"Should I call you Henri during our mutually disagreeable trip?"

"Will you obey me then?"

"Not a chance. On this trip, I am Charles d'Arringnon." Her eyes again were cold and guarded.

Antoine now fully comprehended the headaches his brother had endured during all the visits from the de Brangeltons. Antoine had never had to deal with Charlotte alone, but poor Raoul had spent days and weeks in her impossible company.

11

EN ROUTE

FERRAND – SEPTEMBER 1718

De Brangelton and I are on our merry way from Ferrand to Paris.

Antoine de la Fleure's letter to Laurent de la Fleure – 1718

CHARLOTTE VAULTED INTO THE SADDLE AND PAUSED TO look around the courtyard. The residence was organized for the family's absence. The doors, the windows, and the shutters were closed and the rooms locked, the valuables and important papers hidden, the instructions for the harvest and winter preparations given to Elder Jacques. The letters written to M. Louis and Mme. Constance explained that she had left home with a trusted associate of her father's to meet up with her parents in Paris, and she promised to write upon her arrival. Elder Jacques agreed to withhold the delivery of these letters till Sunday, when they would miss her in church, – *"Monsieur* and Madame will worry less before receiving my letter from Paris," Charlotte explained. And strict orders had been issued not to utter a single word to the ardent Captain de Molienier! Charlotte raised her eyes to the top of the entrance tower and felt an odd pang of detachment. The familiar outline of the buildings, the trees in the courtyard, and the old stone walls seemed distant, like memories. She adjusted her hat. No reason to succumb to nervousness just because today was the first time she had ever left home by herself, present company excluded. Antoine wisely refrained from any comments when his eyes focused on the pistol tucked into her belt. Charlotte waved to Elder Jacques, wheeled Hera around and cantered through the entry. She heard muffled oaths from Antoine when he caught up with her. Armand and Red Jacques followed them without delay.

The weather was favorable, the air was cool, and the puffy sparse white clouds in the sky held no threat of rain. The peak of Pay-de-Dome loomed over their progress, and chances were good that she had left in time to gain a respectable distance in case the impetuous Captain, upon discovering her departure, decided to chase after her. That's why she had chosen the route through Bourges. In his simple reasoning, de Molienier would certainly look at the map and rush through Moulins and Nevers. Her most pressing concern was to avoid de Molienier, his officers, neighbors, or anyone else who knew her, and she chose to ride along the less-traveled side roads until the danger of recognition passed. Without a word, she left the main route and rode through the narrow path across the wood.

"Why are we veering away from a direct route?" her companion vocalized his undesired opinion. "Didn't you state you preferred major thoroughfares?"

"I prefer to prevent a repeat of our argument with M. de

Paulet," Charlotte answered curtly. There was no reason to mention de Molienier.

"Ah..." He searched his memory. "He and Madame are friends of your parents. They will be worried about your disappearance."

"I left a letter for him and Mme. Constance, and I will write to them from Paris."

"Why did you not ask one of the de Paulet brothers to escort you?"

Charlotte howled at the mental image of their horrified reaction, and calmed down only upon contemplating how either one would eventually wag his tongue and she would end up with Captain de Molienier escorting her to Paris. "We don't get along."

"Imagine that." Antoine smirked.

"In fact, they've avoided my marvelous company since the brawl in the tavern."

"Brawl in the tavern?" he repeated in disbelief. "What trouble have you caused?"

"None."

"Your secrecy in leaving leads me to believe that you are escaping from the law," Antoine probed again.

"Nothing that dramatic. Just avoiding be seen with you, isn't that obvious?" Charlotte felt obligated to remind Antoine of his undesired presence.

"I wholeheartedly agree!" His voice rose in defiance.

They wordlessly rode through the stretch of forest, swatting low- hanging branches out of the way. The yellow and russet leaves had started to fall and muffled the sounds of hooves. The shadows deepened in the frail afternoon light, and the autumn smell of dampness lingered in a cooler air. Charlotte led the group through the path down the hill and onto an open country road winding around the fields, where the harvesters toiled and paid no attention to the riders. Her spirits soared despite Antoine's inclination to speak to her.

"I would appreciate knowing what to expect from you on this journey." His comment reminded her of his existence half an hour later. "About that brawl in a tavern?"

Charlotte did not mind narrating how, in a fine moment of inspiration, she had tossed a screeching cat onto the back of one of Henri's opponents.

"That was an excellent idea." Antoine's smile was genuine. "Something to remember for the future, I am certain. My imagination has never extended beyond riding a horse into a dining hall."

"Tell me about it."

Montlucon – September 1718

Dealing with Charlotte de Brangelton caused more and more headaches for Antoine de la Fleure as time passed. He dreaded the crossroads leading to Montlucon since he admitted to himself that his concern for her safety overweighed his aversion to traveling with her to Paris. Last night, after they retired to their respective rooms at the inn, his apprehension manifested itself when he composed a letter to Henri. *"I will stay home through this winter. I had the most edifying chat with the Commandant of a certain harbor."* He tightly sealed the letter, congratulated himself that there was nothing to incriminate him in any way if the letter did not reach the recipient, but his stomach churned upon the thought that his intended messenger may not reach Paris.

He struggled to convince himself that Charlotte comprehended the difficulties of her Ferrand-to-Paris enterprise and that Red Jacques' presence provided a certain degree of protection. Charlotte was an experienced traveler, aware of the dangers and challenges awaiting her on the trip, and yet Antoine would never send her off by herself if she were his sister. Charlotte could pass for a boy of sixteen, no older, not yet the age to be taken seriously. Antoine had been the same age when he left military school to traverse the roads on his own, and he had been relieved to meet up with his father, despite his trepidation of explaining his actions said father. And yet, spending two weeks alone with - allegedly - a woman, young and unmarried, was a superb example of idiocy. Of course, Raoul would scoff at this. By God, Raoul had spent months in her company, and felt no fear about Charlotte laying any claims to him. Antoine had no plans or purpose; he could, and should, accompany Charlotte. In the light of Antoine's discovery in Marseille, catching up with Henri would be a prudent action. Maybe Anaïs would return to Paris this autumn. He would enjoy another month in her company. She certainly knew how to entertain a man despite her peevishness and sharp tongue. Those mild vices were virtues compared to Charlotte's unrelenting stubbornness, single-minded determination to do anything she pleased, wild opinions, uncontrollable actions, unpredictable behavior, and inclination to risk her life, all before noon.

When Antoine and Charlotte paused at the crossroads, he tucked his letter deeply in his pocket and faced Charlotte and her prancing mare. "Any chance you changed your mind?"

"Any chance you will sail to the moon?" A happy grin accompanied the question. Her horse snorted in agreement, as eager to move along as her rider. "Have a nice ride home. Give my best to your parents and Raoul. We will see you in December!" Charlotte tipped her hat, wheeled the mare around and cantered off without looking back. This farewell sequence was apparently an entrenched habit. Red Jacques coughed in the cloud of dust and followed.

Antoine gaped in bewilderment. He had expected a little longer of a departing dialogue. By all means, he should have been relieved that she had no desire for his company all the way to Paris, but she had outmaneuvered him, did exactly what she pleased despite his objections and arguments, left him at the crossroads without a second thought, and, to top it off, she had departed without even affording him a chance to hand her the letter as if he were going to abandon her to her fate!

"Nobody in their right mind will suspect that ... that...over there is a young woman." Armand offered his unsolicited opinion and turned in the direction of Lyon.

Antoine watched the diminishing images of the riders on the road north to Paris. She disappeared from view without even a glance back. He urged his horse to follow and yelled at Armand who almost disobeyed.

Upon parting ways with Antoine, Charlotte's feelings oscillated between relief that she no longer had to worry about compromising her reputation and apprehension about the journey ahead. She had accepted his company until the crossroad at Montlucon since it stopped him from meddling in her affairs She had kept the parting exchange brief and civil. She had no desire to waste time. If Raoul were in his brother's place, Raoul would jump at the opportunity to travel to Paris. She would have a safer trip and more compliant company. Raoul and Antoine looked amazingly alike, but Raoul was a lot more pleasant to be around.

She heard two riders coming fast and hard from behind. Charlotte pulled on the reins, reached for the pistol before turning around to check the commotion, and found herself at an unusual loss for words.

"Shall we?" Antoine said curtly.

"I thought you were heading home," Charlotte fell in step with him. What had made him change his mind?

"I do not want a guilty conscience if something happens to you."

"Suit yourself." Charlotte was again caught up in renewed mixed feelings of relief and uneasiness. Dealing with Antoine caused her a headache. What did she truly know of him? He was a man who was accustomed to having things his way, he was intelligent, and, as she had perceived from their confrontations, he might win an argument or two, or knock her out if it ever came to exchanging blows. Charlotte knew her limitations, and there would be no element of surprise.

She was quite certain that Antoine had not even a shred of any amorous interest in her, and his presence provided solid protection. Antoine possessed an authoritative demeanor which commanded people's respect and obedience. His decision to escort her was obviously made due to the feeling of obligation for family friendship. Henri would do the same, though he would be protesting, complaining, and grumbling all along. *"Henri traveling alone with a young woman?"* Charlotte merriment faded upon the intensification of the nagging concern for her reputation. Considering her brother's loose morals, she had to be very careful in her actions, and yet, here she was, in a company of a young man who was not a relative. Charlotte forced these thoughts out of her mind for now, and consoled herself that a trip with Antoine would be same as a trip with Henri, except, hopefully, Antoine would be less inclined to chase every shapely corseted figure he saw.

"How shall I address you on the road?" His voice interrupted her gloomy thoughts.

"I am still Charles d'Arrignon. Or Raoul de la Fleure. Your choice."

Antoine cheered up at that. "You are my irrational little brother."

If Antoine had a choice, he would only travel in spring or autumn, when he needed neither heavy cloaks, lined jackets, and heavy socks in winter to ward off the cold, nor an endless supply of handkerchiefs to wipe the sweat off his face in summer. By the end of the day, Antoine conceded to himself that, despite his original misgivings, the journey had progressed rather pleasantly. He and his newly discovered relative fell back into the easy comradery of their childhood, forged when his mother banished both of them from music lessons. *"Charlotte screeches like a wildcat,"* Henri explained (the nickname had stuck). *"My brother's singing scares the horses,"* Raoul elaborated. While Henri and Raoul dedicated their time to learning fine arts, Antoine and Charlotte investigated the forest and river life and sung to their hearts' content without care if they kept even remotely close to the tune. Both Armand and Red Jacques fell far behind during one of their duets. To make up for this torture, Armand was assigned valet duties for both Antoine and Charlotte, and the care for all horses was consigned to Red Jacques, much to Armand's and Red Jacques' likings.

By the next day, Charlotte's fierce equine specimen condescended to tolerate Antoine and Armand, and even allowed Antoine to pat its neck and muzzle. "I am surprised your mother did not train Hera out of its prancing habit," he said to Charlotte later in the day.

"There is no particular need for that. I will disclose a

family secret with you." She brought the horse to a halt and waited for the animal to grow agitated in her displeasure and to start prancing in a tight circle.

Charlotte delivered an oration in phrases which Antoine has heard only on the docks in Marseille, and in different languages. Hera seemed to understand the eloquence. She planted her hooves firmly on the ground and stood still, snorting and shaking her head in disgust.

"What? How?!"

"Father vocalized these terms, and, miraculously, Hera took his speech seriously!"

"Only a de Brangelton," Antoine quoted his own father. "Now that I am prepared to communicate with your untamed mare, would you trade horses for a day?"

"Not so fast. Only my mother can borrow Hera on a whim. Father and Henri have to win in cards for the privilege. Best of seven games."

"Cards. Another one of your finely honed manly skills?"

To his dismay, Antoine barely won the honor to ride Hera. For an hour, the mare attempted to throw him off. When he finally achieved a mutual understanding with the beast, he discreetly gloated at this equestrian accomplishment. Needless to say, Charlotte had no trouble with Rainstorm – thankfully, Antoine remembered the name the traders used, or Charlotte would have insisted on naming his horse. She cajoled Antoine into betting on a knife-throw game, and her prize was naming Armand's colorful mount. *"Driftwood,"* Charlotte proclaimed while Antoine recovered from the shock of losing the game to her. No, Raoul had not exaggerated.

Antoine's current tranquil mood was not spoiled by a large flock of sheep crossing – or, rather blocking - the road ahead. The shepherds had brought the sources of wool to marching order when a dozen of the future dinners turned around. Half of the flock bleated in confusion, prompting the shepherds to shout and poke the unruly troops into obedience. Hera twitched her ears at the yelling and bleating, and her spectacular display of hooves-stomping caused Antoine to struggle before he brought the animal under control without resorting to verbal eloquence.

A group of officers watched the show. "That is a mare from hell," a young Lieutenant remarked in the general direction of his companions.

"This is a very fine animal." Charlotte leaned over to gently stroke Hera's muzzle.

The officers conducted a visual inspection of the boy. "I bet you would fly out of the saddle when this horse starts to prance," he sneered.

"I can stand in the stirrups till the count of ten."

"I'll believe it when I see it," the officer said.

"A wager?" Charles tossed a smug challenge.

They gleefully accepted and Antoine relinquished the saddle. The mare pranced around in delight at her owner's return. Charlotte stood up in the stirrups with a wide grin. "One," she counted, holding the reins in one hand and her other arm out for balance. "Two. Three." Antoine joined in. By the count of five, the officers were counting in chorus and Antoine's initial misgivings evolved into conviction that Charlotte could dance a jig on her horse's bare back. "Ten!" Still standing up, Charles gracefully bowed in a practiced manner, swept the hat wide, her hair falling down and forward to completely cover her face. In grudging admiration, the officers whooped, yelled, and opened their purses to pay off the wager.

For the rest of the day, Antoine and Charles traveled with a cadre of officers. Antoine resigned himself to the feeling of pure amazement at Charles' practiced ease in establishing himself as a young cutthroat. Charles won a couple fencing matches, lost one, managed to omit Charles' family name, and not a shadow of suspicion crossed the officers' minds. Upon parting ways, Charles politely declined the offer to enlist with their military regiment, explaining that his future belongs to the glorious path of the Musketeers. Antoine caught himself indeed considering Charlotte his sister. Or a brother.

TWO MUSKETEERS

BOURGES - SEPTEMBER 1718

Take advantage of unlucky coincidence, and it becomes a blessing.

Francis de Brangelton to Charlotte de Brangelton - 1712

AT BOURGES, ANTOINE AND CHARLOTTE SETTLED AT THE Lionheart Inn and met for dinner at its adjoining tavern where the table tops were clean and the tempting smells of roasted meats, baked bread, and spiced wine filled the air. Among the usual varying crowd of merchants, clerks, officers, tradesmen and farmers, Antoine was surprised to see d'Signac and another man in a Musketeer uniform.

Charlotte appraised the distinct blue-gray cloaks with a suspicious look. "I am exhausted. Let me sleep." She reclined against the wall with her feet propped up and pulled her hat over her face just a split moment before d'Signac waved.

"This is my brother Raoul. He cannot manage his wine consumption," Antoine explained to d'Signac and de Rameau. "I prefer to allow him to sleep it off since he cannot hold his disrespectful tongue. May I ask what is the reason for your presence here?"

D'Signac smiled sheepishly.

"Duty, de Flancourt." De Rameau held his hand over his heart. "The most sacred duty known to men, a duty to a woman..."

"Imagine that." Antoine interrupted the prologue to the upcoming monologue of de Rameau's exploits.

Charlotte remained motionless despite the surrounding noise. Her head dropped to rest on her shoulder, and her hat completely covered her face. Was she indeed tired or just being cautious?

"...a lonely, lovely woman whose husband left her here in this sleepy province," de Rameau continued while Antoine eagerly awaited a pause in the narration to change the subject. "She sent me a letter communicating her sorrow and lamenting her boredom. To ignore her plea would be most un-chivalrous. She has been a most delightful and gracious hostess to us."

D'Signac nodded.

Antoine hoped that Charlotte was indeed asleep. He had no intention to ever discuss the subject of love affairs with her, but he had a question for d'Signac. "Is she entertaining *both* of you?" he asked.

"Of course not!" d'Signac refuted in shock. "Do not mistake me for de Rameau." He reciprocated his friend's rude gesture. "Her very attractive cousin just happens to be visiting."

"An enviable arrangement. May I ask how you explained your need for this trip to Captain d'Ornille?"

"All is peaceful in Paris this season, so our revered and

understanding Captain granted us a leave of absence for a couple of weeks."

"And you rode all the way here? Are there no women in Paris this season?" Antoine wondered.

"Would you not take a trip for the company of a very exciting woman?" de Rameau asked incredulously.

"I would not bother beyond an hour's ride."

"You wouldn't? Why not?" De Rameau's curiosity was genuine.

"Is she really worth that much effort?" Antoine inquired. "I mean, so much more than any other?"

"It that the bitterness of a broken heart I do hear?"

"God forbid, no," Antoine scoffed at the notion. "Only misguided fools allow their hearts to be broken, for they fail to run away when they must."

"To each his own." De Rameau had no interest in further discourse and the conversation shifted to general news and gossip. When the meal was served, Antoine elbowed his companion with the hope that Charlotte would have the presence of mind to open her eyes before opening her mouth.

Wildcat did not disappoint. "What?" Despite a startled jump and the heavy drop of her feet to the floor, the hat remained firmly in place. "Ah, finally, the dinner is here. Did they have to catch and pluck it? His Majesty's Musketeers!" She respectfully tipped the hat without dislodging it. "Good evening, Monsieurs. Are you friends of my brother? It is a pleasure to meet you." She spoke civilly, in defiance of his claim of Raoul's disrespectful tongue. "How long have you served as Musketeers?"

"Are you interested in joining our ranks, Raoul?" d'Signac asked.

"Father will kill me if I do not. The son of the famous Lieutenant de la Fleure must carry this duty and this burden."

"Your brother managed to avoid our awful fate," d'Signac pointed out good-naturedly.

"He is a fortunate man." Charlotte grinned.

De Rameau gave her, or, rather, the visible part of her face, a very careful look. "Can you see anything from under this hat, Raoul?" He leaned forward to catch a glimpse of her face.

"More than I care." Charlotte deliberately lowered her head to separate a drumstick from the roasted half-chicken on the serving plate. "How did you become a Musketeer, M. d'Signac?"

"I was cajoled into it by the Comte de Tournelles."

"How did that happen?" she encouraged him.

A momentary surprise flickered on de Rameau's face and he smirked in response to Antoine's studiously blank expression.

"I had a very high opinion of my swordsmanship when I was slightly older than you, Raoul," d'Signac said. "One day, M. de Brangelton claimed that his wife could defeat me in a fencing round. In my youthful arrogance, I laughed at his challenge and accepted the bet. He stipulated an additional condition that if I lose, I would enlist with the Musketeers for a year since his friend, the newly appointed Captain d'Ornille, needed men badly at the time. So here I am, ten years after Mme. Henrietta ruthlessly defeated me on the fencing floor. Her husband advised me to never underestimate a woman."

"In a certain way, you are in the Musketeers' ranks because of a woman. There is always a woman," de Rameau mused. "Our actions and fate are guided by women. I joined the Musketeers because of a beautiful and exciting woman I loved," he added as an afterthought.

To Antoine's relief, Charlotte expressed no interest. She deliberately took another small bite of meat and scooped up the sauce with a chunk of bread. Antoine sliced off a piece of chicken breast for himself and slowly chewed. He had no intention to encourage de Rameau's elaborations on the subject.

"This youthful affair exploded into a significant indiscretion on my part. Her husband found out and he almost arranged to place me permanently in the Bastille." The man was undeterred by the apparent lack of interest from his audience. "Enlisting with the honorable cutthroat regimen of the Musketeers saved me. Let this be a lesson to you, Raoul. Do not ever be indiscreet in your affairs."

"No danger of that for me, Monsieur." She waved a chicken bone for emphasis. "I have learned well from my brother's many deplorable examples."

"I doubt you could have learned anything useful from him," de Rameau commented softly.

Antoine wondered if that comment was directed toward him or Henri.

"My friend, I know more about women than my friend Henri de Brangelton could even dream to find out." De Rameau had apparently recognized her. "Do not ever hesitate to ask my advice about your love affairs. I understand women's hearts and desires."

There was an ominous pause.

"The Comte de Tournelles is a wise man," Charlotte waited till her philosophical statement was acknowledged with nods of agreement. "According to him, only a deluded fool believes that he understands women's hearts and desires." She ignored a sharp intake of air by de Rameau. "No offense, Monsieur, but if you or my brother ever bray an unsolicited piece of advice about love affairs, I will very carefully avoid that pile of manure."

De Rameau's hand rolled into a fist. Antoine realized he mirrored the gesture.

"Take care what you say." de Rameau leaned over.

"Do not threaten me if you value your life." The knife was clenched firmly in her fist.

De Rameau appeared tempted to slap her.

So did Antoine. "Don't take this underage lunatic seriously," he said, attempting to bring some civility to the volatile situation.

From under the hat, Charlotte awarded him with the same murderous look she had bestowed on de Rameau.

"Of course." De Rameau relaxed and a wry smile played on his lips. "Why don't we move on to a pleasant subject, Raoul? Do you know Mlle. de Brangelton?"

Charlotte did not hesitate. "She is a scrawny-looking wildcat with a temperament to match."

Antoine attempted to hide his mirth. Did Raoul himself supply her with this accurate description?

De Rameau was taken aback for a moment. "Are you of the same opinion, de Flancourt?"

"The word insane describes Mlle. de Brangelton perfectly."

"Henri de Brangelton agrees," Charlotte seconded his opinion. "He objects to his sister's habit of running her sword through military men." She raised her head to meet de Rameau's eyes. Her eyes were daggers.

Shortly after that comradely exchange, de Rameau and d'Signac left on their noble mission.

"I certainly hope we will meet no more of your friends!" Charlotte pushed away her plate.

"It does not matter. D'Signac is a reasonable man."

"What about that womanizer de Rameau? He recognized who I am."

Antoine had no answer to that.

Charlotte's opaque eyes brightened. "I will leave by myself ..."

"Do not start that again!"

Charlotte nearly breathed fire. "Don't you understand? If they acquired any certain impressions." She vaguely waved her hand as she continued, "about our travel together."

"I am certain they did not, Raoul!" Antoine slammed his fist on the table. He trusted d'Signac to question – and believe – him, but de Rameau was a stranger. "No sane man will acquire any amorous notions after a single glimpse at you, or after exchanging more than two sentences with you!" he re-assured her and himself.

Charlotte narrowed her eyes. "Yes. But..."

He was in no mood to debate the possibility of ludicrous suspicions. "We have settled that I will deliver you to your parents' house!"

She jumped. "We settled? Who is we? When? I did not ask you to come along!"

"I will kill you if you take off without me!"

"Others have claimed this honor, more than once," she dismissed his threat.

"I am the older brother, and I make decisions, Raoul. You are not traveling by yourself. Do not provoke me to violence!" Once again, Antoine lost control of his temper and the situation. She undermined his decisions with intolerable ease and frequency.

"I will do anything I please. Do not provoke me to violence." She matched his tone, and her cold and measuring eyes from under the hat matched her words.

"I just might beat some sense into you!"

"I will kill you if you touch me," Charlotte de Brangelton said defiantly.

Antoine grasped her shoulder and pushed her against the wall. "Listen carefully. If you leave without me, I will hand you over to de Rameau and d'Signac and beg them to deliver you to Paris. I doubt they will tolerate your outrageous behavior the way I do. Do you understand?"

To his surprise, Charlotte looked away and there was a shred of – maybe not fear, but at least trepidation - in her eyes, but she quickly extinguished it and angrily glowered back at him.

"You are blackmailing me!"

"I am giving you a choice. You can travel with me or with my friends."

Charlotte's fingers forcefully closed around his wrist. "I will think about it, de la Fleure. De Flancourt. Get your hands off me."

He released her shoulder, picked up the bottle of wine, and marched outside to calm down. He was furious enough to slap her, yet he did not care to inflict violence on an – alleged – woman, and besides, he was certain she would retaliate. He drank the wine in the bright moonlight.

Antoine lay in bed wide awake. Earlier in the evening, Charlotte had refused to retire – *"A juggler is coming later,"* she had said. They had waited to see the performance and stayed up late. She behaved in an alarmingly civil manner, which probably meant that she planned to gain a good head start in the morning or possibly even in the middle of the night, and disappear along the way. His threat of de Rameau and d'Signac escort was an empty one, and both he and Charlotte knew it. Antoine could not admit, without losing face, that he needed help dealing with a woman, no matter how unruly and intolerable she was, and d'Signac would probably refuse to acquire such a headache. Antoine helplessly and uselessly swore at the preposterous situation. He worried about Charlotte leaving him while he barely tolerated her fine company! Antoine rose, half-dressed, went over to the stables, picked up all four bridles and brought them to his room. He immediately fell asleep until a loud pounding on the door woke him up at the crack of dawn.

"Monsieur!" The terrified Armand was out of breath, and his hair stood up higher than normal. "Please give me the bridles! I must bring them back within a quarter of an hour!"

"Tell Raoul if he needs the bridles, he has to pick them up himself," Antoine said before realizing that he had no desire to see her at his door. "No, actually, tell him he has to wait until I am ready!"

"Monsieur!" Armand grabbed his sleeve. "Please, please do not send me out there by myself! She threatened to kill me if I return without bridles! She woke me up with a kick in the ribs—"

Antoine pushed him away. "Go. She will not kill you."

"Monsieur! You have not seen her in a rage! She is a tigress! Please, I beg you!"

Charlotte had an explosive temper, but her violent tendencies were inevitably curbed by reason. Red Jacques obeyed her whims not out of fear, but because she generously fed him. "Stay out her reach to prevent a black eye."

Armand whimpered and slowly shuffled his feet toward the door. "Monsieur. What should I do if she comes up to your room?"

"What?!" Since a similar thought had already dimly occurred to Antoine, Armand's vocalization of it made him shudder. "On second thought, stay here." Charlotte could wait by herself, and maybe cool off. Besides, if she did show up at his door, he needed Armand in the room to discourage any amorous notions.

"Thank you, oh, thank you, Monsieur!" Armand exclaimed.

In the first gray light of the morning, Antoine unhurriedly

finished dressing when a sharp knock at the door caused Armand to jump behind Antoine.

"Have the courtesy to inform me if you plan to sleep until noon," the loud boyish voice demanded.

Armand shook his head with a look of desperation. The banging on the door continued without a pause, the wood reverberating.

Antoine swung the door open before she woke up half of the people in the inn. The hallway was barely lit by a single candle which dully reflected off the metal bucket in Charlotte's hands. She had thoughtfully brought it along to use as a battering ram and drum.

"What do you want?" Antoine blocked the entrance.

She stepped back. "Bridles." Her voice was crisp as a crack of a whip.

"We will wait for my friends."

"Did they take our bridles?" Charlotte managed biting sarcasm.

"You were planning to leave without me."

"I was planning to leave before your friends showed up again," she explained with exaggerated patience. "I have no desire to face them in the bright daylight. Maybe, just maybe, there is a wild chance they will doubt who I am. Is this asking too much, brother?" She had outmaneuvered him. She was not a liar, but she was creative.

"Armand. Saddle the horses," Antoine instructed with as much composure as he could manage.

Armand wasted no time. He picked up the bridles and scampered by the seething Mlle. de Brangelton as fast as he could, bounced off the wall down the hallway, stumbled on the stairs, but did not slow down till he ran out in the yard.

"I will not wait for you," Charlotte, on her way to supervise Armand, tossed over her shoulder.

Antoine slammed the door closed.

13

CATHEDRAL OF BOURGES

BOURGES – SEPTEMBER 1718

Dual loyalties invite disasters.

Francis de Brangelton to Marquis de Louiviers - 1710

THE IMPOSING TOWERS OF BOURGES' ST. ETIENNE'S Cathedral dominated the landscape for miles. Through the spyglass, Antoine could discern the intricate carvings on the side of the entrance tower, the elegant flying buttresses, and the deep colors of the glass in the upper windows. He and Charlotte traveled on the main road, which turned into the main street, and the cathedral loomed directly ahead. Antoine envisioned the exploration of the cathedral, but Charlotte acquired other ideas. For the past few miles, she had watched the cloaked rider ahead of them. When he reached the square in front of the cathedral, he dismounted by the ornate triple doors of the main entrance and casually looked over his shoulder before carefully tying his horse to the rail. Instead of climbing up the steps, he briskly walked to the side entrance on the left and waited, without knocking, till the door opened.

Charlotte expertly stalled Hera's steps until the man disappeared. Without any explanation, she tossed the reins to Red Jacques and rushed to the stairs. She did not hesitate to follow her own agenda while Antoine wavered in his former intent to indulge in an hour of sightseeing.

"Don't you -" Antoine caught up with her at the door on the right. Charlotte frantically signaled with her hand for silence and walked inside. She deliberately crossed herself while noiselessly moving between the columns on the right side and keeping up the pace with the cloaked man in the left aisle. He was careful to remain in the shadows, but his steps faintly reverberated in the surrounding quietness.

"Time for a brief prayer," Charlotte whispered softly.

"I did not realize we were on a pilgrimage."

"I must pray for the patience to deal with you."

"Pray that my angelic patience does not run out either," Antoine retorted.

The sound of measured steps stopped. Charlotte boldly stepped in the middle of the nave and piously bowed her head, letting her hair fall over her face. Antoine joined her sudden spiritual fever, but kept an eye on the motionless man half-hidden behind the column.

Antoine and Charlotte slowly approached the altar and kneeled among a dozen of worshipers absorbed in their prayers. A few minutes later, the cloaked man backed toward the cloister and disappeared from their sight. The bells rang the hour. Between the pelting sounds, Antoine caught the distinctive creak of iron hinges before silence fell.

"Who and why?" he asked Charlotte under his breath.

"Information for my father."

"I will probably regret this." Antoine's curiosity won over

annoyance. After the count of ten, they simultaneously rose and carefully followed where the man disappeared. A narrow door led into the ambulatory and the hushed murmur of voices escaped through the carved wood, but the words were not legible. Antoine and Charlotte exited through the door which had admitted the man, and retracted their steps till they could clearly hear the echoes of the conversation. The flying buttress loomed above. Antoine pointed to the flat ledge above their heads, it was just wide enough for a foothold. Years ago in Lyon, they had climbed and crawled on many roofs, balconies, fences, walls and trees, and those skills became useful again. Antoine cupped his hands, hoisted her up and heaved himself up next to her. The space was tight, and Charlotte flattened herself against the wall to make room for him. Antoine eased forward, but she grabbed his sleeve, shook her head, and indicated, by gestures, that the man would look up. They settled back to listen.

"A little more time, Monseigneur, that's all I am asking," a studiously modulated and slightly gruff voice said.

"I have been patient for five long years. Do you no longer care to burden yourself with a post at Bourges' bishopric?" The voice of this speaker had rich and melodious inflections. He was clearly accustomed to public speaking.

"Serving Bourges' bishopric is my sacred dream, my inspiration, my goal in this life, Monseigneur!" the first man pleaded. "I took an oath upon my life that I would deliver the holy relics as soon as the dispute with the Knights of Christ is resolved."

"How can I be certain that the Knights of St. John still have St. Elias' relics in their possession?"

"Monseigneur!" There was a hint of desperation. "The Knights of Christ brought Rome into the dispute. Retrieving these holy relics right now will raise heavy suspicion from my superiors. I am concerned, Monseigneur, a rash decision would be made for the permanent location of St. Elias' relics. Tours, Rouen, and Reims are still very much interested in this honor."

The silence lingered.

"I must have St. Elias' relics soon. There is nothing else we need to discuss."

Antoine judged that they had heard enough, and indicated to climb down. Charlotte shook her head. He held her arm above the elbow and pulled her to the edge. In close quarters, he had the advantage of raw force and Charlotte understood the threat, but indicated, by a roll of her eyes, that not for a moment she believed he would expose them. Antoine clasped his hands over her wrists and lowered her to land softly on her feet. He missed a beat while he swung himself down, and Charlotte escaped back inside the cathedral. She glided back to the altar, and kneeled in a pew again.

Antoine caught up with her. "Lord, grant her the common sense to stop improvising."

"Lord, grant him the wisdom to stop complaining. " Charlotte echoed.

The door from the ambulatory creaked, and once again Antoine watched the shadow of the cloaked man in the passage. The man approached the altar, kneeled in the first pew, bowed his head, and prayed. And prayed. Charlotte fidgeted. The man prayed. Antoine's knees protested. The man prayed. Charlotte squirmed. The man prayed. Antoine's neck stiffened.

"What now?" Antoine mouthed to her.

Charlotte crossed herself, stood up, and sauntered to the main entrance.

"Wait outside." Antoine propelled her toward the corner by the door. Rows of candles separated him from the cloaked man, who remained at his spot for another quarter of an hour before slowly unfolding his limbs and shuffling his feet toward the doors.

Armand and Red Jacques waited at the corner of the façade. In the middle of the square, Charlotte and Hera brazenly perused a map. The cloaked man paused at the stairs and stiff-legged walked toward his horse. He reached to untie the rains, but suddenly raised his head to the skies and, sharply spinning on his heels, ambled back to the entrance.

Antoine turned his back and, lowering his head, rummaged through his pockets. He hurried to intercept Charlotte who almost collided with him.

"Stop! Have you lost your mind?" Antoine expostulated. "I have no desire to meddle in a dispute between the Church and two disagreeing militant religious orders!" Then he remembered her explanation why she was following the man. "How important is this business to your father?"

Charlotte's desire to follow the man suddenly diminished. "Not that important." She spun on her heel to and vaulted into the saddle. Had she just exhibited common sense, or was it was just a coincidence, or, maybe her desire to shine in Paris had overcome her curiosity about the holy relics disputed by the Knights of St. John and the Knights of Christ?

"Did he suspect anything?" Her concern explained her unexpected reasonable action. "I cannot imagine... Did we go back to a different pew?"

"Yes, we switched from the right to the left." Antoine belatedly recognized their blunder. "We must cover our tracks." Many unpleasant possibilities raced through his mind. "All of us turn right and slightly speed up, just enough for people to remember if questioned later. Two blocks down, you, Red Jacques and Armand ride ahead, and I will follow behind. Turn right after three blocks and take a detour around the city for a quarter of an hour before riding out to the main road. I will be waiting for you." He outlined the path of retreat. "I will not tolerate any improvisations."

Antoine circled the streets a block away from the cathedral. All was quiet. There was no sign of an alarm or preparations for a chase. He slowly rode in a northern direction and caught a glimpse of Charlotte confidently leading the group along the unfamiliar streets. She had the skill to navigate by the position of the sun. Or had she memorized the map of Bourges, just in case? Along with a map of every major city in France? Antoine rode ahead and waited behind a massive oak tree.

He motioned for Armand and Red Jacques to fall behind beyond hearing distance. "What is your father's business with this man?" he asked again and braced himself for an argument.

"I suppose I owe you some explanation." Charlotte's eyes focused on the horizon. "Have you heard about St. Elias' relics?"

Antoine searched his memory. "Not before today."

"Five or six years ago, the Knights of St. John obtained those relics from a monastery in Dalmatia. Three or four cathedrals in France stepped forward with bids for these relics, and, I think, Bourges was one of those. Before the Knights of St. John arranged the final destination of these holy bones, the Knights of Christ challenged the legitimacy of the ownership and claimed that the relics belonged in Portugal. The Knights of St. John objected, their dispute heated up, and St. Elias' relics just... disappeared."

"You are not serious," Antoine said absent-mindedly. "Did the Knights of St. John lose those precious relics to the Knights of Christ and are covering up the embarrassment?"

"No one knows for certain. No cathedral in France, Portugal or Spain ever boasted their acquisition of St. Elias' relics."

"Which means the Knights of St. John – or Knights of Christ   may have hidden the relics. Why?"

"That man is a Knight of St. John. Two years ago in Montpellier, he searched the records of ships docked in Marseille at the time the relics might have arrived there. My father would like to know his name, but it isn't important enough to risk our necks. This is all strictly between us old friends, you understand."

"Yes," Antoine knew the expression. It meant this information was only for a handful of people - his father, Captain d'Ornille, Henri...and now Charlotte. "I trust you will inform your father of this excursion?"

"Of course," Charlotte promised.

Later in the day, Antoine and Charlotte entertained themselves by conversing in English when within anyone's hearing. Charlotte had the ingenious idea to imitate an English accent while speaking French to Armand – their newly hired French guide and valet, and Red Jacques, their temporarily mute bodyguard.

In this theatrical manner, they proceeded until an overturned large cart blocked their path. A friar and his donkey had stopped perfectly abreast with a cart, and the donkey refused to budge. The cart owner and his men helped the horse on its feet and were frantically gathering the spilled load of barrels, bags, and hay stacks. There was no visible damage to the cart. The retrieval of overturned cargo and the restoration of passage should take no more than an hour. Moving the donkey might take longer.

The afternoon was hot and muggy, the trees still provided plenty of shade along the shallow banks of the Loire, and the travelers - merchants, clergymen, couriers, servants, soldiers, and clerks resigned to endure a long wait. Antoine and Charlotte found a comfortable patch of dry grass and exchanged occasional sentences in English to discourage any communications with a neighboring group of clergymen. Antoine laid down his cloak and stretched upon it. A sharp poke to his ribs woke him up. He raised himself on his elbow and beheld the profile of his traveling companion outlined against the bright blue sky.

"Beware of distinguished company," Charlotte whispered.

The sound of conversation in English drifted over. "Shall we continue?" asked the older nobleman who carried a sturdy sword on his side and a pair of pistols in the saddle holsters.

"No, we shall wait." His companion's objection carried a cadence of command. His maroon doublet and breeches were of a fashionable style, the plume in his gray hat was colored to match, and he was generously accessorized with jewelry around his neck and in his ears.

Full awareness instantly descended on Antoine. The peace with England, signed in 1714, had seemed to last. Regent Philippe d'Orleans encouraged trade and exchange between the countries, the Jacobites no longer stirred up unrest, and thus English visitors no longer were a rarity. Yet, the countenance of the richly dressed gentlemen commanded attention.

The Englishmen dismounted. Their two valets instantly took the reins with the speed and efficiency acquired from long service in a large household.

"God save us from another group of heretics." A friar woke from his slumber, sat up, and crossed himself. "The Sun King expelled them from France, and now they are invading."

"Bloody jackass," Charlotte commented in English. Her aunt had married a Huguenot, her grandfather had married a Protestant English lady, and both her father and Antoine's own father deeply distrusted religious zealots.

"Narrow-minded bigot," Antoine seconded her sentiment in English.

The younger nobleman fixed his shrewd eyes on Antoine and Charlotte. "I see you speak my language well, gentlemen."

"Good day, my lord!" Charlotte popped up to her feet to present a deep, elaborate bow. "Are you enjoying your journey?"

Antoine refrained from expostulating his unflattering opinion about his self-inflicted travel companion.

"Pardon my liberty, my lord, but meeting Englishmen in the middle of France is a pleasant surprise. May I ask if we can be of service?" Charlotte, inconveniently, spoke English well, but Antoine had no delusions that their accents had betrayed them at the first word, and he passively expected the farce to unfold with fireworks.

"Who are you?" the armed man – a bodyguard? - inquired with curiosity and suspicion.

"My name is Charles d'Arringnon. At your service."

Antoine desperately struggled with the overwhelming desire to kick her for this innovation. He could control his younger brother in public, but Charles was an independent reprobate and could follow through on any reckless whims.

Charlotte firmly placed her hat back on her head, and both men beheld it in thoughtful silence.

"Pardon my impetuous friend. I am Comte Antoine de Flancourt, at your service." Antoine formally bowed to the richly dressed man.

"The notorious Comte Antoine de Flancourt himself," the Englishman repeated with a thoughtful gleam in his eyes. "Even I recall your name from a couple of years ago."

"My lord, are you warning me to never show my face in London again?"

"On the contrary, Comte. Newspapers referred to you as the Bloody Frenchman, but I wield some influence, and would be happy to present you into the finest circles of society." He familiarly slapped him on the shoulder. "I am Lord Nelson, and this is Lord Stevenson." He glanced at the talkative member of the clergy who was currently absorbed in prayer.

"We are speaking English on a bet, my Lord." Charlotte answered the unspoken question. "The first one to slip back into French buys a dinner and a bottle of rum."

Lord Nelson visibly relaxed. "I heard the name d'Arringnon before." He stroked his chin. "Do you have any famous relatives, Charles?"

"My lord, I have my own claims to fame, but I am not at liberty to discuss my finest moments with strangers." Charlotte galloped out of control.

Lord Nelson, Lord Stevenson, and both their valets gaped at her. "How old are you, rascal?" Lord Nelson asked.

The lonely cloud in the sky reflected in Charlotte's eyes. "I inflicted scars onto a few military men. I am not welcome to a place or two. The Captain of His Majesty's Musketeers refused to commission me because of my slightly frayed reputation, although I am an expert with a sword and a pistol, and my horsemanship can shame a cavalry officer!"

He was, just like Antoine, lost for words. "Aren't you too young to be a famous cutthroat?"

"My adversaries prefer the word infamous, my lord. I am at your service for a demonstration fencing round."

The lord desperately glanced at Lord Stevenson.

"I will teach you a lesson," Lord Stevenson volunteered.

"I doubt it. A bottle of wine for a wager?" Charlotte was true to herself.

Antoine willed himself to be a mere spectator. Once again, he had lost control of the situation, but there was no danger. Lord Stevenson wouldn't hurt a young boy for his impertinence, would he?

Lord Stevenson and Charlotte determined that a flat patch

of grass was adequate for their exercise. Their search provoked curiosity from a dozen spectators, and by the time Lord and Charlotte covered the tips of their swords, bets had been made.

Charlotte charged in a fast, straightforward attack. The speed of her blade forced Stevenson to hurriedly scramble back in surprise, but he recovered and pushed back. His Lordship was a strong and more experienced fencer, although his practice was obviously limited to formal lessons and theory. He had the advantage of reach, and muscle. Charlotte was agile, quick, and a little unorthodox; she was fencing from intuition as well as practice, and his Lordship was hard-pressed to keep her blade away from his hide. Charlotte retreated further than Lord Stevenson's advance warranted, and he was lured into an unbalanced lunge. She parried and followed with a definite touch of her sword against his ribcage.

"Very impressive," Lord Nelson said in stunned silence. "Ah, I recall now. D'Arringnon. Are you related to the devil de Brangelton?" He flaunted his knowledge of French cutthroat society.

"May I ask if you are personally acquainted with him, my lord?"

He was taken aback. Definitely, he was a man accustomed to obedience and respect, but Charlotte was either oblivious to that, or, more likely, purposely and deviously exploited his desire to remain anonymous. "Ah... no, I just know him by reputation only," he admitted.

"Did his reputation... - fame? – Infamy? - reach England?" Charlotte brilliantly managed to avoid answering the question.

Half an hour later, the road cleared and Lord Nelson's entourage of half a dozen men and a cart of luggage arrived. "I am certain we will meet again, Comte. Best of luck in keeping your reckless young friend out of trouble," Lord Nelson bid them farewell. He graciously penned a letter of recommendation to a distinguished resident of Orleans, the Comte de Chambreau, and encouraged them to introduce themselves to the Comte. "He is a very hospitable man, and Orleans is a lovely town," he advised.

"Why did you present d'Arringnon to him? The name is widely known." Antoine hoped to discourage her future attempts to disengage herself from being his official charge.

"Lord Nelson is not a simple Lord." Charlotte carefully guided high-strung Hera among the crowd on the bridge.

"You are Raoul on this trip! Is it difficult to remember, brother?"

"I must be Charles when we visit the Comte de Chambreau," she replied.

She was intolerable, and a reasonable discussion with her was not conceivable. "Who is we?" How was he going to introduce his accidental companion?

"Don't even think about excluding me." She brought Hera close to him. "I recognize a business proposition when I hear one."

"No," Antoine said in disbelief. "You and I part ways in Paris."

Fires of fury danced in Charlotte's eyes. "Of course we will! I have no intent or desire to deal with you longer than necessary, but I deserve to know what business brought Lord Nelson to France. May I remind you that I introduced myself first?"

She was correct. Lord Nelson's insistence on their acquaintance with the Comte could not be just a social nicety.

"What business could it be?" Antoine challenged.

"Think. A highly placed Englishman journeys through France incognito. Lord Nelson mentioned that the Comte is interested in the New World."

"A lot of people are interested in the New World."

Charlotte loudly voiced a variety of choice expletives. He was not certain if it was directed at him, or at a coach which almost clipped Hera. The driver of the coach gaped open-mouthed at her verbal assault. "Does the name *Company of the West* sound familiar to you?"

"What do you know about it?" Antoine uttered before recalling that she was the Comte de Tournelles' daughter, and M. Francis had more than a passing interest in the Company's business dealings.

Charlotte sighed with exaggerated forbearance. "To start, your trip to London with M. Jerome de la Norte was connected to this business, wasn't it?"

Antoine forced himself to calm down. Charlotte possessed sharp intelligence and power of observation, along with the admirable skill of avoidance and omittance. No, it should not be surprising that her father trusted her, and that meant she must be a reasonably reliable associate.

"Very well, we will pay a social visit to the Comte de Chambreau together," he reluctantly agreed. "And no more improvisations. Is this understood, Raoul?"

"Don't fret, brother."

14

THE LOVELY TOWN OF ORLEANS

ORLEANS, FRANCE – SEPTEMBER 1718

An honest accomplice in crime is nearly impossible to find.

Francis de Brangelton to Captain d'Ornille – 1690

THE RAM AND BULL INN, HIGHLY RECOMMENDED BY LORD Stevenson, was located in a quiet neighborhood between St. Croix Cathedral and the banks of the stately Loire. Charlotte and Antoine rented rooms, and, upon cleaning off the dust from the road, regrouped for the visit to the Comte de Chambreau. Charlotte congratulated herself on her foresight to pack a simple set of formal indigo breeches and matching jacket, which she wore over a fine linen shirt with lace trim. Antoine dressed in a precisely tailored full suit. His jacket, waistcoat, and breeches were made of striped blue and black fabric with blue trim on the cuffs, lapels, and collar, and he also discarded the riding boots in favor of red-heeled shoes. He evaluated her outfit with the same critical look he bestowed on her pistol.

"Shall we?" Charlotte forestalled any probable comments. The riding boots did not match the formality of her jacket, but she refused to flaunt her legs by wearing dress shoes with stockings.

Lord Nelson either did not know or forgot to mention that the Comte de Chambreau was hosting a formal reception that day. After Antoine announced their names and handed the letter of introduction to a servant, they were ushered into a small sitting room. A matching set of large landscape paintings of majestic cypress and palm trees decorated the walls, and the crimson cushions of the ornately carved chairs were comfortably soft. Within a few minutes, their host, a middle-aged man with a pleasant demeanor, stepped into the room. He regarded Charlotte with an odd expression but graciously invited them to the festivities. Charlotte shook off a premonition of disaster; what could possibly happen at the formal reception? She got her answer when Guy de Brault bounced in the room. "Charles! It is you!" He swept her into a tight greeting embrace.

Not in Charlotte's wildest nightmares had she expected to meet yet another man who could recognize her under the given circumstances. Hospitality to friends and adversaries from fencing school and future business associates did not justify passionate embraces. She and de Brault had parted on unfriendly terms. Her jumbled thoughts came to order when she realized that he had pressed her body tightly against his, and the position of his thigh could not have left any doubt for him that she was a woman. He was in no hurry to release her. Charlotte stopped herself from reaching for the boot knife, - that would entail unacceptable consequences. She writhed to untangle herself and his hand slid down her back.

Charlotte sharply and resolutely pushed on his stomach with her balled fists. He grunted but persisted until she strategically placed her knee between his legs in a very unsubtle hint. Even de Brault realized her intent and released her, although his arm remained wrapped around her shoulders. Charlotte jabbed her elbow into his ribcage and he finally disengaged herself.

"Pardon my nephew's lack of manners, Comte de Flancourt." De Chambreau hurried with the introductions.

Charlotte thought he should be apologizing to her for his nephew.

"I apologize, Comte de Flancourt." De Brault woke up to Antoine's existence and presence. "It's just that d'Arringnon and I attended fencing school together." His eyes darted between her and Antoine, who barely contained his chagrin. There would be hell to pay if he ever found out the source of rumors in Lyon.

"Apology accepted," Charlotte said. "But if you ever embrace me again, I will hurt you."

The Comte de Chambreau gaped. Antoine almost laughed aloud.

"Is that a promise?" de Brault humored her.

"This is a warning, you dimwit." Charlotte gave up the pretense of civility. "I will make you cry."

His smile wavered. His uncle loudly inhaled. Antoine was no longer amused.

"Or I will run you through," Charlotte added. "My skills are good enough to be a Musketeer. De Flancourt will recommend me to Captain d'Ornille."

"No, I will not," Antoine reacted in his typical manner. "You, d'Arringnon, do not obey orders and have no concept of discipline."

Guy de Brault thoughtfully scratched his head. "Ah...

Uncle? My friends might recognize d'Arringnon's name," he confessed.

That meant that she could not attend the reception. Charlotte confronted de Brault. "What did you bray?"

He desperately struggled to release the lapels of his brown-and-cream jacket from her grip. "Only the story of your expulsion from fencing school..." He adjusted the ruffles of his cravat when she released him. "Ah... d'Arringnon... it's probably better if you forgo the reception. Comte de Flancourt, if you don't mind, I will be happy to keep d'Arringnon company."

"No," Charlotte chopped off that idea. Disappearing with Guy de Brault, while traveling with Antoine de Flancourt, was a terrible course of action. "Your uncle most kindly invited me, and I will not disappoint him." She dropped the pretense and talked in her regular voice. "Comte de Chambreau, will you please introduce Comte de Flancourt first? His appearance will cause a distraction and no one will pay any attention to me. I will stay quietly in the back." She flashed a reassuring smile at de Chambreau.

"Yes, yes, of course." Their host immediately accommodated her. "If the Comte does not mind?"

"Not at all." Antoine's answer left her with the distinct impression that he was happy to rid of her company, and the feeling was mutual.

The high double doors of white and gold closed behind the Comte de Chambreau and the Comte de Flancourt, leaving Charlotte alone with Guy de Brault. As many young noble men were, he was raised to adhere to social protocol, and he seemed at a loss concerning how to proceed with renewing their ... friendship? He possessed only average intelligence, and he certainly had not grown wiser. Charlotte took the opportunity to poke around. "Who is Lord Nelson?"

"His Grace..." De Brault was thrown off balance by her

abruptness, but recovered in time. "I mean... I understand he is an English peer and well placed at Court."

"What is his business in France?"

"I don't know."

"Yes, you do."

"You don't tell me your secrets," he pointed out.

Charlotte debated if she should march past him into the reception room or dig for more information. Curiosity won. She pulled off her hat, leaned her head back, and let her hair fall back and away. "I might," she said wistfully. "If you tell me Lord Nelson's name and explain his business in France."

Her friend and nemesis from fencing school stood up straighter. "What about the Comte de Flancourt? Is he... are you and he... are not..." he stammered.

Charlotte choked down the answer that implication deserved. "No, he is not, and we are not! He and I will part our ways in Paris," she added and realized her mistake when de Brault's inspirations manifested on his face.

"Lord Nelson lost precious cargo in Marseille a few years ago. The Marshall cousins took it. He is in France to retrieve it," he blurted out and moved closer. "Who are you? Why do you call yourself Charles?"

Charlotte slid behind a chair. "One question at the time. Which one first?"

He did not hesitate. "Who are you? What is your name?"

"My father is well received at Court. He, my mother, and my brother currently reside in Paris. I am on my way to meet up with them."

De Brault's eyes again appraised her figure. It was time to squash any debauched notions which had probably planted themselves into his brain and other parts of the body.

"It's time for me to appear at the reception." To his obvious disappointment, Charlotte tossed her hair forward and put on the hat. She paused at the door with her hand on the handle. "Wait for here for a slow count to one hundred. And stay away from me." She entered the well-lit, festive, music-filled reception room to the accompaniment of de Brault's objections.

The walls of the ballroom were covered with bronzed panels with gold patterns, and the elaborate white moldings in the shape of classical columns separated the panels. Almost every section exhibited a landscape or seascape painting. Had de Chambreau commissioned these painting? Did he display the pictures to impress the guests? Antoine estimated that the little reception included a hundred or more people, including Mme. Jeanne de Chaudat of the pleasing and welcoming disposition. The neckline of her dress plunged low. Even better, within minutes of introduction, she asked him to call her Jeanne and was happy to present him to the other guests. She was a most enticing distraction, Antoine would gladly stay in Orleans for a month for her. Regretfully, he was reminded of his prior obligation and commitment by virtue of his intolerable companion swaggering into the room ahead of her personal friend de Brault. Maybe, Antoine dryly thought to himself, de Brault could become Charles' bosom companion and Antoine's conscience would be clear to hand Wildcat into de Brault's care.

"There is my young cousin Guy." Mme. Jeanne gestured to the furthest table in the back of the room where Charlotte and de Brault were engaged in a heated argument. "He is the young man on the left. Who is the other young man? I never met him before." She took advantage of Antoine's hesitation and pulled him to follow her.

He hoped that Charlotte would decamp to the other side of the room.

"Guy!" Mme. Jeanne exclaimed. "Aren't you going to introduce your new friend?"

Charlotte impassively stood up and politely bowed when his name was pronounced.

Mme. Jeanne's eyes opened widely. "Charles d'Arringnon! Guy has told me so much about you! It is such a pleasure to meet you in person! Will you excuse me, Monsieur Antoine?" She abandoned him on the spot. "My dear Charles," she purred, hooking her arm around Charlotte's elbow and towing her away. Antoine watched Mme. Jeanne's hourglass figure sashaying away. A very willing and attractive woman had just lost her interest in him due to her curiosity about Charlotte de Brangelton.

"Comte de Flancourt," de Brault interrupted his ruminations. "Do you know d'Arringnon well?"

Antoine kept the answer brief. "We grew up together."

De Brault gave him an incredulous look. "May I ask if d'Arringnon were a...a young woman... you would know?"

"I... ah... why do you ask?"

De Brault shifted from one foot to another. "Since you are traveling together...you and she... are you....not–"

"No."

De Brault relaxed.

Charlotte's studiously innocent expression and Mme. Jeanne's nervous manner of fanning herself caused a shiver to ripple down Antoine's spine.

"I hope she won't be jealous if Jeanne takes a fancy to you." De Brault frowned in genuine worry.

"No, she does not care," Antoine answered curtly.

De Brault snorted. "I would not mind watching a catfight, but Jeanne has no chance against Charles."

Charlotte's eyes narrowed. An off-hand comment caused Mme. Jeanne to frown and raise her arm. Antoine dashed forward and so did de Brault.

Mme. de Chaudat waited for Charles to initiate conversation, and Charlotte took the time to evaluate the situation. De Brault's cousin clung onto Antoine de Flancourt's arm. This seemed the perfect opportunity to leave de Flancourt in Orleans for a month. On the other hand, if Antoine were occupied with Mme. Jeanne, de Brault would continue his attempts to impose himself into Charlotte's service. Antoine, in his deviousness, would encourage and attempt to arrange for de Brault to escort her to Paris. That would end in damage to de Brault's health and disaster to her reputation. Charlotte could purchase new bridles, leave unnoticed, and take a detour off the main road - this would add four or five days to her schedule, but she would be free of any travel companions...

"The Comte de Flancourt is a very handsome man," Madame said.

"I trust your judgment of that, Madame," Charlotte answered without thinking. She had plenty of experience with dialogues starting along the lines of *"Your brother is a very charming man."*

"Do you? Monsieur?" There was a slight ironic emphasis in the last word.

Charlotte's mind galloped in different directions. No, she did not care to be in the center of attention here. "Mme. de Chaudat. Do us all a favor and help Guy de Brault learn how to keep his mouth tightly shut, or I will be forced to deprive him of his tongue."

Madame fanned herself. "Charles, you don't mind

discussing Comte de Flancourt, do you?" She switched back to her original theme.

"As you wish." Charlotte resented the proposed subject, but perfectly understood the theme. "A lot of women adore him, Madame. I am at loss as to why." Henri was a bottomless well of fancy compliments, Raoul could sing and play music, but Antoine?

The woman gaped at her. "Don't you?"

"I do respect his fencing skills." Charlotte chose the ready path of boredom to rid of Madame's company. "He has tremendous accuracy in the backhand parry of a thrust into the second quadrant–"

"Charles, my dear," Madame interrupted. "What would you say if I were to invite the Comte de Flancourt for a private visit with me after the reception?" She was shameless, even by the standards of Henri's passions. Or was she trying to provoke a reaction?

Charlotte hesitated. On other similar occasions, she had cheerfully offered to convey the invitation, but Antoine de Flancourt deserved payback for keeping the horse bridles with him. "Mme. de Chaudat? You could not possibly mean to invite a stranger in your bed?"

Madame gasped at the insult. A bright crimson color spread on her face, and the woman had the nerve to raise her hand to slap her.

Charlotte effortlessly caught Madame's wrist. "The Comte de Flancourt abhors a display of bad temper." She released Madame's hand, presented an exaggerated bow, executed a perfect military turn-around, and found herself facing a very excited Lieutenant.

"Monsieur! Are you bothering Mme. de Chaudat?" He bleated.

"Not at all, Lieutenant," Charlotte denied. "I left as soon as

Madame indicated her displeasure with my delightful company."

De Brault jumped to her side and his arm draped around her shoulders in another variation of a friendly embrace. "Lieutenant, I assure you, my friend has no interest in Jeanne."

Charlotte kicked de Brault in the leg and he wisely released her.

"Your friend bothered Mme. Jeanne," the stubborn Lieutenant claimed.

"Mme. de Chaudat will be very disappointed in you, Lieutenant, if you take this underage reprobate seriously." Antoine joined the fray. "Is that so, my dear Madame?"

"Jeanne, Lieutenant, shall we drink a toast?" De Brault's left arm wrapped around the Lieutenant's shoulders, his right arm supporting his cousin. He led both of them away.

"Do not leave my side," Antoine said.

Charlotte opened her mouth to ask if this command would apply in case Mme. de Chaudat invited him for a private visit later on, but wisely refrained from inspiring him with any amorous notions.

He mistook her silence for obedience. "And no more improvisations, my brother Raoul, do you understand?"

"You obviously do not."

Antoine's clenched his teeth and fists.

"Suppose I told Lord Nelson that my name was Raoul," Charlotte latched to the theme. "May I ask you, dear wise older brother, how would we explain that to the Comte de Chambreau and de Brault?"

"Stop provoking me," he snarled for the lack of better response.

"You could not kill me if your life depended on it."

Antoine de Flancourt feelingly articulated his opinion of their situation.

Charlotte had attended several similar affairs as Charles, and had valued the lack of some ardent admirer trailing her every step. Ironically, today her escort was even more intolerable than de Molienier and de Seveigney combined, although for a different reason. De Brault chatted with two young men who suddenly spun around with stunned expressions. Their hesitant shuffles, the whispers, the elbows to the ribs – the maneuvers preceding young men's self-introductions to unsuspecting females – were painfully familiar and unwelcome. De Brault wisely disappeared from the room when his friends set on the path to approach her. Antoine seemed oblivious to their campaign, and Charlotte braced herself for yet another display of idiocy.

De Brault's friends did not disappoint. "May we have the pleasure of introducing ourselves, Charles d'Arringnon?" the braver one smirked.

"Are you seeking a challenge for a duel, Monsieur?" Charlotte countered.

Antoine twisted her arm behind her back. He also slid the crook of his elbow under her chin to press on her neck. "Pardon me," he apologized to de Brault's shocked friends before snarling in her ear, "Don't even think about it." He hauled her away.

She could not see his face, but she fervently hoped he would not acquire any ideas. De Brault's embrace had been unpleasant enough, although de Flancourt was considerate enough to leave a space between their bodies.

"Think... what?" Charlotte asked as aggressively as she could while gasping for air.

He removed his elbow away from her neck, but gripped the collar of her jacket. "I will be unable to face your parents, or my parents, if you manage to have yourself killed while in my custody."

"Don't be a simpleton. None of them will draw a sword at a woman," Charlotte said.

"A miracle of common sense from you," Antoine released her and pushed her toward the door.

"I am not leaving." Charlotte dug in her heels.

"Yes, we are. Don't make a scene."

"Mlle. de Chambreau and Mme. de Chaudat are prepared to treat the audience with songs. To depart during their performance would be a prime example of rudeness."

Antoine had no choice but to claim the same remote table Charlotte and de Brault had occupied in the beginning of this disastrous evening. The musical entertainment provided the benefit of silencing the chatter and useless arguments, and Antoine was no longer inclined toward any discussions, lectures or any other communication. When Mlle. de Chambreau announced the final song, de Brault plopped in a chair next to Antoine and whispered to him.

"Stay right here till I return," Antoine issued the order to the tune of the last note of the song and disappeared behind the door of their original entrance.

Charlotte uneasily noticed the – damn it! - look of admiration on de Brault's face. "Where did de Flancourt rush off?" she asked.

"My uncle requested his presence in the library." He licked his lips. "Ah, you know, I always liked you." De Brault apparently remembered their school days in a different light than Charlotte. "I apologize if I acted like an ass. Frankly, not knowing.... I envied your knowledge about girls..."

"I still know more that you do," Charlotte said. What was the business between de Chambreau and de Flancourt? It must be related to Lord Nelson's letter. It had been written for both the Comte de Flancourt and Charles, but since de Chambreau knew that Charles was an alias...

"I learned more things since then." De Brault's smirk hinted at more than Charlotte ever wanted to know.

"Did you learn to fence better?" Charlotte redirected the conversation. Has she lost her mind earlier in the evening? Did de Brault forget about his rivalry with Charles on the fencing floor? Or did he bet his friends on an affair with her?

"I won the competition in school!" he whined.

"It is a pity I was not there." Charlotte dismissed his boast.

De Brault leaned over to her. "What would it take for you to stay and lose a fencing round?" he pleaded.

Considering Mme. de Chaudat's grip on Comte de Flan-court earlier in the evening, Charlotte thought that Antoine might be sleeping late tomorrow if he had enough sagacity to compliment her singing. "Tell me Lord Nelson's real name."

"I cannot." He gave her a miserable look. "I gave my word."

"It is good to know that you are a man of your word." Charlotte smiled.

"Will you tell me your true name?" he pleaded.

"Is the Duke's name a tight secret?"

He nervously wrestled with his doubts and conscience. "I suppose not. Lord Nelson is an alias for Duke Collingstone."

"My father is a Comte," she confided.

He jumped at that revelation. "Does your father– I mean, what...are you...is your mother the Comtesse?" he ventured.

"Yes. I am the legitimate and favorite daughter. What's in the lost cargo?"

"I cannot tell you. Is your given name Charlotte?"

"Here is a deal." Charlotte leaned forward. "How about a fencing round tomorrow morning at, shall we say, nine o'clock? When you lose, you tell me all you know of the lost cargo. If I lose, I will tell you my real name."

He groaned. "But I cannot tell you!"

"You concede that you cannot win a fencing round with a

woman?" Charlotte reverted to Charles' finest provoking manner to shake de Brault out of his enthrallment.

"Deal," he hissed. "If you vow to keep it a secret."

"Deal, my friend the adversary."

He closed his eyes and crossed himself.

Antoine returned to the scene of the reception in a thoughtful mood. De Chambreau had confidentially claimed that the Great Mogul Diamond was stolen by the Marshall cousins – *"they practically arranged a battle in Marseille Harbor to cause this diversion and to avert attention from their conspiracy with the Indian warrior named Kumaryan,"* the Comte had explained. Antoine cautiously and vaguely promised to assist in search for both the Great Mogul Diamond and Kumaryan without committing to seek out the Marshall cousins. De Chambreau's other errand - to deliver a dispatch to the Navy - nicely led him into a department of the Navy, and due to that, Antoine had every intention to further investigate the Marseille affair. That dispatch would not be ready until eleven o'clock next morning, which meant a delayed start to the day.

Antoine briefly envisioned Charlotte's reaction to the change of plans, firmly reminded himself that her happiness was the least of his concerns, and realized that she was nowhere to be seen, despite his very explicit instructions. He had been gone for only half an hour; how much of a disaster could she cause in this time? The answer was *"an endless amount".* He panicked, but the quarrelsome Lieutenant was firmly attached to Mme. Jeanne's side. At least Charlotte was not engaged in a brawl with a military man. Antoine circulated around the room until he found de Brault.

"Where is d'Arringnon?"

Her friend startled. " She... he was looking at the music sheets."

Antoine choked at the absurdity of this excuse. Charlotte's musical abilities were just as non-existent as his own. He and de Brault hurried into the street and absorbed the scene of apparent peace and tranquility.

"Please give my best regards to your uncle and Mme. Jeanne, and tell her she sings divinely," Antoine was no longer in the mood for civil chatter. He marched into the dining room of the Ram and Bull Inn, and repeated the experience of discovering that Charles was missing again. Antoine checked the stables, rejoicing that all the horses were in their stalls and the bridles were in his room. Incensed, he pounded on the door to her room. There was no answer. He could not return to the Comte de Chambreau's reception, no matter if Charlotte was there or not. Antoine stomped down to the Ram and Bull dining room, and beheld a familiar brown hat with a blue feather.

"What did the Comte want from you?" Charlotte pushed her tankard towards him.

Antoine gulped down the wine. "He explicitly requested to exclude you from the knowledge." He gleefully exploited the chance to forestall any other questions.

"Does not matter to me. By the way, I have committed to stay in town till noon tomorrow."

"What?!" Antoine's temper flared upon her casual and sudden rearrangement of their schedule. It suited him very well, but she should have consulted with him first. "What happened to your desire to reach Paris as soon as possible?"

"The horses need a longer rest." Both her falsely innocent air and the logical explanation were equally aggravating.

"In that case, why don't we stay for the whole day?" Antoine collected all his willpower to calm himself. He almost inquired if she had developed a passion for de Brault, but the apprehension of possibly triggering any amorous feelings toward himself checked that comment in time.

"Why waste the whole day?" Charlotte retorted, the challenge flashing in her eyes.

"Why not?"

"I am leaving at noon," she spat out. "You do anything you want without me."

Antoine woke at eight o'clock, in a mood not improved from the previous night. He lay in bed for a quarter of an hour and briefly entertained the thought of paying a late morning visit to Mme. Jeanne. He cancelled that idea when he realized that he could not explain Charlotte, and besides, he could not leave Charlotte alone to create chaos. Why was Charlotte not interested in de Brault's company? Why could not she stay here, in Orleans, with her friend from fencing school? What a blessing that would be for Antoine! He would kill the intolerable Charlotte if she acquired any amorous inklings about him... What was he thinking?

"Armand!"

"Monsieur Charles left his room early," Armand greeted him with this bright report.

"When? Where?" Antoine glanced at the bridles, all still hung off the hook in his room.

Armand regretted not having any more information, but Monsieur Charles had left on foot. The horses were still in the stable, and there were no messages for the Comte de Flancourt. Antoine resumed cursing. He could not have cared less where and who she spent her time with, but the sheer audacity of blatantly ignoring him was beyond the limits of even his patience. Fortunately for Charlotte, he had no clue of her destination. He again deliberated upon the possibility of making amends with Mme. Jeanne, but the hour was still early for a social visit. There was plenty of time before his appointment with de Chambreau. Antoine dressed, swallowed down a slice of dark rye bread with cheese, and marched off to find the fencing hall where he was greeted by the happy smile of Charles d'Arringnon and the sour countenance of Guy de Brault.

"De Flancourt, you missed a glorious round this beautiful morning. I won a bottle of wine from de Brault," Charlotte boasted.

Antoine almost vocalized his desire to murder her, then noted worry on de Brault's face - de Brault might perceive his reaction as jealousy, and, God forbid, so might Charlotte. "I am disappointed to have missed your excellent performance," he answered, noting that his upper lip was beginning to hurt from biting on it. "You should have woken me up."

Charlotte's stare was cold enough to give frostbite to a bear.

Charlotte was happy when Antoine and his murderous mood departed - did he regret a missed opportunity with Mme. Chaudat and go to make amends? De Brault had insisted on providing her with a meal of veal stew at the Bull and Ram Inn. Over the meal, he informed her that de Flancourt had a meeting with his uncle and offered to escort her to Paris since she was parting ways with de Flancourt anyway, and finally gathered the nerve to propose that he would trust her with any information and he would do anything she asked if they were lovers.

"When an avalanche occurs in hell a dozen times." Charlotte ended that tiresome conversation.

She was happy when Antoine reappeared. He had no silly notions about their relationship, and he was in a slightly better mood than he had been earlier in the day. Charlotte vaulted in the saddle before de Brault could even think of parting embraces and rode away before the men finished exchanging polite farewells. Antoine, aggravated at having to catch up with her, kept blessedly silent.

Charlotte mulled over the information she had gleaned from de Brault. The search for the portraits did not seem a plausible excuse for traveling incognito in a foreign country. Portraits of former mistresses just could not command that much sentimental value. Maybe de Brault had lied, or maybe he did not know for certain. Her next challenge was to find out what de Flancourt and de Chambreau had discussed.

"Did you find out Lord Nelson's real name?" she asked.

To her satisfaction, he shook his head. "Do you know?"

"Yes."

"Is it a name you recognize?"

"What is it worth to you?"

He awarded her with a scathing scowl. "Nothing."

"A pity. I would tell you his true name and mission in exchange for a reason why the Comte de Chambreau wanted to speak to you alone," Charlotte bargained.

"I know his mission, and I am not discussing it with you."

For what mysterious reasons had he been infuriated at her since last night? She had stayed out of his way. He had had plenty of opportunities to pay more attention to Mme. Jeanne, and he had only himself to blame.

15

RAINY NIGHT

LONJUMEAU- SEPTEMBER 1718

No, of course not, you never look for trouble. You don't have to. You are a bright seashore beacon in the night, and trouble is a ship sailing toward you.

Henri de Brangelton to Charlotte de Brangelton – 1714

THE APPROACHING AUTUMN STORM ENTICED MANY travelers to take refuge early in the afternoon, and no lodgings were available in the town of Lonjumeau. The steady drizzle, the remote flashes of lightning, and the distant rumble of thunder punctuated the early darkness, deeming the possibility of finding accommodations at this hour even bleaker. Straight ahead, military troops occupied the small town square. The carts and the horses faced in the northern direction, and the soldiers carried lanterns. Antoine reined in his horse to follow Charlotte.

"What can I do for you?" the leader barked at them.

Charlotte stood up in the stirrups for a precise military salute. "If you are on the way to Paris, may we ride with you, Captain? My name is Raoul de la Fleure. May I introduce my older brother...?"

"Captain de Varbes," Antoine greeted his former, most memorable instructor from military school. "Comte de Flancourt, at your service."

"Good to see you, de la Fleure. De Flancourt." The Captain recovered from his astonishment and pointed at Charlotte. "My condolences on this relation of yours. The boy is insolent."

"Very much so." Antoine shook hands with the Captain. "For your own sanity, do not ever offer him a commission under your command."

"In truth, my first choice would be a Musketeer's commission," Charlotte recovered.

"Why are you riding at night and in this weather, de la Fleure... de Flancourt? What is the urgency?"

"Nothing of great importance, except there is no place to stay for the night."

"You are welcome to join us," de Varbes invited them. "We are on the way to a garrison at Bievres. I can recommend much better accommodations in town, though."

"Ah, no, thank you," Charlotte said.

The Captain scowled.

"Actually, we accept your offer with our deepest gratitude," Antoine interrupted her. "Never mind my brother. Be quiet, Raoul, or I will knock you out."

A dozen well-maintained and spacious private houses clustered around the local church of St. Eloy. The owners were accustomed to providing comfortable lodgings for noble visitors and their extended entourages, and the promised accommodations consisted of the rooms in one of these houses. De Varbes made the arrangements for his troops and commanded Armand and Red Jacques to stay with the soldiers. He led Antoine and Charlotte to another building, and explained over the noise of the downpour that the owner was a friend of his.

"I will make room for you and your friends, Captain, do not worry." The owner's head bobbed up and down. "I will provide a comfortable pallet for the small room upstairs, and another one can be placed in my own bedchamber."

Antoine's hair stood up at the prospect of sharing the room with Charlotte, but what were his other choices? Send her to share the room with their host?

"No." Charlotte's nervous and strained hiss interrupted his thoughts. Apparently she felt just as awkward as he did. "We keep on riding."

In principle, Antoine agreed with Charlotte, but shreds of common sense lingered in his mind. "At night and during a thunderstorm?" he whispered back to her. "Can you even find your way from here back to the main road?"

Her answer was lost in the sound of thunder. To emphasize his point, the lightning struck outside and illuminated her pinched face.

Antoine was in no mood to prolong the argument. "Believe me, Mlle., I have no desire to share the room with you, but I am not willing to risk our lives for no good reason!"

The host and de Varbes watched them with puzzlement. "What is your brother's problem now?" Captain inquired.

"Never mind this young reprobate." Antoine turned away from Charlotte, but watched the shadow of the motionless figure out of the corner of his eye. "Monsieur, thank you for your hospitality. My brother and I appreciate it."

He expected Charlotte to argue further, but she took a

deep breath and relaxed her fists. "Very well, brother. We will roll dice to determine who sleeps in the bed."

"You can have the bed," Antoine said in relief.

They would have eaten dinner in silence if de Varbes had not entertained them. During the first course of bread and salted fish, he reminisced about the years he was in charge of the military school. At the second course of vegetable pie, he moved on to his marriage, complained about how he was duped into matrimony and narrated that, after his darling wife recovered from the lesson he had taught her, she behaved well for a while and he felt doomed to spend an eternity with her. By the time cheese and pears were served, he had reached the point in his narration when she strayed again but he had become much wiser by then and threatened to kill her lover in a duel, unless his wife would divorce him, which she finally consented. The Captain had generously forgiven her lover and returned to the freedom and excitement of military life.

"Congratulations," Antoine concluded as they rose from the table. Charlotte's silence during the whole evening made him nervous. So far on this journey, Charlotte had indicated no interest toward him, but experience with fast and easy women did not encourage staying in the same room and he hoped she did not acquire any grateful feelings for to him, or any other stimulus from the Captain's unsolicited narration.

The room, formerly an attic, was oddly shaped with opposite walls of uneven width. It was sparsely furnished with a narrow bed positioned against the longest wall, and a small table and a single chair tucked under a small window across from the bed. The washstand with a water jug, basin, and towels occupied most of the wall opposite from the door. The pallet with a pillow and blankets was dropped in the middle of the floor, and a single candle barely illuminated the space.

"Hold it." Antoine handed the candleholder to statue-like

Charlotte. He pushed the table into the corner to move the pallet under the window as far from the bed as possible , and placed the chair at the foot of the pallet.

"This is much better," Charlotte said approvingly and sat the candle back on the table. "Will you please leave for a few minutes?" she asked.

"Yes." Antoine heard her lock the door behind him and leaned against the wall. Once again, he regretted his decision to visit the de Brangelton family, and, ironically, he hoped Mlle. did not kick him out for the night. Her sudden politeness unnerved him.

Charlotte locked the bolt after Antoine, took a deep breath, and knocked her head against her fists. When Antoine had carelessly accepted sharing the room, she had almost asked the Captain for an escort of a couple soldiers with lanterns, but realized in time that she would have to explain why and might as well reveal that she was a woman. Besides, as Antoine had ruthlessly pointed out, she probably could not find her way to the main road and risking her life and Hera's limbs in tonight's thunderstorm was a very unappealing prospect. Upon this realization, Charlotte spent the evening thinking of other options, but there were none. "He is a de la Fleure, just like his brother," Charlotte reminded herself. "So far, he has been disinterested. I can trust him to remain so." She shook off the damp doublet and hung it on the hook in the wall. She would have to sleep in her shirt and breeches, but she took off the special garment she wore – it was made from stiff fabric to bind and flatten her breasts. This un-corset was her mother's own invention. It was practical and comfortable during the day, but not so at night. Charlotte folded it and placed it under the pillow, finished her toilette, brushed her hair, and tightly wrapped a warm wool blankct around hcr shoulders. She placed her boots next to the bed and hung the sword on the head post, within easy reach.

Charlotte crossed the small space and opened the door. She almost tripped over the pallet when she backed off, but Antoine did not seem to notice. He re-locked the door, placed his sword against his pallet, put down the pistol down on the floor by the pillow, and unbuttoned his doublet. Charlotte sat back on the bed and watched the yellow flames of the candle. Antoine hang the doublet on the chair and kicked off his boots. He ran through the motions of his evening toilette before unfolding the blankets.

"Good night." He lay down in his shirt and breeches.

"Good night." Charlotte hoped she hid her relief as she lay down on the bed and pulled her hat over her face.

"Do you always sleep in your hat?" he asked.

"Yes."

Antoine laughed and immediately fell asleep.

Sleep evaded Charlotte. She tossed and turned, marveling at the chain of perverse coincidences during this trip with Antoine de Flancourt. They had managed to encounter Rameau and d'Signac, Lord Nelson and his entourage, de Brault and the whole lovely town of Orleans, and now this! In all her travels with Henri, they had met fewer people who recognized her. Charlotte selected suitable words to honor her brother. He should have been riding with her. She added more colorful epithets for de Molienier, and dedicated the rest of her extensive vocabulary to de Flancourt and de Brault for good measure. Maybe she should have stayed home. She shook her head at the realization that by now, the situation with de Molienier would certainly have deteriorated to exchanging blows, and M. Louis de Paulet had no influence on the possessed Captain. Charlotte contemplated tip-toeing toward the peacefully sleeping Antoine and punching him for his unsolicited chivalrous help. This trip was one disaster after another. She muttered creative expletives, and Antoine moved in his sleep. Luckily, she congratulated herself, she had successfully avoided any personal conversations with him. He did not even know why she left home. Charlotte punched the pillow. It was Henri's and de Molienier's fault that she was traveling with the Comte de Flancourt.

The faint clank of pewter jarred Charlotte awake. Her fingers curled around the grip of her sword before she recalled the previous night's arrangements and opened her eyes to peek around.

The newly lit candle on the table flickered in the translucent light of the early morning. Antoine, dressed only in breeches, was washing his face over the water basin. Charlotte's heart skipped a beat, and her face suddenly warmed up in the cool room. Why was she panicking? She was no stranger to the sight of shirtless men after she had attended numerous fencing halls and military garrisons where half-naked bodies were a common exhibit during the warmer months. Except never in her life had she shared a room with a man not related to her. She had seen Antoine half naked a hundred times, during those summer swims in the Saone, when he, Raoul, and Henri had stripped to the breeches, and she had kept on breeches and a shirt. His body was lean but his muscles were solid and there was a scar on his shoulder. Two necklaces hung from his neck. One was probably a crucifix, but what was the other? Antoine wore only a signet ring, so what did he value enough to keep next to his heart? Was it a gift from a woman? How many women had watched him dress in the morning? Did he ever stay the night? Or did he prefer to leave afterwards? How his skin would feel under her touch?

Charlotte caught her breath at these sudden wonderings at the moment he picked up the towel. She tightly shut her eyes, and focused on keeping her breathing light and steady, focusing on today's problems. They should arrive in Paris by mid-afternoon, so she would not have to deal with Antoine much longer. *"And not a moment too soon,"* Charlotte added. He quietly moved around the room. She peeked through her eyelashes. Antoine tucked in his shirt, buttoned up his doublet, and pulled on the boots. He loudly banged his sword against the table on the way to the door.

"Rise and shine," he said loudly in his most brotherly manner. "I will have Armand and Red Jacques saddle the horses."

Charlotte raised her head. "I will meet you by the front door in a quarter of an hour."

He left the room before Charlotte even finished the sentence. "I will complain to mother that de Molienier harassed me." She combed her hair. "She will forgive me for leaving home. They will have to take me along or leave me with Henri, and that will serve my brother right. He trapped me into staying home alone to deal with the Captain."

Antoine and Charlotte, having paid for the lodgings the night before, quietly slipped out and briskly rode back to the main road. The storm passed and the strong gale blew away the clouds. The rays of sun reflected in the shimmering large pools of water on the ground. There was no way to tell if the water was deep or shallow. Antoine and Charlotte gingerly steered around the puddles. At Gentilly, water covered a large stretch of the road. Riding around through the deep sticky mud was problematic at best and foolhardy at worst. Antoine and Charlotte backtracked half a mile to the Red Boar Inn to fortify themselves with bread and sausage and to wait for the water to drain into the fields.

The yard was crowded and the men were sulky and impatient. Most of them were already delayed by the night's rain and late for their business appointments, affairs, and duties. The word spread that an extended train of carts and carriages with Royal crests was moving from Paris, and that procession would take another hour. Men called for more wine, and the general mood drifted further and further from peaceful. Antoine's disposition did not improve when Charlotte employed a vocabulary that would make a drunk sailor pay attention.

"I am not happy about this road closure either," he said.

"I will check on Hera," she tossed over her shoulder and disappeared in the crowd.

Antoine repeated her speech until Charlotte led agitated Hera outside. The mare snorted and tossed its head in response to sternly taking Charlotte. Hera stomped her hooves and all heads swiveled to watch the animal and the owner trying to bring the half-wild horse under control.

"A spirited mare, isn't it?" a junior officer commented to another.

"Reminds me of that brazen wench from Ferrand." A senior Lieutenant stomped back inside.

The first officer winked at another young man. "Every misbehaving female reminds him of her."

Antoine had an odd suspicion that it could be a reference to his travel companion.

"Now he will be in a foul mood for the rest of the day," the other officer predicted.

Antoine's curiosity took over. "I beg your pardon, but I could not help but overhear. That was an interesting comment, Monsieur. She must have been quite a wench."

"The rumor is that she ran a sword through his shoulder," they explained.

Antoine's mouth fell open in bewilderment again upon the realization that his guess of the wench's identity was probably correct.

"He is obsessed with her. Swears that one day he will even the score."

"I would stay away from any woman who can run a sword through any part of my body," Antoine said. He now appreciated Charlotte's judgement in physically staying far away from the Lieutenant. "I imagine that the men in her family must be capable fencers as well. What is the name?"

The first officer shook his head. "Don't know. He will not tell."

In the distance, the Lieutenant re-appeared with a bottle in his hand. He watched Hera and Charles with distaste, gulped the wine, and marched toward them. His men exchanged knowing glances and pushed their way through the crowd. So did Antoine.

The Lieutenant spoke.

Charlotte wisely ignored him.

The Lieutenant fumed. "You, the little bastard with the blue feather, answer me!" he raised his voice.

She made no indication she had heard him.

The Lieutenant reached out and knocked the hat off Charlotte's head. The crowd in the yard fanned out to vacate the area around the spectacle when she spun around with a blade at the ready. The Lieutenant swung the bottle to block her thrust, backed off, retrieved his sword to deflect her next move, and lunged forward to press his advantage of strength. Charlotte retreated, but the space was tight and her back was pressed to a tree. Antoine shoved men out of his way and jumped over the one who fell. The Lieutenant seemed poised to pin her arm to the wood behind her. Antoine was just a step away when she twisted her body aside and the Lieutenant's blade splintered the wood. Before the pieces of bark had fallen to the ground, Charlotte knocked the sword out of the Lieutenant's hand. He jumped backwards and scrambled away from Hera, who snapped at him. His swearing was lost in the cheering from the audience.

"Pick up my hat." Charlotte held her sword steadily against the hapless Lieutenant's throat.

One of the younger officers picked up the hat and held it out to Charlotte. She paid no heed.

The Lieutenant suddenly gasped. "You. Must. Be. A relative of that wench."

"What wench?" Charlotte almost succeeded in sounding perplexed.

Antoine retrieved her hat. He grasped the wrist of her sword hand and jerked Charlotte back. He slapped the hat on her head and squeezed her shoulder to spin her around, and he pushed her away from the Lieutenant. There was a sudden movement behind him when the Lieutenant rushed to retrieve his sword. Antoine sidestepped to gain a split moment to free his blade and slammed the Lieutenant's weapon down with enough force to make the man lose his grip again. Charlotte recovered her balance and direction, shoved Antoine out of the way, and advanced toward the Lieutenant. Antoine caught the collar of her doublet to unceremoniously haul her backwards and trip her over his foot. She sat down on her behind.

"Don't meddle!" He ordered her before focusing on the outraged Lieutenant. "Leave my brother alone!"

The Lieutenant took advantage of this interference to

retrieve his sword. His fury blinded him and he viciously attacked. Antoine parried a couple of wide, uncontrolled lunges. Trying to finish the quarrel quickly, Antoine took the first opportunity to run his blade across the Lieutenant's forearm.

The man dropped his sword for the third time and growled. "Arrest them," he ordered his men.

"I protest." Antoine brought aristocratic authority to his voice and stance. "You, Lieutenant, attacked me."

The officers hesitated. Charlotte, in almost imperceptible movements, positioned herself shoulder-to-shoulder with him but facing in the opposite direction. Across the yard, a Musketeer and a broad-shouldered man stopped by the fence to view the spectacle.

"Leave," Antoine urged Charlotte. The Musketeer and his friend were likely to catch her, and she would easily obtain an audience with Captain d'Ornille.

"I ordered the arrest!" The Lieutenant picked up his sword with his other hand.

Charlotte slid behind Antoine to cover his back, and suddenly they were against five men. Antoine armed himself with a dagger he carried hidden. The men regrouped, three aligned against him and two focused on Charlotte. The Lieutenant held back. The Musketeer and his friend jumped over the fence and were running toward the fray. Antoine frantically parried three blades and took advantage of his adversaries' split-second pause to overreach and slash the side of the officer who was circling around Charlotte. The clashing sound of the blades indicated that she was holding her ground against her other opponent. Antoine could not completely sidestep the renewed attack by the three men around him and felt a sharp pain in his upper arm. He commanded all his willpower not to drop the sword.

"Stop in the name of His Majesty!" the Musketeer hollered.

"Forward!" Lieutenant counter-commanded.

Without slowing down, the tall newcomer connected his fist with the Lieutenant's jaw. The uniformed body sailed up in the air and landed, motionless, on the ground.

Antoine gripped the dagger tighter to block the second thrust at his arm, and forced himself to move the sword in a wide arc to shear the shoulder of another assailant. It provided Antoine with a brief reprieve, then the Musketeer drove one of Antoine's assailants aside and again bellowed the – ignored - order to stop fighting in His Majesty's name. Antoine focused on his two remaining adversaries. The wounded man lunged once, before recognition of authority – or pain – registered in his mind, and he retreated away from the fight. Antoine's remaining opponent pressed his advantage. Antoine's control of the blade was faltering, and his grip on the dagger was slipping. He lured the man into a close stance and, catching the opposing blade between his sword and the dagger, kicked his foe in the knee. The man staggered back.

Antoine caught his breath and glanced behind to behold the tall newcomer holding the back of Charlotte's collar in one hand and parrying the blade of the officer with the other hand. He tossed her out of harm's way and dispatched the winded officer with an impressive backhand.

Antoine felt movement over his shoulder and raised the hilt of the sword in time to block the resumed attack by the bastard bent on finishing him. The unexpected sudden and awkward move offset Antoine's balance. He dropped to one knee and twisted to trip his foe. The man flailed his arms, which gave Antoine the opportunity to punch him in the stomach, and the man's weapon clattered onto the ground upon the impact. Antoine barely refrained from driving the sword into the man's gut, but confined his actions to slamming the hilt into the man's jaw. His eyes glazed over and he sunk to his knees. The flames of Antoine's fury burned out of control. He dropped the sword to avoid temptation, kicked the man to the ground, and solidly trashed him.

"Name. Rank." The Musketeer demanded of the conscious officers. The carnage was significant – three officers were wounded, two were unconscious, and only one remained relatively unharmed. The spectators prudently drifted away. There would be no witnesses to a brawl between military officers and civilians with a Musketeer on their side. Antoine picked up his sword and dagger and focused on formulating a speech of gratitude to the Musketeer and thus extricating himself and his brother on virtue of being known to Captain d'Ornille, but a glance at Charlotte made him forget the burning pain in his arm.

16

ARRIVAL

PARIS – SEPTEMBER 1718

He is a man of many faces,
Born to wander Seven Seas.
Dire danger he embraces,
When he sails, the Colors flee! –

From a popular song, - c. 1712

CHARLOTTE AND THE TALL MAN MIRRORED EACH OTHER'S
stance, except he was glaring down - the top of her head barely
reached his shoulder. She managed to glare up. Both tightly
gripped their swords, although thankfully the blades pointed
down. The man was about Antoine's age, half a head taller and
broader in the shoulders, and a fighter of formidable skill.
Antoine picked up his weapons and stepped to her side. "What
now, Raoul?"

Puzzled apprehension replaced the man's initial curiosity,

and Antoine frantically raked his own memory. He knew the measuring, expressionless dark eyes.

Antoine collected his thoughts. "Monsieur, I am much obliged to you for extracting my young brother out of this scuffle..."

"Your brother." There was a distinct note of amusement.

Antoine cringed. Here was another cutthroat familiar with his companion. "The boy with no discernable common sense."

"I wholeheartedly agree with you regarding the lack of common sense," the man observed Charlotte, who busied herself by cleaning the blood off the sword by carefully sticking the blade in the soft ground. "Why are you here?"

"None of your business." She piped in without a glance in their direction.

The corner of man's mouth twitched.

Antoine suppressed the impulse to kick her. "Monsieur, I regret to cut our pleasant conversation short, but we must continue without delay."

"No need to cut our pleasant conversation short. I will join you on your merry way," the man replied.

"Save yourself the trouble. I am not speaking to you." Charlotte wiped the dirt off her sword with her glove.

"I am not speaking to you either." The man flicked off crimson droplets of blood from his sword and addressed Antoine. "I assume you are heading to Paris?"

"With all my deepest appreciation of the offer, we require no company." Antoine's arm stiffened. He could barely move it. The blood seeped through the sleeve and dripped into his glove.

"I am delightful company," the man insisted.

Antoine prayed for Charlotte to stay out of their discussion. "Find yourself a more receptive audience."

Their eyes locked in mutual confusion.

Charlotte made certain no one could overhear them. "Oh, daft, overbearing, annoying brothers of mine, are you planning to exchange this nonsense all day?" she expostulated. "I must bandage Antoine's arm. Are father and mother still in Paris?"

Antoine felt sincere happiness as recognition dawned. Did his own week-old stubble alter his looks as much a trim moustache and extra height disguised Henri de Brangelton?

"Did you just insult us both in the same breath?" Henri asked the back of his departing sister. "Give me that." He confiscated Antoine's bloodied weapons, put his arm around Antoine's shoulders, and propelled him to follow her. "So she is Raoul today? He will kill you both for that," he cheerfully predicted.

"He will be fully justified for his actions. This Raoul is insane, irrational, and belligerent." Antoine fervently hoped that Henri's imagination did not extend to thinking that he would have any amorous interest in Charlotte.

"Am I correct to assume that this brawl is her fault?" Henri cleaned Antoine's sword.

"Amazingly, not this time." Antoine shook his head and winced. Now that no danger loomed, the pain was intense and he had to focus to maintain lucidity. "Despite her apparent habit to challenge military men. Is that a common occurrence?"

"Regrettably, yes. Will either one of you explain why are you here?" Henri handed the dagger back to Antoine.

"I had the misfortune to stop at Ferrand just when your sister finished packing her saddle bags. She tried to punch me for my efforts to dissuade her." Antoine begun to explain.

"Your friend had this delusion that I am not capable to find my way to Paris by myself," Charlotte interrupted with sincere indignation. "This conceited, stubborn, unreasonable friend of yours threatened to break my arm -"

"Unreasonable? I?!" Antoine spat. "What do you understand of reason?"

"I have no doubts that my friend has regretted his inane soft-hearted motive since then." Henri returned Antoine's sword.

"More than once. Take your insane sister off my hands, and I will be a happy man. My saintly patience with her just ran out."

"What possessed you to leave home?" Henri caught up with his sister, draped his arm around her shoulders, and gave her an affectionate light squeeze. Charlotte threw her elbow into his ribcage and spun around to face her brother.

"It is all your fault! In fact, I am not speaking to you," she remembered and surveyed the group of officers. "Deal with the damn Lieutenant over there." She pointed to the unconscious form on the ground. Her brother spread his arms in a resigned gesture, grumbled appropriate words about her inappropriate demeanor, and left to join the Musketeer.

"Lean against this tree." Antoine assumed that Charlotte was talking to him. The pulsating pain in his arm was severe, the sleeve was soaked, and the blood trickled down on the ground, yet he needed to conserve his strength for the ride.

Charlotte removed her gloves to retrieve a small bundle out of her saddlebag and carefully unwrapped the contents. "Hold out your hands," she commanded Armand, covered his hands with a clean handkerchief and placed a few strips of bandage and cloths on top. "Don't drop it," she added and Armand turned into a statue.

Charlotte pulled out her boot knife. "Put your arm up," she instructed Antoine.

"I will be fine," Antoine assured her. He did not need her to take care of him.

"Don't be a dimwit. We still have a long ride ahead of us,"

Charlotte unceremoniously grabbed the wrist of his wounded arm and forced the palm of his hand up against the tree. She slashed open the bloody fabric of his sleeve and wiped the blood off Antoine's arm to inspect the cut.

"It's not deep." She pressed a clean cloth against it. "Hold it for a moment." She tossed the knife on the ground and picked up a vial. "Besides, how will I explain to my parents, or yours, why I neglected to treat your wound?" Charlotte soaked a piece of cloth with thick liquid.

"What is it?" Antoine asked.

"The same mixture my mother uses. Ready?"

Antoine leaned against the tree and braced himself. He knew from experience that this mixture would hurt more than a wound, but it would help it to heal fast. He removed the already saturated cloth and Charlotte resolutely wiped the wound. Antoine managed to stifle a groan. Charlotte handed him a strip of bandage to hold against his wound while she soaked another bandage with the mixture. Antoine waited till she nodded and she quickly replaced the drenched bandage with a medicated one. Antoine grunted in pain, praying for the strength to remain standing, but he knew that pressure had to be applied for a full minute. Charlotte's lips moved to the count of hundred before she removed the bandage, and Antoine exhaled in relief.

"I know it hurts. I screamed when Henri slapped this poultice on my leg." Charlotte once again wiped the area around the wound with a piece of clean linen.

"What happened to your leg?" Antoine asked to divert his mind from the pain.

"I did not completely deflect a thrust. Left a huge scar, twice as big as this one will be." Charlotte applied the fresh bandage.

"A blade?" Antoine barely noted the burning on his arm this time. "You actually fought?"

"Yes, we were outnumbered and I was forced to leave Charles to fend for himself." Henri picked up this sister's knife and cleaned it. "That brawl almost forced her into proper behavior."

"Proper behavior?" Antoine repeated. Did Henri mean it as a joke? Such a concept was impossible to imagine.

Henri paid no attention to the interruption. "Unfortunately, it did not happen."

Charlotte tightly wrapped Antoine's arm to hold the bandage in place. "I could not see myself trading the sword for an embroidery needle." She handed him the last piece of clean cloth.

Antoine tossed away his sodden glove and cleaned the blood off his arm and hand. "Why did you stay when I told you to leave?"

"And what would you have done against all of them?" She carefully re-packaged the vial, placed it back into the saddlebag, and retrieved the handkerchief from Armand. "You may breathe now," she humored him.

"A few of them would have chased after you." Antoine speculated. "That would have bought me time to deal with the rest."

"And what would you do if they did not?"

"Why don't you two revel in this futile debate along the way?" Henri's suggestion bailed Antoine out.

"We are finished debating," Charlotte said. "Can you hold your arm perfectly still?"

"Explain to me why you assumed that they would not chase you?" Antoine had no desire to allow her to control all their conversations. Why did he feel compelled to continue their pointless discussion ? Had the blood loss affected his mind?

"He needs a sling for his arm," Charlotte informed her brother.

"I don't." Antoine put an edge in his voice, placed his foot into the stirrup, and hauled himself into the saddle.

Half way through the gardens of Faubourg St. Michel, Antoine started to feel lightheaded and he was grateful to de Bonnard for riding ahead since his Musketeer's cloak cleared the way along the road. They passed Luxemburg and crossed the Pont St. Michel without any delays. Henri rode at Antoine's side with occasional questioning glances at Antoine and backwards – presumably, Charlotte followed. Their speed diminished through the Ile de Cite. De Bonnard slowed down in the crowd, but Charlotte rode to his side, and the two unyielding riders forced the unwilling pedestrians to clear the way for Antoine and Henri, with Armand and Red Jacques closing the column. By the time they rode onto Rue St. Dennis, Antoine's full attention was condensed to staying in the saddle. He even failed to recognize the turn toward the Comte and Comtesse de Tournelles' townhouse. He felt dangerously weak when they stopped at the door, slowly dismounted, and realized that he was staggering. Henri supported him. Charlotte trailed behind. Antoine felt a sudden panic. How would she explain their journey together?

"Antoine!" Mme. Henrietta's smile faded when she saw the bandage. "What happened this time? Sit down." She hurried toward the side door leading to the kitchen. Henri eased Antoine onto the settee, took a decanter out of the cupboard, and poured brandy for himself and Antoine. Charlotte and her father wordlessly beheld each other, his expression displaying mild curiosity without the slightest hint of surprise, hers as innocent as an admission of guilt.

"The Captain ran me out of town," she declared with defiance.

Her mother froze in mid-step and mid-sentence.

"He," Charlotte gestured toward Antoine, "happened to stop at Ferrand the day before I left, and since he considers me an incompetent, insane–"

"Unreasonable." Antoine felt obligated to wedge at least one word into the conversation.

"Lord, give me patience," Mme. Henrietta muttered. "I assume you did clean Antoine's wound?"

"Yes, mother." Charlotte held out the vial of poultice. "Use this. I mixed it right before leaving home." She set the vial on the table.

"Antoine was wounded in a brawl at the Red Boar Inn when he protected his brother Raoul," Henri's brevity was commendable. "We did some damage, father. De Bonnard will warn Captain d'Ornille about the two cutthroats. What kind of trouble have you caused in Ferrand?" He turned his attention to his sister.

"Your friend the Captain caused all the trouble."

Henri grunted. "What have you done to him?"

"Run a sword through his shoulder."

Henri's expression bordered on terrified, and Antoine suspected his was no better.

"You did what?!"

Antoine could relate to the anxiety in Henri's tone. A fleeting shadow of a smile crossed M. Francis' face.

"I mean, I desperately wanted to run the sword through his shoulder," Charlotte clarified.

Henri loudly exhaled. "What happened?"

"What do you think?" Charlotte retorted.

"What did he do?"

"It is your fault. I am not speaking to you."

Mme. Henrietta brought back a stack of clean bandages and sat them on the table. "Charlotte, what are your grand plans for the next few weeks?"

"I will come with father and you."

There was a sharp air intake from Mme. Henrietta and vigorous head-shaking.

"I will stay with Henri."

"No, you will not," he refused. "You are not speaking to me."

"Charles will request hospitality from Captain d'Ornille." Charlotte put on her hat. "Will you take me to Vincennes, Henri?"

"Have you lost your mind?" Her brother blocked the door. "Do you hold the delusion that no one will recognize you as a de Brangelton? One glance at you was enough for de Bonnard."

Charlotte glared at him. "I will leave, then. Right now, while my saddlebags are still packed! I will sail to the New World, and stay there. Move out of my way!"

Henri leaned against the door frame, daring her to pass. She promptly kicked a chair toward him. Henri secured her wrist. She picked up a bowl off the table and swung it forward. Her brother reached with his other hand to retrieve it. She twisted and kicked. He released her and both leapt toward the door at the same time. Charlotte dropped the bowl and managed to halfway open the door, but Henri overpowered her and slammed the door shut. Charlotte stepped back to gain momentum for a fruitless effort to push her brother out of the way with her shoulder, but she bounced off his chest. She jumped away and over the chair, grabbed an empty tankard from the table, and hurled it toward him.

Henri expertly caught it in the air and placed it back on the table. "Father. How long do you expect me to put up with your tempestuous daughter?"

Charlotte picked up the tankard again and tossed it at Henri. He twisted out of its way and the pewter slammed into the wall with enough force to chip off large pieces of plaster.

Antoine watched this exchange with his mouth wide open.

"Charlotte, stop ruining household items," M. Francis ordered. "One is enough."

"Can I stay in Paris, father, please?" Charlotte carefully set the bowl back on the table and embraced him. "I missed you."

"Henrietta?" M. Francis kissed the top of his daughter's head. "What shall we do with our beloved daughter?"

"Lord, give me patience," Mme. Henrietta repeated. "We can decide later. Henri, help Antoine take off his clothes. He needs a clean bandage."

A few hours into the night, Henrietta quietly entered the bedroom and watched Antoine in the dim light of a single candle. His breathing was light and steady, and his forehead was cool and dry. He had no fever to indicate an infection from the wound.

"Antoine," she called softly and was pleased to see that he immediately moved, tensing up for a moment while he remembered where he was. He opened his eyes and blinked in the light.

"I hope for an easy recovery this time, Mme. Henrietta."

"So do I. Time to change your bandage." Henrietta pulled up the chair and unwrapped the cloth. Antoine had suffered a bad wound on their trip few years ago, and it was a memory no one cherished.

"Did you ever tell your mother about Tours?" she asked.

"No," Antoine winced as she pulled the bandage. "Father asked about that scar, but I doubt he shared with her."

"I suspect you are right. Bear with me." Henrietta tightened the clean bandage.

"It will take a week before I can defeat Henri in a fencing round," Antoine claimed with a weak smile when she was finished.

"I would wait a couple of weeks, and he still might win," Henrietta said. "I am expecting an invitation to that event."

"Of course. We will wager a bottle of brandy for the occasion, and dinner as well." Antoine reclined back, his lids heavy.

"Good night." Henrietta lightly touched his forehead with her lips. He was half asleep, and her memory brought the image from years ago, when the brown-haired boy lay on the settee at the de la Fleure house, in the same position as now, one eye swollen shut. Wide-eyed Raoul and Charlotte had sat cross-legged on the floor, listening to his tale of how he and Henri won a fight while Henri only nodded because the cut on his lip hurt. The boys matured to be men, Henrietta thought, but her daughter... *"Charlotte must be the only young woman in France elated that Antoine paid her no attention,"* Henrietta reflected. *"Fine daughter I have, a cutthroat to the core who did not hesitate to travel across France in pursuit of adventure. De Molienier's persistent attention is just an excuse."* Henrietta did not understand Charlotte. The girl did not have to have this way of life. She was the beautiful daughter of a comfortably well-to-do Comte, but nothing mattered. Her arrival coincided with Francis' plans to escort Jerome de la Norte safely out of the country via La Rochelle, and now Charlotte was coming with them. As she had probably planned. Henrietta felt a familiar pang of worry about her daughter, but pushed the recurring concern out of her mind. They had more immediate business to manage.

Antoine woke up with a stiff and sore arm, but his mind was clear. The night before, he had drifted in and out of semi-consciousness while Mme. Henrietta re-bandaged his arm. He indistinctly recalled M. Francis' firm hold on his shoulder, Henri assisting him upstairs, and Mme. Henrietta's night visit to re-bandage his arm. Bits of conversation fluttered in his mind. Hopefully he had not complained about Charlotte. Any unflattering statements about Charlotte never found a sympathetic ear with her (or his own) parents. The only vivid memory from last night was the glow of Charlotte's eyes and her attentive stance with the mixture and bandages.

Antoine opened his eyes. He was in bed. He looked around. The room was unchanged from his previous stay. It contained simple but sturdy furniture and was bare of any decorations. Armand sat on the pallet across from him and, as usual, he was anxious to impart his observations.

M. de Brangelton was expected to arrive shortly, the Comte de Tournelles would be home around noon, and the Comtesse would be out all day, but she had forbidden M. Antoine to leave until his arm was healed, and everyone was instructed to make his stay comfortable. The Comte de Tournelles had ordered Armand to remain with M. Antoine at all times. Mlle. de Brangelton slept on the settee downstairs. She had already awoken and ordered a bath in her parent's room; she was finished and waiting for him and her brother in the sitting room downstairs.

Antoine carefully stood up. He was apprehensive about explaining to Charlotte's parents their traveling together, but apparently her complaints had sufficed to justify his presence, and, besides, her family must realize that no man in his right mind would have any amorous interest in Charlotte. He washed his face and drunk the watered wine Armand offered. He pondered upon the events of the previous day, and grudgingly acknowledged Charlotte's courage to fight when the odds were stacked against them. She had not even been aware of the Musketeer's presence, let alone her brother's, or she would have called for their assistance. It was a pity that she was born a woman; she would have made an excellent fighter. Henri's arrival interrupted his philosophical foray.

Charlotte unceremoniously followed her brother. "How is your arm?"

"Much better. Thank you for giving up your bed for my comfort."

"The settee is quite comfortable." She waved off his gratitude. " I will re-bandage your arm while we wait for the meal."

Antoine was pleased with the condition of his wound, and so was Charlotte. Armand helped him dress, and he descended downstairs where brother and sister waited for him to do justice to generous amounts of ham and fresh bread.

"What is the plan, Charlotte?" Henri asked over the baked apples.

"You and I leave tomorrow. Mother will meet us in Dampier in two days. You are most welcome to stay here," she told Antoine before turning her attention back to her brother. "We can probably stop at Versailles for a day."

"My wounded arm, along with the distinctive description of this participant-" Antoine pointed at Henri. "-will raise realistic speculations about the events at the Red Boar Inn."

Charlotte shook her head. "Not at all. Where is your younger brother?"

"How many of Henri's and my acquaintances did we meet yesterday on the way?"

Charlotte helped herself to another serving of sweetened apples. "Maybe you should stay with Captain d'Ornille. No one would dare to question the Captain of the Musketeers' guest about his connection with a brawl."

"Sounds reasonable." Apparently, Henri was accustomed to accepting most of his sister's plans.

Antoine leaned back. "And may I ask how I will explain my wound?"

"A dispute over a horse. You were outnumbered," Charlotte suggested.

"Must have been quite a horse," Henri scoffed. "Give her a name. Anne?"

Charlotte glared at both of them. "You two contrive a better story!"

They ate in silence while Antoine desperately taxed his mind for a better plan. He was unwilling to impose on Captain d'Ornille.

"I have a proposition for you," Antoine heard himself say. "All three of us leave Paris. A week later, my wound will have healed, and the brawl at the Red Boar inn will be forgotten."

Charlotte narrowed her eyes. "I have had enough of your company."

"I have the same complaint," Antoine retorted, "but a trip takes less effort than inventing a story!"

Henri dropped his head into his hands and shook with laughter. "Which one of you is Raoul?"

Charlotte forestalled Antoine. "He is more annoying than Raoul. I could never have fathomed that it was possible!"

"She is more aggravating than Raoul described. I could never have fathomed it was possible!" Antoine mocked her, aware that he, once again, had completely lost control of conversation. "Henri, can't you talk some sense into your unruly sister?"

"Why waste time?" Henri asked. "I need to prepare for, I am certain, a most entertaining trip, so I shall see you tomorrow morning.

"Charlotte stood up and blocked his way. "I am coming with you."

"Yes, please, go away." Antoine wholeheartedly supported the plan.

"Where do you think we are going?" her brother inquired.

"I will help you prepare for the trip. To pack, and to bid farewell to your ... What is her name?"

Henri gave up. "Very well."

Charlotte flew upstairs and immediately returned, buckling her sword belt on the way down. "See you at dinner, Antoine," she threw over her shoulder from the door.

"Where will you cause havoc until dinnertime?" Henri followed Charlotte.

Henri's apartment was located a short walk away between the Rue St. Martin and the Rue de Temple. "Explain Antoine de la Fleure. De Flancourt," he asked as soon they entered inside.

Charlotte curiously looked at the carelessly arranged surroundings. A shirt was tossed over the chair, unopened bottles of wine were lined up on the writing desk, and there were no fancy glasses; no, he had not started to entertain his women at home. She sifted through the pile of papers on the desk and picked up a heavily perfumed appointment note. "I already explained to you, my imaginative brother, but I repeat, pay attention and remember, your friend insisted on accompanying, in his opinion, the incapable and insane me. This letter is signed G. Have you acquired a new passion? Does she always drench her correspondence in perfume? What happened to Cybille?"

"What will de Molienier and the others imagine if they

ever find out about Antoine?" Henri sorted through the contents of his wardrobe and folded a cloak.

"We agreed to never mention de Molienier." Charlotte carelessly tossed a copper drinking tankard at him.

Henri caught the projectile and placed it on the chair out of her reach. "They will ask why a man follows a woman across France if he does not care for her?"

"You would not think twice about accompanying Raoul."

"Explain Antoine to those who have not met Charles in all his glorious insanity," Henri stubbornly persisted.

Charlotte pulled a clean shirt out of the wardrobe and handed it to him. "Start packing. I am not planning to stay here all day."

"M. Patrice de Seveigney resides in Paris. He recently inquired if the evil spirit of Charles has been exorcised from Charlotte, and even so, I detected the smoldering embers of his almost-forgotten passion."

"More accurately, the question was prompted by his unrequited lust." Charlotte tossed a black powder flask from hand to hand. The good-looking, sweet-talking, playful and scatter-brained youngest son of Dowager Duchess de Seveigney had shamelessly flirted with Charlotte, she flirted with him, and his mother eagerly anticipated the wedding bells until a fencing match doomed it to perdition. Charlotte won by two points, and M. Patrice demanded Charlotte stop wearing men's clothing and to forgo the fencing. Charlotte retorted that wearing skirts would be impractical when sailing the Spanish Main on the ship under her command. M. Patrice lost all his desire. Duchess Helene almost wept in disappointment, but Charlotte's mother was relieved. "Father never wanted me to marry him," Charlotte reminded her brother. "He trained me to hit M. Patrice's weak spots and he orchestrated the fencing match when M. Patrice was reluctant to cross blades with me."

Henri studied the pattern of the doublet he was folding. "Do you regret it?"

"My slightly bruised heart healed nicely when father taught me to shoot a musket. On second thought, do you think I can still entice M. Patrice to marry me now, despite Charles?"

"What? Why? Have you lost your mind?!" Henri sat down to stare at her with a horrified expression. Bringing her brother to such a state was an accomplishment.

Charlotte kept a straight face. "I could use his drinking and womanizing as excuses to travel around the world in any company I choose."

"Did Antoine help you to conjure such an ingenious idea?"

"Antoine is the last man in the world to discuss love affairs or marriage. We are finished talking about him and M. Patrice. Both of them can dance in purgatory for all I care." Charlotte measured the black powder into the flask. "Show me all the places I will not be allowed to attend once I am imprisoned in a dress. Where is the Valiant Fox tavern?"

Henri pointed in the general direction of south-east. "Across the Rue du Temple, a couple of blocks away from City Hall. The tennis courts are at the Louvre, so maybe we should begin the tour there."

"I will kick you if you offer to promenade in Tuileries. Where is the fencing hall?"

"A block away from the Arsenal." He added a pair of breeches and a handkerchief to the clothes.

"Very well." Charlotte tossed his clothes in the saddlebag. "First, to the Valiant Fox! Can we gain admittance to the Arsenal?"

"I hope you are not planning to gain admittance to the Bastille," Henri replied.

An hour later, Charlotte paused at the entrance to the Valiant Fox to view the sign hanging over the door – a red fox standing on its hind legs and wielding a broadsword. Only the front room, wide and narrow, was relegated to regular tavern services. The owner of this fine establishment had dedicated the back main room to card-playing only and served simple but hearty three-course dinners in a smaller adjacent room. The card stakes were limited to the amounts written on the wall in manuscript-style letters and numbers, and this house rule effectively weeded out the unscrupulous gamblers in search of quick fortune. The regular patrons of this thriving establishment congregated to enjoy recreational card play, sophisticated conversations, and either quiet or social meals accompanied by the excellent selection of wine, brandy, and rum. It was a perfect place for Charles.

"De Brangelton!" A young man, impeccably dressed in a gray outfit with gold and russet trim, stood up and waved at them. His golden-brown hair was carefully arranged, he was tall and lean like Antoine, and he possessed the same easy elegance, but the resemblance ended there. His hazel eyes expressed none of Antoine's arrogance, deviousness, and stubborn determination.

"Do not embarrass us both," Henri whispered to her. "What brought you here so early, de la Norte?" he asked his friend.

"I could no longer ignore the buzz of rumors about the brawl at the Red Boar Inn yesterday." He glanced at her with mild curiosity and gestured to the table. "Would you and your friend join me?" He invited them.

"No, I am tracking my father to unload this reprobate on him." Henri curtly nodded in her direction. "What happened at the Red Boar Inn?"

"According to the least absurd version, two young boys decided to teach a hot-tempered Lieutenant a lesson about manners. The scuffle ended when the boys wounded half a dozen officers and Musketeers whisked these troublemakers to the Bastille. In another account, two men with a tame lion defended themselves against a dozen officers!"

"I would have expected a dragon," Henri bantered.

"Or at least a gargoyle," de la Norte laughed. He politely disregarded her presence because Henri did not bother with introductions. Why was she hiding her identity? Out of habit? She was in Paris with her brother, not in Bourges or Orleans with Antoine. An odd sensation settled in her mind and she pulled her hat lower. She preferred to impart a favorable impression on de la Norte.

Antoine cleaned up and shaved, lay down on the settee for a few minutes, and woke up quite refreshed an hour later. He ate a handful of walnuts and washed them down with milk, called Armand to help him dress, and fumbled to buckle his swordbelt with one arm. He finally succeeded, put on his hat, and grimaced at his pale reflection in the mirror.

"I see you are well already." The Comte de Tournelles stood at the open door and critically looked him over.

"Yes, I am, M. Francis, thank you."

"Where is Charlotte?"

"She – Charles - left with Henri this morning."

"Where did they go?"

"I believe your daughter planned a tour of Paris before dinner." Antoine adjusted the hat on his head, searching for a perfect angle. No doubt Charlotte was quite happy to leave him behind, and the feeling was mutual. "Did she mention our little detour of a pilgrimage in Bourges?"

"That detail was almost lost in her extensive complaints about your creative inclination to keep the bridles, but I was able to extract that a Knight of St. John and the Bishop of Bourges are in conspiracy about St. Elias' relics. Where are you going?"

"I have a dispatch to deliver to the Navy."

"Urgent?" M. Francis prompted.

"Probably not, but otherwise it will be delayed for a week. Tomorrow, Henri, Charles, and I will ride to Dampier, and Mme. Henrietta will meet us there."

"Didn't my wife leave strict orders for you to stay home today and recuperate?"

"I pray Mme. Henrietta will never find out," Antoine objected. "That works well with my mother. The less she knows, the less she worries." He placed his hand on the back of a chair to support himself.

"Don't play the idiot. It does not suit you," M. Francis replied. "Most of the time your mother only pretends ignorance. Are you at the liberty to disclose your business?"

Antoine took off his hat and sat down. "I was asked, by the Comte de Chambreau of Orleans, to deliver a dispatch to the Navy. Lord Nelson from England recommended my fine self to the Comte for future business. May I ask if you know who Lord Nelson is?"

"His Grace the Duke Collingstone." He probably knew more about the Duke's business than de Chambreau did.

"M. Francis, are you personally acquainted with the Comte de Chambreau and Duke Collingstone?"

"Never heard of de Chambreau till Charlotte accounted your revelry in Orleans. Are you planning to pursue the business with the Duke?"

Antoine poured himself a cup of water. He did not share the information with Charlotte on principle, but her father was a different story. "It is a search for the Great Mogul Diamond.

It disappeared from Marseille Harbor in 1712. Do you know about it, M. Francis?"

Comte's bright eyes turned opaque. "By any chance, did the Marshall cousins take it?"

Antoine was momentarily startled. He almost forgot what it was like to deal with Charlotte's devious father. "De Chambreau claimed that the Marshall cousins either kidnapped the Indian warrior named Kumaryan who possessed the diamond, or were in conspiracy with him."

M. Francis grinned. "Indeed? I know for certain that the Great Mogul Diamond was nowhere near the harbor in 1712."

Antoine did not doubt the truth and certainty of this information. "So de Chambreau either misled me on purpose, or was misinformed himself, or both. Why? De Chambreau is unlikely to spy for the English."

"Probably no worse than the Marshall cousins," M. Francis commented with a hint of humor. "He seems to be a treasure hunter for His Grace. Frankly, I am quite curious about the Great Mogul Diamond myself, and eager to discover who was the previous owner of this glorious gem. Tell me if you unearth any information, will you?"

"I will," Antoine promised. "Do you know who possesses the diamond now, M. Francis?"

"Yes. It is stored in France and is perfectly safe from the reach of Duke Collingstone, Comte de Chambreau, and Kumaryan."

17

DEPARTURE

PARIS - SEPTEMBER 1719

Compared to Charles, the Marshall cousins are juvenile troublemakers.

Antoine de la Fleure to Henri de Brangelton- 1718

IN THE EARLY HOURS OF THE MORNING, WHEN THE DAY'S first flotilla of barges started to unload the cargo onto the delivery carts, Antoine, Henri, and Charlotte rode along the Seine and crossed the empty Pont Neuf. They took narrow streets through a residential neighborhood to avoid the parade of wagons, pushcarts, and wheelbarrows as well as the throng of workers entering the city on the main thoroughfare, and they pushed their way outside the city gates.

They rode in a single file line till Montrouge, where they were able to ride abreast.

"Charlotte." Henri adopted a serene tone. "You realize, of course, that you have caused me a very painful inconvenience.

Beautiful women desire my fine company, but here I am, wasting my youth and vigor on a meaningless travel with you."

"Women? Plural?" Charlotte echoed Antoine's own thought.

Antoine said nothing. Love affairs were the last subject he desired to discuss with either one of them.

"Yes. My absence is breaking tender hearts, but do not allow the guilt to lie too heavily on your conscience." Henri was undaunted.

"Cybille and the mysterious G? Are women in Paris so desperately bored that more than one misses your unfaithful company?" Charlotte continued the interrogation.

Henri slapped his sister with his hat. "The mysterious G is a beautiful Gabrielle. Why are you staring at me like that?" he asked Antoine.

"I see you have not changed." Antoine privately wondered if Henri was shameless enough to elaborate on his love affairs in his sister's presence.

"No, he still compares his every beloved to Cleopatra and pledges that he would have delivered Rome to her if he were Julius Caesar, then confesses his heart's desire to be her Marc Anthony." Charlotte recited her brother's methods. "Why are you staring at me like that?"

"How do you know that?" Antoine blurted out in horrified curiosity. Just when he thought nothing about Charlotte de Brangelton could surprise him any longer, she proved him wrong.

"A few of his passions confided in me." Charlotte rolled her eyes. "They chirped that my brother is a handsome and charming man. Little do they know he tricks them all. Now, tell me about Cybille and Gabrielle," she ordered her handsome and charming brother. "Do they know about each other?"

"Of course not." Henri had no qualms to plunge into his

favorite subject. "Cybille has the body of Aphrodite, along with unhealthy aspirations to mix business and pleasure. We quarrel often, then passionately reconcile. One more snicker, Charlotte, and I will tell you nothing. Gabrielle claimed my heart last month, I think. She is a very passionate woman, with bright eyes, perfect full lips... I could not resist, besides, Cybille is falling out of love with me. What a pleasant surprise!" He wheeled his horse around.

A richly-decorated carriage had stopped by the roadside inn to rest and to water the horses. The occupant of the carriage was a young, beautiful woman. She looked out of the window with a forlorn expression on her classically beautiful face. Her fashionable hat did not quite cover her honey colored hair. When she beheld Henri, her lips formed into a sensuous pout.

Henri dismounted and carelessly tossed the reins to one of her servants. He kissed her hand with a playful ease and familiarity before he unceremoniously opened the door and held out his arm to assist her descent from the carriage. He ushered her away for a stroll.

"A third passion?" Charlotte's amazement coincided with Antoine's own thoughts again. "Do you recognize the Coat of Arms?" She motioned for Red Jacques to retrieve Henri's horse.

"No," Antoine followed her example and dismounted. "Your brother has changed for the worse. I did not think it was possible," he amended his earlier observation and squashed down the subtly envious feeling.

"He would certainly make a week-long ride for the pleasure of an exciting woman's company. Or two women. Or probably more. What is his limit? And he would certainly dedicate longer than a month to his affairs. He devotes a ridiculous amount of time and effort to chasing women."

Antoine opened his mouth and closed it. He must avoid the

provocation of engaging in any discussion on this subject. His love affairs were none of Charlotte's business. Besides, he had no idea how much time and effort the chase required. He had never bothered because women came to him on their own. He shuddered at the thought of Wildcat possibly acquiring amorous notions about him, realized he was glaring at her profile, and turned his head. His eyes met the languid gaze of Henri's companion. It took Antoine a moment too long to respond to her subtle interest, and she shifted her attention to Charlotte, who swept her a deep, deliberate bow. The tip of the plume trailed on the ground, and the hair fell forward. The woman acknowledged her with a graceful nod, while Henri's face settled in an innocent mask.

"Shall we go?" Charlotte asked.

"Where?" Antoine asked in panic. He suddenly had the sinking feeling that Charlotte, warmed up by their previous conversation and the scene they witnessed, might have made an amorous proposition to him.

She marched away, speaking in her usual manner without turning around. "To order refreshments and play cards at the tables over there. Henri will be occupied for a while." She glanced back, and her mocking grin taunted him. "Unless you are repenting your wooden behavior and would like to redeem yourself with this Venus."

Antoine put his arm on her shoulder and guided her away. "There will be hail and a blizzard in hell a dozen times, before I ever compete with Henri, or anyone else, for any woman's attention, or, worse, ask for your help in these matters!" he expostulated. And if Charlotte ever proposed to him, an even longer time would pass for him to even consider it.

An hour later, Henri's beautiful companion resumed her way to Paris. During this time, Antoine won a bottle of wine from Charlotte and they halfway emptied it.

"Is this Gabrielle or yet another passion of yours?" Charlotte wasted no time.

"That was Marquise Cecilia de Febvre." He helped himself to his portion of the mutton leg which Charlotte ordered earlier, and chewed thoughtfully. "She is attracted to either refined and sophisticated courtiers, or gallant military men in lavish uniforms. I am neither."

"Since when has that stopped you?" Charlotte knew her brother well.

Henri sipped the wine. "Her conquests include Duke Collingstone, a man of significantly higher social standing than myself. I understand Patrice de Seveigney was just as fascinated only half a year after her marriage at seventeen. Her husband lives at his estate with his mistress and brood of children, but this season, he has committed to visit her in Paris."

"Did you recommend she sends for his mistress?"

Antoine was, once again, rendered speechless. Charlotte seemed to be able to read his thoughts.

"She also happens to be the sister of my friend Bertrand de la Norte," Henri explained. Thus I am containing my base desires."

Antoine had recognized the family resemblance. Cecilia de Fabvre seemed to have more character than her spineless brother.

"What a blessing for the Marquise that her brother is a decent man." Charlotte had a better opinion of boy de la Norte.

"She felt slighted by your indifference, Antoine. Take lessons from Charles - his exemplary gallant manners were received well, and she inquired about him!" Henri held up his hands. "I hope she will not recognize Charlotte in the future."

"She will not." Charlotte was confident. "What excuse did you make for Charles?"

"The boy is too young to truly appreciate a beautiful

woman," he said with a straight face and both he and Antoine howled in laughter.

Two days later, the Comtesse de Tournelles, in her usual alias as Henri d'Arringnon, arrived in the afternoon and was anxious to leave early the next day. Henri embraced his mother, then kissed his sister on the forehead. "Take care, Charlotte."

"Take care, Henri." Charlotte stood on her toes to kiss his cheek, then brightly smiled at Antoine. "Take care, Antoine. Thank you for coming to Paris with me," she said suddenly.

"You are welcome," Antoine heard himself say. For a moment, her countenance softened and he caught a glimpse of a mischievous face, but the image disappeared in the next moment when she plopped her hat on her head and followed her mother outside. Charlotte vaulted into the saddle, and wasted no time in wheeling her horse around and riding away. Her mother followed her, and neither one of them looked back as Antoine and Henri watched them disappear around the bend of the road.

Henri's face reflected concern mixed with guilt and regret.

"You seem uncharacteristically worried," Antoine probed.

"My sister is riding to La Rochelle and back with my father, after two weeks on the road. I pray she will not forget how to wear a dress, or how to behave when wearing one."

"Your mother manages well," Antoine pointed out. "Didn't Wildcat learn from her?"

"My mother is the most reasonable person in our family, whereas my sister is more of a de Brangelton than our devil of a sire," Henri explained with affection. "Are you ready to return to Paris? There are beautiful women for me to console before my next departure. I have been summoned to play nursemaid to Patrice de Seveigney." He apparently brushed off his worries and they wheeled their horses around. "When will you be presenting your fine self to the beautiful Marquise Cecilia de Fcbvrc?"

"When she invites me," Antoine replied.

"Don't want to seem easy and eager, do you?" Henri was correct in his accusation. "Raoul shared the wisdom of your teachings, if I can call it wisdom. I took it upon myself to correct his distorted views. Do you indeed leave your women after a month? Have you had any regrets?"

"Only about the *Anne Maria Jane*," Antoine channeled the conversation into a more meaningful direction.

Henri's eyes darkened, and he brought his horse closer. "Charlotte cajoled me into visiting Marseille last year. Did she tell you about it?"

"No. The subject of the Marshall cousins never came up. What does she know?"

Henri dropped his head into his hands. "With her unerring intuition for trouble, she discovered the tale of the Marshall cousins. On our first day in the city, mind you. She was duly impressed by their notoriety and she suggested searching for them."

Antoine almost fell out of the saddle. "You didn't agree, did you ?"

"I irrevocably refused to involve my sister into affairs of piracy. Thus we did not speak to each other, and Charles, in his finest manner, ventured on his own."

"Can't you control your sister?! " Antoine could not restrain himself.

"How much success have you had lately in controlling Charles?" Henri asked. His horse neighed.

"Never mind," Antoine regretted his outburst. "Charles could have blown up the whole harbor by himself. Herself. Did she try to repeat the cousins' not so glorious performance, just to see if it was possible?"

"Charles cultivated a friend, a Lieutenant of the guards. Apparently, a year or so after the incident, a Musketeer and a representative from the Navy showed up to investigate the Commandant's report from that day. Charles' friend had the misfortune to greet that man."

"What was his name?"

"That is the odd part," Henri said grimly, and the man driving the cart on the opposite side of the road steered his horse as far away as space allowed. "The Lieutenant had a glimpse of his official papers before the Navy representative forced his way into the Commandant's office. Charles surmised that the Navy representative terrified everyone, but amazingly, neither the Lieutenant nor the Commandant caught the name."

"A Navy representative and a Musketeer? Why both?"

"I have been asking myself the same question." Henri pulled his hat low to shield his eyes from the sun. "To confuse matters?"

"Two men from two different branches, to prevent anyone from tracing the inquiry," Antoine picked up Henri's trail of thought. "Is this a private investigation?"

"By someone powerful enough to pull the strings at the Navy and the Musketeers," Henri vocalized the bothersome but logical conjecture.

"Do we have a description of these men?" Antoine asked.

"The Navy representative has blue eyes, he is average built and height, and he wore a formal wig. The Musketeer did not say a single word. He was clean shaven and his hair was powdered."

"The description of the Marshall cousins is more extensive than that!"

"I could not investigate further without involving my sister!"

"God forbid," Antoine exclaimed. "By any chance, did she happen to discover any connection between the Marshall cousins and the Great Mogul Diamond?"

"What is the Great Mogul Diamond?"

Antoine launched into the narration of his acquaintance with Commandant Marcoux and Comte de Chambreau.

THE BENEFITS OF DECOROUS BEHAVIOR

PARIS – OCTOBER 1718

Antoine and I?! No, no, no! I will be on my best proper behavior to make certain that no one will connect my name to his!

Charlotte de Brangelton to Henrietta de Brangelton - October 1718

CHARLOTTE SETTLED IN THE SADDLE, A SIDE SADDLE! - newly purchased only yesterday. *"This is a waste,"* father had cheerfully commented. He was probably correct in his assessment considering her first public outing in Paris. Henri yearned for the miracle, and after weeks on the road, - and at the hectic pace of the last four – Charlotte returned to Paris exhausted with fatigue. Maybe she learned her lesson, Henri thought, and her insatiable desire for adventure will be replaced by reason. So far, so good, for three days in a row, his sister behaved in a relatively acceptable manner.

"The Musketeers' Headquarters," she proclaimed.

"The Musketeers' Headquarters are an inappropriate place for a young woman," Henri countered. "A gentle ride along the Avenue de Neuily–"

"Captain d'Ornille of His Majesty's Musketeers is my godfather, my father's best friend, and a man highly respected at Court. There is nothing inappropriate about my desire to visit uncle Paul."

Henri could find no objections to that. He expeditiously escorted his sister through the mercifully small gathering of men in the courtyard. Uncle Paul laughed to tears upon learning about the purchase of the side saddle for her gentle horse and Charlotte's intent of staying on her best behavior. Henri had high hopes of leaving without delays, but this plan was shattered the moment he and his enlightened sister stepped outside and de Rameau scurried to greet her. She tensed, muttered derogatory phrases which most young noblewomen never heard, and glared at the Musketeer with her usual defiance. She had already forgotten Henri's numerous warnings that young noblewomen were not supposed to and did not dare to stare the men down.

"De Brangelton," de Rameau wasted no time. "If you venture to bring a beautiful young woman to our Headquarters, you must introduce her." An air of a tacit challenge descended between him and Charlotte.

"Do not nurture any amorous notions about my sister," Henri brushed aside polite niceties. "Charlotte, my friend de Rameau is a notorious womanizer; his disreputable infamy almost matches mine. D'Signac is almost dull and respectable."

De Rameau possessed himself of her hand and slowly, deliberately kissed it. "It is a great pleasure, a dream come true, a blessing from Cupid, Mlle. de Brangelton, to welcome you to

Paris," he said softly, and there was an odd, even for him, a gleam in his eyes. "May I?"

"No," Charlotte cut off the flow of nonsense and her fingers closed in a fist to prevent him from kissing the palm of her hand – the man certainly had a lot of nerve and no shame.

"Ah... no? May I ask what is it you refuse before I ask?"

"Your company and your attention, M. de Rameau."

"You are breaking my captive heart, Mlle. Charlotte!" he exclaimed with the most artistic flourish.

"Better I break your heart than your head, M. de Rameau," Charlotte no longer abided by the confines of proper conduct. "M. d'Signac, does the dubious honor of being the most disreputable womanizer in Paris belong to M. de Rameau or to my brother? Or is it disputed between them?" She finally managed to free her hand from de Rameau's grip.

"Mlle. de Brangelton, you have no heart!" de Rameau declared with exasperation.

"Of course, my brother is wise enough to realize when to stop wasting his time. What about you, M. de Rameau, do you possess a grain of intelligence?" she asked over the sound of his grinding teeth. As a precaution, she positioned her hand for easy reach of her hidden dagger.

Very nice, dear sister, Henri thought. There was a benefit to her unconventional style, since these comments left even de Rameau speechless. Henri put a restraining hand on de Rameau's shoulder. "Take my advice and save yourself a lot of distress. Stay a cannonball shot away from my volatile sister. She is capable and willing to run a sword through any of her lunatic admirers."

"Mlle. Charlotte. May I rescue you from the company of these two unrepentant womanizers?" D'Signac pushed his friend out of the way and offered his arm for Charlotte. "Is this your first visit to Paris?"

He led Charlotte away, de Rameau growled at their backs, and Henri conceded that father was, as usual, correct. What genteel behavior? With de Rameau's provocation, she would be throwing punches within a day. Or just an hour of his company.

Bertrand de la Norte and Geoffrey de Contraille eyed de Brangelton's new horse in admiration. The large, spirited chestnut mare with black mane and tail pranced in place, forcing the rider to balance himself to compensate for the horse's unpredictable moves.

"It's a fierce beauty," Bertrand said.

"This disorderly beast belongs to my sister," Henri de Brangelton explained. The mare stomped her front hooves in a continuous elaborate dance. "I am just borrowing her for a day."

Bertrand politely refrained from his comment that, judging by its behavior, this horse was better suited for a cavalry officer.

"Mlle. Charlotte, isn't it? Is she here?" de Contraille asked in surprise.

"Yes." De Brangelton affectionately stroked the neck of the horse and the animal finally condescended to stand still.

"Your sister is not married yet, is she?" de Contraille asked.

Bertrand felt a slight embarrassment at his own imagination. It painted a very unflattering portrait of Mlle. de Brangelton.

De Brangelton sighed. "My sister escaped to Paris to flee the attention of a certain Captain. He begged her to marry him one time too many."

There was fleeting disbelief on de Contraille's face. "Did your father dislike him?"

"My father indulges her whims," de Brangelton elaborated. "So here she is, determined to make me pay dearly for my endeavors to marry her off."

The half-wild mare loudly snorted at that.

"Have you ever met his sister?" Bertrand asked after Henri de Brangelton left.

"I am not certain." De Contraille was lost in thought. "De Brangelton's parents visited him at fencing school and brought along a boy named Charles. The Comte de Tournelles introduced him as his protégé. The boy looked just like him, so I figured he must have been a cousin or a nephew. That Charles-" de Contraille shook his head "-accompanied Henri de Brangelton to school, set bets on every fencing bout. He won some, and lost some and promptly paid up, until the Headmaster found out and warned de Brangelton to never bring Charles to school again."

"What does it have to do with Mlle. de Brangelton?"

"After his family left, de Brangelton claimed that Charles was, in fact, his sister Charlotte. I doubted it, but then de Flancourt confirmed it. He called her a scourge of his younger brother because his brother's purpose in life was to keep up with Charles." He smiled apologetically. "I suppose it could be true. In retrospect, neither the de Brangelton family nor de Flancourt allowed the boy out of their sight."

Bertrand felt his mood darkened by the mentioning of de Flancourt. His intense dislike for the young Comte had intensified into simmering resentment when Bertrand's sister Cecilia de Fabvre encouraged de Flancourt's attentions. Bertrand felt nauseated upon recalling each and every cynical statement freely dispersed by the Comte., The men of higher social status showered Cecilia with their adoration and vied for her attention, but de Flancourt's conceited attitude was unforgivable, and Bertrand was relieved when the arrogant Comte suddenly left Paris and Cecilia was spared from another scandalous love affair.

Her Grace Helene de Seveigney attended the theater with a small retinue of two ladies-in-waiting and an unknown young woman, slim and agile, dressed in a modestly cut dress of dark red and the bodice sparely decorated with silver embroidery. She carried herself with assurance and poise, her shoulders and long neck were shapely, and her pale, translucent skin was set off by her black hair arranged in a simple style.

Bertrand's heart skipped a beat when her eyes, glowing in the dim light, momentarily met his and a tentative smile touched her lips before she averted her gaze to survey the crowd.

"My God," de Contraille exhaled. "This must be Charlotte de Brangelton!"

Bertrand caught his breath. He now discerned the resemblance to her brother. She had the same profile, the black hair, and the same peculiar way of turning her head.

"Have you ever met Mlle. de Brangelton before, M. Geoffrey?" Cecilia asked.

"No, I don't think so." His voice was slightly coarse. Bertrand tore his eyes away from Mlle. de Brangelton and realized that de Contraille and an uncountable number of men in the neighboring boxes and the audience had noticed her. Her Dowager Grace de Seveigney was known for the introduction of young noblewomen to society, and he could hear agitated speculations asking, "Who is she?"

"De Brangelton and de Flancourt must have played a joke on me," de Contraille whispered when the curtain went up.

"Yes. No man in his right mind could mistake Mlle. de Brangelton for a boy." Bertrand was certain of it.

Henri's eventful day started with a social visit from de Contraille who observed that Mlle. Charlotte had blossomed, then politely inquired if her interest in fencing had faded since Charles' visit to fencing school. Henri explained that Charlotte's swordsmanship was suitable for a glorious career in the Musketeers, except Captain d'Ornille would not allow her within a mile of the Headquarters. In the early afternoon, matters deteriorated further. De la Norte sought him out and politely inquired if he might call on Mlle. de Brangelton.

"Why?" Henri could not hide his astonishment. Of course, Charlotte was on her best behavior, but Henri had no desire to set de la Norte up for bitter disappointment.

"You do not trust me to behave honorably?" de la Norte exclaimed.

"Of course I trust you. Besides, my sister will not hesitate to set you straight in case you stray off the honorable and respectful path." Henri recovered from his surprise. Didn't de la Norte recognize her from that meeting at the Valiant Fox? "It's just that...why?!"

De la Norte's countenance bordered on exasperated.

"I apologize, it's just that I am not accustomed to chaperoning my sister," Henri improvised. He was accustomed to accompanying Charles. "Why don't you join us for a ride?" There was no harm in a casual outing. De la Norte would be cured of his infatuation soon enough even if Charlotte were to stay on her best proper behavior. If she understood what that meant.

"Thank you, de Brangelton." De la Norte visibly relaxed. "I promise on my honor that I will watch out for Mlle. Charlotte's interests."

"You may do so," Henri thought as he nodded. *"But she will do anything she pleases."*

The enchanting Mlle. de Brangelton held a fashion newspaper in one hand and idly tossed a fan up and down with the other hand. At least, it was not a knife. This time.

Henri poured himself a measure of rum, plopped onto the chair, and waited for her to discard the newspaper. "I understand you have impressed M. de la Norte."

"Duchess Helene was kind enough to present me to Parisian society at the theater. M. de la Norte introduced himself and his sister," Charlotte said with exaggerated innocence. "M. de Contraille gawked at me with an incredulous expression. M. de Chassigneau announced that he was dedicating his fine self to my service, and the M. de Vergne promised to compose an ode to do justice to my charms."

Henri ignored the mental images associated with this story. "What is your impression of de la Norte?"

"M. de la Norte is a handsome and polite man. Neither he nor his sister suspected any resemblance between me and Charles. De Contraille was astounded. De Chassigneau imagines he is a prized catch. De Vergne is rather harmless."

"Who is de Chassigneau?"

"He is a very flamboyantly dressed young courtier of much conceit and little intelligence. He wears enough lace to make a couple of petticoats. He claimed his father and our sire are on excellent terms. His father aspires to an alliance with the Comte de Tournelles and thus he, Chevalier de Chassigneau, would be happy to make a match with yours truly." She flicked the fan in a military salute.

"Did you refuse his romantic proposition a with sword through his shoulder or a punch in the face?"

Charlotte cast down her eyes and almost succeeded as an image of modesty. "A sword, Monsieur? A punch? Indeed, how dare you imply such a thing!" Her eyelashes fluttered.

"You scare me. Stop stalling. What did you do?"

Charlotte abandoned the playacting. "Since I am burdened

by proper manners, brother, I vowed that I will not marry him this century." She tossed the fan from hand to hand. "He did not understand. A boiled pigeon is smarter."

Henri pushed away the image of a man with a bloody shoulder or a black eye. It was only a matter of time before one or other happened to de Chassigneau. "Who is de Vergne?"

"He is a frequent guest at Duchess Helene's household. You may have met him – he has a cherubic face, innocent brown eyes, and he sparingly applies rouge to his cheeks and lips. He is prolific in writing songs and sonnets, he plays the lute and harpsichord, and he authors romantic stories."

"A perfect match for you indeed."

"He showed up here the next day, and within half an hour, he declared, in complete seriousness, that he was madly in love with me! His family is very respectable, he is the only son, and his life is meaningless without me, that sort of thing. Did you ever realize that my eyes are brighter than Indian sapphires?"

Henri could not choose between laughing and cursing. "Bertrand de la Norte agrees. He humbly begs you to honor him with your company on a ride."

"De Rameau bleated that his existence depends on my – ah, exquisite - smile. De Vergne sung a more embellished version of the same nonsense. I left home because de Molienier visited every day. De Chassigneau threatened to wither if I didn't appreciate his taste in fashion." She helped herself to a sip of rum. "What does de la Norte want?"

Henri confiscated the rum from her. "You are as hopeless as Antoine de Flancourt!"

"In what respect?"

"The beautiful Cecilia de Fabvre favored him with attention, but the man is unwilling to exert the slightest effort. When she complained about his apparent indifference, his response was *'May I ask what led you to such an unfair conclusion?'* "

"No! He is worse than Raoul. Compared to Antoine, you arc a perfect gentleman."

"Comparing to Antoine, de Rameau is a perfect gallant. Of course, de la Norte is indeed a gallant knight of legends." Henri raised his voice to emphasize the point. "He lives to accompany you for a ride through the Champs Elysees. Or would you prefer a stroll in Tuileries?"

"Do you expect me to ride with him alone?" She deliberately fanned herself. "No. With a brother like you, I must be very cautious to maintain my impeccable reputation."

Henri caught the fan his sister flung at him. "I will chaperone."

"You? Chaperone?" Charlotte fell back into her chair in unholy merriment.

Much to Henri's surprise, Charlotte exercised her best behavior, but Hera exhibited her usual behavior. The mare suspiciously watched de la Norte, and, for a while, obediently trotted along before raising her front hoofs off the ground. De la Norte quickly reached to grab her reins. Hera snapped at him and his horse startled away, thus diverting his attention so he did not catch Charlotte's elaborately obscene speech. Henri himself ordered the horse to stop her prancing and ignored de la Norte's horrified frown. The language to communicate with Hera was indeed most unsuitable for the ears of young noblewoman, and hopefully de la Norte did not grasp half of it either.

"Mlle. de Brangelton." De la Norte regained control of his speaking facilities. "This mare..."

"Hera is distrustful of strangers," Charlotte explained. "I apologize that we did not warn you."

"May I recommend to have her trained better, Mlle. de Brangelton?"

"I beg your pardon?" Charlotte's tone did not bode well for de la Norte.

Henri kicked his sister. He had warned her: no profanities, no staring, no punches, no kicks, no discussions about swordsmanship, privateering, weapons, etc. He should have added Hera's habits and history to that list.

"This mare is an excellent animal, but we had no time to train it out of this habit. Fortunately, Charlotte is an excellent rider." In fact, his sister could ride standing up in the stirrups and swinging the sword.

De la Norte frowned in confusion. "Yes, of course, Mlle. de Brangelton's equestrian skills are beyond doubt, and yet, it is dangerous for Mlle. de Brangelton to ride an unpredictable horse."

"M. de la Norte," Charlotte interrupted again. "I assure you that I am very comfortable riding Hera. I picked her out myself. The dealer honestly warned my father about that the mare."

Henri kicked her again to shorten the narration. "You know our father, de la Norte. The excellent introductions failed to discourage him."

Hera shook her head and snorted.

"She snapped at father." Charlotte gently pulled on the horse's ear, distanced herself from Henri's foot, and continued the story. "Off we went looking for another, but I lost my heart to this mare. When we came back, Hera had smartened up and allowed me to pat her neck. The dealer was astonished."

Henri silently prayed that his sister would refrain from a demonstration on how to stop Hera's prancing.

THE DRAWBACKS OF DECOROUS BEHAVIOR

PARIS – OCTOBER 1718

What do we have here - de la Norte, de Chassigneau, de Rameau, de Vergne?
a dreamer, a schemer, a whore, and a poet.

Francis de Brangelton to Henrietta de Brangelton –
1718

To disperse a lingering superstition associated with Francis' generally accepted nickname *"devil de Brangelton"*, he and Henrietta attended Mass every Sunday, or as time allowed. It was a prudent, although time-consuming action, and Francis had learned to put the sermon time to a practical use. Many of his greatest schemes were hatched in churches, under the guidance of angels. Lately, his daughter's infatuation with a fine young courtier presented him with a challenge. Francis' gaze slowly traveled the nave of the Notre Dame cathedral. Looking up, he picked a window to focus his eyes on, set his features in the most attentive and pious expression he could manage, and blocked out the sounds made by the preacher for the duration of the service.

At first, Francis had dismissed Charlotte's interest in Bertrand de la Norte as a temporary infatuation, only to realize to his shocked surprise that he had made a severe error of judgement. De la Norte's matrimonial intentions did not scare Charlotte off. To Francis' astonishment, Henrietta's bewilderment, and Henri's gloating, Charlotte curbed her unconventional activities. From her perspective, de la Norte's demeanor must be a pleasant juxtaposition to the straight-forward approach of the mule-headed de Molienier. What a trip it must have been for Antoine and Charlotte, when his attempts to gain control had shattered under her determination to conduct her own affairs in her own way. They developed a wariness and resentment of each other and only miraculously remained on speaking terms. Henri's wasted efforts to protect her from de Rameau's declaration of a sudden desire for matrimony were ridiculous when Charlotte had already established a very reasonable time to accommodate de Rameau's passion. Francis dismissed de Rameau as a minor annoyance and focused his attention to the problem at hand. Bertrand de la Norte was madly, passionately, even desperately in love with Charlotte, but his shortage of self-assurance, his fear of dishonorable actions, and the lack of encouragement by Charlotte doomed his courtship to proceed slowly. Unlike Patrice de Seveigney, Bertrand de la Norte neither besieged her with unrelenting declarations nor begged for her love.

The reason for the young man's reluctance must be his father - Bertrand naively strove to convince his father to accept Mlle. de Brangelton as a match for the heir of the exalted de la Norte family. No doubt his father rebuked him unconditionally, but the son optimistically hoped that his father could be converted. Francis did not dislike the young man. In a crowd of young courtiers born to titles, privileges, and money, Bertrand stood out as an honest, intelligent, and genuinely kind man. Bertrand possessed courage and an odd mixture of stubbornness and a philosophical streak, along with the abundance of family pride ingrained into his soul by his father. Overall, he was a fine young man with many virtues and few faults, but how would he react if disowned by his father? Would he philosophically acquiesce to his fate, or would he suffer from self-imposed guilt of a perceived betrayal? Would he feel that Charlotte and her untraditional ways were worth the sacrifice, or would he loathe his decision to abandon his family?

"Amen," Francis repeated in chorus with congregation as he made the decision.

Jean-Paul de la Norte, the Marquis de Louviers, entered through the front gate of the Vincennes court yard. There was a long checkered history between Francis and him. Occasionally they were on the same side, but adversarial situations were more frequent, and the Marquis did not take his losses lightly. Francis purposefully walked to intercept him, and the Marquis – reluctantly, as usual, - stopped and waited. Francis approached and allowed the silence between them to linger.

"Comte," de Louviers finally greeted him.

"Marquis." Francis formally inclined his head. "How do you feel about our children's optimistic outlook on life?"

De Louviers steeled himself. "I admit that your daughter is a beautiful young woman, but I vow by everything sacred in this world, I will disown my son if he marries her."

"I have no doubt of that," Francis said. "Remember, I witnessed the day when your father disowned your older brother for disobeying his orders."

A shadow passed across de Louviers' face. He begged his older brother Jerome to yield to their father's orders, then abandoned his appeals when father disowned Jerome. De Louviers took over his brother's life, married for money, and made his way to the Court. His brother achieved success and happiness in life, but he and de Louviers remained distant and distrustful of each other.

"You can certainly do better for your daughter." The pleading note was almost undiscernible.

"I understand you bestowed on your son more money than either you or I had at his age," Francis reminded him.

"I warn you. I will not allow my son to throw away his future over..." he faltered, searching for the right word to finish the sentence. He would probably sell his soul to save his Bertrand from Charlotte.

"... an adventuress, in your refined opinion," Francis finished his thought.

De Louviers had the grace to flinch. "I don't want de Brangelton blood in the veins of my grandchildren. I don't want you to meddle in my affairs!" His face colored as the unguarded words escaped.

"I have no desire to deal with you, either. You and I are in perfect agreement about the future of our children."

"I beg your pardon?" De Louviers failed to keep his voice steady. "You don't want this marriage for your daughter?" The courtly mask dropped.

"Your son is a fine young man, but I do not care for a son-in-law who may or may not be loyal to me." That was the truth, along with the fact that Bertrand and Charlotte would be just as mis-matched couple as Charlotte and Patrice de Seveigney, although for a different reason. "You and I have parental responsibilities to arrange our children's futures far apart from each other."

De Louviers fought for control of his emotions. There was delight that his precious son would be saved from an awful fate, and indignation that a recently anointed Comte would refuse his daughter to marry a son of an old noble and titled family. That unhealthy mix was spiced with suspicion and curiosity.

"Will you forbid your daughter to associate with Bertrand?" de Louviers finally croaked, leaning against the wall with the air of a man relieved of a debilitating burden.

"That will be useless. My girl does not obey commands," Francis replied. "Wrecking their illusions will require more finesse. Do you trust me to orchestrate the breaking up of this not-quite-affair?"

"Yes." To his credit, he did not hesitate.

"You and I need to play our cards carefully, my accomplice in crime."

Charlotte, Henri, and Bertrand de la Norte leisurely rode to Bois de Boulogne in the warm afternoon. She contemplated enlivening the picnic with a game of throwing knives, but it would be unfair to de la Norte. His courtly skills did not include those valued among cutthroats.

"Who is riding with you?" Father asked.

"M. Bertrand." Charlotte inspected her gloves.

"Ah. The dreamer."

Charlotte still could not read his thoughts as clearly as she could Henri's. "You don't care for him, do you, father?" she asked directly.

"I don't dislike him." His voice was perfectly bland. "Among your admirers, he is the most acceptable contender for your hand. Are you are in love with him?"

Charlotte mulled it over until father's mouth twitched in a mocking grin.

"I do like him." She winced at the lack of conviction in her tone. "He is considerate, thoughtful, honorable -"

"- delusional, unaware of your true self," father helped out.

"Henri suggested introducing him to Charles gradually," Charlotte said defensively.

"God help us. Henri advocated a subtle approach. Was it successful?" Father's intonation had progressed from bland to mocking.

"Not yet." Charlotte slapped the gloves on the table. She felt apprehensive about Bertrand's raised eyebrows upon her choice of milder language, his uneasiness about her frequent visits to the Musketeers' Headquarters, and his pained discomfort when the three of them stopped at the Valiant Fox. She welcomed Bertrand's company, but he would be even less accepting of Charles than Patrice de Seveigney had been.

"Will you abandon Charles for de la Norte?" Father ruthlessly cut straight to the core of the matter. He obviously shared her pessimistic expectations. So did Henri.

"No!" Charlotte felt a mounting frustration upon realizing how little it took to denounce Bertrand de la Norte. "I will never give up Charles."

He thoughtfully regarded her. "A wise decision, my girl, you will never be happy without Charles. You owe yourself the truth. Do not involve yourself with Bertrand de la Norte in any way, unless he truly comprehends who you are and has proven he has accepted Charles. Will you promise me that?"

"Oh, yes, father," Charlotte promised with a vague feeling of reprieve. "Upon my word."

On that beautiful day, Hera pranced more than usual in her eagerness to frolic. Charlotte's attention was focused on holding onto the side saddle – staying on was never a problem when riding astride! This pretense started to grate on her nerves. Why, oh why, was she subjecting herself to the torture of continuously twisting around to see what was happening on her right? Her riding dresses were designed with slits to allow riding astride, and to carry her special dagger on the right, but she had to forgo the dagger in favor of the side saddle. Maybe she should add a hook to the side saddle to hold a sword scabbard?

Bertrand cast worried glances at Hera as the horse snorted and stomped her feet in a more elaborate dance. He moved his hand toward the bridle and Hera bucked and snapped. Charlotte backed Hera off, Hera objected, Charlotte hopped off and ordered her horse to stop her deplorable performance. Henri raised his voice to preclude Bertrand from hearing that monologue. What was her brother thinking? This would be the perfect opportunity to introduce Charles. Hera, seemingly in conspiracy with Henri, firmly planted her hooves on the ground. During Charlotte's tirade to Hera, Bertrand dismounted, but Henri promptly extended his hand and pulled Charlotte back into the saddle before Bertrand had a chance to provoke Hera's wrath again. Hera's snorting was the only sound during a tense pause.

"And that's why de Flancourt advocates renaming this equine Loose Cannon," Henri said.

"Is he back in Paris?" Charlotte heard herself inquiring. That was news to her.

"As of three days ago. He has been pre-occupied." Henri's grin explained his friend's business.

Antoine, out of common politeness, should have sacrificed a few minutes for a brief social visit. He could not possibly spend all his days and nights with whomever it was. "Who is the unfortunate woman?" Charlotte asked.

Bertrand tensed and Henri ignored her question with an apologetic glance at de la Norte. Was Antoine still pursuing Cecilia de Fabvre?

"Are you acquainted with de Flancourt, Mlle. Charlotte?" Bertrand asked.

"When we were children, Henri and I resided in Lyon for months at the time. His parents were our guardians." Why was she compelled to justify her association with him?

"Our first meeting with Antoine and Raoul became part of the family lore," Henri elaborated. "Within moments of their introduction, Charlotte challenged Raoul to compete who could jump farther."

Charlotte felt silent. She could not care less for the indifferent, arrogant, controlling Antoine de Flancourt. She hoped Mme. Cecilia would be disinterested in his advances. The way he had treated Mme. Jeanne in Orleans was shameful and when a couple unlucky women caught his attention during the trip, he looked them over in the same manner he evaluated Hera. He did not measure up to Bertrand de la Norte, and even de Rameau compared favorably to him.

20

UNEXPECTED COURTEOUS BEHAVIOR

NOVEMBER 1718 - PARIS

The Comte de Flancourt is an arrogant, conceited, ruthless and heartless man.

Bertrand de la Norte to Cecilia de Fabvre - 1718

ANTOINE DE FLANCOURT DAWDLED IN PARIS FOR A COUPLE leisurely weeks before departing to Rouen on an errand for Captain d'Ornille. Once there, Antoine promptly forgot his promise to Cecilia de Fabvre to return as soon as his duties allowed. He toured the Cathedral Notre-Dame and the church of St. Maclou despite the frigid weather. Then a very sociable, brown-haired opportunity availed herself to keep him warm and comfortable for a month. To his surprise, her continuous chatter irritated him after only a couple of weeks. He delivered his well-practiced solemn farewell speech, *"We must part because passionate love causes nothing but disasters,"* illustrated his point with examples of Helen of Troy and Paris and Guinevere and Lancelot, and sent the usual parting gift of an ornamental vase. After completing this ritual, he rode back to Paris. Another week passed before Cecilia de Fabvre forgave him for who knows what transgression and allowed their dance to resume. Antoine anticipated a pleasant month ahead. There was no lack of other entertainment - his time was divided between bouts of fencing and tennis matches, attending theater performances, balls, riding, socializing, playing cards at the Valiant Fox tavern, and other similar decorous pursuits.

The Valiant Fox tavern, a card-player's haven and an excellent dining establishment, was conveniently located less than a mile from his new lodgings off the Rue de Temple. On this fine evening, lively cards games commenced between Antoine, de Contraille, de la Norte, d'Chantal, and de Berteau. De la Norte's idealism and naïveté bordered on ridiculous, but his card game had certainly improved. He must have lost a lot of money to Henri de Brangelton. De la Norte seemed more self-assured and more in control, and Antoine had heard the rumors of his active participation in a brawl, again, at Henri de Brangelton's instigation. Maybe the young courtier was on the way to becoming a man. *"I bet de la Norte still could not possibly measure up to Charles."* Antoine smiled to himself at the odd thought.

"Have you yet met a woman to lose your head over, de Flancourt?" de Contraille asked in order to liven up the conversation.

"God forbid!" Antoine exclaimed. "Love is an inconvenience. This is my game." He laid his cards on the table.

De Contraille folded his cards. "Still never dallied with anyone longer that a month?"

"On occasions, the usual female demands pop up even earlier and force me to leave even sooner." Antoine picked up the cards and shuffled, ignoring de la Norte's grimace of distaste. Hopefully, his refined sensibilities would prevent him from repeating this discourse to his sister.

"Have you ever engaged in a philosophical discussion with de Brangelton on this subject?" d'Chantal inquired.

"I have suffered through his extended monologues on this subject," Antoine cheerfully replied.

"Speaking of de Brangelton," d'Chantal slapped de la Norte on the back and winked at others. "I heard you are no longer on speaking terms with de Chassigneau on account of Mlle. de Brangelton?"

"His attention is not welcomed by Mlle. de Brangelton," de la Norte said with an edge.

Antoine almost dropped his cards. Apparently, Wildcat was tamed enough to be presented in society. When did that happen? Was it even possible? Or did she need protection due to her inclinations for a fight?

"I trust you are not contemplating challenging him." De Contraille sounded genuinely concerned.

Antoine put down his goblet of wine. De la Norte recognized and appreciated female charms. Charlotte de Brangelton was no vessel of femininity. Antoine suspected he had drank excessively and had not heard the name correctly. This conversation could not possibly be about his former travel companion.

"Shall we change the subject?" The underlying tension in de la Norte's voice was palpable.

"Beautiful women always cause discord among men," de Berteau retorted. "Don't you agree, de Flancourt?"

"Charlotte de Brangelton?" Antoine knew he made a mistake the moment he spat the name out.

"Are you on a given name basis with her?" de la Norte bristled.

Why did he have to justify his connections to Wildcat?

"She was five years old when we first met. Addressing her formally did not occur to me at that time."

"She is no longer five." De la Norte's objection was lost upon the audience.

"Tell us, de Flancourt, has Mlle. Charlotte always been so beautiful and enchanting?" De Contraille's tone conveyed a warning and a plea.

Antoine felt the familiar sense of bewilderment and exasperation, which had become very common in his dealings with Charlotte and now arose upon the mere mentioning of her name. Was de Contraille reluctant to bring up Charles because he still did not believe that was Henri's sister? Or did de Contraille forget Charles' visit to their fencing school? Unlikely, since he'd talked about it for weeks. Charles was memorable even at that tender age. "Charlotte has always been a lovely and spirited girl," Antoine quoted his mother.

"Is she spirited in the same way as her mother?" D'Chantal's pointed question rendered everyone silent.

Antoine acquired a distinct feeling that he was missing a lot of information about Charlotte. "She will never be offered a Musketeer's commission," he found an ambiguously dismissive answer.

"That was uncalled for." De la Norte's hands gripped the edge of the table.

"What was?" Antoine stared at him in astonishment.

"Besides de Chassigneau... and besides de Vergne... the Musketeer de Rameau also declares his love for Mlle. de Brangelton....too loudly for de la Norte's taste," d'Chantal, de Bearteau, and de Contraille explained in chorus.

Antoine did not know de Chassigneau or de Vergne, but de Rameau had recognized her in Bourges and had acquired his own interpretation of their relationship. From his perspective, Charlotte would be fair play.

"May I ask what her brother has to say about that?" Antoine ventured.

De Contraille answered. "De Brangelton constantly complains about his duty to chaperone his sister."

"Henri de Brangelton chaperoning!" Antoine's laughter bordered on hysterical at the absurdity of such a concept.

"Yes." De Contraille stopped to gulp for air. "We all agree that Mlle. Charlotte's mare is a better chaperone! The animal does not allow anyone to approach Mlle."

Antoine almost fell out of the chair. Only much later in the evening did it occur to him that he should have paid a brief social visit to Mlle. since his return, but what would he say to her? Maybe ask if she still sleeps in her hat?

"I wonder if Mlle. de Brangelton is enjoying her stay in Paris as much as she expected," Antoine said aloud within Armand's hearing distance. The wealth of information followed.

Although it had been only slightly over a month since the Comte and Comtesse brought their daughter to Paris, many men had started to admire Mlle.'s beauty and to value her sharp wit. She favored M. Bertrand de la Norte. She was often seen in his company - with her brother's presence, of course, - although his father detested Mlle., and, the rumor was, the feeling was mutual. M. de la Norte had already warned off M. de Vergne and M. de Chassigneau. Mlle. forbade any arguments on her behalf. Of course, no one dared to displease Mlle. de Brangelton. M. de la Norte was not delighted with M. de Rameau's attention to Mlle. Of course, M. de Rameau was a Musketeer and he did not care for M. de la Norte's opinion, and M. de Rameau claimed that his friendship with Mlle.'s brother allowed him certain privileges, which, in turn, infuriated M. de la Norte.

"Armand, are you talking about the *same* Mlle. Charlotte who traveled with us in September?"

Yes, he was. A week ago, when M. Henri de Brangelton borrowed Armand's service for the evening, M. Henri expected to leave the ball with one of his mistresses (he had two or three). Armand did sneak into the ballroom, although M. Antoine had declined to attend, and the only way Armand had recognized Mlle. de Brangelton was because M. de la Norte stayed at her side. When it was time to leave, M. Henri escorted his sister toward the carriage. She was vexed by her brother's explanation. She did not need an extra footman for her safety because she was Charlotte de Brangelton.

"You know, M. Antoine," Armand finally winded down. "I feel guilty that I did not believe Red Jacques when he informed me that the commander of the garrison in Ferrand was in love with Mlle. de Brangelton."

"Another one?"

"Please forgive me! I would have mentioned it before, but I thought Red Jacques was mistaken! That Captain was determined to marry Mlle. de Brangelton, but she did not care for him."

Antoine poured himself a measure of rum. Armand's information was always accurate, and it corresponded with tonight's conversation. And yet he could not imagine Mlle. de Brangelton as a young beautiful woman. He could not even picture her face. The only images etched in his mind were a reckless grin under a brown hat with a blue feather or measuring, cold, guarded eyes.

Antoine eagerly anticipated the appointed hour with the beautiful Marquise Cecilia de Febvre in Tuileries. He left his lodgings early, stopped by the tennis hall in the Louvre to watch a game, and arrived on time to greet her with all the gallantry he could muster. She took his hand to descend from the carriage and gently leaned her shoulder against his arm when he tucked her hand in the crook of his elbow and complimented her angelic beauty. The ginger-colored hood she wore emphasized the soft glow in her hazel eyes, the matching gloves clung to the contours of her dainty hand, her feet in soft leather boots treaded daintily on the graveled path along the tree-lined path by the Seine, and Antoine was elated. There would be plenty of opportunities to see each frequently; after all, their social paths crossed often.

"I am contemplating inviting you to Comedie de Françoise tonight, M. Antoine."

"I wish you would do so, Mme. Cecilia."

"Call me Cecilia." Her hand tightened around his elbow and her body moved even closer. "It will be a very pleasant night. My brother invited your friend M. Henri de Brangelton and his sister," she continued confidentially. "You know, M. Antoine, my brother is very much in love with Mlle. de Brangelton."

"Is he?" Antoine inquired with polite indifference, wondering once again what de la Norte saw in Charlotte.

"Yes." Cecilia ran her gloved finger along his forearm. "I have never seen Bertrand so infatuated."

The cozy picture of love-stricken de la Norte and Charlotte had an effect similar to a sudden gust of cold air enveloping him. Antoine could not imagine himself entertaining Cecilia de Febvre in Charlotte de Brangelton's presence, enduring Wild-cat's taunting grin - God forbid, if Charlotte perversely decided to help him out! The Marquise did not miss the abrupt change in his mood.

"What is it?" she asked sharply.

"Cecilia," Antoine pronounced in his best reassuring manner. "Henri de Brangelton is a very close friend of mine. I…

I am concerned, my beautiful Cecilia, that unfortunately Mlle. Charlotte finds my company annoying." he improvised.

"It is very noble of you, Comte," she said, her voice slightly chilled, "although surprising."

"Yes, I do not understand myself why would she resent me." Antoine said with as much wounded pride as he could manage while choking a strong desire to express his unflattering opinion about Mlle. Charlotte. He expected Cecilia to reassure him that she could not understand how Mlle. Charlotte could possibly find his company unpleasant, but instead she thoughtfully regarded him while he imagined slapping Charlotte for all the headache she had ever caused him. This noble intention very vividly reminded him of the moment at Ferrand when Charlotte's fist flew up and he barely scrambled away from its trajectory.

Mme. Cecilia subtly distanced herself so she was no longer leaning against him. "Does Mlle. Charlotte enjoy the attention of a certain M. de Rameau? I have heard he has quite a reputation," she said thoughtfully.

"I doubt it," Antoine bit his lip. Explaining Charlotte de Brangelton was not his ideal of a pleasant discourse.

"Indeed." The Marquise completely released her grip on his elbow. "Will you please escort me back to my carriage, Comte de Flancourt?"

Antoine fumed all the way. He had not seen Charlotte de Brangelton for weeks, and yet his life was disordered by her existence. He turned left from the Rue St. Honore to St. Dennis, hurried past the Comte de Tournelles' residence, then came around and knocked at the door, only to discover that no one was answering. The wait sobered him up, and he realized that he had no business discussing anything in his piqued state of mind. He could not comprehend why he was apprehensive about spending an evening with her and Cecilia de Fabvre.

The opportunity of a pleasant affair with Marquise Cecilia evaporated through no fault of his. Paris was not large enough for Mlle. de Brangelton and himself, so Antoine decided to head to Troyes and ride home with Raoul for Christmas Mother would be happy. This plan was destroyed by Henri's father, who proclaimed *"I expect a short trip in December, are you available?"* Antoine committed himself and spent his time wisely cultivating his contacts at the Navy and perusing the records and reports. The formal report by Commandant de Marcoux of the incident in Marseille consisted of a few sentences. *"Shortly after midnight, a gun accidentally discharged on a private ship. Only one shot was fired. Two private ships and three merchant ships erroneously believed they were raided. The retaliation was limited to defensive actions only. Limited property damage reported. No severe injuries. Order restored within four hours. Names of the ship that caused the incident are unknown at this time."* There was no mention of the Marshall cousins, there were no records of an award posted for their capture, and there was no indication of damage claims. The battle in the harbor had been covered up and forgotten.

Antoine and Henri hurried along the Rue St. Honore to meet up with their former tennis game opponents who, having lost, were hosting a drinking event in a - relatively far away, for their thirst – tavern on the Rue St. Roch. Straight ahead, three riders were proceeding along the Rue St. Vincent toward Tuileries. Henri's mother waved at them,. De Rameau, proudly displaying his splendid Musketeer uniform, acknowledged their existence with a curt nod and maneuvered his horse to block their view of a woman in a burgundy cloak. She rode a chestnut-colored horse and the animal pranced a familiar dance. Antoine was astonished to realize that the horse was Hera, and the woman in the side saddle must be Charlotte. He suddenly and very vividly remembered the exchange in Montlucon when Charlotte rode away without a single glance back.

"Do you have another sister besides Charlotte?"

"Why do you ask?"

"What is that nonsense I hear about the beautiful and enchanting Mlle. de Brangelton?"

Henri kept an admirably straight face. "When wrapped in a dress and not discussing fencing techniques or musket accuracy, my sister is a very beautiful young woman. You have not noticed?"

"Does removing the hat make that much difference?"

"None of her admirers met Charles-Raoul-Wildcat-Charlotte. De la Norte lost his head, heart, and reason over her. So did de Rameau, de Chassigneau, and de Vergne,. After that I stopped counting."

Antoine was stunned at this confirmation. "You are not serious. Have the men of Paris gone mad? De la Norte is in love with Wildcat?!"

"De la Norte is truly and desperately in love with Charlotte. Can dreams be passionate and respectful at the same time? Amazingly, so far, she has managed to properly behave in his presence."

The familiar feeling of disbelief enveloped Antoine upon another reference to Charlotte's proper (?!)behavior. His imagination failed at that. "Is she in love with him?"

Henri stopped in the middle of the street. "Help me convince de Rameau of that! Charlotte promised to reciprocate his passion when her Hera sings an opera. Father said that he will not lift a finger to help de Rameau if his bothersome passion provokes Charlotte into violence. Father claimed he lost count how many ardent admirers she nearly skewered. After that disclosure, de Rameau asked for her hand!"

"You are not serious."

"Father laughed. Mother proclaimed she will pray daily to prevent her daughter from committing herself to such a disastrous match. I explained to de Rameau that if Charlotte married him, he would have no time to even look at other women, let alone dream about anything else, and he is still undeterred," Henri complained. "I introduced him to a beautiful, golden-haired, unburdened by intelligence, young, and willing diversion. What more could a man desire?"

"A challenge?" Antoine ventured a guess.

"Yes. De Rameau, in his righteous indignation, delivered a speech to the effect that he was not an inexperienced simpleton, Mlle. Charlotte would never forgive him if he strays, his heart belonged to her, and he was determined to win her love. I shall never repeat all this nonsense to my sister on his behalf, though I might steal some of it for my next conquest. His brilliant eloquence almost convinced me that he had acquired honorable scruples!"

"Maybe he did," Antoine said sarcastically. "Miracles happen."

"Speaking of miracles, de la Norte and de Chassigneau clashed in St. Paul-St. Louis church when both offered her holy water after Sunday mass. These polished courtiers nearly challenged each other right there. My sister had the presence of mind to threaten that she would request Captain d'Ornille to throw both of them in the Bastille if she heard any more, I quote, 'uncivilized threats or violent actions.' They wisely reconciled, at least on the surface," Henri paused. "Just think, Charlotte established peace and order!"

"Enchanting," Antoine muttered.

Bertrand de la Norte woke up in eager anticipation of his ride with Charlotte de Brangelton. However, the feeling of dread, which had settled in his stomach when Antoine de Flancourt spoke her name last evening, had not abandoned him. Upon de Contraille's urging, de Flancourt had provided a vivid account about how he and his brother met Charlotte and her brother for the first time. Bertrand gave no indication that he already knew that tale, but he was caught off-guard by the unexpected glimpses of warmth and even affection in de Flancourt's voice during the narration. Bertrand rolled out of bed, called for his valet, and pushed apart the window curtains. The sun shone brightly with a promise of a beautiful day. Charlotte would be in high spirits, and nothing else mattered.

Henri de Brangelton pointed to his sister's mare. "What is that?"

"Don't you recognize Hera?" Mlle. Charlotte answered with her usual carefree mixture of innocence and challenge.

Her brother frowned. "What happened to the side saddle?"

"Father sold it. Help me up."

Henri held out his hand for his sister. She swung herself in the saddle with a practiced ease, kicked the folds of her skirt out of the way, and pulled the fabric back to cover her legs. She wore breeches and high boots of the Cavalry style. Bertrand was rendered speechless and motionless. Her horse pranced, and the rider balanced in the saddle with an ease of long habit.

"Next, I will convince Captain d'Ornille to approve a Musketeer's commission for me," Charlotte proclaimed.

Bertrand's heart sank. Her brother's face settled in a mask of innocence, the expression as deceiving as a mercenary's piousness.

"A few years ago, I asked to join the regiment, but he refused in no uncertain terms." She held the reins loosely in her hand and steered the horse with her knees. "I resented it, and father had to reconcile uncle Paul and myself."

"Yes, I cannot imagine..." Bertrand faltered. "I mean, you, Mlle. Charlotte, as a Musketeer?"

Her beautiful eyes narrowed. "Don't you agree that a Musketeer's cloak would suit me?"

Bertrand struggled for words. *No, no, no,* he wanted to scream, but he knew that was not the answer she expected.

"Are you appalled at the notion, M. Bertrand?"

"Ah, no, no," he hurriedly and insincerely denied. Charlotte was not deceived. Her mare, sensing the mood of the rider, stomped her forelegs.

"Charlotte, military life means obeying orders. That would never suit you," her brother said, breaking the uncomfortable silence. "Shall we ride to Montmartre Heights today?"

For the rest of the ride, Bertrand managed to control his inner turmoil. His jumbled thoughts and feelings swirled like the fallen leaves underfoot. Charlotte's sudden disregard for convention and acquisition of the men's saddle made him feel dizzy. She was obviously accustomed to riding in this manner. She effortlessly handled her ferocious mare, and that explained why the mare was never trained.

"My father would have fainted if he heard Mlle. Charlotte jest about joining the Musketeer troops," Bertrand said to Henri de Brangelton as soon as they left Mlle. Charlotte at home. "Not to mention the saddle."

For a moment, regret and pity flickered in Henri's eyes. "She is Charlotte de Brangelton," he emphasized the family name. "She takes after our father. She will not change her ways for anything or anyone. De la Norte, you have no idea." He hesitated. "Ask her how she discouraged– how she scared off Patrice de Seveigney!"

"I don't want to know as long as he stays away from her," Bertrand replied.

"Here is my advice to you, de la Norte. Ask her about Charles d'Arringnon."

"No," Bertrand closed his eyes. D'Arringnon was the family name of Charlotte's mother. Charles d'Arringnon was the boy in de Contraille's recollection.

"Don't be a fool." Her brother's countenance was hard, and his face seemed carved in stone. "I guarantee Charlotte will not lie, although I am certain you will not welcome the truth."

No, it cannot be, Bertrand thought later in the evening. Charlotte passing herself for Charles? That must have happened years ago, when Charlotte was just a child. She could not possible measure up to her mother. The Comtesse de Tournelles was a tall, broad-shouldered woman with a formidable reputation. Charlotte was unlike her mother, and if she was... No, Bertrand decided, he did not want to know.

21

BREAKING STRIDE

PARIS - NOVEMBER 1718

I never have a peaceful moment when Charlotte is
around. You are lucky she is not your sister.

Henri de Brangelton to Antoine de la Fleure - 1712

THE RECEPTION HELD BY THE DUKE DE SEVEIGNEY WAS A
notable event. The Comte Antoine de Flancourt arrived early,
which was a highly unusual occurrence for him. To his own
aggravation and amazement, he thought about Charlotte de
Brangelton all day long, feeling strangely disturbed by Henri's
narration. He had felt uneasy since learning that the alluring
vision he had seen yesterday was *that* Wildcat. Antoine vividly
recalled the figure confidently marching with a rogue's swagger
and a sword riding on her side, and he could not imagine Charlotte wearing an evening gown.

Antoine positioned himself by a sculpture of Diana and
idly surveyed the room, uncertain if he would recognize Char-

lotte. A slim female figure dressed in a cornflower-blue English-style dress commanded his attention. She faced away from him, but her lovely neck, small waist (he could encircle it with his hands), and porcelain-white shoulders hinted at youth and exquisite beauty. A young man passionately spoke to her, his eyes shining in admiration. Antoine looked around the ball-room again, but he was drawn to the young slim woman with black hair. There was something familiar about her posture. Had they met before? He would certainly have remembered that graceful incline of the head down and to the side. It appeared she was listened for a sound from behind her, not to the chatter of courtier facing her. A familiar image formed in Antoine's mind - the slightly inclined head, the dark blue eyes shaded by a brown hat, the blue feather fluttering in the breeze. She was the same height as Charlotte, and her un-powdered hair, arranged in a simple style, was just as black. It could not be her. The resemblance was just a coincidence. To prove himself correct, Antoine concentrated on locating Wildcat.

In the center of the room, Henri was entertaining one of his passions and a half-dozen of her friends. Beneath a palm tree planted in a gilded pot, de la Norte, de Contraille, and a dozen courtiers had formed a circle, but no woman in their midst even remotely resembled Charlotte. Half-hidden by a marble column, Cecilia de Fabvre flirted with M. Patrice de Seveigney. Antoine had heard rumors they were lovers few years back. If she cared to rekindle that romance, Antoine did not care. He glanced around again, gave up his futile search for Charlotte, and gawked at the slim figure across the room. The man blocked her way. She feigned a step to the left and slid past the man like a fencer would, with the speed and grace worthy of a finely honed, quick and decisive fencing maneuver. The man reached for her arm. She twirled around and, with a deceptive appearance of playfulness, shoved him away with her extended arm. She skillfully bore her weight behind the move, and he staggered backwards upon the impact. Antoine's heart leapt upon that instantaneous glimpse of her face with the high cheekbones and glowing eyes. She completed the twirl and sauntered away, and the skirts alluringly swayed with her steps. Her movements were unrestricted; her corset must be loosely tied. The neckline of her dress was modestly, even prudishly high.

Antoine found himself following Charlotte, but stopped the moment de la Norte caught up with her. She turned her head to greet de la Norte with a heartbreakingly affectionate smile, put her arm through the bend of his elbow, and he led her away.

It had been a long time since Antoine de Flancourt was last knocked unconscious, but he remembered a feeling of disorientation afterwards, and he experienced the same feeling now, courtesy of Charlotte de Brangelton. She was indeed a very beautiful young woman, very much a woman, a very fine, attractive woman, and no one in his right mind would mistake her for a young man. De la Norte was not daft. De Rameau was not deceived. De Boucher noticed it years ago. De Brault recognized it. Antoine was no wiser than Raoul.

Outside, Antoine leaned against a cool marble column and gazed at the bright silver moon. She could not be the same Charlotte who had planned the trip to Paris by herself as a young man. She could not be Wildcat who almost obliged him with a black eye upon their meeting. She could not be the same Charlotte who called herself Raoul for two weeks and no one ever suspected she was a woman. She could not be the same Charlotte who, without any hesitation, stood by his side and drew her sword against the officers at Red Boar Inn. She could not be the same Charlotte whose swearing was up to the high standards of her father. She could not be the same Charlotte who shared the room with him ... and only now Antoine realized that, for two weeks, he had never paid any attention to her. He never pressed for the answer why she was anxious to ride Paris, but now he understood. The reason for her determination was named Bertrand de la Norte. Antoine shivered from the chilly air. Maybe he was lucky that she had kept the hat on. Otherwise, he could not have touched her without marrying her. He was not an accommodating, spineless Bertrand de la Norte. Damn him, no matter how she felt about de la Norte, there was no reason for Charlotte to completely ignore Antoine. After all, they grew up together. Antoine returned to the ballroom and found himself face-to-face with Henri de Brangelton.

"What is wrong? Have you fallen off a horse?"

"That is not an aspiring cutthroat Musketeer over there!"

Henri shook him by the shoulders. "Yes, it is. She still dreams of joining the regiment. Or sailing the Spanish Main. She is Charlotte de Brangelton. My insane sister. Wildcat. Raoul. Charles. You know her as well as I do. When the hat goes on, the common sense disappears. Your sudden admiration frightens me. I am staring to think that dealing with Charles is easier!"

"How does she manage to pass for Charles?"

"Years of practice in belligerent behavior." Henri handed him a glass of wine. "You and I contributed to that fine skill by encouraging her rivalry with Raoul."

"I cannot possibly imagine de la Norte's delight upon meeting Charles."

"De la Norte has not had the honor – pardon, horror – of dealing with Charles yet."

"De la Norte just might faint when it happens," Antoine spat out. "I wish to witness that encounter."

"I hope to be miles away from it, and even further from the

aftermath of that disaster. De Rameau will be more than willing to take his place."

"Take his place exactly where?" Antoine knew that he should have refrained from such an inquiry, but his speech was ahead of his reason. "In her heart or her bed?"

"My murderous sister will not allow anyone within a cannon shot of her bed until after marriage," Henri said confidently.

Oddly, Antoine felt elated at that.

Across the room, Charlotte absent-mindedly tossed her fan from hand to hand, each toss making a wider and higher arc, and each movement reflecting in the high window behind her. The Marquise de Fabvre used her fan more conventionally and fanned herself. Charlotte tossed the fan straight up and grabbed it sideways. She innocently looked at her stunned audience, lowered the fan in a deliberate manner, the same way she would move the sword in a perfect arc, and saluted with it to everyone's stunned silence. De la Norte helplessly gaped at such a breach of refinement.

"At least, she did not throw the fan at anyone's head," Henri commented. "This time."

"Maybe she will throw the fan at de la Norte's head," Antoine thought. That evening, his dislike for Bertrand de la Norte intensified tenfold.

Charlotte was a graceful dancer. Antoine recollected the dancing lessons in Lyon, when Charlotte and Raoul made a game of tripping each other over while practicing dance moves, and she even extended her efforts of mayhem when dancing with Antoine and Henri. The room warmed up when his mind resurrected the scene of himself tumbling along with a laughing Charlotte. *"Her dancing is as fine as her swordsmanship,"* Antoine reminded himself to whip his thoughts into the orderly route. He very much yearned to ask Charlotte, in de la

Norte's presence, if she had dueled with any military officers lately. He was unable to stop himself from devotedly watching Charlotte (who was ignoring his presence), and he was at a loss about what course of action to take. It was a painfully familiar situation for a completely different reason. He resented every step of her dance. When the music ended, her current partner M. Patrice de Seveigney remained by her side and held her hand. Apparently, he had confused her with Cecilia de Fabvre. Charlotte's shoulders squared, she held up the palm of her hand, and M. Patrice's amorous enthusiasm was immediately dampened by a comment Charlotte made. Charlotte freed her hand, motioned toward the other side of the room, sent him away, turned her head, and smiled at Antoine. To his own surprise, he realized he was hurrying across the room toward her.

"Charlotte de Brangelton." Antoine raised her hand to his lips and kissed it. Her eyes slightly widened when his fingers caressed the patch of skin on her palm roughened by hours of handling the sword hilt.

"Antoine de Flancourt." She wore a bracelet displaying the de Brangelton Coat of Arms - the golden leopard's head was suspended between the burgundy and black enamel links, and the ruby eyes seemed to wink at him from her wrist. "Stop staring." Her voice was flat, but her dark blue eyes twinkled with pleasure.

"I am not." Antoine stopped himself from arguing the obvious. "Pardon me for repeating what every man in Paris must have stated, but you are beautiful. Must be the absence of your hat," he corrected himself.

Charlotte's quick glance from under her eyelashes could render a man senseless even more effectively than a punch in the head. "More beautiful than insane, or the other way around?" she asked.

"Charles is insane. Charlotte is beautiful. Who is the real Mlle. de Brangelton?"

"It depends on when and where."

Antoine almost asked why he had the headache of dealing with Charles when everyone else had had the pleasure of Charlotte's company, but caught himself in time. "I hear de Rameau is praying for Hera to sing," he said instead.

"I am praying Hera will never produce a single note for I have made too many promises I do not intend to keep." A familiar, reckless, taunting grin flashed on her face.

"May I ask what promises you made to de la Norte?"

Her eyes took a familiar, guarded expression. "May I ask what the Marquise de Fabvre has to say about it?"

"Will de la Norte will value your swordsmanship and your other manly skills?" Antoine heard himself suddenly announcing what he was thinking.

He relished the guilt in Charlotte's narrowed eyes. "That is none of your business."

"Of course. I apologize. May I ask you, Mlle., if you have ever attempted to punch him?"

"May I point out to you, Comte, that he has never threatened to break my arm." Charlotte matched his tone.

"May I ask you, Mlle., if you ever crossed swords with any Lieutenants in his presence?"

"May I point out to you, Comte, that he never threatened to knock me out?" Charlotte reverted to her finest manners and exhibited the familiar, cold, defiant glow.

"May I ask if you ever pretended to be his brother?"

"May I point out that he never choked me?"

"May I ask if you ever provoked him?!" The pain in Antoine's upper lip signaled that, as commonly happened in conversations with her, he had nearly lost his temper.

Charlotte clenched her fists and glared at him. "Stop provoking me!"

"Fortunately for me, you are at a disadvantage due to the bounds of genteel behavior," Antoine reminded her.

Charlotte muttered a few improper words about it.

"You could challenge me for a fencing round," he proposed and his anger faded away at the conspiratory gleam in her eyes.

"My depressingly good behavior has not forced me into embroidery. Henri, or father, or mother regularly rides with me to the Bois de Boulogne to practice. Don't challenge me, Comte, unless you mean it," she added in her deepened voice.

"I am at your service, Charles. When?" Why was he so easily coerced into associating with Charles?

"Henri and I are planning such an outing tomorrow."

"Where and when shall I meet you?"

"At Porte Maillot, ten o'clock. Just keep it a secret, will you?" Charlotte asked.

"You know you can trust me with your secrets. Besides, no one would believe it, anyway." Antoine wanted to caress her fine neck and naked shoulders. "I am having troubles myself."

Charlotte glanced behind him and subtly took a little step away to distance herself. He did not bother to turn around. Maybe the renewed demonstration of her fencing skills would bring back his sanity.

"Comte de Flancourt," de la Norte formally greeted him. "Mlle. Charlotte, you promised me the next dance."

"Of course, M. Bertrand." Charlotte took his outstretched hand. "Excuse me, M. Antoine." She suddenly behaved in a formally polite and prim manner.

"Of course, Charlotte." Antoine formally bowed. De la Norte cringed at his familiarity of address, but she firmly pulled him away.

Antoine again walked outside and leaned against the same cool marble column. "What am I doing?" he asked himself. "I am chasing an untamable young woman who does not care for me. I cannot have an affair with her. I know better. I know *her*. She is in love with de la Norte. He is a decent man, and will blindly follow her commands and whims. Maybe he can even find the nerve to stand up to his father. Do not ruin it for her," he ordered himself. "I should leave Paris now, but I made a commitment to her father," he debated with himself. "If she marries de la Norte, maybe it will be easier for me to forget about the happily married Charlotte de la Norte." This notion evoked the feeling of fury and distress in his heart. Antoine left the ball shortly after, in a gloomy mood. He woke up a dozen times that night, tossing and turning before falling asleep again. His treasonous dreams continuously brought images of Charlotte through the years: Charlotte running across the yard, shrieking with delight upon being the first to set her footprints across the freshly fallen snow; Charlotte curled asleep in the chair in his father's library; Charlotte fearlessly jumping off the fence into his arms; Charlotte's shadow on the ground when she dried herself after a swim in the river while he, Raoul, and Henri sat with their backs to her; Charlotte singing off-key during their wanderings in the woods, Charlotte's face shadowed by the hat, riding at his side during their trip from Ferrand. Finally he heard Henri's comment that *"She likes de la Norte."* He rose with a hollow feeling of abandonment and disappointment.

"I see Charles wasted no time in recruiting you," Henri greeted Antoine the next morning. "Don't allow it go to your head."

"Of course it will. I believe I am the only man, outside Mlle. de Brangelton's immediate family, who has the honor to fence with her, to sort through her impressive repertoire of profanities, and to participate with her in brawls with military men." Antoine tipped his hat to Charlotte. She wore her black-and-gold trimmed burgundy cloak, the hood stylishly framed her face, but the sturdy black boots and the riding gloves were of men's fashion. They rode into the Bois de Boulogne to find a clearing suitable for fencing practice. It did not take long. The park held many hidden small arenas for more malicious forms of exercise.

Charlotte accepted Antoine's help to dismount. "I miss Charles," she confided. "I miss my hat, my sword, and my saddle. I miss playing cards, and everything else you two have freedom to enjoy. Almost everything," she added with a sly grin at her brother before noticing the package he carried. "Why did you bring a blanket to a fencing outing?"

"I am taking the opportunity to catch up on my sleep while you fence with Antoine," her brother explained.

"Cybille and Gabrielle are wearing you out?" Charlotte asked.

"Cybille, Gabrielle, and Eloise," Henri corrected her.

"Who is Eloise? Two passions are not adequate for you anymore?" Charlotte vocalized the sentiment Antoine completely shared.

"She is a beautiful woman with golden locks who preferred me over de Rameau. He bleated that I could not handle three affairs at the same time, and I had to take up the challenge. Besides, Cybille is *finally* nearing the end of her forbearance for me." Henri yawned and looked around in search for a flat dry place to lay down.

Charlotte snatched his hat, pushed the hood back, and jauntily placed the hat on her head. She adjusted it over the pulled-up hair, and her face became shaded in the usual manner. She untied the cords of her cloak and Antoine removed the cloak off her shoulders, forgetting the hat and the reason for their outing until Charlotte pulled the sword carefully concealed in a custom sheath out from under the side of the saddle. "Shall we?"

She did not court any chance of misunderstanding. No fine feminine behavior in his company; such was the legacy of comradeship gained during shared childhood. Although the thought bothered him, Antoine managed to convince himself that it suited him just fine. Away from de la Norte and the constraints of society, with a sword in her hand and the hat on her head, Charlotte was behaving in her usual fine manner, and they parted with an agreement to meet again on Tuesday.

De Rameau finally succeeded in persuading Charlotte to accept his persistent, long-standing invitation for a romantic stroll in the vast Park de Vincennes, and Henri was committed to dutifully chaperoning his sister and her ardent misguided admirer. Granted, Charlotte was intelligent, but de Rameau possessed years of experience and viewed her as a challenge to conquer. Henri suppressed a shiver of disgust at the concept of Charlotte's marriage to his womanizing friend. Henri mumbled unflattering words about de la Norte, who allowed Charlotte to intimidate him, then felt sorry for Bertrand since Henri himself would have no clue how to deal with her either.

"If your purpose in life to make me happy," Charlotte declared, "find yourself another object of everlasting affection."

Excellent suggestion, dear sister, do continue in this vein.

"And then, adorable Mlle. Charlotte, you will throw the unjust accusation at me that I never loved you," de Rameau dismissed her rant.

"I hope you will have no time to annoy me." Charlotte kicked a small pebble into an iron bench and the sound reverberated in the chilly air. "Find yourself a couple objects of your devoted affection, and you will leave no room for me in your thoughts and heart."

Henri relished the exasperated look in his friend's eyes. Adorable?

"Then again, why don't you match your friend passion by passion?" Charlotte gestured in Henri's direction while de Rameau struggled with substantially less tender emotions.

"You fell behind my brother in your womanizing reputation. Can you handle the pressure of four passions, Monsieur de Rameau?" She threw the figurative gauntlet.

De Rameau wisely chopped off the forthcoming verbal flow of uncomplimentary epithets and stepped close to her. Henri marveled at Charlotte's firm stance and her readiness to draw a dagger.

De Rameau had the presence of mind to secure the hilt of his sword with his hand before softly hissing, "I will take this challenge only if you are the reward."

Henri marveled at the magnitude of that blunder on de Rameau's part. Was he beyond reason in desperation? Luckily for him, there was no room for Charlotte to throw a punch, but there was no barrier to her oratory abilities.

"Go to hell," she answered.

"Is this what you said to de Flancourt, Mlle. Charlotte?"

Charlotte made an indeterminate sound, halfway between a choked exclamation and a growl. The air was cold, and the cloud of her breath brought the image of a dragon to Henri's mind.

"That would explain why he no longer tolerates your delightful company." De Rameau took advantage of the next tense moment, swiftly leaned forward, and firmly kissed her on the lips without touching her otherwise. Henri was rendered motionless by the shock of surprise at de Rameau's audacity.

Charlotte kicked him in the knee and her arm shot out for the punch.

De Rameau grunted in pain, but he managed to jerk his head aside. Her fist barely missed his cheekbone. His hat flew off and bounced off the bench. He reached for her, but Charlotte twisted away from his outstretched arms. Henri held his sister across the shoulders to restrain her, tightly gripped her right wrist to prevent her from utilizing her dagger, lifted Charlotte off the ground, and pulled her back.

"Do not ever provoke her," he advised de Rameau over his shoulder. "This is the first and last time I am saving your hide." He clasped his hand firmly over his sister's mouth when she freely expressed her feelings toward de Rameau, his passion, and his actions. No need to provoke the man to violence.

"Maybe you, de Brangelton, could explain to de Flancourt–" De Rameau was undeterred.

"Leave. Or I will allow her to run her sword through your shoulder," Henri threatened. Struggling with his sister to prevent her from committing a murder and containing his joy at her fury toward de Rameau was enough of a challenge for the day.

To alleviate the boredom, Charlotte sorted out the tangle of ribbons and inspected the blade on the boot knife. She even perused the pamphlet on fashionable styles and absent-mindedly peered out of the window. For some odd reason, thoughts of Antoine de la Fleure, Comte de Flancourt crowded her mind. A knock at the door was not welcome either. She was in no mood to receive any visitors – God forbid, it could be de Rameau again. He had made a spectacle of himself the day before when he showed up, dropped to his knees, apologized profusely, vowed that he had lost his mind in desperation, and creatively handed her his sword to run him through if she was still displeased with him. Her father ordered him to stop emitting such nonsense and threatened to pour a bucket of water over him, and father's unceremonious intervention checked de Rameau's passion for an hour. But today, no one besides herself was home, and she would be cornered. Uncle Paul would be upset if she ran a sword through one of his Musketeers in cold blood, but if she continued to engage in such scruples, de Rameau could try to kiss her again. The front door closed. Red Jacques brought in a plainly wrapped package, handed it to her, and left without a word.

Charlotte suspiciously inspected the package. Small attentive gifts from Bertrand de la Norte were wrapped with ribbon and sealed with the de la Norte family crest stamp and a note attached to it. De Vergne limited his tribute to flowery sonnets written on apricot-colored paper; he sealed his masterpieces and wrote her name in fancy lettering on the outside. De Rameau delivered candied fruit in person. De Chassigneau occasionally sent her unobjectionable trinkets, but this package was much heavier and a larger size. She tossed it from hand to hand, and felt through the wrapping. There was something familiar about the weight and feel. Charlotte carefully cut through the wrapping with her boot knife. She ran her fingers over the soft brown leather of the elegant but practical sword shoulder strap, adorned with a simple pattern in blue embroidery. Who would buy it for her? Puzzled, she unrolled the strap and found a note tucked into the gilded buckle.

"Charlotte de Brangelton, I believe the colors of this sword shoulder strap perfectly match your favorite travel hat. Antoine de Flancourt."

He was the only man, outside of her family, to buy her such a gift, and it probably cost more than any ornamental vase.

Charlotte sat down at the writing table and labored to compose the appropriate note of gratitude.

"Antoine de Flancourt, the colors of my new exquisite sword shoulder strap indeed perfectly matches my favorite travel hat. Charlotte de Brangelton."

Charlotte sent Red Jacques to deliver the note, carried the shoulder strap into her bedroom, and hung it on the peg under her hat. "I will never give up my sword, not for anyone, not even him," she muttered to herself. Upon that revelation, Charlotte launched the wooden bowl containing newly sorted ribbons against the wall and watched the contents drift and scatter all over the floor. "This is not a gift from an admirer. It is a devious way to challenge me to introduce Charles to Bertrand de la Norte," she confided to her reflection.

22

CHILL IN DECEMBER

PARIS – DECEMBER 1718

*Few people succeed in suppressing the undesirable
traits of their character. Even fewer succeed in
cultivating the better ones. More often than not,
their true character comes through, and usually at
the least opportune time and with quite disastrous
results.*

Francis de Brangelton to Paul d'Ornille – 1705

ON A CHILLY WINTER EVENING, CHARLOTTE RODE IN THE
carriage with Bertrand de la Norte and Cecilia to the theater.
Cecilia invited the Comte de Bearteau and Mme. Gabrielle to
the private box, and d'Chantal invited himself. Charlotte
invited de Bonnard upon Cecilia's encouragement, and de
Contraille completed their group. Cecilia engaged d'Chantal
and de Contraille, de Bearteau and de Bonnard entertained
Gabrielle, and no one paid any attention to Charlotte and

Bertrand. They sat close together in the overcrowded box and leaned close to converse. The play was a loud farce and the wine was flowing freely. The aristocratic life did afford fine entertainment.

When the curtain fell at the end of the play, Cecilia and Gabrielle sailed away with men in tow, and Bertrand held out his hand for Charlotte. He pulled her up and into the shadows of the box's curtains.

"Mlle. Charlotte." He raised her hand to his lips. "I am in love with you."

Charlotte, surprised by the sudden declaration, did not realize that she returned his gentle squeeze of her hand.

"I have the most honorable intentions." His voice was tense with sincere emotion. They were alone, and Charlotte must have smiled at his earnestness, since he took it as encouragement, embraced her, and leaned forward for a light kiss on her lips. Charlotte did not object. She liked Bertrand and the tender touch of his lips tracing a path down her neck. His fingers caressed her cheek, and he kissed her on the mouth, with more passion than she had expected. Charlotte gently pushed him back. To his credit, he immediately released her.

"I will ask my father's blessing to marry you," he promised with fervor.

Charlotte put her hand into the crook of his elbow and propelled him outside. It was indecorous for the two of them to linger alone in the theater box.

On the ride home, Cecilia chatted about the play. If she noticed her brother's high color, she had enough tact to overlook it, but the inconvenient truth of the situation highly alarmed Charlotte. At her door, Bertrand helped her down the steps and very properly kissed her hand. Thankfully, he could not leave Cecilia in the carriage and follow Charlotte inside.

Charlotte acknowledged to herself that she was guilty of

inadvertent but enormous deceit. Bertrand was in love with a shallow image, a pretense, a public picture of a genteel noble woman who did not exist. He was a kind and decent man, but her duplicitous behavior had misled him into a delusion of love. A peevish voice with Lyonnaise inflections intruded in her mind: *"He will resent Charles."* Charlotte paced around the room. *"Maybe he will not mind Charles,"* she argued with the devil's advocate inside her head. *"When snowdrifts pile up in hell a dozen times,"* the derisive voice said. That was the same time frame in which Bertrand's father would allow him to marry her. Only a naïve mind like Bertrand's could nurture that dream, but that left them where? Did she want to marry him?

When the *"no"* answer sprung to her mind, Charlotte sat down to unpin her hair. Bertrand would have to defy his father for her. She could not, in good faith, expect him to sacrifice his family ties for her, and she did not want that sin to weigh on her soul.

She slowly untied the ribbons and her hair fell down around her shoulders. She brushed it forward. From inside the mirror, Charles sneered. Charlotte's eyes fell onto her hat. She twisted to untie her dress laces. Did she love Bertrand enough to marry him? What was love?

"I knew that I would follow your father to hell and beyond," mother had answered this question.

"I knew Louis and I were destined for each other since I was twelve years old," Mme. Constance had said.

"I could not resist his smile," Henrietta de Paulet had babbled about her handsome, but hare-brained husband.

"He is so brave and strong and smart," Eliza de Paulet had enthusiastically prattled about her rather average specimen of manhood.

"I would not have married anyone else," Antoine's mother had declared.

With a sinking feeling in her stomach, Charlotte leaned forward to unlace her dressy shoes. What were her feelings toward Bertrand? He was indeed intelligent, handsome, and honorable, but Charlotte was well aware of his insecurity, his tendency to brood in philosophical musings, and his romantic views. She did not mind his kisses, but beyond that... Would he travel, in good faith, with Charles to the New World? Or even to Venice or London? Patrice de Seveigney had imagined himself in love with her, until that infamous fencing match. There were buds of chivalrous conduct even on Antoine de la Fleure's part, which had disappeared after the fencing outing. Oh, yes, Antoine knew Charles very well.

Charlotte kicked the shoes off her feet. It was time to eliminate de Rameau's nauseating persistence, de Chassigneau's irritating presence, and de Vergne's pathetic endeavors to seduce her. A sword in her hand would send de Chassigneau and de Vergne running, and might even affect de Rameau. It would also convince Bertrand de la Norte that his heart had erred.

On the road to Paris – December 1718

On this bright, snow-covered morning, Paris lay ten white miles ahead on a surprisingly clear road. Francis, Henri, and Antoine rode as fast as the conditions allowed. Francis felt as elated as his young cohorts. He glanced at his son with a healthy dose of paternal satisfaction. Henri had carefully cultivated the image of a light-headed womanizer, and used it to his advantage. He might be perpetrating this myth on purpose or subconsciously for his own benefit, Francis realized. He lacked subtlety, but, when Henri bothered to apply his practical mind, shrewdness, and decisiveness, he achieved moments of greatness. Henri managed his cross-dealing affair with Cybille very efficiently. Henri made no secret that he preferred his other, light-minded passions, so there was no danger of Henri acquiring a taste to combine business and pleasure. That was a dangerous road to follow, unless, of course, both man and woman had the same goals. *"Overall, I am proud of my son, heir, etc,"* Francis dismissed his philosophical foray and turned his ear toward the young men's conversation.

"... rotate them in order, and entertain in the same manner," Henri was saying. "If I take Cybille to Pont Neuf, it's unlikely she will be there the next couple days when I take Gabrielle and then Eloise."

"Quite a military drill. What will happen when one of them shows up unexpected?" Antoine was a fine young man with occasional lapses into sins of misplaced scruples or inconvenient honorable notions, just like his father.

"Blame my sister, of course!"

Antoine seemed at a loss. "Will you ask Charlotte to concoct an explanation for you?"

"No, I prefer to keep Charlotte out of my affairs. She tends to entertain herself by wreaking havoc with my passions. My noble excuse is that I must chaperone my inexperienced sister - she is so young, don't you know, she has not mastered the art of flirting yet?"

The sarcasm was lost on Antoine. "She mastered it just fine in de la Norte's company."

"She barely mustered the willpower to contain her cursing," Henri complained. "And it lasted only a month. What is more likely to happen, father - you sail to the moon, your daughter abstains from swearing for the whole day, you concur she is insane, or she will be married?"

"Married to whom?" Francis asked.

"The only decent man in her entourage is Bertrand de la

Norte," his son informed him.

Antoine threw Henri a murderous glance.

"Unlike you, I would rather see her marry de Rameau," Francis added oil to the fire.

"What?!" Henri and Antoine exclaimed in chorus.

"At least, de Rameau should be able to keep up with Charles."

"You are not serious!" Antoine accused him.

"De Rameau is just as worthless as Patrice de Seveigney!" Henri uttered a profound statement.

"Patrice de Seveigney?" Antoine abandoned his pretenses.

"My sire incited my juvenile sister to terrify M. Patrice out of his limited wits," Henri complained. "My sire does not think any man in his right mind is worth his precious daughter."

"Certainly not de Rameau or de Seveigney or de la Norte!" Antoine offered his unsolicited assessment.

"And since we are debating the worthlessness of your sister's matrimonial prospects, should we include de Vergne and de Chassigneau in the lists?" Francis asked.

Antoine almost contributed his opinion, but closed his mouth before any words escaped, and tactfully steered his horse behind, but failed to remove himself out of hearing distance.

"What do you plan for her, father?" Henri asked. "You know that old goat will disown his son if said son marries your daughter, so you will never have to deal with him! Bertrand de la Norte is an honorable, intelligent, valiant man. He will never dare to contradict Charlotte and she will do anything she pleases. This man is a saint!" Henri stopped to catch his breath.

Francis locked his eyes with his son whose spine tightened, but Henri defiantly held his look. A fine young man indeed, with only occasional moments of obtuseness.

"Are you finished spewing this nonsense?" Francis inquired

with exaggerated calmness.

"Obviously, yes. Why waste more effort?" Henri barked back and dropped his head into his hands. "You are worse than Charles." He fell back to ride with Antoine.

Antoine's hands tightly gripped the reins. "What happened with de Seveigney?" he asked after a prolonged pause.

Paris – December 1718

"I no longer can tolerate the continuous declarations of love by de Rameau, the machinations by de Chassigneau, and the sonnets by de Vergne." Charlotte was distressed by the amount of notes from Bertrand de la Norte. She hoped his love would not develop in an obsession. He begged her forgiveness of his absence due to the demands of the season in Court, he was consumed by his family's commitments and obligations, etc. Bertrand must have asked his father for permission to marry her, and, reading between the lines, Charlotte surmised that Bertrand hoped his obedient execution of his duties would pacify his father. Charles should present himself before Bertrand confronts the old goat.

Mother acknowledged her remark with a nod, but continued to read.

"Why do women indulge in love affairs?"

Mother's head sharply turned in her direction. "Did de Rameau inspire you to ask this question?"

"It is probably the only excitement available to them," Charlotte reflected.

Mother closed her book. "The acceptable entertainment activities include gentle promenades, occasional riding, playing music, embroidery, visiting each other to gossip, purchasing new outfits, maintaining beauty regimens, dining, balls, outings to theater and church, and doubtless many more. I am exhausted by these listings, indeed, how does anyone find time for household duties, let alone affairs?"

Charlotte chuckled. "Do not reprimand me, Henri d'Arringnon, that I followed your path and have forsaken music, embroidery, and gossiping about men for fencing!"

"I read books and engaged in correspondence while you, Charles, added card playing to your repertoire." Mother crossed herself in her most theatrical manner. "God help me. My de Brangelton girl is wallowing in boredom and searching for entertainment. What shall I do with her?"

"The weather is nice." Charlotte glanced toward the beam of sunshine peeking through the departing clouds. "We could ride out to meet father and Henri on the road." And Antoine.

Mother looked outside of the window and placed her book on the shelf. "I am committed to accompanying Duchess Helene on a brief trip to Versailles."

"Can I go as Charles? When?" Charlotte jumped up in excitement. She no longer cared for anyone's opinion or passion. She yearned to don her man's clothes, put on her hat, strap on her sword, and to revel in precious freedom.

The soft, shimmering blanket of freshly fallen snow covered the ground and the roofs, clung to the walls and fences, and wrapped around the tree branches. The white snow shrouded the Sun King's statue with a sparkling mantle, concealed the dirt and grime of the city streets, and hushed the horses' neighs and brisk human voices. The opaque winter air hung like a veil, and the pale winter sun caressed the layers of pristine white. The sharp contrast between bright whiteness and the dark and muted colors of buildings, the quiet, and the stillness made the city a fanciful woodcut. The sharp sound of the bell striking the hour resonated in the crisp air. Hera softly snorted steam out of her nose and stomped her hooves in eager anticipation of a trip. Charlotte took off the glove and patted the horse's warm neck. Duchess Helene's small entourage, under the expert command of M. Henri d'Arringnon, finally set out from the Place de Victories, crossed the Pont Neuf over the iced Siene, weaved through the quiet streets, cleared the city gate, and finally reached the open road to Versailles. M. Henri d'Arringnon assigned Charles to lead their group, and mother fell back to quietly converse with Her Grace. The snow fell for the most of the night and no one ventured out this early for pleasure, so the only traffic was a stream of peasants, workers, and peddlers to and from the city. They made excellent time.

The court was no longer located in Versailles, but official business was still conducted there. The palace and the gardens were guarded, maintained, and visited. Charles, armed with a descriptive pamphlet and his formal position of a courier in Dowager Duchess de Seveigney's service, was granted complete freedom to roam the most glorious royal residence in the world. Charlotte stood in the center of the echoing Marble Courtyard. Here, under the watchful eye of the Sun King, hunting and boating parties gathered, troops held their exercises, courtiers conspired, and ambassadors arrived and departed. Is this why the King, with so much power and wealth, had chosen the apartments facing this stony hub? She squinted at the overcast skies. The courtyard faced south-east. The sun peeked in only in the morning, before anyone awoke. Charlotte began her indoors tour in the luxurious Apollo salon. She dutifully studied the paintings, examined the frescos, viewed the gold ornaments, and marveled at the eerily real marble sculptures. She explored the Mars room before moving on to the Venus room. Then her eyes and mind could no longer distinguish one extravagant image from another. Near-permanent dizziness settled in. Mars and Venus looked like twins in their ostentatious robes among the lush surroundings. Charlotte left the visual overabundance for the peace of the somber winter palette of the expansive gardens. The fountains were silent. The only sounds were the chirps of birds and the crunching of snow under her feet. Neptune and his sea horses wore white puffy mantles, and the wisps of snow fell from the bare tree branches when a bird or a squirrel hustled along. Charlotte followed a trail of deer tracks to Colonnade, roamed along the symmetrical snow mounds covering the hedges, read a story of a fox's successful hunt recorded by the paw prints in soft mud among scattered feathers, and reached the Grand Canal. Charlotte imagined boats sliding along the water, but wondered if the enjoyment of such parties was poisoned by the excessive formalities, venom, envy, idleness, hypocrisy, and mindlessness of the Sun King's Court. Now, the Court was ruled by the Regent Duke d'Orleans. The times were merry and wild, but no one could foresee what Louis XV's reign would bring. The denizens of the New World had the right idea to carry themselves off as far from royal reach as achievable. It was fortunate that her uncle Batiste, her aunt Violette, her maternal grandfather, and her uncle Richard resided in the New World.

Charlotte's nose and cheeks tingled from the wintry air. She rubbed her face and returned to the terrace for a view of the vast gardens. She entered the famous Hall of Mirrors and stopped breathless in that grand room of glass, gold, and crystal. What a place for fencing practice! Diffused light, deceiving multiple angles... She squared her shoulders, drew her sword, and paused to study Charles' image in the mirror. She felt strangely detached from the non-descript young man staring back at her with a feral expression. What did others – namely, young men of her close acquaintance - see? Henri's words, echoed by Antoine and Raoul, haunted her mind: *"No man in his right mind will tolerate Charles. Think of the de Paulet brothers, de Clouet, the de la Fleure brothers, de Seveigney, de Contraille...*" Charlotte stepped back, drew an imaginary circle in the air with her sword, and sharply sliced it in vertical and horizontal lines.

"From this day forward, the young men of my close acquaintance will be positioned within these fencing quadrants," she announced into the emptiness around her.

"High Outside – those that pursue Charlotte because they have not met Charles. De Chassigneau." She delivered a sharp pass, followed with an additional one for de Vergne, and moved to the next mirror.

"Low Outside – those that resent Charles, although they lapse into pursuing Charlotte. De Rameau, de Seveigney and de Molienier." Charlotte brought the sword point straight toward the mirror until its reflection converged into a single point. She held the position, then executed a perfect lunge and two repeats for good measure. She saluted to her image and stepped to the next mirror.

"Low Inside – those who do not care for Charles." A simple thrust forward sufficed for this group. "De Chassigneau, de Vergne, de Seveigney, de Molienier, and de Rameau have lingered between High Inside and Low Inside for an excruciatingly long time. It's high time they permanently decamp here."

She moved on. "High Inside - friends of Charles. De Contraille, d'Signac, de Rousard, Raoul de la Fleure." Charlotte stumbled as Antoine's name leapt to her mind. "Friendship and resentment with occasional forays into love of Charlotte?" Her image in the mirror froze.

The fencing outings with Antoine occurred twice-a-week unless the weather conspired against them. On other days, he showed up at the doorstep to play cards, or to join her and either one of her parents for an errand. Their paths crossed at all social outings. In fact, Charlotte spent more time with Antoine than with Henri and Bertrand de la Norte combined.

Charlotte sheathed her sword, hurried to the next mirror, and exercised her imagination to picture the crowds of courtiers within this magnificent hall, every one waiting for the Sun King to notice them, all of them entertained on royal expense, and being discreetly served by legions of servants. She thought about the upcoming Regent's New Year ball at Palais Royal. All the noble families in France would be represented. *Bertrand de la Norte will definitely spend a significant amount of time at his father's side,* Charlotte thought. *Mercifully, de Rameau will be on duty, and Henri will alternately attach himself to his passions.* She would have to deal with de Vergne and de Chassigneau. Charlotte marched to the next mirror. *"Charles, my friend, I will never forsake you, not for anyone,"* she whispered and abandoned the gilded room for the cool winter sunshine.

"I have welcome news for you, Bertrand." Father rubbed his hands as soon as the valet left the room. "The de la Decourcelle family finally arrived in Paris."

"Yes, father?" Bertrand answered absently. The family name was one of the oldest and richest in France, but why was he expected to rejoice upon their arrival? His mind was filled with thoughts about Charlotte de Brangelton and the memory of the kiss in the theater. She had disappeared without any warning, and he panicked at the suspicion that the Comtesse de Tournelles took her daughter away to separate him from Charlotte. He was elated when Cecilia found out that the Comtesse de Tournelles had escorted Duchess Helene to Versailles and his spirits lifted, but there was no mentioning of the Comtesse's daughter in Duchess Helene's entourage.

Father's sanguine mood vanished. "You don't even remember, do you?"

"I apologize, father," Bertrand answered cautiously. "No, I don't."

"You don't bother to remember the obligations and commitments of our family, Bertrand?"

Bertrand twisted the family seal ring on his finger. "Please remind me, father, what is this regarding?"

"Your future, Bertrand!"

"No!" He now recalled the name. Long ago, his father had extracted a promise from the de la Decourcelle family that their oldest daughter, Mlle. Anne-Louise, would be married to Bertrand.

Father's face flushed red and he slowly raised himself from his chair. "What do you mean, no?!"

"I...I mean..." Bertrand steeled himself for the imminent confrontation, this had to happen sooner or later. He had been waiting for the right moment to bring up the subject of his heart's obsession to marry Charlotte. "What is the reason for their presence, father?"

"To conclude the negotiations of the marriage–your marriage, a very prestigious marriage, Bertrand!–and to draw the contract."

"To draw the contract? Now?"

"Yes, now! Before you are goaded into compromising Mlle. de Brangelton and will have to marry her!"

"She will not allow herself to be compromised!" Bertrand raised his voice, but he did not care.

"How reassuring," father spit out. "Nevertheless, I shall not allow you to be trapped, in some more elaborate manner, to squander your future and family name for the adventuress!"

"Charlotte de Brangelton is not an adventuress!"

Father dropped into the chair. "Do you realize she partici-pates in her father's business?"

"We don't discuss business."

"I certainly hope you don't!" Father slammed his fist on the side table. "Will you have enough willpower to withhold infor-mation from her when she inquires of our family affairs?"

"Yes." Bertrand heard the uncertainty in his voice.

So did father. "There will never be peace between de Brangelton and myself. What will you do if she forces you to choose between her and our family interests, Bertrand?"

Bertrand felt nauseous. His father's words reaffirmed exactly what Charlotte's father said to him in confidence. "Do not nurture any delusions. You will have to choose between your family and ours."

Father regarded him with hostility. "Don't you understand that the future, the honor, the glory of the de la Norte family are at stake, Bertrand? The King is yet young, but he will rule soon. I have spent years building up my, and mind you, your position at Court. You are no longer a child. You must consider the de la Norte name, our standing in France, and your obliga-tions and duty to our family! Look at your uncle Jerome," father reminded him. "He made his disastrous choice to forsake his life in France! For what? For a home in the barbaric New World? For the company of privateers and cutthroats there? Is this what you wish?! Or is this her desire?! Will you love her dressed up in men's clothing?!"

"She does not wear men's clothing!" Bertrand shouted back.

He thought his father would strike him, but his father gained self-control and loudly exhaled. "How can you be so certain?" he hissed. " What do you truly know about her, Bertrand?!"

Bertrand left without uttering another word. What did he

know about Charlotte de Brangelton? She was beautiful, intelligent, outspoken, and he was certain she liked him; he had witnessed her icy demeanor toward de Chassigneau. In his mind, he again saw the smooth, controlled arc of Mlle. Charlotte's fan. Fencers honed their skills to perform this deliberate move, and she performed it effortlessly. She did not flirt. She dressed modestly, but her interest in the New World and her knowledge of weaponry made him uncomfortable; she was more knowledgeable in these matters than he was. His love of music and interest in philosophical sciences held no meaning for her. Did Charlotte leave Paris because of the de la Decourcelle family's presence? Bertrand rode home, watching the twisting shadows projecting from the lanterns and reflecting the turmoil in his mind.

The Dowager Duchess de Seveigney returned to Paris only three days before Christmas. Bertrand desperately struggled to tear away from all his obligations, but he was unable to leave the Court and the de la Decourcelle family. Charlotte's single brief note indicated no reassurance or even a hint of any emotion toward him. *"Thank you for your kind thoughts. My mother and I went to Versailles. It is truly a magnificent place. I enjoyed the visit immensely and hope to visit in the summer. I am looking forward to the festivities of the season,"* was all she wrote in her precise, exquisitely fine handwriting.

Bertrand arrived at the Regent's ball with the hope and determination to detach himself from his obligations and search for the opportunity to speak to Charlotte alone. He swallowed his pride and decided to ask her brother to entertain Mlle. Anne-Louise. Bertrand located an uncharacteristically solemn Henri de Brangelton who stood with his parents, but there was no sign of Charlotte. Bertrand frantically looked around and felt a cold grip of desperation on his heart when he saw the man at Charlotte's side.

23

BALL AT PALAIS ROYALE
PARIS - DECEMBER 1718

*I want a committed, reliable, level-headed man to escort
my precious daughter to the Regent's ball. A man
capable to stop her from punching one or another of
her admirers in case their passion flares up beyond
her short patience.*

Francis de Brangelton to Henrietta de Brangelton –
1718

"WHAT IS IT?" HENRIETTA FINISHED READING HER
correspondence and focused on Charlotte, who, for the past
half an hour, had been mumbling, sighing, tossing letters left
and right, and emitting a variety of derisive sounds.

"This." Her daughter gestured at the pile of papers in
distinct handwriting and small packages which bore de la
Norte's seal. "Bertrand de la Norte has become almost as
prolific as de Vergne in his writing. Mercifully, de la Norte does

not compose sonnets." She tossed a sheet of de Vergne's verses to Henrietta. "How am I an irresistible nymph in a sizzling sea of love?"

"What did Bertrand de la Norte have to say?" Henrietta put aside de Vergne's latest rhyming endeavors.

"I certainly hope he does not expect me to answer every one of his articulate missives." Charlotte shuffled the papers around. "I have no desire, no time, no literary talent, and no patience for that."

"Did he mention the name de la Decourcelle?"

"Somewhere here, he apologized because his father insisted he must entertain a family of this name." Charlotte searched for the letter and re-read it. "Why?"

"There are rumors his father is arranging Bertrand's marriage to Mlle. Anne-Louise de la Decourcelle," Henrietta had obtained this recent intelligence from Duchess Helene's household.

"Indeed?" There was more surprise than hurt in her voice. "He neglected to mention it in his epistles." She carelessly gathered all the notes in one large pile. There was only a trace of disappointment in her eyes, but mostly relief.

"Do you love him?" Henrietta asked.

"Who?" Charlotte asked absent-mindedly.

"Obviously not Bertrand de la Norte," Henrietta kept her thoughts to herself.

"What does Antoine truly think of Charles?" Charlotte pondered.

Henrietta was taken aback by that sudden change of subject. "Would you give up Charles for him?"

"What? No, no, not for him, not for anyone. I don't want to talk about him. No man is worth giving up Charles!" Papers floated down when Charlotte slammed her fist on the desk.

"There is a rumor of Duke Collingstone's upcoming official

visit to Paris," Henrietta said. Might as well bring up another piece of bad news since Charlotte was already in a tempestuous mood. "How will you explain Antoine de Flancourt to His Grace and his entourage?"

The chair overturned when Charlotte jumped up. "I certainly hope His-Womanizing-Grace, along with his cohorts, will remember my fencing skills. That should preclude any debauched notions." She glanced at her correspondence and tossed a tankard at the wall. It was thoughtful of Francis to keep only the broken tankard within her reach.

"Has your swordsmanship discouraged either de Rameau or de Molienier?"

"Mother!" Charlotte kicked the abused tankard to hit the usual target spot on the wall. "How do you manage? No one dares to bother you with any amorous nonsense."

"I have never been even half as beautiful as you are, I am married to your father, I have years of formidable reputation, and I am significantly older," Henrietta counted out on her fingers. "Even so, occasionally, a silly man will make himself a nuisance. Those Englishmen witnessed you and Antoine together– put that goblet down!"

"I am moving to the New World!" Charlotte hissed. "This continent is not large enough for Antoine and myself."

"Are you expecting to repeat the success of your enterprise from Ferrand to Paris?" Henrietta unwisely reminded her.

Fortunately, the hurried steps at the door – Henri and Antoine had showed up for dinner much earlier than expected - prevented her daughter from an explosion. While greetings were exchanged, Charlotte firmly planted herself between the young men and the desk, and her foot pushed the papers under the table.

"Mother and I visited Versailles," Charlotte launched into an excited narration.

"What is all this?" Henri was not to be deferred.

"This?" Charlotte eyed the desk with an innocent sense of surprise. She casually shuffled the papers – in the process, hiding the boxes and de la Norte's letters on the bottom of the pile. She picked up a literary composition - seemingly at random, but it just happened to be from de Vergne - and unfolded it. "You know, brother, Monsieur de Vergne rhymes his compliments."

"Favorably comparing my women to Cleopatra is poetic enough." Henri reached for the letter, but Charlotte held it away. Henri snatched another one from the desk and struck a theatrical pose. "She is a moonlit lily from a heavenly garden," he read. "She holds the beacon star of his happiness in her gentle - gentle? – hands..."

"Her fist has not flown toward his face yet," Antoine chimed in.

"Her smile is sacred nectar to nourish his zest for life." Henri gave in to laughter. So did Antoine.

Henrietta admired her daughter's opportunistic actions. During the brief moment of distraction, she deftly scooped up the gifts and papers into a basket and motioned to Red Jacques to take it away.

"The rest is worthless." Henri eyed the rest of the sonnet. "A reference to Aphrodite is useless to me. Greek goddesses are de Rameau's realm."

"Not any longer," Charlotte said. "Not after I warned him to keep his hands off Hera."

Henri and Antoine hooted in perfect harmony.

Henri explained, to all three of his beautiful women, not at the same time but sequentially, that he, a responsible son of a

Comte, was expected and, in fact, ordered by his father, to dedicate the Twelve Days of Christmas to his family or he would be disinherited. Gabrielle uttered a sarcastic *"Hmmm..."* but did not pursue the subject, Eloise complimented his devotion to his family, and Cybille expected him to escort her to the ball at Palais Royale. Henri insisted on the compromise to accompany her for the banquet only, citing the obligation to escort his sister. With luck, his passions would decrease in number next year.

Antoine spent all Twelve Days of Christmas with the de Brangelton family. His presence shortened and effectively precluded frequent attendance by all Charlotte's admirers. While various nuisances were present, Antoine engaged the beautiful Mlle. in a discussion regarding geographic locations of Caribbean islands for de Vergne's education, in a debate about medieval weaponry for de Chassigneau's reference, in childhood reminisces for de Rameau's mercifully brief visit, and in speculations of piracy during de la Norte's visit. At some moment of insanity, or perhaps the influence of rum, Antoine suggested that Charles should attend the ball at the Palais Royale. Even father disagreed, and took the precaution to safely yoke Charlotte with a formal noble escort, the only man able to anticipate her behavior. At least, for the occasion.

The splendid, glittering, titled, and rich crowds congregated at the Palais Royale. All the oldest and noble names were in attendance. Thousands of candles basked the room with a glow equal to summer daylight. Elaborate, expensive, fashionable attires were on display. Clothes of rich deep colors were adorned with elaborate embroidery and lace woven with shiny threads of gold and silver. Bright diamonds, vivid red rubies, vibrant blue sapphires, and blood-colored garnets shone and sparkled; large and small pearls shimmered. Henri appreciated the jovial ambiance, father exercised his usual inscrutable courtly demeanor, mother reveled in festivities, and among the illustrious crowd, Charlotte and Antoine made a handsome couple. Henri ceremoniously bowed to Cybille from across the room, exchanged longing and despairing glances with Gabrielle, bestowed an admiring smile at Éloise, winked at Charlotte and Antoine, and firmly planted himself next to father.

"I am touched to tears by your dedication to family, duty, protocol, etc.," father commented dryly while Henri's eyes swept across the grand hall to momentarily pause on Cybille, Gabrielle, and Eloise.

"I am touched to tears by your fatherly understanding." Henri set his face in a serious expression for the duration of formal pre-dinner socializing. Per unwritten protocol, that's when alliances were formed, friendships were renewed, news was exchanged, and everyone moved in circles, greeting and acknowledging each other. Across the room, Charlotte decorously engaged in the routine of polite chatter in the glorious company of the Comte de Flancourt, who, representing his noble family, was highly in demand. She ignored pleading glances from Bertrand de la Norte. Indeed, what did he expect her to do? Should she bring herself and Comte de Flancourt over for introductions to the de la Decourcelle family? Mlle. Anne-Louise was a very young, not yet fully developed, beauty. She possessed chiseled classic features, but what a pity that the appearance was only a shell. The excess of proper upbringing would extinguish any fire under the skin. Beautiful as a Greek statue, and probably just as passionate, Henri decided.

"Are you certain that pairing Antoine and Charlotte is a good idea?" he asked his father.

"Are you concerned about the feelings of your philosopher friend?"

"He is emotionally quartered between his unrequited love

for Charlotte, his obligations to his family, the protocol of entertaining Mllc. dc la Decourcelle, and his desperate jealousy of all Charlotte's admirers," Henri quoted mother's assessment. "Granted, he deserves to be chomping at the bit, but aren't you worried he will perceive Antoine's role tonight as provocation?"

"Neither de la Norte nor Antoine will cause any disturbance here." Father dismissed Henri's concerns. "For the future, de Louviers will hire a nursemaid for his son to prevent any exchanges about Charlotte's affection to any of her admirers or travel companions."

"Are you certain of that?"

Father exchanged commonplace pleasantries with yet another couple. Henri smothered a yawn.

"De Louviers needs the connections with the de la Decourcelle family, and he will not allow my girl to interfere with his ambition. His son's happiness does not matter to him, either," father said.

"What matters here is that you, my devious sire, don't want Charlotte married to de la Norte."

"What matters here is that Charlotte, your sensible sister, does not love him," father retorted.

Henri dropped the subject. Father did not care for Bertrand de la Norte as his son-in-law, and father did not intend to bless such a union unless Charlotte begged him, which was highly unlikely if father's assessment of her feelings was correct. The current of the so-called social river carried de la Norte and Mlle. de la Decourcelle on a collision course with the Comte de Flancourt and Mlle. de Brangelton, and Henri briefly and feelingly wished for civility within the cozy foursome. De la Norte stiffly made formal introductions, and, surprisingly, animated, maybe even friendly, conversation continued between Charlotte and Mlle. de la Decourcelle with occasional contributions by Antoine. It lasted longer than Henri expected. De la Norte's eyes apprehensively shifted between the unconcerned Charlotte and Antoine. None too soon, in Henri's opinion, the couples went their separate ways and Henri breathed a sigh of relief. Until Charlotte faced off with the Marquise de Fabvre.

For the formal ball at the Palais Royale, everyone dressed in the finest clothes. Father wore a formal black suit with burgundy and gold trim, his Coat of Arms embedded on the lapel. Mother dressed in a cherry-red dress with black with gold embroidery; she looked handsome and dignified. Henri presented a stylish figure in his elaborate suit of black breeches and burgundy jacket with generous embroidery of black and gold on the lapels and wide cuffs. The feathery pattern repeated on the waistcoat, and he had even opted for a lavish lace cravat. Antoine displayed a dark green formal suit, and the lapels and sleeves of his jacket were decorated with a spare amount of gold braid. His golden waistcoat was embroidered with white diamond and square shapes, and the snow-white cravat and the lace at the cuffs was immaculate. Charlotte had ordered a new dress in a formal French style. The fabric was blue-green like the sea with subtle black and gold stripes. The trim of the overskirt and the front of her bodice were adorned with simple gold bows. Her hair was pulled back with matching blue-green ribbons and a gold necklace completed her outfit.

"Comte, Mlle. Charlotte, you have reconciled," Marquise Cecilia de Fabvre chirped after a perfunctory introduction of her husband, a stout middle-aged man whose countenance clearly indicated a strong desire to be miles away.

"Yes, Charlotte and I do not dwell on our quarrels," Antoine answered.

Cecilia fanned herself. "Mlle. Charlotte, what crime has the Comte committed to upset you?"

"Numerous," Charlotte claimed. If Antoine aimed to provoke jealousy in Cecilia, he should have the decency to leave Charlotte out of it. She would never be an accomplice to his affairs. There would be no praises from her to impress another woman on his behalf. In fact, he deserved just the opposite. Both the Marquis and Marquise de Fabvre expected an explanation which was not forthcoming.

"Charlotte, that is an unfair exaggeration," Antoine reproached her. "Indeed, I cannot fathom a single action on my part to incur your wrath."

"No? You are indeed a very discourteous man." She tossed her fan in the air.

Cecilia's wide-open eyes darted between Antoine and Charlotte with horrified curiosity.

Antoine caught the fan in mid-air. "May I ask when you acquired such an unflattering opinion of me?"

"My opinion of you formed years ago." Charlotte matched his tone.

"Will you excuse us, Marquis, Marquise?" Antoine hastily bowed, gripped Charlotte's elbow, and indecorously pulled her away. "Discourteous? I?" he pointedly glanced in the direction of de la Norte and his obligation.

"Confiscating the bridles on the road deserves payback," she fumed. "What did you tell the Marquise de Fabvre? We reconciled? After what quarrel?"

"Apparently, after I confiscated the bridles," Antoine snapped back.

The memory of the morning at the house in Lonjumeau

flashed through Charlotte's mind. "You... you told her about our trip?"

"Why would I tell her about it?"

"Didn't you plan to spend a month with her?" Charlotte never meant to blunder into that discussion. No man in his right mind would tell a woman about a trip with another woman, Antoine's affairs were none of her business, and yet the notion of an affair between Antoine and Cecilia infuriated Charlotte beyond reason. "Never mind! Give back my fan. It's not a bridle!"

Henri solemnly led Cybille to their seats only to discover that Gabrielle and her husband were seated on his other side, and Eloise and her husband across the table. Father must have had a hand in seating arrangements here, Henri grudgingly acknowledged the genius of his deviousness and ignored Charlotte's and Antoine's unbridled amusement. De la Norte, occupying the chair next to Mlle. de la Decourcelle, was completely out of Charlotte's sight. Henri's sire was, as always, unerring in his observations and actions. Charlotte seemed to have forgotten about Bertrand de la Norte's presence, and maybe his existence altogether.

The sumptuous multi-course feast consisted of cream chicken and leeks soup, whole geese and turkeys, stuffed carp and jellied pike, baked carrots and apples, hard and soft cheeses, roasted venison and pheasants, mutton, beef and mincemeat pies, dried apricots, fig and date tarts, sugared plums, honey-covered cakes, custards, and even fresh oranges. The crystal goblets were filled with fine wines, strong brandy, and spiced rum. The feast was accompanied by musicians, opera singers, acrobats, jesters, bards, and jugglers. After the last course of fruit ices was served and consumed, most of the dignitaries, the officials, those in formal attendance, and those who did not enjoy festivities left right after the departure of the royal family. The dining tables were cleared to make room for dancing, additional groups of musicians were brought in, and the mood shifted to carefree and festive. Those who remained late in the night comprised a younger, more boisterous crowd. Monsieur Patrice de Seveigney, with his current mistress (What was her name? Adelaine? Amelia?) on one hand and a goblet of wine in another, sought Henri out.

"What are our plans for the night, de Brangelton?" His head bobbed toward the intimately darkened room off to the side. Sofas and chairs were arranged in a wide circle. Rum and brandy decanters and glasses, dice and cards were laid out on the side tables, and M. Patrice's wink inferred exactly his own thoughts were. Didn't the man ever tire of these silly games? Henri nudged Gabrielle toward the half-sober M. Patrice, smiled at Cecilia de Fabvre, bowed to Cybille, and winked at Eloise. Henri just hoped that Charlotte and her escort would not make use of the billiards in another side room. No, Antoine would not dare to introduce Charlotte to yet another manly occupation. Henri mentioned the assembly to de Contraille and d'Chantal and peeked into the cozy room where a couple dozen people had settled by now. Gabrielle, Cybille, and Eloise were present and on the different sides of the room. Henri escaped unseen into the hallway, rounded the corner, and collided with Antoine and Charlotte.

"If you, a delicate lily of womanhood, stray away from my overbearing company, you will have to run a sword through one or other of your unworthy admirers," Antoine predicted. "Such rash actions will displease your father and upset your mother."

"Charles, my friend, where are you?" Charlotte bantered.

"Yes, I miss that cutthroat," Antoine goaded her. "He and I

could play billiards."

"If you encourage Charles in his manly pursuits, prepare to accompany him to the New World when he is exiled from France," Henri interrupted.

Antoine bit his lip in dismay.

"Oh, no, you will beg Charles to keep you company when you escape from the fury of all your passions upon their discovery of each other," Charlotte took offence on Charles' behalf.

"A fast road from heaven to hell," Antoine added.

"You two seem to have a delusion that my three passions will discover each other," Henri said.

"Bet you Cybille will realize his unfaithfulness first." Antoine winked at Charlotte.

"Gabrielle," Charlotte retorted. "She watches him like a hawk."

"And if it is Eloise, Henri will buy us a bottle of rum."

"Here is my wager to you two," Henri proposed in his turn. "None of my beautiful women will suspect me of unfaithfulness. You and Charlotte will buy me dinner." He would not mind if one of his passions dropped her desire for his company, but losing a bet on women to Antoine was preposterous. Henri sunk into a chair, pondered the irony of his situation, and settled to map out his course of actions to fulfill his commitments to all three of his passions. He could leave the ball shortly and go to Cybille's house before she left the ball. Then visit Gabrielle for a short time since she must be exhausted after dancing all night. Then move on to Eloise. Maybe she would be asleep; if not, he would apologize to her that he had to reconcile his sister and the Comte de Flancourt. Henri's mood slightly brightened. He did not care if the plan was good or bad. Frankly, he would have preferred to go home and sleep. Blissfully alone.

24

REVELATIONS

PARIS, FRANCE – JANUARY 1719

*Mlle. Charlotte's militant inclinations and skills terrify
de la Norte and intimidate even de Flancourt.*

Patrice de Seveigney to Henri de Brangelton – 1718

ANTOINE TOSSED AWAY THE NEWSPAPER AND SHUFFLED through the letters on his desk. None required immediate attention. He organized the papers in neat piles, inspected the shine on his pistol's barrel, and stared at the morose gray skies outside. Antoine checked the condition of his hat - it bore traces of dust. Armand must have brushed it in a hurry, expecting Antoine to leave early in the afternoon. He had not, because yesterday his visit with Charlotte ended when she catapulted the much-abused tankard into the wall. As far as Antoine was concerned, she had no excuse to be piqued when he politely inquired if Charles' fencing skills had impressed de la Norte and offered to be of service and schedule a fencing round between Charles and de la Norte. The conversation went downhill at a gallop after that when Charlotte's father supported the concept, Charlotte could not dispute the right-fulness of it, and resorted to *"none of your business"* statement. Antoine had departed with an icily polite, *"At your service, Charles, when you gather enough courage,"* to the accompaniment of another projectile hitting the wall. Antoine fastened his cloak. He and de Contraille had scheduled a fencing round for this afternoon. He should have mentioned that to the beautiful Mlle. de Brangelton. Maybe that would entice her to grace the fencing hall with her enchanting presence. Antoine glanced at the clock. There was no time to see Charlotte now.

De Contraille and Antoine arrived at the fencing hall and were unpleasantly surprised by the presence of Henri de Brangelton and Bertrand de la Norte. Despite a strained pause in the buzz of conversations, de Contraille's worried frown, de la Norte's stony face, and d'Signac's raised eyebrows, Antoine marched toward the group. De Bearteau scattered out of his way.

"I am surprised you found time for a fencing round, Henri," Antoine said loudly. "Aren't hearts of beautiful women shattered this afternoon by your dedication to the art of the sword?"

"When did you become an expert of the mysteries of women's hearts?" Henri asked without glancing back, in the same manner his sister had perfected.

"Am I wrong, oh expert on the matter?"

"Flattery? Are you in need of my counsel?"

"God forbid!" Antoine exclaimed in mocking horror.

Henri flicked the sword at Antoine. "A fencing round for such disrespect! Usual wager."

Antoine locked eyes with de la Norte. "Why don't we settle

it right now? You and de la Norte against de Contraille and myself. D'Signac and de Bearteau will arbitrate."

"An excellent plan." Irony dripped from d'Signac's voice.

Antoine and de Contraille removed their cloaks and hats and discarded their doublets and boots. The floor had been cleared and all four participants had taken their positions when the familiar brown hat with the blue feather bounced into the viewing gallery. What was she doing here?

Upon arriving home after the morning promenade at the Pont Neuf with her father, Charlotte was informed that she missed another visit from M. Bertrand de la Norte. He had left her a note to the effect that the Fates had cruelly conspired against him. He promised to come back after his fencing match with her brother, and Charlotte felt a slight discomfort at his persistence. Ever since the Regent's New Year Ball, he had attempted to contact her at home. Once she was out for a fencing outing with Henri and Antoine, the second time she and mother were ambushed by de Rameau on their way from the dressmaker, and the third time she was at the Musketeer's Headquarters with Henri and Antoine. Another time she went to Vincennes with father. She had only briefly seen Bertrand at the Louvre where she was with Antoine and de Rousard, and at the theater where Antoine and de Contraille steered her away. She still fumed about last evening's squabble with Antoine. Much as she hated to admit it, he was right; what did Bertrand de la Norte expect from her? Was he forced to part ways, or was he thankful? Charlotte paced the room until it occurred to her that Charles' appearance would speed up Bertrand's decision if there was any doubt in his mind or heart. It would also ease her guilty conscience. She discarded her dress, donned a men's shirt, buttoned up the leather doublet, and completed the outfit with her new embellished sword strap. She wrapped herself in her plain winter cloak thinking that she should have it decorated to match the shoulder strap, and stepped into the dreary winter day outside.

The viewing gallery at the fencing hall was crowded. What was happening? Charlotte carefully weaved her way toward the front and froze upon the sight of Antoine in the center of the fencing floor. He wore only breeches and a shirt with rolled up sleeves, and the image of him at the room at Lonjumeau on that fine September morning rose in her mind. Charlotte's immediate inclination was to leave. She bounced off an officer standing next to her, but regained her wits. Antoine was unaware of her presence; he was focused on conferring with de Contraille. Charlotte snuck around the officer for a better view of their opponents. Henri was checking the cover on his blade, and de la Norte completed the group. Antoine's presence effectively cancelled any introductions of Charles to de la Norte, but there was a promise of a very fine display of swordsmanship. Charles leaned against the column in the shadows to watch.

The participants squared off. Antoine relentlessly pressed de la Norte. Henri was forced to abandon his offence against de Contraille and to move into the breach left by de Norte. Antoine and de Contraille had a slight advantage, and when d'Signac signaled the time, all participants remained on the fencing floor, although Henri and de Contraille prudently positioned themselves between Antoine and de la Norte –

"They should have invited Mlle. de Brangelton to this exhibit," a young Lieutenant remarked.

"To distract de Flancourt and de la Norte?" his friend speculated.

"Don't care for either one. I would be eager to investigate what makes her so desirable!"

Another officer poked him in the ribs. "You fancy yourself more desirable than a Comte?"

"What?" Charlotte heard herself exclaim.

"What did you squawk?" the first imbecile asked.

Charlotte no longer cared for caution, or causing a scene, or starting a duel right there in the fencing hall, in front of courtiers, Musketeers, Antoine, and de la Norte. "What right do you have to bray about Mlle. de Brangelton?"

The instigator casually leaned on her shoulder with his elbow. "I hear that Mlle. de Brangelton is a beautiful young woman. She strings along a troop of admirers, but one man will breach her defenses one day."

"The Devil take you." Charlotte threw his elbow off her shoulder.

"Damn your impudent tongue!" He raised his voice and heads turned. "On whose behalf are you insulted? De Flancourt or de la Norte or de Rameau?"

"I will not tolerate any disrespect toward Mlle. de Brangelton," Charlotte spat out. Their exchange caused a commotion, and she could feel Antoine's stare. No, she could not explain the cause of this quarrel either to him or Henri.

"You?" Lieutenant smirked. "Why?"

"I am a relative of the Comtesse de Tournelles."

"Why don't you claim you are Mlle. de Brangelton?" he sneered.

"Not today," Charlotte declined.

"Afraid that one of them will take offense that you would use her name?" His friend jeered with a gesture toward the fencing floor.

The crowd sensed that a brawl was brewing. Row by row, the men fell silent to catch every word of the conflict.

Charlotte had to end this exchange. "Go to hell, Lieutenant, and take your friends with you!"

Purposeful steps behind her broke the brittle silence in the fencing hall.

"Don't even think about it. Especially you," d'Signac's precise, commanding voice sounded at her ear as he squeezed her shoulder in warning. He and two other Musketeers lost no time pushing their way into the viewing gallery. Henri and Antoine were unsympathetic to her plight. They had suddenly become law-abiding citizens.

"Please deliver my greetings to your Captain." Charlotte removed d'Signac's hand, bowed, and marched toward the door.

The Musketeers blocked the officers' path. "I will arrest anyone stepping outside for a breath of fresh air," d'Signac warned.

Charlotte marched toward the door, past Antoine, who was putting his boots on.

"Where are you going, de Flancourt?" d'Signac bellowed.

"To make certain this aspiring cutthroat causes no trouble," Antoine answered. "Charles!"

Charlotte raised her arm in acknowledgement, but neither glanced back nor stopped and sauntered along the Seine into the viciously cold wind.

Antoine ran to catch up with her and thrust his cloak, gloves, and sword into her arms. "Hold it for me." He finished putting on his doublet and buttoned it.

"Never imagined the sight of de Flancourt dressing in the street," d'Signac appeared behind him and winked at Charlotte. "This is more de Brangelton's style, isn't it?"

"Why did you follow us?" Antoine strapped on his sword belt.

"I did threaten to arrest anyone leaving the fencing hall.

Consider yourself detained. What was the argument about, my quarrelsome friend Raoul?"

"I am Charles d'Arringnon."

D'Signac was undaunted. "What was the reason for the disturbance, Charles?"

Charlotte's irritation mounted. "M. d'Signac, this is none of your business."

"May I guess? Did you plan to introduce de la Norte to Charles?"

Did Antoine set him up for that? Charlotte gripped him by the front of the cloak. "You owe me a fencing round for this affront!"

"It will be my pleasure," he assured her with a wry smile. "Shall we return to the fencing hall now?"

Antoine finished wrapping himself in his heavy velvet cloak and pulled on his gloves. "D'Signac, will you allow Charles to settle his differences with the Lieutenant on the fencing floor?"

"No." Charlotte did not elaborate. They had definitely conspired against her.

"Don't have the heart to present Charles to de la Norte in front of an audience, do you?" d'Signac shrewdly asked.

"Go to hell."

D'Signac rolled his eyes. "Charming company I have this afternoon."

"Shall we play cards at the Valiant Fox?" Antoine asked.

The events at the fencing hall had convinced Henri that peace between Antoine and Bertrand de la Norte would flourish around the same time that Charlotte embroidered a waistcoat. Antoine's arrival had been ill-timed. The tension between him and de la Norte hung in the air like a screen of thick fog. De la Norte was still brooding about the ball at the Palais Royale, Antoine was unsympathetic toward de la Norte's tender feelings, their unspoken contempt of each other alarmed de Contraille, and the fencing round had been sliding toward disaster unless a compelling distraction occurred. Charles was magnificent. In his vigilant desire to maintain law and order, d'Signac had claimed control of the situation, an enterprise he accomplished as well as could be expected. Antoine's unperturbed expression and subsequent abandonment of the fencing round indicated that he had invited Charlotte. Henri would have washed his hands off, but the incensed Lieutenant required pacification in case he met Charles again. Henri's conversation with officers was illuminating, de Contraille wisely fled from the fencing hall in a hurry, de la Norte left in a pensive mood, and de Bearteau repeated his question about Charles. At the Blackheart Tavern afterwards, Henri vaguely owned that young miscreant was a relative of his, bought half of a roasted pig and bottles of wine, making the Lieutenant and his friends generously forgive Charles's impudence and drink to the boy's fiery spirit.

Later in the day, Henri stormed into his parents' residence and found his sister in the sitting room. She still wore men's clothing, and the mud on her boots had not dried yet.

Henri helped himself to a serving of rum. "Is this your interpretation of proper behavior?"

Charlotte hurled the much-abused tankard at the wall. "What do you expect me to do? Sit at home all day? Learn embroidery? Maybe take singing lessons?" She paced around the room with the wild look of a caged animal. "I cannot tolerate this way of life, Henri! I do not want to! I will not!"

"Charlotte!" Henri shook her by the shoulders. "You

cannot flaunt your ways in Paris as you do at home! Take an example from mother. She maintains appearances here."

"Yes, so do I. I pretend to be a prim young woman for a while, but then I choke." Charlotte leaned her forehead against his shoulder. "Henri. Shall we ride to Chantilly?"

"No," Henri said firmly. "Everyone will think you are jealous of Mlle. de la Decourcelle."

Charlotte's fingers grasped the front of his doublet. "What are my other choices? How long will I be able to tolerate de Vergne's company?"

"An hour," Henri estimated.

"How long will it take de Chassigneau to provoke me?" his sister continued.

"A quarter of an hour." Henri felt a headache coming.

"Of course, there is de Rameau, whose company will gloriously benefit my reputation!"

Profanities leapt to Henri's mind and tongue.

"Then again, Mlle. de la Decourcelle will stay in Paris for only a month. What will everyone conclude if the disreputable Comte de Flancourt were to escort me for a month?"

Henri's mind painted a vivid vision of a bored Charles on the loose and Antoine encouraging Charles' outrageous predilections. "Chantilly? When are we leaving?" he asked. Wildcat could never be tamed.

Chantilly – January 1719

The ambitious project to build the grandest stables in France was a scene of organized chaos. Charlotte and Henri decided to watch the whirl of activities. They brought mincemeat pies and flasks of spiced wine, wrapped themselves in heavy fur-lined cloaks and found a comfortable stone bench, a block which was discarded because of a large crack in the middle. Masons rhythmically chiseled the stones to fit into neat rows while architects, their secretaries, and their clerks reviewed the rolls of papers. The apprentices carried tools and orders, handymen bustled between scaffoldings, lifts, covers and carts, and groups of noblemen gaped at the spreading structure. Charlotte and Henri overheard English, Spanish, and half a dozen other languages.

A young nobleman briskly walked along the façade of the building. His heavy cloak was made from expensive velvet cloth and elaborately decorated with fur and gold embroidery. The hilt of his sword was gilded, a bodyguard trailed him, and a cloaked man approached. The newcomer barely had time to utter a single sentence before the nobleman engaged in a monologue until the cloaked man responded with a gesture of negation and managed to contribute another sentence. The noblemen again launched into a tirade in obvious displeasure, and the cloaked figure vigorously nodded this time. The nobleman dismissed him and gestured to his bodyguard. Without delay, the bodyguard brought a fine bay horse of an English breed. The nobleman seated himself into the richly decorated saddle and rode away.

"An arrogant bastard," Charlotte cheerfully concluded. Her thoughts wandered off toward Paris and Antoine. How was he occupying his time? Hopefully not by pursuing Cecilia de Fabvre again. Charlotte should have thought about visiting Raoul in fencing school. Needless to say, Antoine would join them, and her brother would probably send Charles off with Antoine. Mercifully, Henri interrupted her disorderly musings.

"It will be Versailles for horses, packed with equines as elegantly as Versailles was overrun with courtiers."

"It will probably smell the same," Charlotte agreed.

The cheering and jeering crowd blocked the road, and Henri rode ahead to check the source of the commotion. Charlotte stayed behind to spy on the occupants of an expensive and freshly painted carriage. In the descending dusk, she did not recognize the quartered Coat of Arms on the door, but the main colors seemed to be blue and yellow. A lantern was lit inside the carriage. Charlotte caught a glimpse of the nobleman from the construction site. Next to him sat a woman with an ample bosom that was generously exhibited despite the freezing air, while the rest of her body was tightly bundled with a fur throw.

The driver of the carriage stood up to see what had caused everyone to stop. "A cockfight and a man-fight ahead, Monsieur," he reported. He leaned toward the window to inform the nobleman. The sun was setting behind him, and Charlotte could not make out his features.

"Are you planning to ride through it?" the nobleman asked. He was French. His voice rung with aristocratic control and a trace of impatience.

"I would not recommend that, Monsieur. The officers are waging on the outcome. They will resent any interruptions."

"So we wait?" the nobleman scowled.

Hera chose this moment to prance.

The nobleman stuck his head out of the window for a better view. He was probably close to thirty years of age. His hat, gloves, and cloak were trimmed with fur and gold stitching. "You, young man," he addressed Charles. "Will you dare to ride your monstrous mare through this crowd?"

"What will I gain by it?" Charlotte respectfully touched her hat. "Will you hire me, Monsieur?"

The nobleman gave her an appraising look. "What can you do for me?"

What was the most undesirable trade for employment in a

nobleman's household? "What use do you have for a mercenary?"

"None." The nobleman's gloved fingers brushed the woman's bluish skin when he reclined back to murmur to her.

"Your loss, Monsieur." Charlotte tipped her hat and pushed her way forward to catch up with Henri.

ABOUT THE MARSHALL COUSINS
PARIS - JANUARY 1719

*About twenty years ago, Black Caesar ran his slave
business out of Marseille. His guards were African,
cursed by voodoo. They had no life in them except to
serve him. Until one day, they turned on him and
burned down the warehouse. People whispered that
a boy named Francis Bradforde brought Black
Caesar's ruin, but the boy could not have been more
than fourteen years of age. More likely, the devil
himself came to claim Black Caesar*

-A tale from Marseille - c. 1 7 1 2

THE MUSICIANS PLAYED FLAWLESSLY, THE WINE FLOWED
freely, and the hundreds of crystal chandeliers brightly illuminated the grand room. The servants darted around, the malicious gossips flourished, the lovers conspired, the enemies
plotted; in other words, the reception was as magnificent as any
expected at Luxemburg Palace. The young men were in high
spirits, and the women flirted, that is, all women save one.

Charlotte's wistful look at the cards tables and the clock was followed by a grimace of disgust, and then a gleam of inspiration. Conveniently, M. Bertrand was not present to raise his perfect eyebrows, and tonight was a perfect opportunity to set yet another precedence of Mlle. de Brangelton's acceptable activities.

"Are you planning to play chess, father?" Charlotte asked with false innocence.

"Will you watch the game?"

"I suppose playing is much more entertaining than watching." She emitted an exaggerated sigh.

"I will teach you to play chess."

"Yes, father, you taught me to play cards," she pursued her original thought. "What good does it do for me? I have not played a game outside of home since last autumn," she launched into a tirade. "I am certain playing chess is just as improper and I might as well learn embroidery and possibly how to play the lute." She stole a measuring look. "Shall we play just one game of cards?"

"Is that proper behavior for either one of us?" Francis teased her.

Charlotte's attention was suddenly distracted. "The middle-aged man with a neatly trimmed moustache, dressed in a russet jacket with red trim, on your left, by the column. He is the Knight of St. John from Montpellier," she whispered.

"He might be evaluating the possibility to play chess," Francis noted.

"Chess is a very exciting game to watch."

"Indeed. Such a sudden interest," Francis countered. He held a healthy respect for the Knights of St. John, a militaristic and self-righteous (though that was all of them) organization built on reverence and dedication to God, gold, and glory. This efficient brotherhood of well-trained knights did not hesitate to attack a ship at sea and appropriate most of the goods in the name of their order, Christianity, safety of the trade routes, and filling their own coffers. It was a very efficient and ingenious operation, despite the limits imposed by the rigid structure which was necessary to maintain the status of a religious order.

"I suspect the man will discuss no business in your presence," he said to Charlotte.

"Should I provide singing entertainment?"

"Follow me." Francis steered his girl toward the table where the game was just finished. He requested d'Chantal's and his partners' permission to allow his daughter to play with them while he played a game of chess, and thanked them for the indulgence. They assured him it would be their pleasure, and Charlotte merrily settled down.

"Pay attention, Monsieurs," he warned them. "I taught my girl well."

He left the men to contemplate the veracity of his claim and situated himself by the chess tables, in a position to witness the predictable progress of Charlotte's card game. The condescending smirks on the men's faces evolved into disbelief, concentration, amazement, and again stunned disbelief.

The Knight of St. John watched the card game, albeit with a disapproving frown.

Francis casually approached him. "Pardon me, Monsieur, you look familiar. Have we met?"

The man's eyes flickered to the scar on Francis' forehead. "I regret to say, I do not know you, Monsieur. I am Honore de Courbet, a Knight of St. John," he introduced himself.

"I am the Comte de Tournelles, at your service. By any chance, do you play chess, M. de Courbet?"

Yes, he did. In fact, de Courbet was a decent player and a gracious loser.

"That was a challenging game. Please accept my compliments on your skill and competence," Francis said. "Are you planning to stay in Paris long? We could have a rematch."

"Yes, I would greatly appreciate that as time allows, but my duty and matters of business must come first."

"Of course. Do tell me, what are the latest exploits of the Knights of St. John?"

De Courbet kept his answers vague. "Protecting Christian pilgrims and legitimate shipments in the Mediterranean keeps us fully occupied."

"Has *Swan Song* been restored to her owner? My information is lagging behind by a month."

De Courbet was startled. "You are very well informed, Comte. My own information is no more recent."

"Common sources?" Francis gestured to the chairs arranged for a private conference. De Contraille had joined Charlotte at the cards table. His skills would liven up the game and keep the girl happily occupied for a while. "I have some personal interest in marine commerce, M. de Courbet."

"It is quite unusual for a man residing in Paris, Comte."

They cautiously sparred for a while, and Francis casually dropped names and hints.

De Courbet fidgeted in his seat. "By any chance, Comte, were you in Marseille in the autumn of 1712?"

"Ah, you must be referring to the ill-famed day when the harbor was set ablaze. Regrettably, I was not there to witness the spectacle." Francis ruefully shook his head. "I only read about it in the newspapers. Incidentally, I heard rampant gossip about the Marshall cousins lately. Have you ever encountered these cutthroats in the Mediterranean?"

"No," de Courbet smiled and confidentially leaned forward. "Did you know they appropriated the Great Mogul Diamond?"

"The Great Mogul Diamond?" Francis feigned surprise.

"What is that Knight of St. John's business, father?" Charlotte asked as soon as the carriage door closed and the wheels rolled.

"He is searching for the Marshall cousins."

Even in the dim light of a small lantern, her eyes shone bright. "The connoisseurs of Duke Collingstone's - I mean, his mistresses' – portraits. What does a Knight of St. John have to do with it? Did he have an affair with one of those women?"

"Don't judge all men based upon your brother's pathetic example," Francis admonished her. "M. de Courbet's luggage was lost in the chaos."

Not a moment was wasted. "So he tracked the shipments in Montpellier. The cargo intended for the Bishop of Bourges was probably lost during the skirmish, wasn't it?"

"Probably."

"Did the Marshall cousins take it as well?" She was lost in thought. "No, this is preposterous. Who would be interested in secular pictures for the Protestant Duke in England and holy relics for the Catholic Church in France?" Charlotte slapped her fan against the palm of her hand. "Marshall is an assumed name. Is that so, father?"

"It seems likely."

"You know who they are, don't you?"

Misleading his girl was a close-to-impossible task. Her intuition and perceptiveness were developed to perfection, except when a certain young man was concerned.

"What is your guess?" Francis asked.

Charlotte's eyes gleamed with excitement. "I suspect they hunted for Duke Collingstone's portraits, to sell those in the New World. These dovetails with their alleged background. Or they might have been hired by the Knights of Christ to appropriate the Bishop of Bourges' cargo. No, on second thought, the Knights of Christ would never resort to the services of the unknown cutthroats from the New World. They would hire infidel corsairs."

Francis admired her reasoning. "Why don't you find out who they are and why they caused such a chaos in the harbor of my misguided youth?"

Charlotte enthusiastically accepted the challenge. "When I do, will you buy me a new pistol?" she bargained.

"I will think about it, but no promises," Francis teased her. "You are dangerous enough without adding more firepower to your arsenal."

Francis purchased a pastry filled with almonds and raisins, tucked away a flask of spiced wine, and showed up at the dressmaker's shop in Faubourg de St. Jermaine just in time to praise his wife's selection of a new dress of the latest fashion; yes, that sienna color suited her to perfection. He articulated his solicited and favorable opinion on the golden shade of the petticoat, and whisked Henrietta into the soft winter sunshine. The warm air and soft light lured them into a leisurely stroll along the banks of the Seine by Tuileries. As he expected, Henrietta hadn't had time to eat at midday, and she did full justice to the pastry while he recounted the news from his visit to Vincennes.

"Paul d'Ornille received a distinguished visitor who brought up that wondrous event in Marseille." Francis handed her the flask. "M. de Courbet lost priceless family heirlooms when his luggage disappeared during the chaos. Did you know that the poor, sworn to poverty Knights of St. John carry their belongings in large trunks?"

Henrietta carefully wiped her lips with a handkerchief. "Do their belongings include huge single diamonds?"

"De Courbet vaguely alluded to having ownership of the diamond. He speculated about its fate after its disappearance from the Marseille harbor. Don't you agree that carrying the

Great Mogul Diamond in the same trunk as spare breeches makes perfect sense?"

"I suppose he meant it as a decoration to his breeches?"

"Don' be flippant, my dear. That notion is worthy of our son."

Henrietta poked his ribs with her elbow. "What exactly did de Courbet ask of Paul?"

"De Courbet mostly lamented the loss of family heirlooms, and blamed it on the Marshall cousins. I believe it's a ruse. Do you recall Rabatin's letter? A man claimed that contents of his large trunk were switched in Rabatin's warehouse. The description of the man fits de Courbet."

Henrietta almost whistled. "Amazing, indeed, how many objects slipped away from suspicious ownership. We have clandestinely obtained Florentine religious paintings, illegally appropriated intimate portraits, the legendary Great Mogul Diamond, and now a very curious trunk of valuable personal possessions belonging to either a single Knight of St. John or to the whole order," she counted off on her fingers.

"The Knights of St. John have been disputing the ownership of St. Elias' relics with the Knights of Christ since 1713. After - this is important- *after* these relics were officially purchased by the St. John order. We know that de Courbet sailed incognito into Marseille in 1712, as a passenger on a merchant ship. He carried a trunk large enough to hold a casket with religious relics, and he is in conspiracy with the Bishop of Bourges - one of the claimants for St. Elias' relics. So the latest entry in the list of the Marshall cousins' glorious achievements is the disappearance of religious relics along with the Knight's breeches," Francis amended her account. "Don't forget the charges of spying, revenge, and piracy that are also attributed to these oblivious miscreants."

Henrietta handed the flask back to him. "I am concerned

about the involvement of the Knights of St. John in the search for the Marshall cousins."

"So am I."

"When are you planning to enlighten them?"

Francis finished the wine and placed the empty flask into his pocket. "Not yet. There is nothing to do now but wait for de Courbet's next move. Collingstone's nudes can wait. Did I mention to you, my dear, that our daughter will entertain herself by searching for the notorious Marshall cousins?"

Henrietta laughed all the way home.

Honore de Courbet was losing faith. His time was running out, but all his efforts had proved unsuccessful. Captain d'Ornille was sympathetic, but unhelpful. The thought of dealing with the Comte de Tournelles made Honore break into a cold sweat. The man was cordial enough, but Honore could not shake off the impression that the Comte knew more than he let on. In the back of Honore's mind, there was a continuous unease about two men he had noticed in Bourges last September. He distinctly remembered that they came inside and left at the same time as himself. When he exited from the cathedral, they rode away without paying any heed to him. He had searched around, and discovered that if someone was agile, determined, and lucky enough to discover an open door, someone could have climbed up and overheard the conversation in that side room. Honore shivered each time he pictured the deliberate gait of the taller one, and the swagger of the small-framed man with black hair. Who was the young man who jumped from the rafters at the Happy Goat tavern in Montpellier? He obviously was in league with an experienced accomplice, judging from that masterly retreat. Was there any connection between these events, and if so, what was it? And yet no one had ever contacted Honore. He was not inclined to panic, but he felt that an invisible net was tightening around him. His dream of obtaining a respectable post within the Bourges bishopric would disappear if he did not deliver the relics by the summer. His superiors in the order were prevailing over the Knights of Christ. The delivery of St. Elias' relics could be expected any moment, and he could not possibly explain how the pictures replaced St. Elias' relics.

In Montelimar, after a fruitless chase, Honore had examined the canvases closely. The pictures were, without a doubt, precious works of art, and he recognized the style. If these were original paintings, they were of immense value. Who owned those? Were they misplaced on accident? Honore introduced himself into various artists' communities and expressed a vague interest in owning Old Masters' paintings with religious themes.

"I would like to have a picture of Saint Mark with Venice in the background," he claimed. "There are many excellent paintings of Saint George and the Dragon. But most of all, I dare to hope for a sacred Holy Night at Bethlehem." He loosely referred to the paintings from his unexpected collection. He received many offers for commissioning paintings, but no clues to Renaissance masters from his accidentally acquired masterpieces. He despaired, but stubbornly continued his search. He soldiered on this dreary day, and descended the stairs into another shabby tavern frequented by artists. Honore drunk various vile concoctions and listened to chatter around him. A man with a short beard entered the room. His stained hands and speckles of oil paint on his shoes identified his occupation, and he was jovial and talkative. Honore introduced himself and brought up the subject of the Florentine paintings within minutes of conversation. He had become extremely skilled at that.

"Yes, yes, I can vividly imagine such paintings." The newcomer, whose name was Bourzat, stroked his moustache. "Old Masters of the Renaissance painted so magnificently that the pictures survived even in the barbaric New World! I have had the pleasure of purchasing quite a number of Florentine paintings on my patron's behalf...." He coughed. "Most magnificent. Monsieur prefers to decorate his residence with landscapes, not that I mind, of course. Two of those landscapes are mine. I confess, my talent is well recognized."

"So Monsieur does not display Renaissance pictures?" Honore barely kept his voice even as his heart pounded in his chest.

"No, not at all. Such a pity. He left them in the warehouse. He plans to sell them. I hope I will be able to behold these paintings once again."

"Sell them?" Honore asked. "What a blissful coincidence. I might be interested in purchasing them."

"Monsieur is negotiating with a prospective buyer," Bourzat revealed.

Honore left the tavern in rapture. He barely noted the brightness of the sun shining into his eyes as he hurried to the Cathedral of Notre Dame, kneeled at the altar, and praised God, Providence, and all the angels for guiding him toward Bourzat. With the incentive of a monetary reward, Bourzat promised to send an urgent message to Honore if and when these magnificent pictures were to be removed from Rabatin's warehouse. Bourzat did not disclose his patron's name, only that he resided in Orleans. That was Honore's next destination in his quest to recover St. Elias' relics.

26

END OF DECOROUS BEHAVIOR

PARIS – FEBRUARY 1719

*No woman is worth fighting over. Love them for a
month and leave them forever.*

Antoine de la Fleure to Bertrand de la Norte – 1716

THE REQUISITE MUSIC, THE ABUNDANCE OF WINE, THE
bright light from the mirrored chandeliers, the multitude of
servants, the fashionable attires, and expensive jewels of the
courtiers - all components necessary for a dazzling reception were
on display at Palais Royale. Small tables and chairs were arranged
among the containers with tall thick greenery to create shadowed
corners of privacy, and all the men and women were in high spirits. *Almost everyone,* Antoine amended his observation.

In the group gathered around a table, Cecilia de Fabvre's
fine-featured face indicated a vivid interest at the story
narrated by de Chassigneau. De Vergne listened with an air of

resignation. Both men possessively framed the high-backed chair of Charlotte de Brangelton, who was in danger of dozing off from boredom. Her demeanor toward Antoine never improved; she treated him with as much affection as she dispensed on her brother.

"That's an idyllic scene," Antoine commented to Henri.

"The tranquility of this scene will shatter if either one of these jackasses leans closer to admire the view of my sister's décolletage. I wish de la Norte was here."

"Why?" Antoine bit out.

"Because his presence ensures her proper behavior. Why are you not attending to his sister? Your strategy of taxing a woman's patience will never bring her good will."

Listening to Henri's lecture on womanizing did not appeal to Antoine. "Does de la Norte's presence ensure Charles' sane behavior?" he said acidly.

Henri grimaced at the unspoken truth behind these words. "It is not humanly possible. At best, de la Norte's attentions prevent de Chassigneau from provoking her. Spilling blood at the ball is undesirable, even by my father's standards. Or maybe he claims so only to placate mother."

Antoine's incredulous look was lost on Henri. "Why don't you or your father explain to de Chassigneau how the matters stand?"

"Chassigneau's father encourages his son to pursue Mlle. de Brangelton. My father trusts Charlotte to deal with her lunatic admirers. I refuse to fight all de la Norte's battles for him. I took upon myself the task of restraining de Rameau."

"Successfully, no doubt," Antoine interrupted. "Do you suppose Charles will take it upon himself to teach de la Norte to take charge of his own affairs?"

"Don't give Charles any ideas."

Charlotte briefly contributed to the conversation, and shocked stillness descended on her companions.

"We should disband this fine assembly in order to save your beautiful and enchanting sister from becoming bored to tears." Antoine led the way.

"Judging from her tart countenance, she abandoned the concept of blunt weapons and is contemplating the sword," Henri grumbled behind him. "Do me a favor, and keep an eye on her tonight, will you? De Chassigneau harbors a delusion that rumors about de la Decourcelle and de la Norte might send Charlotte into his arms."

Antoine unceremoniously removed Charlotte's feet off the ottoman to sit down. He helped himself to her goblet of wine.

Henri leaned on the back of Cecilia's chair.

"Mlle. Charlotte, why do you say the man lied?" De Vergne mercifully continued the conversation her comment and their arrival must have interrupted.

"Chartres is about fifty miles from Paris." Charlotte flicked her wrist and tossed her fan to hit Antoine's arm. "It is more than a hundred miles round trip. No horse or rider can cover that in half a day."

Henri whispered to Cecilia while bestowing a smoldering look at Gabrielle. The men flanking Charlotte's chair exchanged alarmed glances.

"The man was in love," de Vergne ventured.

"The horses were not in love," Charlotte pointed out with an admirable lack of delicacy on the subject.

When the dancing commenced, Antoine absent-mindedly lead Henri's Cybille while watching Charlotte and de Chassigneau. From across the room, Antoine could read Charlotte's favorite statement on her lips the moment before the music stopped. She carelessly tossed another sharp remark over her pearl-white shoulder and sauntered away to the narrow gallery which extended between the ballroom and the outside balcony where Antoine hurried. In the deserted garden below, the trees stood bare, and the sparse snowflakes slowly twirled to the hushed music. Through the tall windows, he clearly saw Charlotte's swaying figure, the stormy expression on her face, the squared shoulders, and the clenched fists. She briskly curtsied to a lonely couple and continued on her way in the dimly lit and deserted gallery. She stopped, and the steps echoed behind her.

"You bastard. Why the hell are you following me?" she asked de Chassigneau.

His face twisted in anger and he wisely stopped a few paces away. "Your unpardonable rudeness and penchant for foul language -"

"You are a pompous jackass, de Chassigneau." The hardness in her voice could cut the marble balusters. "I repeat, for the last time, leave me alone! I will never marry you. I don't give a damn for your or your father's wishes."

His body twitched. "You despicable little wench!" De Chassigneau's posture was tense and menacing. "I will teach you." He reached forward.

Charlotte punched him in the face. He staggered backwards, fighting for balance and consciousness. Charlotte took advantage of his disorientation. She leapt toward the door leading inside the ballroom. She was a hair's breadth ahead of de Chassigneau, who had partially recovered and dashed after her.

In an instant, Antoine climbed through one of the open windows. He landed behind de Chassigneau just as a steel weapon gleamed in Charlotte's hand. De Chassigneau desperately lunged forward to disarm her. The sharp professional sweep of the blade forced him to recoil in panic.

"Damn you," he hissed. His hands groped against the wall at his back, and he remained oblivious to Antoine's presence.

Antoine covered the distance between them in quiet strides. "What was that, de Chassigneau?"

"None of your business." The man did not even bother to turn his head to speak to him.

Antoine reciprocated by a punch to the side of de Chassigneau's head.

Charlotte hid away her weapon in a hidden pocket at the side of her dress.

"Why did you go out here?" Antoine laced their fingers together and led her away from the motionless shape on the stone floor. "Did it occur to you that he might follow?"

"Why were you outside?" Indignation, defiance, and amusement mixed in her voice. "Did you follow me?"

"Did you bring your hat for the occasion of bloodshed?" He marched fast, furious at himself for coming to her aid. He should have allowed her to run the curved dagger through de Chassigneau's shoulder. That would have been the end of de la Norte's romance. He was equally angry at Charlotte for taking charge in this matter. He would have been delighted to deal with de Chassigneau on her behalf, and he should have done it in a more gracious manner, instead of turning the exchange into a common brawl.

"Why did you meddle?" Charlotte asked.

"I am practicing gallant behavior." He barely restrained himself from articulating his opinion about her enchanting ways.

"Since when? Why?"

"Maybe tonight I can believe, along with other fools out there, that you are a woman!" Antoine raised his voice over the sounds of church bells announcing the hour of midnight.

"I am Charlotte de Brangelton," followed the familiar explanation.

Antoine spun to face her, with the intent to communicate his opinion about the duplicity of her words and deeds. Would she be spoiling for a fight and bloodshed if de la Norte was present? In his exasperation, Antoine did not release her hand, and the sudden pull on her arm threw her off balance. He caught her in an embrace, his arm wrapped around her waist and her body pressed against his. Charlotte's glowing eyes opened wide, and the palms of her hands rested against his chest. Her skin felt cool and soft under his caress, and he leaned forward to kiss her. Her hands moved up his chest to his shoulders, but suddenly there was a flicker of panic in her eyes, the same expression he painfully remembered at the tavern in Bourges, and she pushed him away. Antoine released her and staggered back. The time stood still. Antoine's mouth was dry, his heart beat fast, and his mind was in disarray. The empty air between them sobered him into desperation when Charlotte wrapped her arms around herself and gazed at the clear crescent of the moon outside.

"I thought... ah...that you maintain the appearance of proper behavior," Antoine managed in a hoarse voice.

"This prim and decorous behavior brings me nothing but hassle and headache!" Charlotte shook her head. "I am no longer myself!"

"Charlotte, you cannot live all your life as Charles." Why did he discourage her to introduce Charles to de la Norte?

"I am not a courtier, and will never be one." She was defiant. "I will not be imprisoned in a fancy dress. It is a miserable existence, Antoine, when you have to worry about every step."

"Is this why you prefer to be Charles?"

"As Charles, I enjoy the freedom you have, and I guide my own fate," she said softly. Her sparkling eyes focused on the bright stars in the sky. "I will never give that up. Not for anything. Not for anyone. Never," she repeated with iron determination, her jaw set in defiance.

Antoine's heart leapt at that. He nodded his encouragement.

"Can you imagine me traveling from Ferrand to Paris as myself?" She spread out her arms, and Antoine shook his head, unable to phrase his thoughts into a coherent response. "I dream of visiting faraway places - Venice, London, Amsterdam, Edinburg, and the New World. Charles can journey anywhere unnoticed, independent, carefree."

"I will accompany you." Antoine's tongue disconnected from his racing mind at the vivid image of Charlotte and himself alone.

She smiled and nodded before her eyes flashed and narrowed. "No! Don't even think about it!"

"About what?" Antoine' heart sunk again in the knowledge that the reason for her refusal was named de la Norte.

"Never mind." She shook her head.

Antoine stepped closer to her. After all, there was nothing for him to lose. "I will accompany you anywhere in the world. Your choice is where to start."

"You are not serious," Charlotte accused him.

"I am serious. Damn serious." He reached to embrace her. His fingertips brushed her shoulders, and he thought she would come into his arms, but Charlotte vehemently pushed him back.

"Stop it!"

"Stop what?" Antoine asked. The touch of her hands against his chest rendered his mind void of any coherent thought.

"Never mind! It's freezing out here," Charlotte headed toward the door into the ballroom. Antoine, oblivious to the cold, watched her swaying figure when she turned her head to favor him with a wistful glance before she hurried inside.

"What shall I do about you, Charlotte de Brangelton?" Antoine asked the empty air between them. She did not take offense at his disjointed rumblings. Maybe she did not care for de la Norte after all.

Henri made the mistake of investigating why a group of people were fussing around a man reclined on the floor. He regretted his curiosity upon realization that de Chassigneau had a compress against the right side of his head, while his left eye was starting to swell.

"That perverse wench de Brangelton..." De Chassigneau had regained the ability to speak.

"What was that?" Henri interrupted. "Are you referring to my sister?"

"No, of course not!" He bit his tongue, conscious enough to understand the implications. "My apologies, my minds is addled. I don't know what happened. I went outside for a moment."

Henri listened to the speculations before contributing his guess that de Chassigneau must have slipped. When everyone to agreed, or at least pretended, Henri returned to the peaceful ballroom and a single glance at Charlotte's innocent face and Antoine's unperturbed face confirmed his suspicions.

"Charlotte?" Henri asked.

"What?"

"What happened to de Chassigneau?"

Charlotte shrugged her shoulders. So did Antoine.

"Charlotte de Brangelton?" Henri repeated.

"I encouraged the bastard to move out of my way."

Henri deeply inhaled to control his flaring temper. His sister could provoke a saint. "What exactly was the extent of your encouragement?"

"I threatened him with an embroidery needle."

Henri had a sinking feeling that Charlotte's proper behavior was a lost cause. "Antoine, what happened there?"

"Antoine interfered before I had a chance to run my blade through de Chassigneau's shoulder," Charlotte explained. "Are you satisfied?"

"I cannot leave you alone for a moment!" Henri remonstrated. "Can you imagine de la Norte's reaction if he witnessed your performance?"

Both grimaced with annoyance. "I wish," Antoine responded.

"You still have told me nothing about your trip last December." Cybille's lips caressed Henri's ear.

He was amazed that their affair had lasted. She must have realized that no information was forthcoming and turned her efforts to blackmail. When would she finally tire of him? She had a perfect body, but bringing business to bed and using it as a payment for passion was a recipe to cool off a man's desire.

"Did I take a trip last December, love?" Henri perused the gaudy-painted panels of bucolic springtime pastures painted on every wall in her bedroom. No matter how many times he viewed those pastoral scenes, he still marveled at how tasteless they were.

"Yes. You, your father, and your friend left Paris for a couple of weeks." She physically distanced herself from him.

"Ah, that trip must have been uneventful." Henri did not

bother to close the space between them. "Except my moustache grew back."

"Marshall cousins, love?" Henri asked innocently.

Gabrielle's very vivid imagination lately has been ignited by the outrageous gossip about the cousins' imaginary exploits. Spying! Revenge for Port Royal! A vendetta from India! A random act of piracy on a dare! The conjectures were becoming more and more absurd. "No, I have never heard of them till now."

"Henri!" she pouted. "They are such intriguing young men! So daring!"

"Ah, that is unfortunate. I avoid danger, and embrace the life of pleasure." He wrapped his arm around her waist, but she wriggled out, leaving almost a visible screen of her exotic perfume.

"But this is so exciting!" she sang. "Just think, two young men blew up Marseille Harbor and pillaged over twenty ships in one night! Don't you wish you were one of them?"

"Not at all. I am a lover, not a fighter." Henri lost all desire to stay with her. He never cared to pay attention to conversation in bed. "But since their exploits excite you so much, tell me everything you know about them." He uttered with a feeble, even to his own ears, impression of wounded pride.

"The Comte de Flancourt is in love with your sister," Eloise repeated the outrageous gossip.

"I don't think so, love." Henri brushed off the subject.

"Didn't the Comte de Flancourt knock out M. de Chassigneau?"

"Love, that is an indelicate question to ask." Henri refused to engage into speculations about who knocked out de Chassigneau. Who would guess that the enchanting Mlle. de Brangelton was perfectly capable of single-handedly dispatching a man?

"Must be difficult for you to chaperone your sister." Eloise paid no attention to his comments. She rummaged in the bowl of sweets, found a piece, and nibbled on it. "The Comte de Flancourt and M. de la Norte and M. de Rameau are your friends, aren't they?"

"My sister will make her choice." He played with Eloise's golden hair. "It is always a woman's choice, isn't it, love?"

Henri felt miserable due to the headache of his hangover and the plain fatigue since he had prowled till dawn again. He had lost count how many days in a row. He barely stayed in the saddle upright at the early hour of noon. Cybille, Gabrielle, and Eloise were beautiful women, but their continuous claims upon his time were increasing and thus encroaching into other aspects of his life, such as sleep. Why did he commit to taking his sister fencing? Was it indeed necessary? Antoine waited for them at the Bois de Boulogne, and Henri was grateful for his friend's dedication to the art of swordsmanship and honing Charlotte's skills. Henri brought a blanket for himself. He anticipated slumbering for a couple of hours there. The clear blue skies and bright sunshine meant dry ground, and he counted on borrowing Charlotte's lined cloak for added warmth.

"Henri, I endured enough diplomacy in dealing with Bertrand de la Norte," his sister announced without any preface.

Henri moaned, partially due to her timing, partially due to the immediate increase of his headache. He was in no shape to discuss de la Norte or anything else. "I thought you considered marrying him."

"Marrying him?" Her inflection betrayed the familiar aversion upon the subject. "I will live my life my way. Not he, not anyone else will ever change me!"

Henri rubbed his forehead to awaken his mind. "You no longer care for him, do you?"

"I can live my life without him." She was edgy, and she was concealing the cause. What happened between them? But Henri himself had heard enough of de la Norte's complaints about her visits to the Musketeer's Headquarters, about Hera, and about who knows what else that Henri dismissed. De la Norte perceived her demeanor as wild, and Henri could not imagine de la Norte's reaction and disappointment upon meeting Charles. And if Charlotte had decided to trade de la Norte for de Rameau, Henri did not want to know.

"Antoine is the only lunatic encouraging Charles," Henri changed the subject. "Even de Rameau -"

"The devil take de Rameau!" Charlotte twisted in the saddle and her mare pranced in response. "Antoine... Never mind, I do not have to explain him to anyone! I bet no one dares to question him!"

"Who, besides my dim-witted friend de Rameau, asked you about him?"

Charlotte narrowed her eyes. "Never mind," she repeated. "I do not want to talk about Antoine. Oh, there he is." She waved and sent Hera trotting toward him.

DISPUTE

PARIS, FRANCE – MARCH 1719

Most of the time, you can get away with dueling as long as there are witnesses that your foe draws the sword first.

Paul d'Ornille to Henrietta d'Arringnon – 1694

BERTRAND PULLED UP A CHAIR TO THE HARPSICHORD AND absent-mindedly tapped the keys. "Mlle. Charlotte knows that my formal obligations are not my heart's desire," he said with more confidence than he felt. Charlotte de Brangelton's thoughts and feelings were as indefinable as her perfume. She switched and mixed the fragrances every day.

Cecilia reclined on the spacious settee and absent-mindedly drummed her fingers to echo the rhythm. "Even if she cares for your heart's desire, she knows that you are a much less attractive match if father disowns you."

"You are repeating father's sermon." Bertrand played a short march.

"Father married me to the Marquis de Fabvre to promote you in the world." His sister snapped her fan for emphasis. "Do not belittle my sacrifice."

Bertrand's stomach churned. How could he defy his father and distress his sister when he was not certain about Mlle. Charlotte's feelings toward him? "Am I a fool to hope that she loves me?"

Cecilia's grim expression reminded him of their father. "Has she ever exhibited any jealousy of Anne-Louise?"

No, Bertrand thought, Charlotte ignored his looming engagement to Mlle. de la Decourcelle. Jealousy was his lot. Ever since the Regent's New Year Ball, the phrase *"de Brangelton, his sister, and de Flancourt"* had become more common in idle conversations. Charlotte's mare, who still suspiciously eyed him, nuzzled de Flancourt in the most domesticated manner.

"Are you aware that in December, Duchess Helene's escort to Versailles included a boy named Charles d'Arringnon?"

"Yes, I heard about it, more than once." He hit a dissonant key a few times. He could not banish from his mind the image of the swaggering boy from the fencing hall, the understanding glances between the Musketeers, Henri de Brangelton's elusive answers, de Contraille's pained silence, and, most persuasive of all, the sudden, no-hesitation departure of de Flancourt. Had she come to meet with de Flancourt there?

Cecilia smoothed the pale yellow fabric of her dress. "What happened to M. de Chassigneau last week?"

"I don't know," Bertrand admitted.

"Everyone believes the Comte de Flancourt knocked him out." She fanned herself.

Bertrand played *"Pretty Maiden, don't you know..."* and winced when he hit a wrong note.

Cecilia waited till the sound subsided. "Charlotte de Brangelton is the only woman in the world capable of extracting a range of emotions from the self-possessed Comte de Flancourt within a span of a few moments."

Bertrand turned away from the harpsichord. "They argue." *And reconcile.*

Cecilia leaned forward. "He is very attentive to her."

"He is a friend of her brother."

She was troubled. "I hear they are seen together every day."

"Are you insinuating that de Flancourt and she...No!" Bertrand found himself standing up in front of his sister. "No, Charlotte is... she is not..." He searched for words to say without offending Cecilia. "I am certain that Charlotte is not having an affair with him!"

Cecilia lowered her head. "I agree with you. But I am certain this is precisely the subject of their arguments."

Charlotte, the most inconsiderate young woman, has eluded Antoine for the second day. Yesterday she had accompanied her father on his errands, and today she had scheduled visits to a dressmaker, shoemaker, and a merchant of fine linens. Antoine spent an hour at the Louvre watching a tennis match and loitered at the Pont Neuf for another hour. Late morning extended into afternoon, but Charlotte still did not return home. He headed in the general direction of the Musketeer's Headquarters when de la Norte appeared from the Palais Royale. Despite the never-ending constructions on the Rue St. Antoine, the street was generally wide enough for two men on opposite sides to politely ignore each other, but not today. De la Norte purposely crossed the street to intercept him.

"De Flancourt."

"De la Norte."

"I heard you and Mlle. de Brangelton traded horses?"

Hearing Charlotte's name from de la Norte immediately set Antoine's nerves on the edge and pushed the boundaries of his self-control. "How does it concern you?"

"I understand her horse does not trust strangers." De la Norte surprised him with an unexpected display of nerve. His inflection echoed Antoine's sentiment.

"We are not strangers."

His eyes flashed with anger. "How well do you know Charles d'Arringnon?"

"Have you finally had the pleasure of meeting Charles?" Antoine attempted to keep his voice level, but could not cover his disdain.

"I know of him," de la Norte said sharply. His courtly polish was wearing thin. Was it courtesy of Charlotte? Had he witnessed even one tenth of her wild behavior?

In the distance, across the Bastille square, de Rousard and two Musketeers suddenly stopped in their tracks. Antoine's mind wrestled between obeying common sense and the overwhelming desire to boast of his close association with Charles. "Charles stood by me in a fight when we were attacked and outnumbered." His upper lip hurt when he realized how much he had disclosed.

De la Norte paled. "What happened?"

"I do not have to answer your questions."

"Yes, you do." His hand rested on the hilt of his sword.

Antoine mirrored the other man's pose. "No, I don't." Out of the corner of his eye, he noticed that a man in a Musketeer's uniform stepped to his side.

"I must know the truth about you and her." De la Norte's eyes were feverish with desperation.

Antoine's control of his temper and any lingering good

intentions disappeared in a whiff of smoke. He would never admit to anyone, least to de la Norte, what a fool he could be. "I will save her the trouble of introducing Charles to you. She is easily accepted as a cutthroat among the cadre of military officers. She is an excellent fencer. She is more courageous than most men I know. She knows her mind and her loyalties."

De Rameau broke the terse silence. "If you, de Flancourt, de la Norte, are unclear about the tender feelings of a certain high-strung Mlle. toward either one of you, I will be happy to abolish any illusions you might have."

Neither Antoine nor de la Norte acknowledged de Rameau's intrusion in their conversation. De Rousard and his cohorts briskly marched toward them through a surrounding crowd. Men even climbed up on the construction scaffolding in anticipation of violence.

"Her loyalties are not with you!" De la Norte's voice was coarse with suppressed emotion. "She deserves a better man."

"You are not worthy of her!" The hot rage clouded Antoine's mind. He could not tell if he or de la Norte moved first, but their blades had crossed just as the Lieutenant and his men arrived to the scene. One of the Musketeers gripped de la Norte's wrist while de Rousard and another Musketeer moved to restrain Antoine. He dug in his heels, pushing de Rousard back and kicked out with his left foot, tripping the Musketeer. De Rousard recovered from the maneuver and twisted Antoine's sword arm back. The blade scraped on the ground and slapped against de Rousard's boot.

"Stop acting like a love-stricken jackass," his friend the Lieutenant advised quietly. "I am under orders to arrest anyone for dueling."

Antoine had no choice but to allow de Rousard to relieve him of his weapon. De la Norte's sword was already unceremoniously confiscated.

"This was just a simple misunderstanding. Everything is in order now," de Rousard stated for the benefit of the public.

"We were just admiring the many virtues of a very alluring, but fickle young woman." De Rameau studiously avoided his officer's eyes.

"Fickle?" Antoine spat. Charlotte may be uncooperative, impulsive, stubborn, reckless... "She knows damn well what she wants, and she will do anything she damn well pleases!"

"This conversation about Mlle. is finished!" de Rousard bellowed.

The Lieutenant's understanding of the situation collided with de Rameau's perception of it. "We shall see who will help her to do anything she damn well pleases!"

Antoine's "To quote Mlle., go to hell," coincided with de la Norte's meek "Not you, Monsieur."

"Not a word from either one of you!" de Rousard roared.

"When did Mlle. address this sweet statement to you, de Flancourt?" de Rameau sneered.

"How many times did she address it to you?" Antoine disregarded de Rousard's punch to his shoulder. "She has an excellent vocabulary, doesn't she?"

The Lieutenant's vocabulary was just as excellent, but his tirade was trounced by de Rameau's desire to continue this debate. "How did she dismiss you, de Flancourt?"

Restrain abandoned Antoine. "Didn't she compare your filthy overtures to a pile of manure?"

"Silence!" de Rousard thundered.

De Rameau's eyes blazed murderously at Antoine. "I recall your uncouth and boorish-"

"Hand over your sword!" the Lieutenant commanded his Musketeer.

De Rameau opened his mouth to argue further, but a vague sense of discipline belatedly prevailed.

"Upon His Majesty's authority, follow me. All three of you," de Rousard ordered. "If anyone utters a single syllable, I will gag him."

The onlookers hastily cleared the path.

Bertrand de la Norte was aghast upon being escorted, together with de Flancourt and de Rameau, to the room behind the Musketeer's Headquarters. The room contained half a dozen chairs and a table with a pitcher of water and drinking cups on it, but the bars on the windows, locked door, and the two guards outside clearly indicated that was no plain waiting room.

What had possessed him to converse with de Flancourt about Mlle. Charlotte? Had he expected de Flancourt to bow out and leave her alone? Bertrand's throat contracted when he thought about the scandal this adventure would cause and his father's reaction. He resented that his only course of action at this moment, due to the lack of any knowledge and experience in such situations, was to follow de Flancourt's lead.

De Rameau straddled the chair along the wall. De Flancourt, his face a blank mask, positioned himself on the opposite side. Bertrand took the place under the window.

After waiting for what seemed to be an eternity but according to the clock was only slightly over an hour, the door opened and the Captain of His Majesty's Musketeers, along with Lieutenant de Rousard, entered.

"Report for double duty this evening, remain within the Headquarters between the second and third double duty," Captain d'Ornille spat into de Rameau's direction. De Rameau made a sound of indignation, wisely choked the impulse, saluted, grabbed his sword from the Lieutenant, and stormed out. The Captain focused his attention at Bertrand and de Flancourt.

"One of you hot-blooded reprobates will leave the city tomorrow for a month," he continued. "The other one will stay under house arrest for a week."

Bertrand didn't quite understand the details. Who was staying and who was leaving?

De Flancourt spoke. "I am not leaving Paris."

"Neither am I," Bertrand added.

"Would you prefer to be guests of the Bastille? I can arrange for you to share a cell," Captain d'Ornille threatened. "What will it be?" he prompted after a few moments of word-lessness.

"I have a proposition," de Flancourt half-growled. "A fencing round, de la Norte? First one to touch the opponent wins, and the winner stays in Paris."

Bertrand never expected Captain d'Ornille to accept de Flancourt's solution, let alone merrily. Bertrand was flabber-gasted by the expeditious and efficient manner in which it was arranged. Within half an hour, bales and ropes defined the makeshift arena in the Headquarters' inner yard. The dusk was yielding to the evening darkness, and lanterns were hung from the high windows to provide the light.

Captain d'Ornille and Lieutenant de Rousard covered the blades of the swords before handing the weapons back to Bertrand and de Flancourt. It was difficult to judge the number of men loitered along the walls, but Bertrand was certain there were at least a hundred.

"Do you prefer to start with the light on your left or right?" de Flancourt asked him.

Bertrand vaguely remembered the theory that fencing in the darkness greatly depended on interpreting the distortion of the shadows. What was it? *"If you are right-handed, position yourself with the light on your left."* Or was it on your right? De Flancourt obviously knew the answer, and doubtlessly, he had more experience of fencing under those conditions. He was also a better fencer with his left hand, and if he chose to use his left hand, Bertrand's chances of winning decreased even more. "Does not matter to me." He hoped that his tone was just as blank as Comte's.

The Captain and Lieutenant blended with the shadows. Everyone seemed to know the protocol, leaving Bertrand to wonder just how many arguments were settled this way. The assembly in the yard hushed. The distant sounds of the evening in the city – laughter and singing, dogs barking, horse hooves - drifted overhead, and a single bird laboriously chirped on the roof. De Flancourt put the light on his right.

Bertrand took his position and focused on his strategy. His training was classic, with deep and long lunges and parries. In the deceptiveness of shadows and the uncertainty of light, he reasoned that he should open by keeping his adversary at a distance.

"Go," Captain d'Ornille sharply commanded.

Bertrand barely blocked the fast long lunge from de Flancourt, which forced him to fall back. He had the advantage of position in the shadows. In dis-engagement, de Flancourt moved into the center of the light circle. Bertrand lunged forward with a thrust toward the left side of the stomach, but de Flancourt sidestepped and almost knocked the sword out of Bertrand's hand. For a split moment, Bertrand lost his balance. He was now in the center of the light circle. De Flancourt's blade flashed and Bertrand spun around to block it. He was at a disadvantage, unable to see his opponent's face. Bertrand retreated, inviting de Flancourt to step up toward the light. De Flancourt's fencing style was tight; he usually excelled in efficient movements, but seemed to hesitate. A moment later, the blade flickered toward Bertrand's collarbone, and he panicked. He lost a split moment in deflecting it, and realized de Flancourt's strategy to position himself to deliver the thrust from the side only when the covered tip of de Flancourt's sword painfully hit him from the left side.

28

FAREWELL

PARIS, FRANCE - MARCH 1719

*I had a lingering, naïve hope that I underestimated
Antoine's reason and overestimated young de la
Norte's lack of such, but once again, I am proven to
be correct in my original assessment.*

Francis de Brangelton to Paul d'Ornille - 1719

Fury and embarrassment enveloped Bertrand de la
Norte. He had had no business to question de Flancourt about
Mlle. de Brangelton! Bertrand did not know what devil had
possessed him earlier, but his word of honor to Captain
d'Ornille bound him to leave the next day. He had no doubt
that after a week of confinement, de Flancourt would be at
Mlle. Charlotte's side. Bertrand had no time to adhere to
conventions. Despite the lateness of the hour, he headed
directly to Charlotte's home and his heart leapt for joy when

his arrival was announced and he heard her clear voice, "Bring him in."

"Charlotte," He kissed her hand and for the first time noticed the hardened skin on the palm and the fingers, exactly where the sword grip would cause calluses. "I apologize for such a late visit, but I have no other choice. I must speak with you."

"What is it?" Her eyes were wary and measuring.

"I must leave Paris tomorrow." He paused, waiting for her reaction, but she showed no emotion. "Before I go... I must tell you... I crave to ask you...Charlotte, will you marry me?"

"No." She shook her head.

"Charlotte!" His mind plunged in turmoil. "Why do you say no? Is it because of my father's threat to disown me? I am certain I can provide for us," he blubbered.

Charlotte pushed him away. "Bertrand, you don't know me."

"I do. I love you." Bertrand embraced her, but her dark eyes took on that disconcerting, dreamy glitter. Her thoughts were hidden, her feelings veiled.

"We should have had this conversation sooner, Bertrand." Charlotte inhaled and visibly braced herself. "Have you heard about Charles d'Arringnon?"

"No... yes," Bertrand stammered.

"You don't believe it." She faced him with a rueful little smile. "You did not even recognize Charles when you saw him."

"When?" Bertrand gripped the back of the chair for support, his conflicting emotions of despair, embarrassment, denial and desire clouded his mind. "How could I possibly not recognize you?"

"Do you recall meeting a boy named Charles?"

"Yes," he faltered. "I guessed it was you at the fencing hall. Why?"

"To practice my fencing skills."

Bertrand felt a chill down his spine. "I hoped you had no such interest."

Her back stiffened. "May I ask why you nurture that hope?"

"I desire to marry you, Charlotte, but if you pretend to be a man... it is ... is not acceptable ..."

She clenched her fists. "You must understand that I can, and will, do anything I please. I am Charlotte de Brangelton."

Bertrand took her hands in his. "I understand, but I will never prevail upon my father to accept it!"

"Your father will never accept me," she said flatly. "If you marry me, Bertrand, he may never speak to you again."

Deep in his heart, he knew it was the bitter reality. "But why, why would you insist on being Charles?"

She looked beyond him. "Charles enjoys the same freedom you have, the freedom to act as I please. I will never give that up. Not for anything. Not for anyone. Never. Will you, Bertrand, accept Charles' decision to head out on my father's business, or will you regret severing your ties with your family on my account?"

Bertrand kissed the palm of her hand. "Charlotte, I will do anything for you." He forced himself to ignore the chill in the pit of his stomach. "Anything."

Her features hardened. "I will make no promises, Bertrand, until you know me as Charles."

"I must leave Paris for a month." Bertrand wrapped his arms around her. "Please, give me hope and faith, till I come back." He kissed her temple, but Charlotte unceremoniously removed his arms from her waist.

"What is the reason?"

"I have to, I must, I promised. But I will return, Charlotte."

"Bertrand. Do you not trust me, or are you under an obligation to keep a secret?"

"This is no secret, but no, I beg you, do not command me to admit..."

Charlotte's eyes narrowed. "May I ask you, Monsieur Bertrand, if the same answer would be acceptable coming from me?"

"Yes." Bertrand no longer knew what he was saying. "Anything, except..." he trailed off.

"Except what?" Charlotte's hands were clenched into fists again. She stood like a fighter prepared for hand-to-hand combat. "Except tolerating Charles?"

Bertrand gathered his courage. "I will do anything for you, Charlotte, except tolerating your friendship with the Comte de Flancourt."

Charlotte's heated glare almost physically burned his heart. "May I remind you that Antoine de Flancourt and I grew up together? I consider Raoul de la Fleure my younger brother. I cannot disown either one of them any more than I can disown Henri."

Bertrand tossed away all caution. "Do you consider Antoine de Flancourt your other older brother?"

He jumped back when Charlotte picked up a misshapen tankard from the table and tossed it at the wall, precisely in the center of the chipped spot on the wall he had always wondered about. The tankard rattled back, the splinters of plaster floating to the floor.

"That is a ludicrous question!"

"Please answer me!" Bertrand heard himself raising his voice.

Charlotte kicked the tankard up, caught it with one hand, and hurled it back precisely at the same spot.

Bertrand took her hands. "Please, Charlotte. This is all I ask of you," he begged in desperation.

"I will never give up our comradeship," Charlotte's eyes held a disconcerting, warlike gleam. "Antoine de Flancourt and I fought together. I will never forgo a friendship bound by blood."

"Fought together?" He repeated. *"Charles stood by me."* de Flancourt had said.

Charlotte freed her hands. "Yes."

"No," Bertrand's thoughts scattered to the seven winds upon her statement. "Why would you...?"

"He and Charles were attacked upon our arrival to Paris last September." Charlotte's face set into an emotionless mask.

Bertrand's heart sunk. "You care for him more than you will ever love me," he accused her. His own voice sounded hollow even to his own ears.

"If that's what you believe, suit yourself," Charlotte kicked the tankard precisely to the same spot on the wall, ascended the stairs, and slammed the door shut behind her.

Bertrand focused his eyes on his father's disapproving frown. The room and the ceiling chandelier swayed, and he dropped into a chair without waiting for father's permission. He pondered if his appearance was as dis-arrayed as his rum-infused thoughts.

"Explain yourself, Bertrand."

"I was ordered to leave Paris," Bertrand answered.

"What were you thinking, to challenge de Flancourt on the account of his mistress?" father asked.

"She is not his mistress!" Bertrand's voice cracked. How could he be certain? Did it even matter now? Charlotte – no, Mlle. de Brangelton – had made her choice clear.

"It is irrelevant." Father leaned against the table. There seemed to be two of him.

In Bertrand's cloudy mind, another question formed. "How do you know about it, father?"

"Giles followed you. You are fortunate that Lieutenant de Rousard and his men prevented you from splitting yourself on de Flancourt's sword!"

"Did you order Giles to spy on me?" Bertrand tried to stand up, but lost his balance and dropped back into the chair.

"It is for your own good." Father's face darkened, doubled, and floated again. "You are a de la Norte, Bertrand. It does not suit you to behave like an irresponsible cutthroat."

"Or a coward," Bertrand spat out. "I am a coward, father, unable to accept the truth."

His father cringed, probably at the hysterical notes in his tone. "You are drunk out of your mind."

"And I am elated about it," Bertrand sneered. He never dared to speak to his father in this manner, but he did not care today. "Do you know anything about love and happiness, father?"

"You shall not marry the Devil's daughter!" Father slammed his fist on the table, and the candleholders rattled.

"No, she will not marry me. Who did you assign me to marry, father?"

Father leaned over and put his hands on his shoulders. "Bertrand. I will soon secure a dukedom for you."

"Will Dukedom give me happiness?" Bertrand raised his eyes to the ceiling.

"It will bring you power!"

"Ah, yes," Bertrand pushed father's hands off his shoulders and rose unsteadily to his feet. "Yes. But Charlotte de Brangelton will never be mine."

Henrietta paused at the entrance to the sitting room to behold a caged lioness in the image of her daughter. Charlotte alternated between pacing around the room, kicking and hurling a former tankard, and indulging in sips of rum from the bottle. Large pieces of wall plaster were scattered on the floor. The stone wall beneath the plaster was chipped as well.

Henrietta surmised that either Bertrand de la Norte or Antoine had stopped by. Hopefully, not both at the same time. Paul d'Ornille had extracted an oath of peace before releasing them, but the truce between young men on account of a young woman would always be fragile.

"Charlotte," Francis called her attention. "What now?"

"He must have expected me to trade my sword for an embroidery needle." Charlotte tossed up the unrecognizable tankard and flung it precisely into the center of the target.

"You must be speaking about Monsieur Bertrand de la Norte."

Charlotte sat down, punched a pillow against the back of the settee, and jumped up again. "The Devil may choke on my proper behavior! It's all Henri's fault. Why did I ever listen to him? This masquerade has caused nothing but headaches. I have suffered through Antoine's implications, twice - twice! - that I was lying to de la Norte! And then he had the nerve to offer to escort me to Lyon."

"I assume Antoine offered to take you to Lyon," Francis stated slyly.

Charlotte took a deep breath. "Never mind that, father."

"An excellent suggestion," Francis grinned. "I am certain Laurent and Marguerite will be happy to see you."

"Antoine is an impossible man to deal with!" Charlotte spread her arms. "He is devious, stubborn, arrogant, and inconsiderate. I have had fencing round challenges with de Bonnard and d'Signac because of him." Every loud sentence was punctuated by the clatter of pewter hitting the wall. "I cannot appear in the fencing hall because–" At this point, Charlotte primly sat down and dreamily stared in the distance. "Why not? It's time for Charles to show up in Paris!"

"Why do you –or Charles – object to Lyon?" Francis inquired.

Charlotte made a sound suspiciously resembling a growl. "Very well, I will suffer further imprisonment in these dresses," she said with air of insulted dignity, unsteadily climbed the stairs, and slammed the door to her room.

Francis grinned at Henrietta. "What do you have against sending our daughter off to Lyon?"

"Nothing at all," Henrietta found her voice. "Yes, it's perfectly acceptable for a young woman to travel with a young man. Why just Lyon? Marguerite and Laurent just might instill some respectability to the situation. Maybe Charlotte and Antoine should depart to the New World? For certain, a longer trip will cause less gossip!"

He embraced her. "My dear Henrietta, I am ashamed that I underestimated Antoine's deviousness. Very well, I will take care of this incident."

"How?"

"Take Charlotte to Versailles with detours to Poissy and Conflans. A week of sightseeing will calm her down. Antoine's detention should cool off his temper. Then maybe these two worthies will bother themselves with a meaningful discussion."

Charlotte peeked outside her door. "Not for a moment I did believe that he would ever accept Charles!"

"De la Norte? Of course not." Francis sipped the rum. "Are you depressed or relieved?"

"De Rameau will become intolerable now. I will ask Uncle Paul to send him away." Her eyes fixed on the bottle of rum and she descended the stairs. "Maybe we could visit Raoul in Troyes."

"You and de Rameau?" Francis inquired.

"No!" Charlotte picked up the bottle of rum. "Henri, Antoine, and I."

Henrietta cringed at the amount of rum flooding down Charlotte's throat.

Francis confiscated the bottle. "What happened here?"

"He made an idiotic accusation about Antoine and me, and never apologized for it." Charlotte resumed her artillery practice. Her aim remained amazingly steady. "Father, why must Bertrand de la Norte leave Paris?"

Henrietta caught a glimmer of amusement and surprise in her husband's eyes. "Would you like to ride to Versailles with me tomorrow?" he invited her.

"Yes!" Charlotte carefully placed the twisted pewter on the table. "What time are we leaving? For how long?"

The satisfaction of winning the fencing round and thus ensuring his stay in Paris did not provide happiness and satisfaction for Antoine. Despite the quantities of wine he consumed, he had spent a restless night. He was in no way romantically involved with Charlotte, but he had nearly fought a duel on her behalf, he had committed himself to roam the world with her, he sought her company every day, and he could no longer ignore the feelings of dismay and apprehension at his own inexcusable behavior. He refused to forfeit the company of the beautiful and enchanting Charlotte. He had lost his head over the most impossible woman in France, and probably the whole world. In the bleak pre-dawn hours, it occurred to him that if de la Norte possessed even a shred of intelligence, he would see Charlotte before leaving Paris. If she were to come with him ... At this thought, a chair broke against the wall and all hopes of sleep eluded Antoine altogether. The rising sun found him marching back and forth in the room and vowing to kill de la Norte if that happened. Antoine could not bear the thought of de la Norte touching Charlotte. Why had de Rousard interfered? Antoine had just found choice words to honor the Lieutenant when Henri arrived.

"My sister is insane. De la Norte has lost his mind. De Rameau is a fool. What happened to you?" Henri had thoughtfully brought along a bottle of brandy, which he handed it to Antoine.

"De la Norte refused to believe in Charles' existence, thus implying that I had lied," Antoine found a logical justification for his actions.

Henri dropped his head into his hands. "My apology. Charlotte would have introduced Charles a long time ago, but I advised her to do it gradually, and de la Norte must have been shocked upon finally realizing the truth." He sat down and looked for another chair to put his feet up. "She is quite infuriated at you and me."

"Why?" Antoine almost dropped the bottle.

"She blamed me – and you - for something either I - or you - did or failed to do. She was generously using unflattering epithets, so I escaped and did not quite catch why we are annoying, dim-witted louts. And why is she mad at me? What did I have to do with your unprecedented chivalrous activities last night?"

Antoine did not care why she was upset at Henri. "Where is she now?" he asked with trepidation.

"Charles is on his way to Versailles."

No, she could not possibly have left with de la Norte.

Antoine splashed brandy in a goblet and gulped a generous measure. "What is there for her?"

"A brief excursion with our father. He probably wished to avoid the expense of fixing the hole in the wall. There is no plaster left." He eyed Antoine's glass.

"I trust your father will not marry her off to de la Norte." Antoine needed to be certain.

"Oh, no." Henri helped himself to brandy. "De la Norte is not good enough for Charlotte. Neither de Seveigney nor de Molienier is good enough for Charlotte. I just do not understand–"

"Who is de Molienier?" Antoine managed to stay in his chair.

Henri sat his drink down. "She did not tell you?"

"Tell me what?" Antoine barely contained his temper again. *Another admirer?*

"Captain de Molienier, commander of the garrison at Ferrand. He was the reason she left home. You did not know?"

"No, I had no idea. Your sister is a master of evasion. What happened?" he asked.

"His persistence in asking for her hand and his presumption that he could pry a sword away from her hand infuriated her. I just cannot imagine how a sensible man, who has met Charles, could possibly lose his head over Charlotte?"

That explained her urgent desire to leave home last September and her unwillingness to return to Ferrand now. Armand had mentioned a Captain before, but Antoine never had given it much notice. "Anyone else I should know about?" he heard himself asking.

"Why?"

"How many challenges do I to expect if it ever becomes widely known that I accompanied Raoul... I mean, Charles...

pardon, the beautiful and enchanting Mlle. de Brangelton to Paris?"

"Patrice de Seveigney no longer desires her or her hand. You disposed of de Chassigneau. De Vergne gave up. De la Norte has been disillusioned. I trust you and de Rameau will tolerate each other on civil terms."

"His passionate attention displeases Charlotte beyond words, even with her colorful and extended vocabulary."

"Have you lost your mind? Have you not provided enough reasons for gossip?" Henri asked pointedly. "Your name has been permanently added to the list of her insensible admirers."

Antoine winced at the implications. "Tell de Rameau I will accept the dictum that Mlle. de Brangelton will do anything she pleases on her own enchanting terms."

Henri's busy day commenced early when his father rudely woke him. *"Henri, the ever-ready stallion, have you serviced all your mares last night?"* The vivid inquiry was accompanied by the sound of unlocking shutters, and when Henri opened his eyes to the pale morning light, he correctly judged that he had slept only a couple of hours.

"If the reason for your visit is not worthwhile, I will follow you around until you hear the complete narration of all the explicit details from last night," Henri threatened and stayed in his bed without moving.

Father tossed him a shirt and breeches. "Yesterday, three of your dim-witted friends contemplated running their swords through each other on behalf of your sister."

That immediately woke Henri up. "Who is the third lunatic?" He started to dress.

Half an hour later, father finished his colorful narration

with *"I trust you to reconcile Antoine and de Rameau. I will deal with my girl."*

Henri was pleased to be assigned the easier task. He first stopped at a coffeehouse and heard more rumors than he could tolerate. He made the mistake of checking on Charlotte who, conveniently for him, cut his visit short by calling him, along with de la Norte and de Flancourt, names of dubious distinction. He used her ramblings as a reason to leave with a theatrical display of hurt pride and feelings, hopefully to never discuss with her what had transpired between his dim-witted friends. Next, Henri caught up with de la Norte, politely inquired what happened last evening and listened to a - thankfully short, due to the imminent departure - monologue of conviction which ended with *"Mlle. de Brangelton never loved me, never will, and if she wants de Flancourt, the Devil take him, she can have him."* No sense in wasting time here. Henri wished him a safe journey and left to pay a visit to Antoine, after which his mood drastically improved. Antoine took this turn of events philosophically, no matter what anyone does or does not do, gossip will flourish. Henri left Antoine with the conviction that Antoine himself could explain his irrational actions to Charlotte, and with this bright perspective on his mind, Henri arrived to the Musketeer's Headquarters to face the sequestered de Rameau.

"I just have one question for you. Why did she and de Flancourt part ways in the autumn? What changed since then?" De Rameau ranted. "Why did she ever travel with him last September?"

Henri was caught off guard. "He came along with her, despite her protestations and arguments. He had no choice. Charlotte left home and he followed."

De Rameau foamed at the mouth. "Why did she leave home with him?"

"To put some distance between her blade and another bothersome military admirer."

"Why did de Flancourt not confront him?"

"They did not know about each other." Henri handed the Musketeer a bottle of rum. That tactic worked well with Antoine.

"How did she manage that?" De Rameau's mouth fell open in surprise.

"I don't know. I was not there." Explaining his sister's actions was impossible, even to de Rameau. "In any case, I trust you and de Flancourt will remain on civil terms while she does anything she pleases."

De Rameau shook his head.

"If there is a duel, I will summon Charlotte to stop it," Henri threatened. "This will be the first duel in the history of mankind when the subject of dispute will personally fight her ardent admirers. Will you raise your sword against her?"

De Rameau opened the bottle of rum, gulped the contents, and sulkily agreed to forget the previous evening. Henri reported his successful campaign to Captain d'Ornille, and, to reward himself, enjoyed a blissful, uninterrupted, day-long sleep at the Captain's apartment.

Armand returned home and launched into a detailed report of wild rumors which varied from speculations that the Comte de Flancourt, de la Norte, and de Rameau, either one of them, or two, or all three, were either wounded, or killed, or in the Bastille, or banished from Paris, or from France altogether. Armand would have come back much earlier, but he had taken the liberty to stop by Mlle. Charlotte's home and check if she had any messages for M. Antoine. No, he had not seen Mlle.

Charlotte, but the Comtesse de Tournelles had kindly conveyed a message to M. Antoine that the Comte de Tournelles and M. Charles would be away for a week.

Starting in the afternoon, and continuing through the next day of his home imprisonment, Antoine received a steady stream of visitors. De Contraille, d'Chantal, d'Signac, de Berteau, de Bonnard, de Rousard, and a dozen other acquaintances showed up one after another, and inevitably tiptoed to a variation of *"May I ask what truly transpired between you, de la Norte, and de Rameau?"*

Antoine responded incredibly calmly. He explained that he was only helping the honorable de la Norte and de Rameau comprehend that Mlle. de Brangelton did not favor either one. Indeed, how could they have failed to realize it? Charlotte must have articulated her opinion very clearly. Besides, de la Norte was destined for Mlle. de la Decourcelle; they made a charming couple, and de Rameau must happily continue his womanizing, or many beautiful women would weep in disappointment. After that articulate tirade, no other questions were posed.

Antoine devoted time to compose slightly belated answers to the family correspondence. His mother had barraged him with many pointed questions. *"Do you see Charlotte de Brangelton often? How is she occupying herself? I hope she has lost neither her spirit nor her loveliness. When are you coming home, or is there a reason for your extended stay in Paris? What are your plans?"* Antoine did not elaborate in his response back. After all, Madame Henrietta's letters to his mother arrived on a monthly basis and usually amounted to short novels. *"Charlotte is lovely and spirited like always. We see each other often,"* was all he wrote.

Raoul had celebrated Christmas at home and he had obviously heard about Antoine and Charlotte's trip. The contents of his brother's epistle provoked Antoine into slamming his fist on the table. *"I hear Wildcat is in Paris, and, amazingly, she might marry soon. Has her conduct improved or does her de la Norte have no common sense?"*

Antoine penned the reply it deserved. *"Bet you a bottle of brandy Charlotte will win a fencing round with you next time you meet. Her swordsmanship is excellent. By the way, she never cared for de la Norte."*

29

SPRINGTIME IN PARIS

PARIS, FRANCE - MARCH 1719

Blessed are those whose ignorance leads them to stumble into glory.

Francis de Brangelton to Paul d'Ornille - 1710

HENRI, CHARLOTTE, AND ANTOINE RODE TO THE PONT Neuf to bask in the fresh breeze and vibrant sunshine of the early spring. The area by the statue of Henri IV was crowded with food and drink vendors, two improvisation stages were set up, a group of musicians played, and a dog performed tricks. Charlotte, Henri, and Antoine had an excellent view over the crowd of a newly painted and gilded carriage stopping on the opposite side of the statue. Antoine recognized neither the nobleman who leaned out of the window nor the Coat of Arms depicted on the door. The nobleman, without taking his eyes off Charlotte, stepped outside. He was of average height and build, fashionably dressed; he had an arrogant bearing. He executed a practiced and graceful bow to Charlotte when she glanced in his direction.

Henri also noticed the man. "Who is that?"

Her face was a model of innocence. "I don't know his name."

"Shall we introduce him to Charles?" Antoine placed his hat on her head. Charlotte pulled the hat forward to adjust it for comfort and glanced in the direction of the unknown nobleman. Hera chose this moment to prance. The man thoughtfully regarded Charlotte and her misbehaving horse, evaluated Henri, and held Antoine's look with matching hostility before climbing back into his carriage and slamming the door shut. Charlotte promptly hit Antoine with his own hat.

The next day, de Brault showed up at Antoine's residence with a letter from the Comte de Chambreau. *"Would you accompany my nephew to London, since Guy has no command of the language?"* De Chambreau's letter read. *"He is entrusted to conduct the business we briefly discussed last September: the purchase of certain decorative art items from a private collection."*

The prospect of an immediate jaunt to England did not improve Antoine's mood. "What is your business in London?"

"I have to deliver very important documents." De Brault crossed himself. "I vowed to keep the secret, but I can tell you this much: it is to confirm a certain business transaction, purely private in nature, between my uncle and Lord Nelson. Upon my word, no politics."

"I see." Antoine folded de Chambreau's letter. He might as well leave Paris. Charlotte was still impossible to deal with. "Very well. We can leave tomorrow afternoon."

"Tomorrow?" de Brault cried out in dismay. "Don't you need time to prepare for the journey?"

Antoine sighed. "Cleaning my pistols does not take as long as arranging a ball, de Brault."

"Ah, yes, of course." He coughed to cover his embarrassment. "May I– that is, if you don't mind...Where is Mlle. Charlotte?"

"What business do you have with her?"

De Brault nervously blinked. "I thought, I mean, she said that you were parting ways upon reaching Paris."

Antoine did not care for this revelation. "All questions about d'Arringnon must be addressed to Mlle. de Brangelton."

De Brault's mouth dropped upon recognition of the name.

"I will even introduce you," Antoine offered. De Brault should have enough intelligence to refrain from greeting embraces.

Charlotte was attending to the Dowager Duchess de Montmurrant at Place de Victoires. Usually Antoine did not cherish the notion of attending Mlle. de Brangelton on the center stage of the reception room (aptly named *"the henhouse"* by M. Francis), but today was the perfect occasion. The buzz of conversation paused when he entered, and heads swiveled.

Antoine formally raised her hand to his lips. "May we step outside for a few minutes? I need to speak with you in private. Pardon us." He bowed and tugged Charlotte outside and toward the statue of the Sun King where de Brault was waiting. The colossal pedestal blocked the view from the fluttering curtains of the reception room windows.

De Brault stopped gaping at the sculpture and froze in astonishment upon setting his eyes on Charlotte.

"M. Guy de Brault is looking for Charles d'Arringnon,"

Antoine informed her." Will you please enlighten us both about Charles' whereabouts?"

Charlotte recovered from her surprise. "May I ask, M. de Brault, why you are looking for Charles?" She attempted to disengage her hand from Antoine's firm grip.

"Mlle." De Brault took off his hat and bowed. "It's a pleasure. I thought–"

"I suspect there is no single intelligent thought in your head right now."

Charlotte's callous statement in Charles' insolent manner had the desired effect on de Brault. He straightened up, plopped the hat back on his head, and scowled at her.

"Will Charles come along with us?" Antoine asked.

De Brault's dismayed "What?" was barely audible against Charlotte's reaction. "Trip to where? When? Who is we?" she asked.

"Paris to London and back. Leaving tomorrow. De Brault, possibly Charles, and me." Antoine gently squeezed her hand.

A strong desire to travel to London manifested itself in Charlotte's eyes. "Why was Charles left in ignorance of those plans until today?" She demanded. "De Brault?"

"I thought d'Arringnon was not available," Antoine said innocently while de Brault desperately gulped for air.

"What gave you that idea?" Charlotte wrestled to free her hand and Antoine released it before their little tussle developed into a full combat. "Since when have you taken the liberty of making decisions for Charles? What is the reason for this trip?"

De Brault backed off.

"Stop right there!" Charlotte commanded.

De Brault obeyed with a desperate glace at Antoine.

"I will arrange to hire horses. After crossing the Channel, we can sail on the Thames all the way to London," Antoine tempted her.

"No! D'Arringnon is not available." There was a firm finality in her tone. "You must prepare for your trip. Good day." She lay her hand on his arm.

De Brault tactfully bolted.

Antoine was not ready to give up. "May I ask, Charles, why are you not available?"

Her eye narrowed. "You had no desire for Charles' involvement back in Orleans," she reminded him.

"Please accept my deepest apologies. That was a severe error in judgment on my part. Allow me to make amends. Come to London."

"No." Charlotte shook her head with regret.

Could her refusal be due to the expectations of de la Norte's return? Or the presence of the nobleman from the Pont Neuf? Antoine pondered. "May I ask why not?"

"I don't trust de Brault to keep my identity secret," Charlotte said.

Antoine could not argue.

The Court was no longer in the Louvre, but the whirl of the usual activities never ceased. Charlotte and father navigated their way across the courtyard among the scurrying messengers, idle officers, harassed vendors and servants, and loitering courtiers. The carriages rolled along, and the occasional rider maneuvered through. In this chaos, Charlotte recognized the nobleman whose terracotta-colored jacket was adorned with enough gold thread and ribbons to glitter in the shade. His hair was fashionably powdered and curled, and he was no more than thirty years of age. When he caught her glance, he placed his hat to his heart and headed toward them in a manner calculated to intercept them.

Father sighed with a theatrical exaggeration. "Am I to suffer yet another new admirer of yours?"

Charlotte pouted. "He met Charles in Chantilly but did not hire him."

"Ungrateful bastard," father quipped.

"Yes. Last week, he shamelessly gaped at me until Antoine slapped his hat on my head," she dropped her voice to an undertone. "He claimed he misses Charles."

"Comte de Tournelles?" The nobleman bowed with polite reverence. "I respectfully beg your pardon for my deferential presumption of boldly requesting kindly permission to introduce myself to you and your lovely daughter."

"I will be quite delighted to dispose of my disadvantage of not knowing your name, Monsieur," father weaved his words while Charlotte waddled through the pattern of the man's speech.

"My name is Maurice de Tavoisier, Marquis deTernille, reverently at your service. Your formidable reputation, Comte de Tournelles, has been a constant inspiration for me for ages. I am greatly honored at this most fortunate opportunity to meet you in person."

"Marquis de Ternille." Charlotte threw a veiled glance from under her eyelashes when Marquis paused in his effusions and father formally introduced her. Might as well play along. Did he recognize her from Chantilly?

"May I?" He raised her hand to his lips. "Making your delightful acquaintance immediately raised my joy of returning to Paris to ecstasy."

"Return?" she dutifully echoed. "May I ask how long have you been away, Marquis?"

His rueful smile was well-practiced. "A few long years, and not by my own choice, beautiful Mlle. Charlotte. Comte de

Tournelles, may I address your breathtakingly fine-looking daughter by her given name?"

Charlotte pulled her hand from his light grip. "May I ask why were you exiled? Is this the right word to describe your departure from Paris, Marquis?"

"I am exceedingly embarrassed to admit that the true reason was a shameful outcome of a rash action on my part. I was unwillingly entangled in an unjustifiable duel on the account of a broken heart, and a highly exaggerated scandal followed." He dismissively waved his embroidered handkerchief. It shimmered. "I am perfectly content to leave this sordid affair far behind me, curious Mlle. Charlotte. Although, I am genuinely grateful it made me significantly wiser and allowed me to experience the decadent life in Venice and London."

Charlotte allowed him to dismiss his checked past. "How do Venice and London compare to Paris, Marquis?"

"Morose and dull, for you were absent from there, dear Mlle. Charlotte," he held his hat over his heart. "I feel extremely fortunate that my unpretentious return coincided with your glorious presence. It must be fate! I will be the happiest man in the world if you generously allow me to entertain you with the modest narration of my extended travels. May I pay my genuine respects to your gracious daughter, Comte de Tournelles? My poor heart will be irrevocably broken if you refuse."

"You may pay her all attention you wish," father allowed, "but beware. More than just your heart will be broken if your admiration progresses out of control."

Charlotte was standing at the entrance door at home when a man on a roan horse rode inside the courtyard, dismounted and walked toward her. He wore the same formal dark green suit he had worn at the Duke de Seveigney's ball in November. His eyes held the same intensity that had manifested itself on the balcony, and Charlotte realized that she was completely naked. She retreated inside, only to find herself at the small room at Lonjumeau, where he stood by the window. Charlotte woke up with a pounding heart and shaking hands, her entire body covered with sweat. She leapt out of bed to disperse the dream and splashed cool water in her face. She shivered in the chilly air, but the images from her sleep refused to fade. She wrapped her favorite robe around herself. The garment was made of padded red silk from the Orient, and lavishly embroidered with brown horses, their manes and tails accented with gold thread. It had been a very intimate gift from Antoine at Christmas, but neither mother nor father, and not even Henri, were perturbed, and she had accepted it with grace. Charlotte closed her eyes, remembering the feel of Antoine's warm hand on her bare shoulder. It had taken all her willpower to push him away that evening. She had been attracted to Patrice de Seveigney and Bertrand de la Norte, and she felt occasional smidgens of tenderness toward Raoul de la Fleure, Andre de Rameau, and a handful of other men, but never in her life had she experienced an instance when her emotions galloped over her reason. She again felt her inner turmoil. She had almost lost her reason and her self-control in that gallery.

What exactly had happened there? she asked herself yet again, *Was that embrace just an impulsive response in an opportunistic situation?* He had readily released her, but after that exchange, the invisible distance between them seemed to disappear, along with physical distance. Charlotte's face warmed up as she thought about his hand on the small of her back, his knee against hers at the theater, and his shoulder against hers while standing by the door, waiting for Armand to bring the horses. Charlotte paced around the room. How would Antoine react to the Marquis de Ternille's interest in her? He would violently object, no doubts, but it was none of his business! And if he was shameless enough to expect any explanations, she would... Her eyes fell on the sword shoulder strap. She had never been to England and now the opportunity was wasted. *Never mind, there was no opportunity,* she sternly reminded herself. Traveling with Antoine and de Brault would be the most idiotic action she had taken, except for traveling with Antoine alone. Charlotte resumed pacing around the room, reminded herself that he did not intend to marry, and she did not intend to engage in any affairs. They could never reconcile these differences, and any discussion about it would inevitably turn their friendship into mutual resentment and hostility which will spill over to affect her parents, his parents, Henri, and Raoul. To preserve peace and friendship between the families, she must never find herself alone with Antoine. Charlotte steeled her resolve to follow this principle and went downstairs with the full intent to chase away the dream.

These hopes shattered when she sat down at the table and shuffled through the scattered maps. Last night, she had occupied herself by estimating Antoine's location and wishing Charles was there.

"What did you say?" she asked Red Jacques.

"This package was delivered for you, Mlle. Charlotte."

She suspiciously eyed a lightweight, cream-colored packet. *Not another poet.* De Vergne had abandoned his quest for her hand after de Chassigneau was discovered unconscious on the balcony. Charlotte squelched her suspicions which, just like every one of her thoughts this morning, had returned to Antoine as a culprit, and cut the ribbons of the package.

If she needed a distraction, that was it. De Ternille had sent her a gift of silk stockings, and Charlotte completely exhausted her cursing vocabulary before noticing that Red Jacques was gaping at her with horrified respect.

"Take it back." She shoved the package in his hands. "Insist on handing it to the Marquis yourself and feel free to repeat anything you heard just now."

"They will hang me if I speak that way to a nobleman!"

"Tell him that." Charlotte sighed.

Red Jacques blinked. "Will you eat, Mlle. Charlotte?"

Just when had he placed the meal on the table? She tore a large chunk of bread, slathered a generous portion of butter on it, and handed it to Red Jacques. He wolfed it down and, now fortified, disappeared on his errand.

Charlotte absent-mindedly took a bite of soft bread and ordered herself to stop thinking about Antoine. Deliberate on the problem of de Rameau for distraction. She chewed on the dry slice, realized that she forgot the butter, and spread extra on the next bite to compensate. She would be ecstatic if de Rameau left her alone. For a moment, Charlotte regretted de la Norte's departure, since it encouraged de Rameau's dreams and hopes. Maybe there was more to the man than it seemed. People perceived Henri as an irresponsible womanizer, but in truth, her brother had perfect control of his affairs, after all. She must get rid of de Rameau before her imagination presented him in a more favorable light than he deserved!

"The Marquis de Ternille conveys his apologies and asks if you would receive him this afternoon. That's what I think he meant," Red Jacques brought back the response.

"Only if he brings along my brother." She dropped her face into her hands. Since when had she been reduced to these infuriatingly silly games, when her swordsmanship was up to par with elite military officers? She, who would have traveled to Paris by herself. She clenched her fists at disgust of all the society confinements she had to endure in Paris, whereas Antoine came and went as he pleased.

Mother was engaged on Duchess Helene's errands, father was hosting visitors from Brugges, and Henri had suddenly left Paris with a pathetically vague excuse. What had lured her brother away from the bedrooms of his three passions? The Marquis communicated his desire to visit, and today was an off-duty day for de Rameau. Charlotte chomped down the remainder of her meal and washed it down with chocolate. A quarter of an hour later, Charles quietly slipped outside. She was Charlotte de Brangelton. She had the option of the cherished freedom of a man, the freedom that most women could not even fathom, and she would never give it up. Besides, her pride and dignity forbade her from sitting at home and daydreaming about Antoine de la Fleure, Comte de Flancourt.

On the Pont Neuf, Charlotte watched a play and dawdled for another hour before heading toward Sorbonne and the Tutor Frog tavern where she played tavern games with inept law students. Afterwards, she crossed the Ile de la Cite and loitered by City Hall. Her feet were tired, but the dream remained vivid in her mind. At the Spice and Song coffee-house, she commandeered a nice seat from which she overheard a conversation between two Englishmen. Last time she had spoken the language, Antoine and she—*what was that?*

"The Marshall cousins will arrive with Duke Collingstone's retinue," the Englishman said skeptically.

"Didn't their booty include His Grace's property?" his companion asked.

"Who knows?" the other man answered. "For all I care, they might be spies. French or ours."

Another bloody ridiculous theory, Charlotte thought in English and inconspicuously slid on the bench toward these men, but they conversed in quiet voices and an argument in the corner turned louder. She slowly sipped the bitter drink. This tale from Marseille about the elusive, mysterious Marshall cousins had reached legendary proportions. Henri had reacted violently to her curiosity about the Marshall cousins. In fact, upon discovering that she had unearthed a bit of information related to these cutthroats, her brother had ruthlessly and abruptly ended their trip. He and Antoine were in Montpellier when the Marshall cousins' day of glory had commenced. Henri and Antoine either had heard rumors, or maybe even spoke to witnesses, or maybe even met the Marshall cousins themselves. She should have asked Antoine. Charlotte was startled to discover that she murmured his name aloud!

The smoke inside the main room thickened to a dense fog, the chatter around turned louder and of little interest to her, and Charlotte strolled to the Valiant Fox tavern.

The hour was still early, and only two card tables were occupied. After a game, the player on her right abandoned the table at the same moment de Contraille stepped into the room, so naturally de Contraille immediately set upon a course to claim the empty seat. "May I join you?" He froze when their eyes met.

"Good day, Monsieur. I am Charles. We met in Montpellier." She kicked him under the table.

He promptly awoke from his stupor. "Yes. What a pleasant surprise. Charles!"

De Contraille's attention wavered, and after a single game, Charlotte led him to the empty table in the dining room. A few patrons were scattered around, but no one she or de Contraille recognized. Charlotte figured that she might as well fend off any questions from him now.

"May I ask you a private question, Charles?" he asked as soon as they ordered the dinner of baked trout and white beans.

"Who else, besides your family and de Flancourt, knows about your presence in Paris?"

"Duchess de Montmurrant, M. de Seveigney, Captain d'Ornille, Lieutenant de Rousard, d'Signac, and de Rameau know me, de Bonnard met Charles, and now you, M. Geoffrey. I am surprised that you recognized me in an instant."

"I had the benefit of meeting you in Montpellier. I was convinced your brother had been joking about his sister. I doubted it even after de Flancourt confirmed it. I confess, I harbored doubts until the day you attended the fencing hall." He cleared his throat. "May I ask... I apologize if it is an indiscreet inquiry... Does de la Norte know?" He held his breath.

"Yes." It was the truth, even if Bertrand had found out too late.

"He did not want to believe it." De Contraille traced the spirals of wood pattern of the tabletop.

"Speaking of disbelief," Charlotte seized the opening to rein the conversation toward the topic of her immediate interest. "Last Wednesday, you seemed disinclined to agree with de Chantal about the Marshall cousins' motives."

He relaxed. "If these cousins had any illicit purposes, I doubt they would cause such fireworks. I am more inclined to follow the theory of revenge for the loss of their ship."

"I have not heard this one."

"It's yet another conjecture." He was at ease now, chatting about the Marshall cousins. "A variance of this theory is they are English privateers and in service of Duke Collingstone."

"Do you have any conjectures of your own invention, M. Geoffrey?"

He leaned forward with a conspirator's wink. "I overheard a man inquiring about them at the Three Diamonds Tavern."

"Only an idiot would be searching for New World English cutthroats in Paris."

"And he is a Frenchman, too!"

"That is absurd," Charlotte said. "What was his name?"

Upon returning home, Charlotte discovered that she had successfully missed both de Rameau and de Ternille and congratulated herself. She slowly ascended the stairs to her bedroom, pretending that her dream from that morning was forgotten. Charlotte hung up the hat and the sword, replaced the shirt and the doublet with a chemise and corset, and put on a house dress. She faced the mirror to pull her hair up. The most logical way to search for the Marshall cousins was by soliciting information from Antoine. Actually, start with interrogating Henri and catch him after a sleepless night. Was that a knock at the door? She tightened the side laces and made the mistake of peeking out of her bedroom door.

"The Marquis de Ternille is requesting to see you," Red Jacques announced.

"Humbly begging to see you, my elusive Mlle. Charlotte." Uninvited, the Marquis walked into the sitting room. He bowed and watched her descend down the stairs, kissed her hand, and frowned at Red Jacques who stood guard at the door.

"I don't see my brother."

"Of course not, my capricious Mlle. Charlotte. I have taken the slight liberty to stop by and respectfully inquire about your brother's whereabouts."

"How would I know? You are a man, Marquis. You certainly have a much better chance of guessing where my brother spends most of his time," Charlotte said innocently.

He regarded her with a hurt expression. "I am not the same kind of man as your brother."

"Yes, indeed. My brother does not send stockings to his mistresses." Henri limited his contributions to inexpensive impersonal trinkets, such as ribbons and candles.

The Marquis' eyes flashed. "May we talk in private, my unpredictable Mlle. Charlotte?"

Charlotte motioned to the disappointed Red Jacques to stand guard outside the door in the unlikely case she needed a backup. Her boot knife was snug against her ankle, and the heavy (and badly misshapen) tankard sat on the table.

"Will you give me your beautiful hand and close your dreamy eyes?" The Marquis interrupted her inventory of weapons.

"Will you stop mistaking me for a whore?"

He was shocked into incoherent sputtering while crimson color creeped to his ears. "I would never! Mlle. Charlotte!" He regained his composure. "I came to sincerely apologize, and to relentlessly beg you to accept this little token of my esteem for unknowingly offending you." He reached into his pocket and held out a bracelet of shimmering pearls with a filigreed gold clasp. "May I have the high honor of placing it on your dainty wrist?"

"Marquis de Ternille. I do not accept gifts from men." Charlotte edged closer to the poker at the fireplace.

"You are the most intriguing woman I ever met, my lovely Mlle. Charlotte." He placed the bracelet on the table. "Please reconsider. It would give me much pleasure."

"Marquis de Ternille. Either pick up this bracelet and put it back in your pocket, or I will throw you and the bracelet out of the house. Have you thrown," she corrected herself.

He possessed more intelligence than she originally credited him; the bracelet disappeared. "Your wish is my command. Will you generously forgive me for my unintended transgressions today?"

There was no polite or gracious way to refuse. "Don't ever repeat these mistakes again, Monsieur."

"I am a quick learner, my beguiling Mlle. Charlotte.

Speaking of learning, may I ask you an unconventional question? How well have you learned sword fighting ?" De Ternille proved Henri wrong. Her brother had once claimed that no man in his right mind would ever ask a woman this question.

"This is an odd question, Monsieur."

"Please, mysterious Mlle. Charlotte, don't be so chillingly formal. My given name is Maurice. Why is my question odd? Everyone in your illustrious family is a master expert, I am certain you have a great talent for it as well, my amiable Mlle. Charlotte."

His creative selections of affectionate address would cause Henri to dissolve into hysterical laughter. "M. Maurice, isn't fencing a dangerous pastime?"

"No, not at all. My delightful Mlle. Charlotte, you have not answered my question."

"Why would I need sword fighting skills?"

"For self-protection, of course," he said softly.

"Indeed? From whom must I protect myself? Should I be concerned for my safety because of my association with you, M. Maurice?"

"No, not at all, I assure you." He reached for her hand. "You have nothing to fear from me, my prudent Mlle. Charlotte."

She folded her arms. "Why do you always have bodyguards with you?"

"It's extremely fashionable. I am a man of high position, my desirable Mlle. Charlotte."

"How disappointing. I hoped you recklessly involved yourself in dangerous adventures."

"What is perceived dangerous by your family standards, my enigmatic Mlle. Charlotte?"

"Nothing by my father's standards. Or by my brother's. Enlighten me, please, on what reasonable people think."

"My dear Mlle. Charlotte. You carry a sword when you are dressed as a young man. It's a dangerous practice unless you know how to employ the weapon." He raised her hands to his lips. "In Chantilly, my sweet Mlle. Charlotte..." His thumb brushed the hardened skin on her palm in a caress similar to Antoine's.

She freed her hands. "Don't waste your time, Marquis de Ternille."

On Sunday, father chose to attend Mass at St. Eustache Church. De Rameau was off duty and caught a religious fever which did not prevent him from shamelessly hinting at his intent to challenge the Marquis de Ternille to a duel. Charlotte, already in a grim mood due to his amorous presence, threatened to officially complain to Captain d'Ornille, her godfather, mind you, to lock up his Musketeer for harassing her. Amazingly, de Rameau's ardor diminished and they entered the church in peace. Charlotte attempted to coerce her mother into sitting between herself and de Rameau for the duration of the service, but mother refused to cooperate. Thus Charlotte, after stomping on de Rameau's foot to remove his knee from the proximity of hers, settled in to devise how to rid herself of his pestilent company swiftly and permanently.

Charlotte's eyes fell on the Marquise de Fabvre's thoughtful, sad face. Was Cecilia thinking about Antoine? Charlotte must have mumbled aloud because mother kicked her. She calmed herself by reviewing the possible routes from Le Havre to Paris and idly noted that Mme. Cecilia's attention was focused on de Rameau. Didn't Henri mention that Cecilia liked men in uniform? Charlotte felt a divine inspiration to lead the man toward temptation and to leave him there. She lowered her head to hide a smile, and waited till the end of the Mass in a much better mood.

"Ah, M. de Rameau." To award the gleam of appreciation

in his eyes, Cecilia de Fabvre extended her hand to him. "You were the third man to involve himself in the dispute between my brother and Comte de Flancourt, weren't you?"

"What dispute?" Charlotte's vocal cords jumped ahead of her mind.

Both gave her startled looks.

"I understand Lieutenant de Rousard and his men stopped my brother, Comte de Flancourt, and M. de Rameau from a duel on your account." Cecilia's expression was of incredulous amazement. "Mlle. Charlotte, didn't your dear Comte inform you of that occasion?"

"My dear Comte... No, he said nothing! He is not my dear Comte!" Charlotte exploded, noting that this had become her habit upon hearing his name. "What happened? When? De Rameau, should I arrange for your extended stay in the Bastille?"

His eyes darted between her and Cecilia. "I assisted Lieutenant de Rousard to arrest both de la Norte and de Flancourt."

"Arrest? Why?"

"I only heard the last part of their conversation. De Flancourt insisted that he is the man to help you do anything you please." He bowed.

Charlotte composed herself and put her hand on de Rameau's sleeve. "I apologize for my outburst," she pronounced, noting an immediate wariness simmering in his eyes. "Of course, you had no choice but to follow Lieutenant de Rousard's orders to detain two friends of my brother for their own safety." The suspicion in his eyes evolved in a smoldering resentment as he might have guessed her game. Charlotte continued before he had a chance to argue. "And I am grateful to you on Henri's behalf." Charlotte discerned the angry exhale at that. She continued, "And I am certain Mme. Cecilia also very much values your brave actions on M. Bertrand's behalf,"

Charlotte concluded with a flourish. "M. de Rameau, my godfather is fortunate to have men like you under his command. Your dedication to duty is commendable. Don't you agree, Mme. Cecilia?"

There was an eloquent pause, during which the Marquise and de Rameau contemplated each other.

"Now, if you will please pardon me, Mme. Cecilia, I will leave you in M. de Rameau's excellent company. My father summoned me." She exchanged air kisses with the Marquise and held out her hand to de Rameau who, at this moment, was undecided if he was irate at his soon-to-be-former passion Charlotte, or grateful to her. She hastened off to obtain an accurate account of that event – almost duel on her account? - from her father.

THE VALIANT FOX AND THE THREE DIAMONDS

PARIS, FRANCE - MARCH 1719

Fortune favors the audacious.

Francis de Brangelton to Henrietta d'Arringnon – 1694

CHARLES D'ARRINGNON LEFT HOME EARLY IN THE afternoon. At the Fountain des Innocents, Charlotte indulged in an eggs and spinach pastry, proceeded to a wine merchant and purchased two bottles for father, then continued to the Arsenal. She stopped by the fencing hall, only to leave when de Bonnard pointed her out to de Rousard. She crossed the Ile St. Louis to the Quay de la Tournelles, and strolled along the Rue St. Antoine toward the Rue St. Martin. Her mind was uncomfortably occupied with contemplating the activities of her dear Comte. She wanted him to explain his inexcusable actions, but she did not dare to start a conversation of such a personal nature. Henri's memory loss deserved payback. Where was her dear Comte? Did he extend his visit in London for a month? Charlotte clenched her fists and stopped when she mistook a young man across the street for Antoine. He stopped to look at the shop window, proceeded up the Rue St. Martin, and a man followed him. Their path led in the general direction of her home and Charlotte followed them. Bertrand de la Norte turned left and knocked at the door of her house. He waited and knocked again. His shoulders dropped in disappointment when no one answered; he crossed the street for a better view of the closed windows, and remained there, waiting. The second man stopped on the corner to scrub the mud off his boot. He must have stepped in a bucket of dirt to take that long. Charlotte eased herself in the shadow of the early evening. She waited till de la Norte hesitantly left and the second man deemed his boot clean, and, out of sheer curiosity, she followed them. De la Norte strode toward the Rue de Temple and stopped to listen to a song by a street performer. The second man paused around the corner, thus unwittingly providing Charlotte the opportunity for action. She noiselessly caught up with the man and pressed the point of her boot knife to the back on his neck.

"Who are you following?"

His body stiffened in an unnatural pose. "M. de la Norte."

"Why?"

"The Marquis de Louiviers ordered me to watch out for him," he chattered freely when the blade pressed tightly on his skin.

Charlotte lowered her weapon. "Make yourself scarce. Run and don't you dare to stop till you reach the Siene, or you will be skewered," she warned him and propelled him in the right direction with a swift kick at his behind. The man sprinted away. Charlotte was halfway to the Valiant Fox. She might as well play cards there.

Bertrand de la Norte was absorbed in reading a newspaper,

and Charlotte retreated toward the door. The Venetian she had met on a previous visit stood up and pointed to the available spot at his table. The eloquence of his body language attracted de la Norte's attention and he raised his head with a puzzled frown. The color drained from his face and he frantically jumped up. Charlotte waved to the Venetian, hastened to de la Norte before he regained the ability to speak, and forced him to sit down by squeezing his shoulder.

"Stop staring." She pulled up a chair. "I do not wish to attract any attention."

"Yes of course," he stammered. "I did not quite expect... I did not quite realize...I should not have been surprised."

"Or shocked and horrified."

"No!" he vehemently denied, but his eyes frantically searched the room again. " Are you here alone?" he asked in disbelief.

"Yes."

"But," he half-raised himself but wisely plopped back down. "It's dangerous for you to be here unescorted."

A vague plan formed in Charlotte's mind. "What danger can be possibly lurking in this respectable establishment?" she asked incredulously. "The Valiant Fox is a society salon compared to, for example, the Three Diamonds!"

"You have been to that dreadful place?" he exclaimed in shock. Was he recalling the dancers from the Near East, or the fight Henri dragged him into, or wondering if Antoine escorted her there?

"No, M. Bertrand. Charles d'Arringnon and Henri de Brangelton stopped at yet another tavern," she corrected him.

He inhaled sharply. "Yes." He twisted his ring. "I apologize. What did you think about the Three Diamonds tavern, Charles?"

That was unexpected, but the honest effort of friendship

deserved kindness.

"Seems to be exactly the place the Marshall cousins would patronize, if they were in Paris."

"The stories about those cousins reached epic proportions." Bertrand slightly relaxed. "I expect to see an anonymous publication of their memoirs!"

He knew even less than de Contraille. After the dinner of jellied pike and lentils, it occurred to Charlotte that such cozy socialization might ignite the ashes of old feelings. She folded the cards. "It was a pleasant evening, M. Bertrand, but I must leave now."

He was on his feet as well. "May I escort you home?"

"No need," Charlotte refused. Had she given him hope for reconciliation?.

He was undeterred. "Please, I insist."

"I am planning to stop at the Three Diamonds tavern," she tossed over her shoulder.

He jumped to her side. "You cannot possibly go there by yourself!"

Charlotte wrestled to dispel the echoes of another conversation on a similar subject, with a man not even remotely this polite. She marched outside and away from the entrance before spinning around to deal with the honorable young man. "I can, and I will, do anything I please!" she reminded him.

"Yes, I know," he inclined his head. "Charles. Please allow me to accompany you. To make certain you are safe."

Charlotte contemplated the offer. She did not particularly relish the concept of attending the Three Diamonds by herself, and if he re-acquired any delusions, there was no better place for Charles to discourage any amorous notions.

The Three Diamonds Tavern was located behind the Arsenal. The crowd was boisterous and loud at any day, and worse on this evening due to the nature of entertainment - a bawdy jester with a fiddle. Charlotte plunged inside. Bertrand de la Norte trailed behind her and winced at every third note played. Charlotte weaved her way toward a small clearing to the left of the door that afforded a fine view of the whole room. De Contraille had not caught the name of the man searching for the Marshall cousins, but had provided a detailed description of him. Charlotte casually positioned herself near a middle aged man with an unusually long face and whose brows merged into a single line.

"Ahoy, my friend," she said. "Quite a place for cutthroats, isn't it?"

He raised his mug. "You are too young to be here."

"Tell that to the Marshall cousins."

He reeled back. "Who are you?"

"Let's just say we might have common interests."

"Do you know the Marshall cousins?" he asked in a trembling voice, and the hand holding the drink trembled.

"I have my reasons to search for them. Different than yours."

"What?" He downed his drink. "Who says I am searching for them?"

"Aren't you?" Charlotte waited until he averted his eyes. "Pity. We could help each other." She turned away.

"Wait!" the man panted. "Can you find them?" The man was not a sailor, he was not a mercenary, and he was not destitute, so why was he searching for the Marshall cousins?

"Is there a monetary reward for the information?" Charlotte asked. Did these cousins even exist outside of the collective imagination of Marseille's inhabitants?

He hesitated. "Yes. Do you know them?"

"Never met them. What is your name?"

The man shifted on his feet. "Can you trace the Marshall cousins?" He was desperate to find them.

"I ask again. How much do you pay?"

"Depends on the information you provide," he bargained.

"Marshall is an English name. Why are you searching for Englishmen in Paris?"

"Why not? I cannot find them anywhere else. What do you mean, I am searching for them? You are!"

"No, I am not. I am only contemplating your offer of money for their whereabouts. Who are you and who employs you?"

The man gaped at her in bewilderment. "You, little bas–I have noticed you are in no hurry to introduce yourself."

Charlotte shrugged. "Very well. I suppose you are not serious about needing their services."

"My name is Rene Prassal." He conceded defeat. "And who are you?"

"You may call me Charles."

After the haze of thick smoke inside the Three Diamonds, the stench of stale water and street mud was sweet and fresh in comparison. She rushed to the nearest shaded house entrance and waited. A couple of reprobates left the premises and disappeared in the distance before Bertrand de la Norte, obeying her earlier instructions, walked outside. He nervously looked around, hesitated, but hurried toward the Fontaine St. Catherine. Charlotte stealthily followed him. His pace increased and he was running by the time he reached the Rue St. Antoine. She whistled to stop him.

"What?" he sputtered.

"Third doorway down from the Three Diamonds." Charlotte grinned at his confusion. "By the way, did you know that a man followed you to the Valiant Fox tonight?"

His face was hidden in the darkness. "I thought that hound was recalled." He sounded embarrassed.

"I sent him away in one piece, don't worry," Charlotte assured him. "Who was it?"

She could detect embarrassment in the two words. "My bodyguard."

"Indeed?"

He fell in step with her. "My father insisted. I objected, and I crroncously believed he relented," he admitted. "I hear it's fashionable," he added lightly. "Why don't you acquire services?"

"I am not in the habit of starting duels," Charlotte retorted without thinking.

Bertrand de la Norte stumbled. "I regret that the argument was interrupted," he spit out, although he could not match even a half-measure of Antoine's peevish tone.

"If that argument was not interrupted, you would be hurt and Antoine de la Fleure would have been thrown in the Bastille," Charlotte pointed out. "Or possibly the other way around," she added generously.

They continued on their way. At the front door, de la Norte exhibited no signs of desire to leave. "Please, may we speak in private?" he pleaded.

Charlotte felt she owned him some gratitude for his assistance and led him into the sitting room. No visitors were expected at this hour, unless Antoine had returned to Paris. The hour was late, but it might not deter him. Charlotte tossed her hat on the table and picked up the solitary candle to light up the others to dispel the darkness of the room. "By any chance, do you know that man from the Three Diamonds?"

"No, I never saw him before. I thought he recognized you, Mlle. Charlotte?"

"He recognized Charles."

He remained standing in the middle of the room and nervously twisted his ring around his finger before raising his eyes. "I apologize for distressing you the last time we spoke."

"No harm done," Charlotte assured him. "My father gave

up on repairing that wall."

"No harm?" His voice cracked in despair. "I lost my reason, Charlotte. I was beyond myself with jealousy."

"Why did you refuse to explain the reason for your exile from Paris?"

He shook his head and clenched his hands together. "No, please, I implore you. I am embarrassed to recall that I stooped to..." He took a deep breath, paused to make a decision, and forged ahead. "I asked you to marry me, and I meant it." His eyes shone.

"Shall we recall the announcement of your upcoming marriage?" she reminded him.

He perceived it as jealousy. "I will break the engagement if you promise to marry me!"

Charlotte was at a loss for words.

"Will you marry me?" He held her hands.

She was caught off-guard. "You ask me to marry you after spending the evening with Charles?"

"Yes. I was wrong about you, Charlotte. I thought I could not imagine you as Charles. I did not want to. But tonight I realized I will do anything for you!"

Charlotte momentarily closed her eyes to hide the confusion in her mind. She had never expected this conversation. He leaned over to gently kiss her, and Charlotte kissed him back, a soft, pleasant kiss, followed by something more passionate. Suddenly she felt a hollow, cold feeling in her stomach upon the realization that she felt not even half of the passion she had experienced with Antoine in the drafty gallery. All her comfort in Bertrand's arms evaporated when her imagination drew a scene of explaining Bertrand to Antoine. Bertrand must have felt the change in her mood and he released her.

Charlotte backed away. "No. I am sorry, Bertrand," she said firmly.

ABOUT THE TRUNKS

LONDON, ENGLAND – MARCH 1719

Lucky coincidence is God's gift.

Francis de Brangelton to Henrietta de Brangelton –
1694

DE BRAULT SAILED (ALBEIT ON RIVER BARGES), HE
traveled extensively (between Orleans and Montpellier), he
understood English (a few words, to be exact), he was discreet
(if you discount the advertisement of Charles' persona), and he
was a better fencer than Charles (though Antoine begged to
differ). Was it necessary to travel at such neck-breaking speed?
(Yes, you don't dawdle on business, according to Antoine.) His
uncle trusted him with important business (his uncle was no
fool and ensured that de Brault did not flounder by himself).
Was Mlle. Charlotte jealous of Jeanne ? (Ask Charlotte if you
dare.) By the time they sailed from Calais, Antoine contemplated gagging his associate. Fortunately for de Brault, the sea

crossing silenced him, and Antoine chose to sail up through the Strait of Dover and up the Thames to London.

Woe to the visitors who do not speak the local language. That notion held truth in any place in the world. Londoners led foreigners for a merry dance as eagerly as Parisians, and the surly inhabitants of London were just as wretched as Parisian rumble. Antoine lost his way twice in the dingy streets before he found the Crimson Rose Inn that he had been recommended by de Chambreau. The room was clean, the ale was strong, and the late dinner was speedily served in the private parlor.

"Tomorrow, we will request an audience with Duke Collingstone," Antoine said.

De Brault faltered. "I suppose we – I - should ask-"

Languishing in London for an extended time did not appeal to Antoine. "You will send him a note tonight requesting the audience for both of us tomorrow."

"My uncle instructed me to negotiate with His Grace!" De Brault held on to the delusion that Antoine would allow him to wander off by himself for the meeting with the Duke.

Antoine had no desire for an extended debate. "On second thought, I will submit the note. Once we are admitted, you can negotiate all you please."

The formal audience with Duke Collingstone lasted less than a quarter of an hour. De Brault delivered the stack of papers from his uncle, His Grace promised to peruse them at his leisure, inquired about happenings in the French court, and invited Antoine and de Brault to stay in London. He proved to be a generous host, introducing them into recreational pastimes of London society, inviting them to a dinner at a private club, to a theatrical performance, to a social assembly of dance and song featuring the attention of the magnificent Lady Jane Pattingham. A week later, Duke Collingstone remembered the busi-

THE LEGACY OF MARSHALL COUSINS

ness purpose of Antoine's and de Brault's visit. Yes, the Comte de Chambreau's papers satisfied his concerns, and yes, the terms were acceptable and the deal would be completed next month when His Grace officially visited France.

After that, Duke Collingstone dismissed de Brault, and Lord Nelson took Antoine to a pugilist match, an uncivilized legacy of gladiators where the outcome depended less on skill and more on whose skull was thicker. For the first time, Antoine was glad of Charles' absence. Charlotte was not fond of recreational violence. After the bout was finished and thoroughly analyzed, the wagers paid off, and the winner cleaned up and toasted, Lord Nelson and Antoine left the stifling hall.

Their footsteps echoed in the thick fog. "De Flancourt, how did you end up saddled with Charles d'Arringnon?"

"Family friendship." How was Charlotte occupying herself tonight?

Lord Nelson spat out the wad of tobacco he had been chewing for the past hour. "What is his relationship to devil de Brangelton?"

Sooner or later, the Duke's and Charlotte's paths would cross. "D'Arringnon is the Comtesse de Tournelles' family name. Charlotte de Brangelton uses it often."

Lord Nelson choked. "You mean? No, it cannot be!"

"Yes, Lord Nelson. I know for certain."

Duke shook his head. He squinted into the fog, turned into an alley on the right, cursed, and backtracked before taking another turn. "You are an adventurous man, de Flancourt. I suppose she is worth it."

"Every insane moment."

"More than Lady Pattingham?" He slapped Antoine on the shoulder. "You weren't subtle in your escape from her, you know."

"I learned that from Charles." How did Charlotte, left on

her own, deal with de Rameau, de la Norte, the nobleman from the Pont Neuf, and who knows what other rabble that had crowded around the beautiful and enchanting Mlle. de Brangelton in his absence?

His Grace answered with a derisive scoff. "Bring him – her to London next time. Have you heard about the Great Mogul Diamond?"

"It is a large diamond which disappeared from the temple in India, isn't it?"

"It's rumored to have resurfaced in the New World, before vanishing again." Lord Nelson stopped to take a snuff box out of his pocket. "Frankly, I doubt if it was ever there."

"Yes, indeed," Antoine said carefully. "The New World is such a vague, convenient, remote place for all unexplained and, quite often, illegitimate occurrences."

"I covet the bloody diamond." He snapped the lid of the box closed. The concoction stuck to his fingertips in the moist air. "De Chambreau found half of my paintings by accident. Will the Great Mogul Diamond emerge on its own?"

"Would you like me to look into this matter, my lord?" Antoine volunteered. "Do you have any clues?"

"None that I believe any more." Lord Nelson nudged him toward the double door marked by a weather-beaten plaque advertising the establishment as yet another gentlemen's club. "Do you play billiards?"

Portsmouth, England – March 1719

De Brault hoped to stay in London longer, but Antoine insisted that the Comte de Chambreau expected the report, so de Brault sullenly rode with Antoine to Portsmouth. *"From Le*

Havre, your ride to Orleans is a short one," Antoine cheered him up and waved de Brault off to sail home.

Antoine returned to his room at the inn and perused a copy of the list of names involved during the night at Marseille. He strolled to the docks in the early dusk of the evening, and his diligence was awarded with a sight of the *Golden Sails*. The blustery wind did not encourage an idle promenade and extended lingering at the docks would raise suspicion. Antoine reviewed his options. It was too late in the day to seek an audience with the Commandant of the harbor to inquire about the *Golden Sails*. Antoine provided Armand with the necessary instructions, stopped at the nearest tavern, and made innocent inquiries concerning if *"that beautiful* Golden Sails *ship"* was taking any passengers. An hour later, he found Captain Mathew Johnson in the smoke-filled dinner room of the Blue Seas tavern.

"The *Golden Sails* is a beautiful ship, Captain," he complimented the man in English.

Johnson evaluated the expensive feathers on his hat and suspiciously lingered on the worn tip of the sword scabbard visible from under his cloak and the military style of his boots.

"Yes, my lord," he answered cautiously in English, his square face impassive.

"May I join you?" Antoine swept his right hand out, affording the captain a glimpse of the pistol in his belt. He kept the sword tightly in his left hand and hidden under the cloak. He slid down on the bench across without waiting for a reply.

"What may I do for you, my lord?" Johnson asked.

"You can tell me your version of a certain event in the Marseille harbor in September of 1712."

Johnson sharply inhaled. "I am afraid I must disappoint you."

"If you disappoint me, customs officers will search your ship," Antoine said sharply.

"Who are you and what do you want?" Johnson bluffed.

"You may address me as Comte. Enjoy your drink, Captain Johnson, while we talk. I assure you that no harm will come to you, if you cooperate." Under the table, Antoine briefly pressed the tip of the sword to Johnson's leg. "Keep your hands on the table."

Johnson twitched. "I don't know anything," he denied, then thought better of it. "I minded my business. What do you mean, my version?" he recovered. "That was five years ago. I don't remember what happened."

Antoine remained silent and impassive.

Sweat amassed on Johnson's forehead and his eyes watered. "What do you want to know?" His voice was gruff.

"What did you lose or acquire on that day? And I don't mean just the two barrels of rum and three boxes of tobacco you claimed in your official complaint," Antoine casually added as an afterthought. The records from Marseille were worth every coin and every minute spent.

Johnson's jaw dropped in horrified surprise. "I lost a prisoner from the brig." He scratched his unkempt beard. "My ship was under attack when he escaped."

"You are lying."

Johnson turned a shade paler. "Lying? About what?"

"No one attacked your ship." Antoine pressed his advantage.

"How do you know?" Johnson asked with as much indignation as he could muster, which was rather limited. "Were you there?"

"I ask the questions, Captain. You were docked next to the *Sacred Allegiance*."

Drops of sweat rolled down Johnson's forehead. "I don't know the ship."

"What a pity. Allow me to arrange a jovial meeting between you and her Captain to figure out how a large trunk was, shall we say, misplaced."

Johnson nervously chewed his beard. "No, I have no reason to relive that day!"

"Do you have no desire to find your escaped prisoner?"

His teeth chattered. Either he stood to lose more, or he was an excellent actor. "Do you know where to find this cursed Kumaryan?"

De Chambreau had mentioned the same name. Was Johnson terrified by a possibility of retribution? Physical or superstitious? The Great Mogul Diamond was taken from a temple in India, after all. "What is the connection between your false claim and your prisoner?"

"None! I filed no false claims!" Johnson pounded on the table with his fist. "I will tell you the holy truth, upon my soul." His voice trembled. "But first, I must know who you are. How do you know about my claim?"

"Captain Johnson. Shall I interrogate you in front of a magistrate?"

Johnson swallowed hard. "No, no, I have nothing to hide. There is no need to involve magistrates. Is it about the portraits? Did you lose five portraits of beautiful women?" he whispered. The man was either a simpleton, or there was a reason behind his obtuseness.

"Isn't Kumaryan a man's name?"

"Yes, yes." Johnson's head bobbed up and down. "He was detained in St. Dominigue. Lost his mind there. I was taking him to London. He stole the Great Mogul Diamond before he disappeared." Johnson inhaled. "It's a very large diamond, you know."

431

"Where is the Great Mogul Diamond now?"

"I am certain Kumaryan has it," Johnson panted. "His Grace the Duke Collingstone wants it."

Antoine scrutinized his face. The man was not completely forthcoming. "Did you allow him to keep the diamond?" Antoine asked.

"No! I kept it safe," he faltered. "The Marshall cousins boarded my ship, they released Kumaryan, and they stole the Great Mogul Diamond from me."

Antoine felt a flicker of irritation at the outrageous lie. "Who boarded your ship?"

"The Marshall cousins. They are infamous cutthroats from the New World."

"What is their claim to infamy?"

Droplets of sweat dripped from Johnson's forehead onto the table. "I heard rumors they were successful privateers. I don't recall any particulars, except their act in Marseille's harbor."

Antoine suppressed the desire to pound Johnson's head against the tabletop. "What is the connection between the Marshall cousins and Kumaryan?"

"I only heard they sailed the Indian coast before they moved to the New World." Johnson did not know when to stop his fabrications. "When I read their names in the newspapers, I assumed they recognized him."

The tip of Antoine's blade pushed into Johnson's leg. "Wasn't he in a brig?"

He twitched. "Maybe they noticed him when I brought him abroad my ship in St. Domingue and they followed me."

"Captain Johnson. Did the Marshall cousins board your ship in Marseille or St. Dominique?"

"I don't know! I was busy. My whole ship was in danger from the explosion and fire!" Johnson howled.

Antoine's patience was wearing thin. "Have you seen them in Marseille?"

"No, no," he shook his head. "I only played cards with them once. In Martinique."

Antoine was fortunate to control the blade at this revelation. In case of more surprises, he pulled the weapon away from Johnson's flesh. "What do they look like?"

"Unexceptional." Johnson let out a gasp of relief. "Frankly, I could not tell them apart from a hundred other English lads."

Antoine's mind boggled at this statement, but it provided a definitive measure of Johnson's inability to lie convincingly and logically. He abandoned the Marshall cousins to their fate. "Besides Kumaryan and the Great Mogul Diamond, what was your cargo?"

"Pelts, tobacco, and rum. I suffered losses in Marseille, but acquired those portraits unwillingly. No fault of mine. The trunk was left on my deck."

"What trunk?"

"The trunk with these portraits. I did not even notice it until the next day." Johnson's tongue loosened. "There were no markings on the outside. I opened it to see if there were any papers inside to help me find the owner. I found nothing except the portraits." His eyes were feverish. "I knew right away to keep their existence a secret. I am a discreet man, Comte! I told no one about these portraits, and no one saw them." He paused to catch his breath. "You have to see these portraits, Comte, to understand why I kept quiet all these years!"

Senlis, France – March 1719

. . .

"*Hire two mercenaries and send them to Senlis. I need to guard the Comte de Chambreau's house till next month,*" read de Clouet's message. Henri chose to ride out, even if that meant leaving behind an inspired-to-spy woman, a perfume-drenched woman, and a scatter-brained woman. In truth, he expected his absence to play out to his benefit. He needed to make his passions comply with his schedule, not the other way around.

"I certainly hope your business here is worth my time," Henri said.

"This business has turned sour." De Clouet promptly poured drinks into the goblets. "The task was simple enough: bring a trunk from Rabatin's warehouse in Le Havre and wait here for further instructions, but now someone aims to steal it from me. I mean, from the Comte de Chambreau."

Henri forgot his wine and his fatigue. Most goods in Rabatin's warehouse had a secret or two attached. "A trunk?"

"Yes. The Comte assigned me to sit on my arse waiting for further directions." He raised his tankard in a toast. "A week ago, the banging on the door woke me up. At first, I thought the neighbor across the street was pounding at his door. His wife sometimes locks him out. Then I realized he was not yelling like usual."

"Did you have the window open?" Henri asked. The Comte de Chambreau's residence in Senlis was unremarkable and compact. The building was square in shape and lacked an inner courtyard. The main front entrance faced a small square, and the back door was located on the opposite side and opened into a street lined with shops.

"Yes. I heard hushed voices. My room is above the back door. I had an excellent view of the scene," he chuckled. "One man was crouching at the lock. He was hitting the wood around the lock with a chisel. Another man was watching over his shoulder, debating if a lantern was needed due to the slow progress. Another man was guarding a cart."

"Why did they not just ask you, through the open window, to provide illumination to their labors?"

"I put on my breeches and slipped downstairs without lighting a candle," de Clouet continued. "Two of the Comte's men sleep in the sitting room, but they are no soldiers. I woke them up, armed one with a poker, and sent the other to check the front entrance. By the time we groped our way in the darkness to the back room, the cretins had lit up the lantern."

"No!" Henri howled in laughter.

"They tore out the lock and swung the door wide open. My eyes were still adjusting to the light, but the lantern bearer was a well fed hog. I held a sword in my hand and charged. They fled. I fired a shot, but missed."

"Are you certain they were scared of your weapons and not your bare chest?"

De Clouet responded with the expected rude gesture. "This is no laughing matter, de Brangelton. Again, I am not an expert on burglary methods, but I would expect any idiot to enter with some caution."

"Why do you suspect they wanted the trunk?"

"What else? The house stood unoccupied for months. Why wait until I and the trunk arrived? I sent the report of this event to the Comte. He instructed me to hire guards as needed." De Clouet scratched his head. "There are no trained men in this town. I organized two stable hands to stand guard." De Clouet sighed. "They are no soldiers. One of them armed himself with a broom."

"I trust you re-armed him with a shovel?" Henri had counted on a few nights of uninterrupted sleep in Senlis, but no such luck. He would have to return to Paris the next day. "What is the cargo?"

"I don't know."

"Didn't you inspect the contents of the trunk at the warehouse?"

"No. The trunk is sealed." De Clouet frowned. "De Chambreau never mentioned what's inside."

"Show me that trunk," Henri said.

Henri brushed off the light layer of dust and cleaned the cobwebs. The lid was sealed with wax to protect the inside from moisture, but there were no seals or marks to indicate the owner. That was typical for goods in Rabatin's warehouse, but de Chambreau did not seem to treat the ownership of this trunk as a confidential matter. The shape and size were common, but the secrecy and the unwelcome outside interest were intriguing. Henri lifted the corner off the ground. The trunk was oddly balanced. There was a heavy item inside. It slightly shifted when Henri and de Clouet lifted the short side from the ground. Was it half-empty to disguise the contents inside? Henri dropped the trunk and heard a muffled rattle. He carefully examined the seams. At some time, the lid had been opened and re-sealed. The faded patches indicated where the large seals were originally placed on all sides.

"How long are you expected to care for this trunk?"

"Till next month."

That coincided with Duke Collingstone's visit. His Duplicitous Grace had traveled incognito in the autumn to ensure that the French monarchy no longer supported the Jacobites, and the search for the paintings was a pretense. The upcoming visit was a formal acceptance of the pact between the French and English monarchies to exorcise the Stuart claims to the English throne, but that did not mean the Duke had forgotten his personal investments.

32

RETURN TO PARIS

PARIS, FRANCE - APRIL 1719

Your son is a very busy young man. Today, Henri,
Antoine, and Charlotte left in the morning for a ride
and have not returned yet. It's dinnertime now.
Yesterday Francis rode to Vincennes. Charlotte came
with him, as did Antoine. On Wednesday, Henri,
Antoine, and Charlotte disappeared in the early
afternoon to attend the theater in the evening. On
Tuesday, Antoine joined Charlotte and me ...

Henrietta de Brangelton's letter to Marguerite de la
Fleure - April 1719

ON THE ROAD FROM LE HAVRE TO PARIS, ANTOINE
congratulated himself on wisely investing a day to make the
acquaintance of a certain pathological liar named Captain
Johnson. Obtaining information about Kumaryan or the
diamond proved to be a challenge, since Johnson was obsessed

with these erotic portraits. Amazingly, the Marshall cousins had not painted them. Yet. Antoine doubted the quality of these paintings to be as described, but Henri, the connoisseur of female beauty, would probably be enthused to evaluate these portraits. And M. Francis would certainly succeed in extracting more information about the Great Mogul Diamond. That was why Antoine had arranged to meet up with Johnson in Le Havre. And Charles would certainly come along. Charlotte would better realize, and soon, how matters stood between her and Antoine. To hell with Johnson, the Marshall cousins, the Great Mogul Diamond, de Brault, de Chambreau, and Duke Collingstone. De la Norte must be back in Paris by now, de Rameau had never left, and the unknown nobleman from the Pont Neuf was smitten and thus poised to evolve into a damn nuisance. Antoine wasted no time on the road.

He arrived in Paris in the early afternoon, but Charlotte was out with her mother. He went home, sorted through the pile of correspondence and invitations, put aside the ones to answer or to send apologies, and stopped his activities upon opening the invitation to tonight's ball at the Louvre. Charlotte would certainly be attending. Antoine hollered at Armand to hurry with preparations for a bath.

Antoine's hair was still wet when he entered the ballroom and immediately faced an unpleasant confirmation. In his absence, Charlotte indeed had acquired a new damn admirer - the man from the Pont Neuf. He stood close by her side, and he was very comfortable, perhaps entirely too comfortable, in her company, and she purposely ignored Antoine's presence. Her brother, taking his chaperoning responsibility as seriously as he could, positioned himself as far from her as possible to entertain a group of women, including two of his own passions. To Henri's credit, upon noticing Antoine, he excused himself from his harem.

Henri made certain no one was within hearing distance. "I stumbled upon an intriguing trunk in Senlis," he whispered. "The trunk is large and lightweight. It is awaiting Duke Collingstone's attention next month. How was your trip?"

"Captain Johnson of the *Golden Sails* has interesting memories, as well a souvenir, of a certain chaotic event in the Marseille harbor."

Henri inhaled sharply. The room full of people was not the place for a long and private conversation. "I have a fencing round with de Bonnard tomorrow morning. We can meet after it."

Antoine focused his attention on his most urgent concern. "What is that?" He nodded toward Charlotte.

"The Marquis de Ternille," Henri said sourly.

"Conceited bastard," Antoine inferred. "Another goddamn admirer of the enchanting Mlle. de Brangelton? Is he also oblivious to Charles' existence?"

"He is aware of Charles, and still undeterred."

"What do you know about him?" Antoine demanded. Charlotte still had not bothered to acknowledge his presence, and not for a moment did Antoine believe that she was unaware of it.

Henri's eyes were as dark and hard as coals. "A couple years ago, he was exiled from Paris in the aftermath of conducting a scandalous affair and wounding a man in a duel. He has a mistress tucked away at Montmartre, although that does not hinder him from admiring my sister. He stands in awe of my father, he deeply respects my mother, he values and fully shares my concern for my sister's well-being, and he worships my sister. So far, she can do nothing wrong. I have an odd feeling he and I have met, but I cannot grasp where and how, and I don't trust him."

"Am I to expect a challenge from him as well?" Antoine asked.

Henri shook his head. "He is no de la Norte. De Ternille has a high concern for his skin."

"And what is Charlotte's opinion of him?"

"I have no idea."

"You, the expert on women, have no idea of your sister's opinion about a man?"

"I no longer presume to second guess my lunatic sister. Either she will marry him, or he will display a black eye." Henri glanced at Charlotte's direction. "I will intervene, for the pleasure of disappointing at least one of them. " Much to Antoine's relief, Henri left on this noble mission, but was distracted by one of his passions.

Antoine bit his upper lip. "I hurry to return to Paris, and this is what I get." He had already walked halfway across the room toward Charlotte when an arresting hand landed on his arm.

"Comte de Flancourt. What a pleasant surprise."

Antoine was of a different opinion. "Madame de Guisse." He would have bowed, but she held on to his forearm.

"So formal?" Her tone carried a shred of peevishness.

At this very moment, Charlotte deigned to notice his existence and acknowledged his presence with narrowed eyes.

"Madame Anaïs," he corrected himself. "Are you enjoying yourself tonight?"

She anticipated a memorable season and excellent company, and she emphasized the latter by leaning against him. He was tempted to spend another month with her. How would Charlotte react to that? He owed no loyalty or faithfulness to a woman who ignored his existence especially when this woman favored the smitten de Ternille with a devastating smile and sly glance.

"Your attention is faltering, M. Antoine." Anaïs tapped his shoulder. "You have not heard a word I said. "Is my attention faltering, Madame Anaïs?" Antoine repeated. She was correct.

"Yes, you have not answered my question."

Antoine realized the error of his strategy. The innocence plastered on Charlotte's face was a cause for alarm. "I did not realize it was a question, dear Madame," he answered absent-mindedly, for indeed he had not heard her. De Ternille held a chair out for Charlotte and sat down by her side.

Anaïs de Guisse's nails dug into his forearm. "I asked you," she hissed, "if you had any regrets about your refusal to escort me to Tours last year?"

"Tours? Didn't you just arrive in Paris, Madame?"

She stammered. Her vocabulary did not expand to even a tenth of Charlotte's collection of expletives. "You are shameless!" she finally said before she loudly exhaled and fanned herself. "Are you acquainted with the Marquis de Ternille? Poor man, he is so much in love with the heartless Mlle. de Brangelton!"

Antoine left Anaïs de Guisse, or she left him. It did not matter. He socialized for a quarter of an hour before walking straight into Charlotte's line of vision to bask in the unwelcome and wary glow of her expressive eyes.

The Marquis stood up to greet him.

"Marquis de Ternille? Good evening. I am the Comte de Flancourt," Antoine formally introduced himself, possessed Charlotte's hand, and raised it to his lips for longer than conventions allowed. "Charlotte."

"You are interrupting a most interesting account of Carnival in Venice," she greeted him.

"My apologies. Marquis, please, do continue." He politely inclined his head and unceremoniously pulled up a chair to the small cozy table.

The Marquis gaped only for a split second. He took up the challenge, planted himself back into the seat on Charlotte's other side, and resumed his narration in a remarkably smooth manner. Venice, the very city Charlotte wished to visit most.

"Everyone says that Venice a jewel of the Mediterranean," Charlotte sounded wistful. "I love the sea. I so much enjoy listening to the stories of seafaring adventures. Have you ever been to Marseille, M. Maurice?"

She was on given name terms with him?

"Yes, of course." De Ternille leaned forward.

"Have you heard of the Marshall cousins?"

Antoine gently kicked her under the table.

Marquis did not miss her curiosity. "Yes, of course. These despicable scoundrels destroyed and robbed a dozen respectable ships. A significant bounty was placed on their wicked heads."

That was old news. The bounty was not large enough to warrant any interest after all those years.

Charlotte's eyes lit up. "May I ask what you know of their exploits, M. Maurice?"

"Regretfully, only as little as I read in the far-flung newspapers," de Ternille answered vaguely with an uneasy glance at Antoine. "No one was able to catch those audacious cutthroats ever since. They mysteriously disappeared."

"I happened to be in Marseille last year, and I dedicated a whole afternoon to figuring out how the Marshall cousins could possibly cause as much trouble as attributed to them," Antoine said. "I concluded, if any newspaper account contains a grain of truth, that there must have been at least a dozen men."

"In that improbable case, ten Marshall cousins must be severely disappointed about their lack of notoriety." There was a certain speculative interest in de Ternille's sharp glance. "Do you have a viable theory, beautiful Mlle. Charlotte, on what exactly these vile cousins planned to accomplish and if they succeeded?"

"I only suspect that a large amount of rum was consumed." Her eyes sparkled with mischief.

"I wholeheartedly agree with you, charming Mllc. Charlotte. What is your opinion, Comte?" The Marquis condescended to acknowledge his presence.

Antoine shrugged his shoulders. "After consuming the excessive amount of rum, the Marshall cousins must have imagined that Kraken attacked, and they felt compelled to reciprocate."

"An excellent theory, Comte," de Ternille allowed. "Their notoriety reached London. I heard irrational conjectures that these cousins acquired the Great Mogul Diamond."

"Indeed? In this case, the Marshall cousins' family - clan? – squadron? - must have increased to twenty. Have you or anyone of your acquaintance ever met a Marshall cousin, Marquis?"

"Regrettably, no. I would gladly trash such vermin for causing such unforgivable havoc in a French harbor!"

"All of them?" Antoine scoffed. "I know only one impudent cutthroat capable of such a feat. His name is Charles."

Charlotte winced before her face settled into an innocent mask as eloquent as an admission of guilt.

De Ternille remained silent after a sharp inhalation of air.

"By any chance, did Charles show up in Paris lately, Charlotte?" Antoine pressed his advantage. "I certainly miss his delightful presence."

Charlotte recognized the threat. "M. Maurice." She unclenched her fist and laid her arm on his lavishly embroidered sleeve. "Will you excuse me? I must reprieve Comte de Flancourt of a certain delusion. He and my brother occasionally suffer this malady."

"So does Charles," Antoine said blandly while de Ternille bowed to kiss her hand longer than was strictly necessary.

Charlotte sailed away without a glance at Antoine. He caught up with her and firmly tucked her hand in the crook of his elbow. Charlotte's body was tense, her eyes were blazing, and her hair was styled differently. Was it a new fashion choice or de Ternille's preference? Antoine laced his fingers through hers. "Did anything interesting happen in Paris lately?"

"No. When did you come back?"

"This afternoon, barely in time for the ball," Antoine answered briskly. Why was she piqued? Certainly not about the interruption of her socializing with the Marquis. "How is Charles?" he asked, tightening his hold on her hand.

"Tell me about your trip," Charlotte demanded.

"You should have come along."

Her fingers gripped his hand tighter. "Did you return the portraits to the owner?"

"What portraits?"

Her eyes narrowed in suspicion. "The ones Lord Nelson was searching for. Or will you pretend you still do not know who he is?"

"Duke Collingstone most graciously received me. He sends his regards to Charles, by the way. I apologized for Charles' absence and promised to bring him to London next time."

"Stop it!" Charlotte said.

"Stop what?"

"Never mind! Stop stalling and explain de Chambreau's business in London."

"De Brault carried detailed descriptions of six old paintings for the Duke to assess and decide if he wished to purchase them. He does, so de Brault arranged a time and place for Lord Nelson to inspect the originals. I suspect de Chambreau was happy for the opportunity to ship his nephew out of earshot."

Charlotte was dismayed. "Did de Chambreau find the Duke's stolen portraits and now is selling them back to the Duke?"

"What portraits?"

"Of Duke Collingstone's mistresses."

"What? By old Florentine masters?"

Charlotte stumbled in mid-step. "What Florentine masters?"

Antoine guided her toward an empty settee by the wall behind the musicians. "Charlotte, the Duke is purchasing two-hundred-years old paintings by Florentine masters. What portraits?"

She grimaced in distaste. "The erotic portraits of the Duke's mistresses. Didn't de Brault tell you? The lout had no qualms in describing those portraits to me."

"Maybe you can re-convey his account?" Antoine's premonition turned to certainty. "You and I seem to refer to different objects of art."

Charlotte hesitated. "De Brault claimed it was a set of a set of five life-size portraits, each one depicting a different woman in bed."

The pain in his upper lip revived Antoine's ability to speak. That matched Mathew Johnson's collection. "Are the women completely naked, spread on a bed in the same pose?"

She nodded.

Antoine had a disorienting feeling that he had entered a tavern when he expected a library. "The backgrounds are blue, maroon, golden, green, and lavender?"

"So you know about it!"

"Charlotte. I have not heard anything about these portraits from de Brault, de Chambreau, or Duke Collingstone."

Now Charlotte was briefly deprived of speech. Her opaque eyes focused on a point in space. "How do you know, then? What did you and de Chambreau discuss in September?"

"De Chambreau asked me to deliver a dispatch to the Navy, and informed me that Duke Collingstone wished to obtain the Great Mogul Diamond. The subject of Florentine paintings only came up on this trip, and I saw the sketches. The only woman in those portraits is Mother Mary. The first time I heard about these erotic portraits was last week in Portsmouth from Captain Mathew Johnson of the *Golden Sails*." He handed her a glass of wine. "We need to sort all this information out later and in private."

Charlotte leaned her head toward him. "What is the Great Mogul Diamond?"

The day after the ball at the Louvre started for Henri much earlier than he had wished or planned.

"Wake up!" Antoine brutally demanded at the first rays of sunrise. "Tell me about the trunk in Senlis."

Henri pulled a pillow over his head. "Go away. It can wait." He had counted on discussing trunks and trips after his scheduled fencing round with de Bonnard, not before it.

His friend was undaunted. "De Ternille bleated about the Marshall cousins and the Great Mogul Diamond. This subject excited your sister's curiosity."

"He did not propose to help her search for these cousins or the diamond, did he?" Henri interjected.

"I will run a sword through him if he does."

"But what if Charlotte likes him?"

"I don't give a damn," Antoine retorted.

Henri didn't care to waste his time explaining a delicate

subject of dealing with women to Antoine. "What did he say about the Marshall cousins?"

"He pranced around the accounts from the newspapers and sung his guesses about their true motives." Antoine inhaled, eyed Gabrielle's letter on the table, and moved away from the lingering scent of the perfume. "Charlotte does not care for him."

"What makes you so confident?" Henri challenged this statement. "Do you know something I don't?"

"One more complaint from you about the bastard, and you can deliver him my challenge - you contrive a reason or ask Charlotte to do it!" Maybe he knew a few things about women. After all, he never believed that Charlotte was in love with de la Norte, and he had been correct in his assessment.

"Charlotte and mother are on their way to Versailles." Henri pulled up the blanket.

"What?!" Antoine spit out. "She never mentioned that yesterday!" He trailed off and no more exclamations followed.

Henri almost drifted off back to sleep when his friend deprived him of his pillow. "We must tell the enchanting Charles the truth about the Marshall cousins."

"Have you lost your mind?" Henri sat up. "Why?"

Henri lost a fencing round with de Bonnard, but the fact did not curb de Ternille's compliments. "It was a most educational and impressive round," the Marquis said. "I pride myself on being an accomplished fencer, but watching your match afforded me a new appreciation for the intricate art and science of it."

Antoine's and de Rousard's approach saved Henri from the necessity of acknowledging the flattery.

"De Brangelton, do you care to judge a friendly fencing round between de Flancourt and the Marquis de Ternille?" de Rousard asked.

"Shall we have every point count, Marquis?" Antoine's murderous attitude did not bode well for his opponent. Did Antoine finally and belatedly realize the implications of Charlotte's involvement in the affairs of the Marshall cousins? Henri had agreed to inform her. By now, Charlotte had gleaned knowledge of every alleged deed attributed to them, and there would be no peace for either Henri or Antoine till she figured out the connection between the Florentine pictures, the portraits, and the Great Mogul Diamond.

"I would prefer a more civilized round, Comte, strictly by exhibition rules." De Ternille's caution stemmed from the recent demonstration of unlicensed combat.

"Of course." Antoine inclined his head in his most arrogant, patronizing manner. "Will three points lead suffice for a win?"

De Ternille took his time to remove his doublet and to put the cover on the tip of his sword, in a vain effort to rile his opponent. Once the bout commenced, Antoine opened with a basic thrust, almost insulting in its simplicity. The Marquis blocked it and hesitated while Antoine waited for the response. De Ternille had two choices, either to continue in the manner Antoine set, or to make it a real match, as the audience anticipated. Antoine remained passive, and his inaction forced the Marquis to repeat futile attacks. Marquis realized that his adversary had not moved across the ground, but remained in the same spot he had started, while the Marquis had to waste his energy on circling around. In the same moment the Marquis realized his opponent's strategy, Antoine went on the offensive. The Marquis scrambled back till he felt the guard rail against his back, and the capped tip of Antoine's blade pushed against his chest.

Antoine won the first point in this round, but in a real combat, this would be the end of a duel and the end of the Marquis.

The fencers took the starting positions again, and the Marquis attacked first. Antoine sidestepped the thrust and his tipped blade jabbed Marquis in the ribs. Second point to Antoine.

The two men again moved to the center. The Marquis executed a basic maneuver, and Henri guessed that the Marquis had decided to use Antoine's tactic. Antoine countered with another insultingly simple move and the Marquis countered with a matching thrust again. Antoine unexpectedly stepped back, took a split moment to risk a salute, and pressed the covered tip of his sword to the Marquis' throat.

"That should ensure peace between them," de Rousard whispered to Henri.

33

DUEL

PARIS, FRANCE – APRIL 1719

Insane, impossible, incomparable, what is the difference?
She is Charlotte de Brangelton.

Antoine de Flancourt to Henri de Brangelton – 1719

THE CROWD AT THE COURTYARD OF THE MUSKETEERS'
Headquarters was no different from any other day. Groups of
Musketeers lingered around, officers from the guards visited,
civilians dropped in, and women joined their men. Valets,
servants, and messengers scurried back and forth. Henri
honestly wished the man in front of him would focus on his
military duties instead of discussing Charlotte's admirers. De
Molienier had come to Paris upon re-assignment, he had
surmised a disturbing amount of information within two days
of his arrival in Paris, and he had cornered Henri half an hour
ago. The Captain announced that he intended to challenge the

Marquis de Ternille about Mlle. Charlotte's affections, and yet he was still here, interrogating Henri.

"And who is de Flancourt?" de Molienier asked.

"He is my friend."

"He spends an extraordinary amount of time with you and Mlle. Charlotte. Why?"

Henri ignored the obvious implication. "He is helping her hone her fencing skills. We have known each other since childhood."

The Captain rolled his eyes. "Family friends are the most troublesome, de Brangelton."

At that profound observation, the subject of conversation entered into the courtyard and stopped to exchange greetings with d'Signac. Upon seeing the Captain and his uniform, Antoine purposely marched toward them. Henri turned away in the hope that he would leave them alone.

"I will buy you a bottle of rum, de Molienier." Henri nudged the Captain in the direction opposite the line of Antoine's approach.

Antoine refused to recognize Henri's lack of desire to socialize with him that moment and increased the speed of his stride to intercept them. He was in his – lately usual - dark mood. He and de Molienier regarded each other with enough hostility to start a war. Henri let them conduct their own introductions.

"I am Captain de Molienier."

"I am the Comte de Flancourt."

"I am looking forward to Mlle. de Brangelton's company." Captain threw a gauntlet.

"Indeed. Did Mlle. de Brangelton invite you?" Antoine inquired in a polite, superficially courtly manner, which never failed to enrage military men.

"And what affords you the right to ask such a question?" de Molienier challenged.

"And what affords you the right not to answer?" Antoine matched the Captain's tone.

"I do not appreciate your attachment to Mlle. de Brangelton," de Molienier stated.

"I do not appreciate your interest in Mlle. de Brangelton." Antoine suddenly acquired a streak of chevalier behavior.

De Molienier's mouth fell open in surprise. "I am a military man, Comte." Either he had not bothered to find out about Antoine's reputation, or he had overlooked any warnings and dismissed him as just another aristocrat.

"I do not give a damn, Captain."

De Molienier put his hand on the hilt of his sword. So did Antoine. Lieutenant de Rousard, d'Signac, and three other Musketeers approached fast.

"De Flancourt, de Molienier," Henri endeavored to bring order and sanity to the situation. "You can argue till you drop in exhaustion, but she will do anything she pleases."

"Captain. Comte. You are familiar with the royal edict forbidding duels," de Rousard formally declared.

"It is not a good time to remind me of that edict. You are dismissed, Lieutenant," the Captain barked.

De Rousard swore. Unofficially, no military officer outranked a Musketeer.

"Will you do me the honor of acting as my second, de Rousard?" Antoine took advantage of de Molienier's blunder. "Should Captain de Molienier dare to challenge me."

"Name the place and time." The Captain jumped at the bait.

"My pleasure, de Flancourt," the law-abiding and law-enforcing Lieutenant of Musketeers accepted without hesitation.

Within an hour, arrangements were made to resolve the dispute behind Luxemburg Palace at three o'clock that afternoon, before the duel became public knowledge. The terms were efficiently arranged; de Molienier's second was intelligent enough to accept de Rousard's proposal to stop the duel at first blood. Henri made a half-hearted attempt to inform father of yet another spectacle of Antoine bestirring himself on Charlotte's behalf, but his sire was nowhere to be found. Henri abandoned the quest in favor of attending the grand event. Among the audience of no less than a hundred men, he brushed off all questions with a gruff *"Don't ask me, ask de Flancourt."* Henri did not involve himself in the final preparations. De Molienier was a respectable fencer, but unless he had greatly improved his skills, his chances against Antoine were slim. Antoine had a slight advantage in height and reach, and he was a more precise fencer, but he was at the disadvantage of understanding that severely wounding or killing de Molienier might send him on the way to the New World or the Bastille. De Molienier was not burdened by any notions aside from the desire to prove his claim on the Mlle. in question – and neither he was concerned that the disorderly subject of his affection would probably award him with a black eye for his noble endeavor.

The combat area benefitted from the long shadows in the afternoon. The ground was flat and dry. Antoine and de Molienier observed all formalities before crossing their blades. De Molienier, in the manner of most military men, predictably relied on sheer force and intimidation. Antoine firmly stood his ground in defense, allowing the Captain to exert himself while evaluating his weaknesses. Antoine fenced cautiously, taking time to calculate his options as he continued to blandly deflect the blade from his skin without losing much ground. They circled each other. De Molienier grunted at each failed thrust. He showed signs of fatigue from maintaining his continuous attacks and exasperation from being thwarted at each thrust. Long and strategic bouts were not his style. Antoine launched a quick attack and drew back at de Molienier's forceful defense, thus provoking the Captain to more aggression and less control. De Molienier obliged, Antoine gave ground again, and de Molienier hurried through with his next lunge, leaving an opening which allowed Antoine to push his blade along the Captain's ribcage. A bright red stain spread over the fabric of the shirt.

"Halt!" sang de Rousard and de Molienier's second, and the men surrounded them. Antoine stood back and lowered his blade, as did Molienier. The Captain touched his ribcage, wiped his fingers, and stood upright. His eyes remained clear as he relinquished his blade to his second.

Along with Henri and d'Signac, Antoine waited for the doctor to examine the wound. In the morning, with a pang of anxiety, Antoine had realized that Charlotte could disappear from his life any time, without notice, and he would have to chase her around the world. He upbraided himself for being such a fool, and arrived at the Musketeer's Headquarters in a vicious mood, which became murderous when d'Signac dispersed intelligence that Captain de Molienier, the man engaged in a lively dialogue with Henri, was inquiring about Mlle. de Brangelton. Antoine followed the urge to assist Henri in providing an adequate explanation, and succeeded.

"You have lost your mind," d'Signac pointed out.

"Not at all," Antoine objected. He should have dealt with de Molienier last September.

"Don't make dueling a habit," de Rousard warned him. "De Molienier's wound is a mere scratch on his skin, but next time you disturb the peace, Captain d'Ornille will toss you in the Bastille."

"Mlle. Charlotte will rescue him," d'Signac chuckled.

"Will Mlle. Charlotte rescue me from a sequestration for the duration of a week or two?" de Rousard asked.

"It is a rare occasion when my sister's absence causes me a headache," Henri mused. "She would have stopped this nonsense. I am not explaining your chivalrous actions, Antoine."

The first bottle of wine was consumed at the Tutor Frog Tavern by Sorbonne to celebrate that no one was seriously injured in the duel. The second bottle was shared while crossing the Isle St. Louis in honoring that no city patrol had interrupted their exercise in Luxemburg. At the Pont Marie, Henri remembered that he was inexcusably late for his appointments with two of his passions and departed. De Rousard, d'Signac, and Antoine continued on to the Arsenal and stopped at the Three Diamonds Tavern to celebrate Antoine's victory with a third bottle. The fourth bottle was accompanied by a dinner of trout and lentils of at the Valiant Fox tavern. The fifth bottle was drunk to award themselves for properly conducting the duel. The sixth and maybe seventh bottle were enjoyed at the Blackheart Tavern by the Musketeers' Headquarters to toast courage, honor, and women, until Captain d'Ornille sent men with an order to bring de Rousard and d'Signac to his office and to escort Comte de Flancourt to his lodgings.

Upon arrival at his apartment, Antoine fumbled as he removed his swordbelt and dropped his hat on the floor. He fell onto his bed and studied the shifting ceiling. The state of affairs between himself and Charlotte de Brangelton was completely out of his control. It needed an immediate solution. The sooner he married her, the better. Charlotte did not seem to notice (or, rather, stubbornly and blithely ignored, he corrected himself) his undivided attention. She managed to avoid any opportunity to discuss the unacceptable state of their affairs in private, without any interruptions. In fact, when he to attempted to do so, she managed to start an argument or to plunge into a different subject. She was impossible. Antoine struggled to raise himself up, but abandoned the effort when the bedpost moved out of his reach.

"Armand! Bring me a bottle of wine!"

And if she harbored any illusions that he would be running off on any other errand of her making (such as his recent trip to London), she was mistaken. He was not traveling anywhere without her. Antoine resigned himself to understanding that Charlotte would never change. She was determined to make him suffer for his rude and brotherly conduct in September, although it was her own fault for pretending to be Raoul during their two weeks together.

"Armand! Where is the wine?"

No wonder she was unhappy with him. He had spent two weeks alone with her and paid her as little attention as her brother would, then failed to promptly claim their friendship, then tolerated de la Norte's presence. *"I will kill her if she thinks of me as her brother,"* he proclaimed. *"She will probably manage to ignore me if I kiss her shoulder in the middle of the crowded ball room,"* he interrupted his own monologue to contemplate that interesting idea.

"Armand! Wine!"

He needed more wine, in order to think clearly. Why was he wearing boots in bed? His thoughts blurred and crossed, but one thread remained constant. Antoine yearned for Charlotte by his side all the time, day and night, and especially the night. Preferably away from Paris, since she had always liked Lyon. The summer was an excellent time of the year, and they could visit Marseille. Had it been six months since he and Charlotte

THE LEGACY OF MARSHALL COUSINS

had left Ferrand together? What happened to the wine? Antoine slowly and somewhat unsteadily rolled over, found the elusive bedpost, and pulled himself up. He stumbled back to the sitting room to behold Armand and the open saddlebags on the floor.

"What are you doing?" Antoine leaned against the wall.

"Monsieur ordered to prepare for a trip to Venice, so I thought..."

"Stop thinking and start listening. Wait. What? When did I order that?"

"I thought I heard you say that maybe a quarter of an hour ago?"

"The Devil takes it, we are not leaving Paris until ...she...I... we... I say so! Bring me more wine!"

"Yes, Monsieur." Armand headed toward the front door.

"Where are you going?"

"To purchase wine, Monsieur."

"What?" Antoine vaguely remembered that he indeed had started to drink early in the afternoon. It was no surprise that he could no longer think coherently. He glanced at the darkened windows, groped at the wall for support, staggered back to bed, dropped in, and passed out.

The next day, Antoine woke up with an excruciating headache, parched mouth, and swollen eyelids. The aroma of stale wine could probably make a horse sick. Antoine fought a nauseous feeling, sat up, and regretted the impulse when the room shifted. "Armand!"

"Yes, Monsieur?" Armand stuck his head into the room. "Shall I open the window, Monsieur?"

"Yes." Antoine closed his eyes and inhaled the fresh air. "Help me up." He had slept in his clothes, but, mercifully, Armand must have pulled off his boots. "Set up a bath. With cold water." The distant sound of church bells reverberated in his head. Was it ten or eleven?

An hour later, Charlotte's father walked into the room. "You look awful."

"More wine than was reasonable, M. Francis." Antoine gulped more water. He finished his toilette, but his mouth was dry, his voice was hoarse, and the words came out with difficulty.

"Ah. What was the reason?"

"I forgot."

"Allow me to refresh your memory." M. Francis stepped over the water puddle on the floor and made himself comfortable in the chair. "I received an official request from the Captain of His Royal Majesty's Musketeers to explain, once more, the edicts regarding dueling to you. He is not certain you understand."

Antoine moaned. "With all respect, you can explain all Captain d'Ornille desires, but I warn you, I am in no condition to comprehend."

"You will be in no better condition after your hangover is cured. So, we might as well continue. De Molienier suffered no serious hurt, and no one cares for the unknown Captain, so your friend de Rousard has only a week worth of double duty to pay for his entertainment. You, starting tomorrow, leave Paris for a week. Preferably longer."

Antoine choked at that. "What? Leave?"

"No arguments. This is the official order from the Captain of His Royal Majesty's Musketeers." Antoine uttered an uncomplimentary opinion about the regulations and official orders.

"When you come back, do not entertain the rash notion to run your sword through the Marquis de Ternille, or there will be a warrant for your arrest."

"I have had enough of his tales."

"I must insist that you restrain yourself from skewering the Marquis," M. Francis warned him. "Neither d'Ornille nor myself will hustle to bail you out, so your father will have the joy of it. I see you are delighted at this bright prospect. In any case, clearing your name would take months."

"I shall not tolerate the Marquis' attention to her." He rubbed his temples and gulped more water.

"How will you pacify her wrath when she finds out about your uncharacteristically chivalrous actions to protect her from the advances of an unwelcome admirer?" M. Francis inquired.

"I don't own her any explanations for my actions!" Antoine's mind caught up with his emotions and he loudly exhaled. "When will she return?"

Her father regarded him sarcastically. "Are you inquiring about Charlotte?"

Antoine bit his lip. "Who else?"

"She returned last night. Antoine de Flancourt. You are intelligent enough to realize that arguments and duels on my daughter's behalf will cause a scandal to her name. That will infuriate her, distress her mother, and inconvenience me." The main reason for his visit became clear. "What were you thinking?"

BACK TO THE TRUNK

SENLIS, FRANCE – APRIL 1719

*Yes, I am a shameless opportunist. A soldier of fortune.
An unprincipled mercenary. And I am proud of it,
for I am a reliable, trustworthy, and discreet
opportunist.*

Francis de Brangelton to Laurent de la Fleure - 1691

HENRI WHOLEHEARTEDLY SUPPORTED ANTOINE'S IDEA TO
take Charlotte to Senlis, but he insisted on departing no earlier
than noon. Five minutes past the hour, they rode out in single
file, wove their way through the crowds of carts, riders, and
pedestrians moving on the Rue de St. Dennis in both directions, continued through Montmartre, and settled to ride
abreast half-way to the town of St. Dennis.

Henri had left his beautiful women to speculate about his
friend's duel without bothering him, and he eagerly anticipated
a few uninterrupted nights of sleep. Antoine would have a

chance to inspect the trunk as well. With luck, Charlotte would never find out about the duel. De Ternille would be deprived of her company, de Rameau would be free to pursue Cecilia, and Charles' presence might encourage de Clouet to leave the trunk in their care and ride to Orleans for more definitive instructions from de Chambreau.

The leisurely pace of the journey placed them at the inn only an hour's ride from Senlis. The hour was late. The inn was clean and quiet due to its location off the main road. After a satisfying dinner of partridge pies and leek soup, the three of them settled for the night in a large room containing three separate beds. Henri stretched out, pulled up the blanket, and almost drifted off to sleep when Antoine's whisper invaded his conscience.

"Charlotte, are you awake?"

"No," she answered.

Henri opened one eye. A single candle flickered on the table in the corner of the room. In its dim light, Henri could barely distinguish the shapes and shadows, but he saw Antoine cross the room and unceremoniously sit on Charlotte's bed. "I want to apologize for my idiocy in Lonjumeau."

"Never mind that!" Charlotte sat up, pulled her knees to her chest, and wrapped the blanket tightly over herself. "Did anything interesting happen in Paris while I was away?" She remembered to ask.

"Nothing of significance. Don't you always slept in your hat?" Antoine said.

"Only on special occasions," Charlotte replied after a brief pause.

Henri sleepily mused that a conversation between a half-dressed man and woman, spoken in soft voices, in the dark room, could sound nothing but intimate. No matter what the subject was or who the participants were.

"How did you acquire that hat?" Antoine seemed to be in the mood for irrelevant questions. Couldn't he save it for some other time?

"It was a gift." Was there a note of teasing? Or maybe it was the effect of the surroundings again. A woman's amiable voice in the dark room would sound seductive.

"From whom?" Antoine asked a little too quickly.

"Uncle Paul. It was his peace offering after his refusal to allow me to join the Musketeers. What are those necklaces?"

Did she almost reach out for him? Henri mulled over an odd but certain feeling that he was overlooking another theme lurking between the lines of their disjointed conversation.

"A crucifix and our family Coat of Arms." Antoine pulled the pendants out from under his shirt.

Henri yawned and hoped that they would refrain from dissecting the meanings of the heraldic symbols.

Charlotte leaned forward for a closer look in the dark. Their heads touched, and she scrambled back. Had she finally realized that he was sitting on her bed?

"Speaking of family. How will you explain the change in Raoul's appearance?" She sounded like herself now.

"To whom?" Antoine asked a perfectly sensible question in a suitably peevish tone. "And why?"

"It is your fault that your brother is somewhat known in Paris without ever setting a foot in the city. If you did not insist on escorting me to Paris–"

Antoine interrupted her. "Since we are discussing our trip to Paris, why did you act in such a dislikable and disagreeable manner?"

Couldn't he find a better time to philosophize about her behavior? Preferably in the morning. Such debate could last the whole day. Or night.

"I did not! What did you expect from me?" Charlotte retorted with indignation.

"I am not Mme. de Guisse!"

"And I am not de Ternille," Antoine spit out.

Was it mutual jealousy or just a trick of the surroundings? Two faceless voices speaking harshly to each other sounded sinister in the dark. And there it was again, an uncomfortable vague thought about a trunk, lately tugging at the back of Henri's mind.

"And we are not discussing our trip to Paris!" Charlotte hissed.

Henri almost interjected his opinion in this exchange, but recognition struck him like lightning. The voice of the nobleman in Marseille, berating Prassal! Henri sat up, but no one paid him any attention.

"Yes, we are," Antoine countered. "Did you not trust me?" Fragile silence settled for a few heartbeats.

"You are not my brother." Charlotte's response was as odd as Antoine's question.

"I am glad you realize it," Antoine said with an edge. "And don't you ever forget it."

Charlotte suddenly gave Antoine a push which nearly sent him to the floor. "Good night, Antoine."

"Good night, impossible Charlotte de Brangelton." Antoine ambled to his bed.

Henri lay down. He would share his revelation with Antoine in the morning, after a good night's sleep. Otherwise, there was a chance that Charlotte would keep them up all night with questions about the Marshall cousins. The disclosure about these renegades was better saved for the occasion when they needed to distract Charlotte from some other enterprise.

"If, by some miracle, Antoine and Charlotte entertain any ideas about each other, they will have to deal with each other

without me." With this pleasant thought, Henri drifted off to sleep.

Charlotte woke up in a quiet room, but as the sleep cleared from her mind, she heard hushed whispers coming from the corner furthest away from her bed. Fully awake now, she strained her ears to hear.

"... remove him," Antoine was saying.

Henri mumbled an unintelligible response.

"Yes, I am perfectly willing." Antoine insisted.

"Keep your voice down," Henri warned him. Charlotte remained motionless, aware that both were watching her. Was there another, besides a precious trunk, reason for their trip that neither one had mentioned to her?

"We can figure it out later," Antoine reckoned. "Go check on the horses while I wake up Charles."

Charlotte's head shot up from the pillow. "I will be ready in a quarter of an hour." She hurriedly sent both of them out of the room and jumped out of bed. She had stayed awake past midnight, and she had not heard when they rose up this morning, missing what must have been a very interesting discussion. Charlotte splashed water in her suddenly flushed face to dismiss mental images of herself and Antoine. The water spilled on her fine linen shirt. She thrust her left arm into a sleeve of the doublet and missed the right sleeve. If her dear Comte had a nerve to - She would press him for information about Marshall cousins! The buttons and holes of her doublet did not align, and she had to re-button it over. Charlotte finally adjusted the brown-and-blue sword holder strap over her shoulder, and once again, firmly ordered herself to keep her mind strictly on the current business.

"Trouble?" Henri inclined his head to indicate the group of four men who loitered by a closed door of a residence closest to the corner. They were soldiers awaiting orders, and they were well armed. One held a small barrel under his arm, which he had almost concealed under the folds of his cloak.

Charlotte subtly pulled on the reins to stall and allow more time for observation.

"De Chambreau's house is on the right, third from the corner," Henri explained.

Antoine halted in believable hesitation, took a piece of paper out of his pocket, and imitated reading a map. Hera's ears twitched, she tossed her head and flared her nostrils to sniff the air, and distinctly snorted.

"There are other horses nearby," Charlotte translated.

"That powder keg is perfectly sized to blow up a door," Antoine said. "Another man is holding a lit fuse."

The men exchanged nervous glances and impatiently shuffled their feet, glancing in their direction. The man with a scar across his face, probably the leader, stood closest to the corner and consulted the pocket watch.

"From the looks of it, they are waiting for a pre-arranged time," Antoine surmised. "We need to stay at their backs while providing an illusion that we are no threat to them."

"Performance time, Hera." Charlotte gave a gentle kick of command. The horse obligingly stomped, and Charlotte flailed her arms in a theatrical display, pretending to lose control of her mount and sliding off the saddle to land in a dry and clean patch of cobblestone. Henri pretended to have difficulty grabbing Hera's reins. Antoine dismounted and kneeled to help a fallen comrade. When the church bells tolled the hour, the leader snapped the watch closed, and there was a distant sound of an explosion.

Henri gathered the reins. "There are two groups. They will

strike when de Clouet's men are most distracted by the first attack. I will take care of the fuse."

"I will take care of the powder. Charles, watch our backs," Antoine seconded.

At the last ring of the bells, the leader signaled to the men to ran around the corner. In a heartbeat, Antoine, Henri, and Charlotte were in the saddles and the horses thundered on. The men, upon hearing the sound of the hooves, lost a precious moment looking behind themselves. The distance was short and the horses covered it to the accompaniment of the musket shots coming from the same direction as the explosion. Henri trampled over the man with a lit fuse and knocked out the leader with his fist. Antoine slashed the arm of the man holding the powder keg and kicked the keg out of the way; the powder keg flew into the air and landed a safe distance away. Another man raised his pistol when Antoine wheeled Rainstorm around and drove the horse to knock the man down. The last man standing reached for his weapon when Charlotte brought the hilt of her sword on his head. The action brought them around the corner to behold the view of the charred front door and the sight and sound of three musket muzzles protruding from the windows and discharging toward the roof of the house across the small square between the buildings.

Antoine, Henri, and Charlotte halted at the corner. De Clouet's men recognized Henri and reset their aim to the rooftop. At the other side of the square, a mounted man carefully eased himself around the corner and paused to observe the scene. He raised his head toward the men on the roof and gestured to flee, turned his horse around, and spurred it away.

Antoine grabbed Hera's reins.

"That was de Courbet!" Charlotte cried out.

"Are you certain the men on the roof are gone? How many men are around the corner?" Antoine countered.

Riding into a likely ambush was indeed undesirable. Charlotte patted Hera's neck to calm her down.

"Who is de Courbet?" Henri asked.

"Charles will tell you later." Antoine watched the street behind them. The men they knocked out were starting to stir, so he pulled out the pistol. "Keep the name to yourself for now."

The commotion raised the agitation in the street. Since musket shots were no longer being fired, people threw open the window shutters and some brave citizens ventured outside and converged in the square. City patrol showed up half an hour later.

"Good morning," Antoine pleasantly greeted the leader. "Are you in charge of this incompetent cadre, Monsieur? May I ask why it took such a long time to arrive at a scene of such unacceptable civic disorder? Are raids on private residences allowed in this fine city?" He masterfully launched into official complaints, smoothly transitioned to issuing direct commands for the patrolmen to guard the captives, and sent the leader scurrying away to bring a mason for emergency repairs of the back door and wall. Henri and de Clouet organized the men to untangle the abandoned cart from blocking the street, and to urgently find someone to repair the damage.

"We can relocate the trunk into the vault at the Valiant Fox," Henri suggested to a council consisting of him, Antoine, de Clouet, and Charlotte.

"The Valiant Fox?" De Clouet scratched his head. "Yes, I see. I suppose no one would mind if de Chambreau conducts his business there."

"Yes and no," Antoine said. "The trunk is too conspicuous for the vault. Why don't we store it at the Musketeer's Headquarters? Later, we shall find another private place for Lord Nelson to inspect the contents."

"We can secure a tent at any army garrison." De Clouet, for all his limited imagination, had been blessed with a sudden inspiration. "What? Why are you looking at me like that?"

"You proposed to bring a contingent of Englishmen to a French military establishment," Antoine explained.

Henri had a different opinion. "That is an excellent excuse to deal with Lord Nelson without his official entourage."

By noon, the abandoned cart was repaired, the trunk was loaded, and Charlotte set out with Henri and the guards toward the Musketeers' Headquarters. Antoine and de Clouet stayed in case de Courbet returned, and in order to find a welcoming army garrison.

Honore de Courbet no longer had time to investigate if the Comte de Chambreau's trunk contained St. Elias' relics or not. He prayed and hoped and trusted providence that it was so, and he meticulously laid out every step of his strategy to retrieve the trunk. It was to commence on Sunday morning, when most of the population was in church and the streets would be relatively empty for a quick escape. He drilled the men until they could account for every moment and move from the distraction of the explosion at the front entrance to loading the trunk on the cart. He set the explosion at the front door perfectly on time. His two men fired warning shots from the roof of the building across the square. The main force, led by the corporal, was to wait till the last hour bell was rung, blow up the back door, charge inside in the chaos caused by the distraction at the front door, retrieve the trunk, and carry it onto the waiting cart.

Honore heard loud yells and more shots. The ringing of the bells stopped, but there was no sound of the second explosion.

What was holding the corporal up? The timing was critical; with every passing second, it became more likely that the force inside the building would realize that had they left the back door unguarded. Honore eased his horse around the corner, and froze in terror upon the realization that three riders, who must have seen the corporal and his men, had paused at the corner. One of them made a move forward, but was held back by another man who cocked his pistol. The explosion at the back door never happened. The men inside the house remained by their posts at the windows and continued to shoot across the square. Honore knew that his plan had gone wrong, terribly wrong, with the arrival of those riders, and he reacted without thinking, motioning to his men on the roof to make themselves scarce. He turned around. "Get out of here, fast!" he shouted to Durrant, who was holding the cart for trans-porting the trunk. Durrant sat motionlessly for a painfully long moment before pulling on the reins to make the horse sharply veer off to the left and almost flipping the cart over. Durrant barely held on.

"Stop it!" Honore's order was lost in the commotion. Durrant was balancing himself upright on the seat, the reins still wrapped around his wrist. He used the straps to pull himself up, and unintentionally commanded the horse to move to the left in a tight circle on a narrow street, with the imme-diate result that the cart became wedged between the stone walls. It was a stroke of fortune that no one came around the corner.

"Leave it!" Honore again hollered at Durrant. The imbecile clumsily disengaged himself from the reins and ran for all his worth away from the cart. Agitated voices and the clatter of open shutters and doors wafted from the square. Honore rode away in the frustration of defeat and prayed that no one would catch Durrant either. An hour later, he realized that leaving the scene had been a costly mistake. He should have pretended to be an innocent bystander, speaking with those newcomers and seeing who they were. As matters now stood, he had to hide his face. Durrant was a worthless simpleton unable to conduct any intelligent search; his intellect was below even his ability to drive a horse-drawn cart. Honore went to the old Cathedral of Norte-Dame and prayed for deliverance, prayed till the light outside of the ornate rose windows faded into darkness.

After a sleepless night, Honore remembered that he had not eaten since yesterday's debacle and went to the common room of the inn for a meal. The corporal, his arm in a sling, was waiting for him, and penitently explained how the three riders had duped and overpowered them. The corporal and his men were detained, but since no injuries were reported, the magistrate only ordered the payment of a fine. The corporal was allowed to leave with a promise to return with money. His comrades were still in jail.

"How did you explain your actions?" Honore asked.

"We never did any damage, did we? I just claimed we were on our way to Chantilly, but that did not fly with these riders. They kept interrogating me. I swore I did not know my employer's name, but they did not believe me. Glory to the city watch who tossed us in jail!" He crossed himself and wiped the sweat off his forehead. "Those riders are an odd bunch. Dressed like noblemen but act as mercenaries," he observed.

Honore discreetly handed the corporal the requested amount to pay off the fine, and hissed that no, he was not going to hand over the other half of the promised fee since the trunk was not retrieved. In fact, he reminded him, the corporal technically owned him further service. The corporal haggled until Honore threatened to contact the magistrate, and they parted with an agreement that the corporal and his men would be available when Honore needed a similar service again.

Honore fortified himself with a large chunk of bread and sausage stew, and returned to the scene of the disaster. The workers were repairing the door of the Comte de Chambreau's house. Honore's risk in stopping and politely inquiring the nature of the damage paid off. He discovered that the trunk had been removed by the Lieutenant and his men, a precious bit of information accompanied with a hand gesture pointing in the direction of Paris. Honore headed south. He made inquiries on the way, but he lost track in Paris. He rode onto the road to Orleans, but there was no indication that his trunk had been carried toward Orleans. At Notre Dame Cathedral, Honore prayed for deliverance again.

35

CONFESSIONS

PARIS, FRANCE- APRIL 1719

There is never enough time, money, or information.

Francis de Brangelton to Henrietta d'Arringnon - 1694

THE WIDE OPEN WINDOWS OF CYBILLE'S ROOM ADMITTED
bright light. The noise and clutter of cart wheels and horse
hooves wafted from the street. The cheerful voices of people
and the deafening chorus of birds filled the room.

"If you love me, tell me about your trip," Cybille purred.

When would she give up? "That trip was miserable. I was
drenched by the rain and suffered from cold for nothing,"
Henri complained. "I am ecstatic to wrap my arms around
you."

"You are evading answering."

"Love, I am telling you about my trip. The food was awful."

"What was the reason of your trip, Henri?" she
interrupted.

"Reason? If I were a reasonable man, I would have refused to leave Paris, and you." He pulled her up to her feet and held her close. "I missed you, love."

Cybille pushed him away. "Did you go away with a woman, Henri?"

"No, of course not, upon my word!"

"Either you no longer love me, or you don't trust me." She theatrically gasped and fluttered her eyelashes. "What is the reason for your rejection of me, M. de Brangelton?"

"Madame! Your unjust accusations break my heart! How can you accuse me of no longer loving you?!" Henri dropped his face into his hands with just as much theatrical flair.

"You tell me nothing!"

"I suspect, Madame, you no longer love me, and you are starting a quarrel to make me leave!" Henri stifled laughter. "If this is what you desire, farewell!" He dashed to the door, slammed it on the way out, and did not allow himself to smile until he rounded the corner.

The open window failed to diminish the intensity of the perfume arising from Gabrielle's clothes, scent decanters, candles, and furniture upholstery. The people in the streets and the cats on the roofs probably reveled in the scent as well.

"I have heard that the Marshall cousins will arrive with Duke Collingstone's entourage," Gabrielle said.

"Indeed?" Henri traced his finger along her collarbone.

"Yes." She and her breasts bounced up and down in excitement. "It is a secret, of course, but I heard the ownership of the Florentine pictures has been restored back to His Grace! Did you know, these pictures were secretly purchased in Florence, and then stolen by the Marshall cousins in Marseille Harbor!" Gabrielle clasped her hands.

"Are you saying that the Marshall cousins graciously returned these pictures to His Grace with a sincere apology and he generously forgave them?" Henri chose the most outrageous guess.

"Do you think they would? Will the Duke will arrange for a pardon of their piracy? They are such daring men. They committed such legendary deeds!"

"I certainly hope, love, that you will not abandon me for either one of these cutthroats," Henri said. The speculations and mysteries surrounding the Marshall cousins grew more outrageous every day.

The pillars of light from the open window highlighted Eloise's golden locks, creating a rainbow of colors in the cover of the crystal dish filled with sweets, and revealed the dust on the gilded fireplace mantle.

"Will the Comte de Flancourt challenge the Marquis de Ternille next?" Eloise thoughtfully chewed a pink confection.

"De Flancourt did not challenge anyone. He was challenged." This question was obviously occupying many gossiping minds. "I am certain that dueling over my sister will never become a habit for him."

"Besides, the Comte has to allow at least one admirer around Mlle. Charlotte. It makes it so much more difficult to guess the truth." Her vocal cords galloped on without any guidance from her mind.

"Love, I asked you before, please leave my sister and de Flancourt alone."

"I am certain they are lovers." Eloise ignored his request for the hundredth time. "He is a handsome man. He is always at her side, and I see no efforts on her part to discourage him."

"Yes, that exactly proves my point," Henri interrupted. "I would be at your side all the time, love, but, unfortunately, the rules of society forbid such obvious displays of love." He rumbled about society rules concerning decorous behavior until she lost interest in Charlotte's and Antoine's affairs.

Two days later, the weather was dreary, the steady drizzle was threatening to develop into rain, and Henri was in an excellent mood. He had not heard from Cybille since their last squabble, Gabrielle's ridiculous speculations about the Marshall cousins had halted in anticipation of their alleged arrival, and his convoluted explanation about subterfuge had overburdened Eloise's mind to the point that she had been quiet about Antoine and Charlotte. Maybe, after all, Antoine's one month limit for the duration of love affairs was an excellent rule to live by. Henri would wager that none of Antoine's women ever demanded to know his business, and none dared to make a scene when no answer was forthcoming. At his parents' residence, Henri observed his friend waking up on the settee in the sitting room, and reversed his opinion. Antoine was the last man to look up to for advice concerning love affairs.

"Couldn't find your way into Madame de Guisse's bedroom?" Henri inquired.

"Charlotte pointed out that resuming an old affair equates to spending more than a month in Madame's charming company."

"Since when are you asking Charlotte's opinion in these matters?"

"Since she volunteered her opinion about Madame Guisse, and I expressed my opinion about de Ternille and de Vergne."

"Are you two still on speaking terms after that?"

"We had an argument that could be considered extensive even by our standards, which ended in a cards game, the stakes being Madame de Guisse's hand versus courting the Marquis de Ternille. I lost, so farewell Madame. Then I offered to reveal everything I know about the Marshall cousins in exchange for pleasure of hearing her favorite three words addressed to the Marquis de Ternille."

For a moment, Henri was speechless.

"Your father assured Charlotte that I know everything about these cousins," Antoine said.

"He probably knows more than we do," Henri grunted.

"I bet he knows the man from the Navy and the Musketeer." A range of emotions including astonishment, disbelief, ire, and finally sincere relief manifested in his face. "Henri, we are dimwits! A blue-eyed, crafty, intimidating Navy representative without a name? Accompanied by a reserved Musketeer?"

Henri did not bother to waste his breath on words as sudden understanding dawned on him as well.

Henri and Antoine flanked Francis on his way home. Why the sudden urgency to discuss, as they phrased it, *"matters of interest"* with him? Whose interests, the Marshall cousins? Did Charlotte send them out in the rain? Each in his own way, the young men were intelligent, but lately their minds had not been engaged properly. Blame that on women, pillars of happiness and the source of downfalls for many men, young and old alike. Judging by Henri's own caustic comments about his three passions, his excessive womanizing had finally caught up with him. His mistresses' whims and expectations had worn him out. Antoine, very much like his father years ago, was consumed by unresolved issues with his dearest Mlle., who was not at home, much to his disappointment and Henri's delight.

"Father, what do you know about the Marshall cousins?" Henri did not bother with preambles.

"The exaggerated rumors of their exploits overshadowed the deeds of Francis Bradforde. I declare my compliments to the boys. Along with a warning that the destruction of harbor should be the least of their worries." Francis threw off his damp cloak.

The innocence on Henri's face and the unperturbed expression on Antoine's were replaced by visible concern as they exchanged meaningful glances. "Why?" Henri and Antoine dropped into the chairs.

"Worried?"

"No, not at all," Henri denied.

Francis deliberately shook the water off his hat.

"Why should we worry?" Henri asked after a pause.

"Allow me to count their exploits. One – the Marshall cousins appropriated the trunk, full of precious Florentine religious art, on its legitimate way to His Grace the Duke Collingstone. Two – the Marshall cousins illegally acquired erotic portraits of naked women which formerly belonged to His Prolifically Womanizing Grace, and these portraits were on the way to re-unite with him. Three – the Marshall cousins also purloined the Great Mogul Diamond, which was nowhere near the harbor at the time. These exploits are only half of it."

"Half of it?" Antoine repeated is dismay. "May I ask what else are we unaware of?"

"Worried now?" Francis prompted.

Antoine's immediate reflex was to shake his head in denial.

"Where is the Great Mogul Diamond, father?" Henri asked.

"You are a master of subtle inquiries, my son. At present, an honorable citizen of Lyon is entrusted with physical possession of that jewel."

The two young men exchanged resigned glances. "May I ask since when?" Antoine finally asked.

Francis selected a bottle of wine. "That marvel of nature reached France's shore when the Marshall cousins painted themselves as New World savages to scare neighbors. Besides the unknown Kumaryan, I still do not know who claims previous ownership of this gem."

Antoine and Henri did not ponder long. "What caused a Navy representative and a Musketeer to descend on Commandant Marcoux of Marseille?" Antoine cradled the goblet in his hands.

"Did the unnamed Navy representative and his loyal Musketeer encourage the hapless Commandant to edit his report?" Henri seconded.

"When I discovered the identity of the cousins, I searched for Commandant Marcoux's original pile of manure. I mean, that original report. It is unbelievably entertaining, and it is archived in the same private collection as the Great Mogul Diamond. Read it someday."

"Another devious piece of work by the master." Henri emptied his cup.

"Thank you." Francis savored his wine. It was unfortunate that his favorite Musketeer Henrietta had missed such an entertaining discourse.

"How long have you known the identities of the Marshall cousins, father?" Henri stretched on the settee.

"My first introduction to these dim-witted ruffians was in 1712, through the newspapers. I would have dismissed it as another example of preposterous nonsense, but the award for their capture seemed to validate the use of ink," Francis recalled. "Interesting and amazing, I had never heard of these two cutthroats, and I flatter myself to believe that I am acquainted with the many, if not all, notorious reprobates on this continent. My brother Batiste had never heard of the Marshall cousins either, before or after their worthy enterprise, and he knows of every brigand in the New World. Besides, why would someone blow up the harbor? Piracy? Unrewarding. Entertainment? Unlikely. Revenge? Maybe. Sabotage? Probable, but inefficient. Stop someone from leaving the harbor?

That seemed most likely, despite being an overly dramatic enterprise, so the transgressors must have been unexperienced."

The defiant silence indicated that, yes, they were well aware of the cousins' shortcomings.

"I was intrigued, and asked Paul d'Ornille and your father, Antoine, to pay attention to any news about the Marshall cousins. As you probably heard in Montpellier, the original accusations included only piracy, sabotage, and plain drunken rampage." Francis paused to enjoy the suppressed grumblings about the Marshall cousin's idiocy. "Later on, the rumors circulated that the Marshall cousin's goal was to appropriate the Great Mogul Diamond."

"So the lie about the diamond caught your attention," Henri interjected. "Otherwise, you would have no interest in the Marshall cousins' deeds?"

"Not necessarily," Francis corrected him. "The time of the event coincided with your extended absence from fencing school and alleged drinking to provoke your expulsion. My suspicion arose when you, Henri, described your visit to Marseille as brief and uneventful. Indeed, you expected me to accept that? You, and later Antoine, denied any knowledge of the Marshall cousins."

"Cannot trick a devil," Henri proclaimed.

"Thank you again, my son. Your admiration warms my heart. So I had the description of the Marshall cousins, the conviction that their age is difficult to ascertain accurately, the memories of your experiments with gun powder, and, most telling, your reluctance to discuss the most exciting event in Marseille which happened when you were in close proximity."

Henri exhibited an acute interest in the lace of his cuff. Antoine studied the peeling plaster of Charlotte's target spot on the wall.

Henri raised his eyes. "What happened to the Florentine pictures? Or was it portraits?"

"De Louviers acted like a broker to purchase the Florentine paintings for Duke Collingstone. It was a legitimate deal," Francis explained. "The portraits have a history of illicitly changing ownership. Thrice."

"Thrice?"

"They were stolen from Duke Collingstone and re-appeared in Vienna, relocated to Venice, and finally disappeared in Marseille."

"Stolen each time?" Antoine verbalized his thoughts.

"Yes."

"What is the connection between the paintings and portraits?" Henri dismissed the history of the portraits.

Francis had no intention to elaborate. "Did Charles inform you of his recent outing to the Three Diamonds Tavern and what transpired there?"

The corner of Henri's mouth twitched.

"Why...when...she...!" Antoine exploded in a short but colorful speech about Charles' habits to venture out on his own and into trouble. "What happened there?" He finally recalled the business at hand.

"Charles acquired a new business associate and made certain commitments. The Marshall cousins were mentioned." Francis paused while Antoine sputtered and Henri articulated his unflattering opinion about Charles' habits and inclinations.

"And yet, this is not the worst of it," Francis said when Antoine gained a semblance of calm and Henri gave up his rhetoric.

"What? How?" they asked in perfect chorus.

"In the same year, the Knights of St. John secretly acquired St. Elias' sacred relics. There are allegations of the relics' disappearance, and it's attributed to the elusive Marshall cousins."

Both young men sputtered exquisite profanities in perfect chorus.

"Bourges." Antoine glanced at Henri. "Did Charlotte tell you about that?"

"No. Another one of her enterprising forays in chaos?" Henri asked with resignation.

The stage play at the Comedie de Francaise was greatly enhanced by Henri's performance. He most artfully divided his attention between Gabrielle and Eloise and claimed to both that he was dedicated to chaperoning his sister because she was overwhelmed by the obliging company of the Comte de Flancourt and M. de Contraille. The said sister added to her brother's script by promising to bring both Gabrielle and Eloise to their box, the brother threatened to sail to the New World without her, Antoine proclaimed a toast to Charles, and they ordered more wine. Charlotte's eyes glowed with mischief, and the evening progressed very pleasantly. After the curtain fell, half of the noble audience converged in the Place du Palais Royale. The warm spring air smelled of blooming flowers, spiced wine, and a mixture of perfumes. The stars in the velvet sky loomed large and bright, and the jewels against smooth skin and colorful fabric twinkled in the white moonlight. De Contraille tactfully bid them farewell, and Antoine pondered why Henri had not left the theater with one or another of his passions.

"I have an urgent matter to attend to." Henri finally validated Antoine's expectations. "I trust you to help my sister find her way home and not to the nearest tavern." He ignored Charlotte's protest accompanied by a move to grab his sleeve, and sauntered off.

Antoine blocked her path. He had no desire to blend back into the crowd. "Charlotte, we need to discuss–"

"The Marshall cousins," she interjected.

"– where matters stand between you and me."

"I must know about the Marshall cousins to make a decision about if I accept a certain business proposition."

Antoine marveled at how skillfully she had cornered him. "I offered you a deal," he reminded her.

"That was blackmail!"

"That was perfectly fair."

"The Marquis de Ternille is quite willing to provide me with information." If she was provoking jealousy, she had succeeded.

Antoine leaned over to her. "At what price?"

Charlotte glowed with false innocence. "To remain on speaking terms with me, the Marquis de Ternille might share his confidentiality without expecting any extreme incentives."

"The Marquis will be so touchingly accommodating when Hera sprouts wings," he retorted. "May I remind you that I know about the Marshall cousins, the Florentine paintings, intimate portraits, the Great Mogul Diamond, and, incidentally, do you recall our prayers in the Bourges cathedral?" He led her away from the crowded square. "Along with our encounter with a Knight of St. John?"

Charlotte made a sound between an exclamation of surprise and a choked expletive. "What did you find out?"

Antoine turned his back to the crowd. "What shall we do about de Ternille?"

"We? Who is we?"

He stepped closer to her. "Yes. We. You and me. Either you rid of him and his attention, or I will."

Charlotte startled. "Have you lost your mind?" She shoved him away.

"Not at all."

"Your exchange with de Rameau and de la Norte already caused enough embarrassment for me!"

"Embarrassment?" Antoine repeated in disbelief.

"What were you thinking?"

It was an improvement over their earlier conversations. She demanded an explanation, and he was elated to provide one. "Charlotte, I–"

"That was uncalled for! You were very happy to have my brother take me off your hands when we arrived to Paris." Charlotte quoted that idiotic statement of his.

"That was after you spend days in continuous efforts to make certain I disliked Charles!" Antoine exploded.

"You also threatened to send me off on the road to Paris with de Rameau and d'Signac," Charlotte reminded him.

"I followed you across France!" Antoine nearly yelled. God knows what other nonsense he had brayed during that trip in September. "Today is different."

"The Marshall cousins do not exist," Charlotte interrupted him. "Marshall is an assumed name. Am I correct?"

"Yes, and stop changing the subject! Back in September–"

"You are Andrew and Henri is Harold."

"What makes you think so?"

The sly grin teased him. "When a certain person described Harold Marshall, he mentioned that Charles reminded him of Harold," she said with triumph. "You claimed that you knew everything about those cousins!"

"Do you trust your certain person?"

Charlotte did not answer and Antoine seized the opportunity to bring up his original intent. "Come with me to Lyon." He was interrupted by the untimely and unexpected return of her brother.

"Gabrielle's husband assigned his loyal valet to escort her

home. I was easily, I mean, heartbreakingly deterred in my endeavors tonight," Henri explained his reappearance.

Antoine was very irate at Gabrielle's husband's discourteous actions to interfere with other people's agendas, and even more incensed at Henri himself. "Have you forgotten Eloise and Cybille?"

"I offended Eloise by dismissing her chatter."Henri paused. "Am I interrupting an argument?"

"Yes. We are assessing the identities of the Marshall cousins and their connection to the Marquis de Ternille."

Henri loudly inhaled. "Charles. To hell with the Marquis, or Antoine and I will tie you up and ship you out to the New World on the fist available ship from Uncle Batiste's fleet. Or we kidnap the Marquis and send him off to the Orient. What is your preference?" he asked Antoine.

"I volunteer to accompany Charles to the New World, and leave the Marquis at your mercy."

"An excellent plan," Henri seconded.

"No!" Charlotte squeezed between them and marched through the crowded square to locate Armand and the horses. She snatched the reins and hauled herself into the saddle before Antoine caught up with her. The folds of her split skirt tangled and Antoine smoothed the fabric over her legs. The horses' hooves against the pavement clanked a marching melody.

"Very well, never mind the Marquis," she conceded when the three of them rode past the Palais Royal. "Start talking about the Marshall cousins' exploits."

"After you explain your recently acquired associate from the Three Diamonds," Henri said.

For some reason, his comment provoked another round of indignation.

Henri claimed the settee and promptly fell asleep. The task

of reciting the Marshall cousins' truthful history fell to Antoine. He accounted for their every step and swim stroke in the harbor, and every accusation of their deeds.

Charlotte reciprocated. "That Prassal was searching for the Marshall cousins at the Three Diamonds."

"What?!" Antoine's yelp almost woke Henri up.

The bells tolled two o'clock in the morning when they exhausted their stories. "Already?" Charlotte yawned and stood up. "I am going to bed. Good night."

Antoine grabbed her, pulling her into an embrace.

Charlotte rested her hands against his chest and he felt the warmth of her touch through the layers of his clothes.

"No, you don't!" She pushed him away.

Antoine lifted her up. Charlotte kicked her feet, he feigned a struggle for his balance, and Charlotte, unwilling to tumble onto the hard floor, calmed down. He carried her upstairs, to the accompaniment of her indignant complaints that she was perfectly capable of finding her way to her own room, and oh, no, he was not welcome, and don't even think about it. At the landing, Antoine realized that someone had to open the door.

"Set me down!" Charlotte ordered.

Antoine wrapped his arm around her waist, but she wriggled out of his grasp.

"Good night." Her face was flushed, but the eyes were clear. Her corset was not tight, but it was laced in the back. She would have to cut the strings to undress.

"May I undo your laces?" Antoine offered.

She looked behind him toward her brother. "Henri! Wake up!"

"What now?" her brother muttered.

"Help me with the laces!"

Henri raised his head and looked at them with bleary eyes. "Antoine is standing right next to you." He adjusted the pillow and settled back. "I am certain he has unlaced a few corsets in his life. Leave me alone." He covered his head with another pillow.

"Are you planning to sleep in your corset?" Antoine asked.

Charlotte planted herself as far from the door as possible. "Just untie the top knot," she instructed him briskly. Antoine's hands shook when his fingers brushed against her cool skin while he fumbled with the strings underneath the fabric of her dress. As soon as he undid the first knot, she dashed into her room and slammed the door shut, and he heard the sound of key locking the door from the inside.

Henri did not wake up when Antoine descended the stairs and confiscated the pillow to spend the night in the chair.

THE VOICE OF REASON
TROYES – APRIL 1719

It's a wager. A fencing round three years from now. If you win, I will confess to my brother the sin of spreading these preposterous rumors about you and him. If I win, you kiss my brother. He will probably kill either one of us. Or both.

Raoul de la Fleure to Charlotte de Brangelton – 1716

RAOUL DE LA FLEURE ENJOYED HIS INDEPENDENCE, THE comradeship of his peers in the fencing school, and his lively social life. In the past year, his voice had deepened to a baritone, he played the lute and harpsichord tolerably well, and thus he never lacked invitations to recitals, salons, and receptions. A very pretty Marie had led a sophisticated and extensive social circle, and he frequently escorted her. On this warm spring evening, Raoul was leaving the Dragon Song tavern early to dress up for yet another assembly. *"My heart will lead me to my love,"* he hummed on his way.

"I do not like your serenade." A man in military uniform blocked Raoul's path.

"I am not singing for you, Lieutenant." Raoul did not recall the man's name, but the man had glared at him last week at a picnic, when Raoul, Marie, and two of her friends had sung for an hour.

"Keep your mouth shut, cockerel," the Lieutenant sneered back.

"Do not presume to command me, jackass." Raoul tossed caution to the wind as his hand closed around the hilt of his sword. There were plenty of witnesses around, yet the Lieutenant did not waste any time in attacking. Raoul parried defensively until he saw the opportunity to drive the tip of his sword into the flesh on the Lieutenant's upper arm. The Lieutenant gave ground, but his friend took his place and Raoul sparred with him. Another man joined the attack on Raoul, but Guy de Boucher stepped up to Raoul's side. One more officer assisted the enemy, but another officer reinforced Raoul and Guy, and more combatants engrossed themselves in a disorganized and loud brawl despite the lonely call for order by an outnumbered Captain. By the time the Captain had rallied reinforcements and his commands penetrated into the consciousness of combatants, tables were overturned, chairs were broken, shards of glass and spilled wine covered the floor, and every participant had at least a scratch or a bloody nose or a bump on the head. The Captain accused Raoul of instigating the quarrel, and ordered him to leave town. Raoul explained that he was bound by his commitment to fencing school. The very next day, Raoul was summoned to the fencing master's office.

"The Captain officially requested to expel you from my school for initiating a brawl with officers of France. I do not tolerate such transgressions," the fencing master spit out.

"Monsieur. I was not the instigator. I am grateful to you for training me on how to defend myself," Raoul flattered him.

The fencing master pounded his fist on the desk. "You have to obtain the Captain's forgiveness for your outrageous conduct, de la Fleure. Otherwise, you must leave."

"It has been a pleasure, Monsieur." Raoul clicked his heels in a military salute and left.

He did not care for fencing school, but departing from pretty Marie was unfortunate. Raoul packed his saddlebags and imagined how his father would take the news. This time, he had been expelled on account of his own actions and there was no convenient excuse of Charlotte de Brangelton's involvement. Raoul shook his head thinking about Wildcat. Was she indeed set to marry that de la Norte? Raoul felt a pang of apprehension. She was like a sister to him, but no husband of hers would complacently accept that. How did de la Norte tolerate her friendship with Antoine? Raoul was surprised at his brother's reluctance to share tales of her antics. Antoine's letter was oddly uninformative. Charlotte was rather pretty on those rare occasions when she wore a dress, he said. Raoul set aside the saddlebag and retrieved his brother's letter praising her fencing skills and denying any matrimonial prospects to de la Norte. Raoul re-read Charlotte's letter. *"You could not win a fencing round with me, even if your life depended on it,"* she boasted, ignoring his question about de la Norte. Had the man smartened up? She wrote nothing about Antoine, although she took time to narrate the state of affairs between Henri and *"his unholy trinity."* Raoul unrolled the map. Troyes was located significantly closer to Paris than to Lyon and he was not anxious to explain his departure from fencing school to his father.

"Why not?" Raoul asked himself. He had just received money from home to pay the expenses for two months in school, and he would stay with Antoine to save the expense of lodgings. Raoul felt the stirring of excitement. He and Wildcat would finally settle their fencing challenge. He no longer feared his brother's reaction to the origin of Antoine's alleged betrothal to Mlle. de Brangelton. *"Pretty maiden, meet me by the river,"* Raoul hummed as he finished packing.

Paris – April 1719

Raoul arrived to St. Antoine's gate, gaped at the Bastille, proceeded to search for his brother's residence, and lost his way among the narrow winding streets. He did not mind the first dozen detours. The wanderings afforded a pleasant opportunity to acquaint himself with the city, its insolent inhabitants, and the landmarks of the Palais Royale and Le Temple. An hour later, he finally found Antoine's home. The landlord procured the key to Antoine's lodgings, stabled the horse, took Raoul's belongings upstairs himself, and ordered his young son to see to Raoul's needs. Raoul engaged the boy as a guide and headed toward the Comte de Tournelles' residence where, to his surprise, he found Armand.

"What are you doing here?" Raoul asked in amazement, partly due to the fact that Armand was much shorter than him now.

Armand explained that M. Antoine, along with M. Henri de Brangelton, and M. Charles d'Arrignon were away on a short trip, so Armand was temporary in the Comte de Tournelles' service, but, of course, he was certain that the Comte would not mind if Armand left to attend to any needs M. Raoul might have. Maybe M. Raoul would leave a note for the Comte? A quarter of an hour later, Armand finally paused in his ramblings, and they headed back to Antoine's apartment.

"M. Raoul, what is the name of your horse? Shall I move it to the stall next to Rainstorm and Driftwood?" Armand inquired.

"Rainstorm? Driftwood?"

"The horses, Monsieur."

"Since when do we use the names referring to horses?"

"Mlle. Charlotte named Driftwood."

"Why did Mlle. Charlotte name my brother's horse?"

"It was a wager. M. Antoine lost a game of knife throws."

Fortunately, Antoine kept bottles of wine in the cupboard. Raoul pulled the cork out of the bottle and took a long gulp. "Are they lovers?"

"I did not say that, M. Raoul!"

"Why don't you explain to me, in plain language, what is happening here?"

"Since you put it that way, M. Raoul..." The dam of silence breeched, and, for the next hour, Raoul listened to the eyewitness account of the events since Antoine's encounter with Charlotte last September. Raoul needed time to mentally recover afterwards. He had always perceived Antoine as a level-headed man, but his actions on Wildcat's behalf proved otherwise. *"But if she were to marry anyone else, I would have to stop calling her Wildcat."* He laughed at the absurdity of this concept.

Among the pile of papers on the desk, Raoul found a hand-drawn map of Paris with Charlotte's handwriting indicating key city landmarks – the fencing hall, theaters, taverns, and coffeehouses. He borrowed that precious piece of paper; she could always draw another one. Just how much time did she spend at Antoine's lodgings? He studied the map, tucked it into his pocket, and went out again, this time down the Rue du Temple toward the Seine. He watched workers unloading of barges; the cargo consisted of wine barrels, stacks of wood, and trunks marked for delivery to the Arsenal. These were carried with utmost care, so they must be ammunition. Raoul lingered by City Hall, continued his pleasant stroll along the bank of the Seine, passed the Port Saint Nicolas and the Louvre, and found himself at Tuileries. He went up the stairs through the gate and entered the park. A crowd of courtiers promenaded along the straight paths lined with stately chestnut trees and the bright green color of young leaves added a fresh tint to the scene. Raoul stopped by the fountain to watch the rainbow play of the water drops against the stone base, and found himself the subject of curious interest by a very beautiful young woman, her escort in a Musketeer uniform, and his comrade-in-arms. Raoul bowed to her, gave a tight apologetic nod to the Musketeers, and resumed his walk.

"Just a moment, young man," an affable man's voice said behind him. "Have we met?"

Raoul spun around. Had they confused him with Antoine? "My name is Raoul de la Fleure."

"Yes, of course," the Musketeer smirked. "My name is de Rameau and this is d'Signac. You would have remembered us if you were sober last autumn. May I present you to the Marquise Cecilia de Fabvre?"

With an alluring smile, the Marquise extending her hand to him.

Raoul made an effort to hide his confusion. "It's a pleasure to make your acquaintance, Marquise."

"M. de la Fleure! Don't you recall our first fleeting meeting?" she pouted in a flirting manner.

"Was I unconscious at that time, Marquise?"

"You did forget me! Monsieur!" she teased him again.

De Rameau and d'Signac studiously hid their amusement.

"Is it possible you mistook me for my brother?"

Her manner instantly cooled. "Not at all. M. de la Fleure. Last September, M. de Brangelton failed to formally introduce your brother and you." She sharply inhaled.

"What?" Raoul stopped his exclamation when he realized who would have used his name, which seemed very likely considering Henri's actions and the time of the alleged meeting!

The Marquise studied him. "I distinctly recall that your hair was black. Andre!" She tapped de Rameau's shoulder with her fan. "Is this the same young man you met in Bourges?"

"Cecilia, I neither recall nor care for his looks. What does it matter?"

"M. d'Signac?"

"Mme. Cecilia, the tavern was very poorly lit. He wore his hat low."

"M. de la Fleure, were you in Bourges last September?"

"I must have been," Raoul muttered.

"Do you recall meeting these men?" She pouted at Raoul.

"It seems like a long time ago, Madame." Raoul continued his evasion tactic.

"You are just like your brother!" She reproached him.

The tense silence settled like a cloud of smoke around them. In his thoughts, Raoul cursed at Armand for omitting some key details, at Charlotte for causing this mess, at Antoine again for acting on her predilections, and at Henri for good measure.

"Tell us, de la Fleure, what brings you to Paris?" de Rameau asked.

"Probably a duel." D'Signac gripped Raoul's shoulder and nudged him away. "Mme. Cecilia, will you excuse de la Fleure and myself? He obviously is no better at conversation than his brother."

Raoul followed the Musketeer's lead. He had no desire to explain Wildcat. "Actually, the reason for my arrival to Paris involves un-appreciated songs and a brawl," he corrected his new friend.

"An excellent introduction. Your brother is a friend of mine. He mentioned that you will enlist in our ranks?"

"The sooner Captain d'Ornille signs me up, the happier I will be," Raoul answered. "Will you enlighten me on what else I have forgotten since last September? What else have I accomplished lately? What disasters have my actions caused?"

D'Signac gave him an appraising look. "You know who borrowed your name, don't you?"

"I suspect a belligerent young person of lean frame, black hair, dark blue eyes, and no discernable common sense. He is my childhood nemesis, partner in pranks, and a relative in spirit if not by blood. His usual alias is Charles d'Arringnon."

"Yes. Your brother is a very brave man."

A few days later, Raoul comfortably settled in the Musketeers' Headquarters and waited for his official commission to come through. Captain d'Ornille assigned him to prepare for the glory of serving His Royal Majesty under the command of Lieutenant de Rousard. Armed with M. Francis's hilarious explanation of Antoine and Charlotte's affairs, Raoul successfully deflected all questions about his brother and his dearest with a simple statement, *"Do not ask me any questions that you would not ask Henri de Brangelton."*

The inseparable triumvirate of trouble, as Captain d'Ornille put it, rode into the Musketeer's Headquarters courtyard in the early afternoon. Charlotte has not blossomed into a breath-stopping beauty, but she was even prettier than Raoul remembered.

"I will kill you if you ever use my name again," Raoul greeted her.

"Good day to you, my ungrateful little brother and namesake," she answered.

A short time later, Henri departed for an appointment with one or another of his passions. Raoul, Antoine, and Charlotte camped at the de Brangelton residence and Antoine sent for a dinner of roasted chicken and tarts with honeyed walnuts. After the meal, the beautiful and enchanting (What did men drink in Paris to lose their minds?) Charlotte disappeared and the impudent Charles joined them for the outing to the Spice and Song coffeehouse.

"What is the problem between you and Charlotte?" Raoul asked his brother as soon as the door of the de Brangelton residence closed behind Charles at the early hour of midnight.

"I will see if my invitation to the hunt in Duke Collingstone's honor can be extended to you."

"What, exactly, is the state of your relationship with Charlotte?" Raoul persisted.

"None of your business."

"Yes, it is."

Antoine stopped in the middle of the street. "Since when?"

"You have lost your head over the most insane woman in the whole world."

"Should I ignore you, or humor you, or punch you in the head?" Antoine did not deny the accusation.

"I would like to understand if you are a saint to tolerate her delightful demeanor, or if you have completely lost your mind." Raoul was undeterred. "Do you need my help to deal with her?"

"I don't need any help in my personal affairs," Antoine expostulated. "How will you explain your expulsion to father?"

"Blame Wildcat." Raoul tested his idea. "There would have

been no brawl if Charlotte had not encouraged me to sing to Mlle. Aline years ago. Or maybe I could just tell him I could not miss the spectacle of Charlotte de Brangelton reducing you to begging." He ducked from his brother's half-hearted attempt to slap him on the head.

37

HUNT

PARIS - APRIL 1719

Never underestimate a chance occurrence.

Francis de Brangelton to Laurent de la Fleure – 1705

HONORE DE COURBET'S PRAYERS FOR DELIVERANCE remained unanswered, so he switched to prayers for inspiration. He did not forgo his mundane efforts, and attended social functions in hopes of gleaning any hint or rumor about the trunk. His toils were awarded with an introduction to the Comte de Chambreau. Before the blunder in Senlis, Honore had been too cautious to approach the Comte, but he had nothing to lose now. Honore took charge of his destiny and requested a private audience with the Comte. He was ushered into a small room decorated with paintings of landscapes and seascapes; none had religious motifs. The paintings were done in different painting styles; Bourzat was not the only contributor.

Comte was politely cordial. "What can I do for you, M. de Courbet?"

Honore summoned all his willpower to appear calm. "Comte de Chambreau, please forgive my impudence in advance, but may I ask you an undiplomatic question? I understand you are in possession of certain Renaissance paintings?"

"Ah, yes." The Comte sounded surprised. "I purchased six Florentine paintings a long time ago." He frowned in concentration. "May I ask how you became aware of them?"

"Purely on accident," Honore said. "When I happened to make the acquaintance of M. de Bourzat, he praised your exquisite collection. Comte, would you part with the painting of the Crusades Battle?"

The Comte seemed satisfied by the explanation. "I regret to say, M. de Courbet, that all these paintings have been claimed."

Honore's mouth was dry. His hopes were crumbling to dust once again. "May I see these paintings, Comte?"

"I am afraid not," the Comte countered. While he understood M. de Courbet's desire to see the Florentine masterpieces, it was impractical –two attempts had been made to steal them. The trunk was secure at the Musketeer's Headquarters and awaiting delivery to its new owner within a week.

From the Comte de Chambreau's residence, Honore went to St. Paul's Church to pray for wisdom and for forgiveness of his sins. He despised himself for his deceit and lies, but if he could not deliver St. Elias' relics, his honor would be lost and his years of service to the Order of St. John forfeited. His life would be over. The Comte was certain that he owned the same paintings that de Bourzat had described, and Honore was certain that they were the same paintings he had acquired from Rabatin's warehouse. Honore prayed for insight; if, by some diabolical play, there existed two sets of the same paintings, what had happened to St. Elias' relics? No enlightenment came over him, and Honore summoned the corporal and Durrant.

The official hunt in the honor of Duke Collingstone commenced in the Bois de Vincennes as well as Charlotte had expected , that is to say, with all dignitaries present. No one paid any undue attention to their quartet.

"I am torn between my burning desire for the company of a beautiful lonely woman and my family duty to escort my sister," Henri complained. "This pompous event will last for a while. If I leave for a couple of hours, no one would notice. Will you two manage to keep Charlotte out of trouble?"

Antoine enthusiastically nodded.

"My brother has nothing better to do. He will happily guard your vulnerable sister for the happiness of your pretty whose-turn-is-it-today," Raoul piped up.

"No, you don't have to," Charlotte objected.

"I have an urgent matter to attend to, so I bid you farewell." Henri disappeared before Charlotte had a chance to invent an acceptable explanation for why leaving her alone with present company was a very undesirable turn of events.

"Your brother is an incredibly irresponsible, and therefore very accommodating, chaperone. I will follow his excellent example." Raoul's teeth showed in a wide smile. "Wildcat, who should I entertain?"

Charlotte was about to tell him to go to hell, but she caught herself before he used it as an excuse to disappear as well. "You are staying with us. We will manage to keep you out of trouble."

"Do you truly enjoy my company? Should I sing for you?

Who should Antoine entertain? Is Madame de Guisse present here?"

The trumpets signaled the formal start of the hunt.

"Two deer," Raoul said.

Antoine handed the spyglass to Charlotte. She fiddled with the sights before standing up in the stirrups for a better view. "There are more deer behind the bushes."

The bucks jerked their heads up, sniffed the air, and darted forward at the overwhelming smells of horses, dogs, and people. The hounds, already tense with anticipation, went into a barking frenzy, and a dozen canines broke loose to chase after the deer. The dogs' paths lead them directly toward His English Grace and his companions. The horses neighed in alarm. More hounds followed the leaders, leaving the handlers behind. In panic, the horses buckled and collided into each other. The riders' attention became focused on bringing the animals under control. The frightened deer bounced in a straight line, and the dogs kept on their collision course.

"Charlotte, chase the deer into the woods! Raoul, back me up!" Antoine shouted over his shoulder and sent Rainstorm to intercept the frenzied pack. Charlotte pressed Hera's flanks to fly at full gallop toward the deer. Terrified bucks stumbled before shifting their direction toward the woods and disappearing among the trees.

Antoine cut in front of the dogs' bared teeth to swing his hat over the snarling mass. The dogs, distracted by the bright green and white feathers brandished in front of their noses, skidded and tumbled over. Raoul fanned their confusion by hollering and beating them off with the flat of his sword. Antoine joined him to gain precious moments for Duke Collingstone and his entourage to bring their horses under control. The dogs, maddened by the interference and the blows, jumped after Antoine and Raoul. The brothers brought the horses side-by-side, one facing to the right and the other to the left, and wheeled in a tight circle. The flats of their swords and the kicks of the horses' hooves fended off the dogs until the handlers plunged into the tangled mass of fur and fangs and slowly forced the pack into obedience.

Into the chaos, another deer trotted into the meadow and froze. Charlotte chased it off into the woods. She stayed at the edge of the woods to patrol the line of trees till the pandemonium subsided.

Antoine and Raoul were laughing. They were unharmed, she realized in relief. When Duke Collingstone conversed with her dear Comte, Charlotte took the opportunity to follow her brother's example. Maybe no one would notice her exit. All the attention was being showered on Antoine and Raoul for stopping the mob of hounds. She casually moved almost out of Antoine's line of vision when he became aware of her maneuvers and excused himself from His English Grace's presence to catch up with her.

"Mlle. de Brangelton, why are you leaving so soon?"

"Comte de Flancourt, this is none of your business."

"My dear heroic Mlle. de Brangelton, His Impressed Grace has generously invited you to adorn his entourage."

"My dear Comte, I have a severe headache. Please convey my sincere regrets," Charlotte articulated. The extended entourage included the notable Patrice de Seveigney, the distinguished Marquis de Ternille, and the honorable M. de la Norte. She wished that there were a mile's distance between them and Antoine.

"Headache?" Antoine repeated with the sarcasm it deserved. "Do you feel faint, by any chance? Will a sword by your side cure it? May I escort you home?"

"No, you may not. You will stay with His Thankful Grace. This is a perfect opportunity to find out more about the paintings." She did not bother to continue. Antoine's tight smile was response enough. She steered Hera toward the Duke's illustrious entourage. Hera snorted and stomped. Out of the corner of her eye, Charlotte noticed Antoine's smirk of content. "It's the New World for me," she said.

"The New World? When are we leaving?" He pounced.

The vivid image of Antoine in the room at Lonjumeau caused her to grip her reins tightly. "What? We? Who is we? Oh, no, you don't." Charlotte almost stopped Hera to debate this point, but rode forward. Hera shook her head and neighed. Charlotte silently prayed that Antoine's deviousness and imagination would not lead to him showing up at her home expecting her to be ready for a trip with him, or threatening to never see her again. Her father might just seize the opportunity and happily send her off with Antoine within an hour, and she could not ditch Antoine's company. Hera pranced. Charlotte used the usual expletives to bring the horse to obedience, and prepared herself to deal with the tersely inquisitive stares of Duke Collingstone's entourage.

Henri had a busy day. His morning with Gabrielle was quite pleasant despite her complaints that he had shaved off his moustache. However, he then made the mistake of visiting Eloise and enduring extended speculations about his sister and the Comte de Flancourt. He stopped at home to reinforce his sanity with a nap and discovered a message from de Clouet, who had received a summons for immediate trunk delivery to Bievres. Henri had to forgo the hunt entirely and went off to secure reinforcements. He successfully ensured the commitment of two more reliable men and trotted back and forth between his parents' residence, Antoine's apartment, and his own. He had no luck in finding any of his cohorts. Where had Charlotte and the de la Fleure brothers disappeared? The hunt should have been over hours ago. Henri repeated his round once more, and rejoiced upon finally finding them at his parents' residence. Raoul comfortably reclined in a chair, while Antoine watched Charlotte and her skirts swishing around her legs as she paced back and forth.

"Don't you understand? Because of you, my reputation is now ruined in Paris and London!" she addressed Antoine. "Wasn't Orleans enough?"

"And Lyon." Raoul tossed more fuel to the fire.

Henri backed out of the room, but his sister grabbed the front of his doublet and pulled him back inside. "Henri de Brangelton, what were you thinking?"

"About what? When?" Henri stalled in anticipation of a severe headache.

"About what? About leaving me alone at the hunt." Charlotte released him. "You are such an irresponsible jackass."

"I left you with Antoine!"

"Since when is that a problem?" Raoul asked.

Charlotte threw her much-maligned tankard in his general direction. Raoul dove on the floor.

"Where were you?" Henri asked Antoine over Charlotte's head.

"Faithfully by Charlotte's side."

Charlotte took hold of Henri's doublet again. "That is what I am telling you. His Assuming Grace and everyone else believes that we...he and I – you know what I mean!"

"Everyone has believed that you and he are lovers since Antoine's duel with de Molienier," Raoul chimed in again.

"What was that?" In a regular woman, that would be a gasp followed by fainting, but Charlotte had produced a growl. Henri backed off with high hopes of placing a closed door between himself and the flying objects, but he could not undo Charlotte's grip. She emitted more unidentifiable sounds before forming the words "Duel? When?"

"Recently," Raoul volunteered. "In case you care, de Molienier fully recovered from his scratch."

"Why did no one inform me of that nonsense?" She locked eyes with Antoine. "Henri?"

"I thought he told you." Henri and Antoine pointed at each other.

Raoul doubled over with laughter.

Charlotte released Henri and marched toward Antoine. "How dare you? You are... you..." Speech failed her, a typical occurrence this evening, though normally fairly unusual.

Antoine prudently covered her clenched fists with his hands. She sprung backward. Instead of releasing her hands, he pushed her off and purposely threw her off balance. He pressed his momentary advantage, pushed on her left hand to spin her around and pulled her toward himself to restrain her with a tight hold across her upper arms and body. Charlotte buckled. Antoine almost tumbled over.

"Get your hands off me!" she screamed. "I am not speaking to you." She wriggled to free herself.

Raoul slid off the sofa in uncontrolled laughter.

"De Clouet will deliver the trunk tomorrow," Henri announced.

Charlotte and Antoine froze in their embrace.

Raoul sat up straight. "What trunk?" he asked.

"His Friendly Grace is quite excited at the invitation to visit, incognito, a French military establishment." Antoine was reluctant to release Charlotte. "De Chambreau and the trunk will greet him there." He regarded the back of Charlotte's head. "I invited Charles to make certain the trunk is transferred into

His Anticipating Grace's possession, but Charles is beyond reason today. Are you coming along or not?"

"Have you lost your mind?" Raoul echoed the question on Henri's mind. Apparently, the younger de la Fleure brother had more common sense. "You are suggesting bringing a girl to a military garrison!"

"Are you concerned Charles will be recognized?" Antoine asked.

Charlotte struggled free from Antoine's hold.

Raoul shamelessly looked her up and down. "Mlle. de Brangelton no longer possesses the ability to pass for Charles," he said, adding the appropriate hand gesture.

Henri corrected himself. No, neither de la Fleure brother had any sense.

Charlotte's narrowed eyes focused on Henri. "What time are we leaving?"

"We?" he repeated. "What makes you think de Clouet will allow you to come?"

"I will deal with de Clouet. Where are we going?"

Henri gave up. He was hopelessly outnumbered. "Bievres."

"What?" Charlotte yapped as she again turned to face Antoine. "Did you arrange that? Is your Captain de Varbes still there? What were you thinking?"

"What does it matter now?" Henri interjected before Antoine began to reason with her. "Are you coming with us or not?"

"Yes. No. Yes!"

"We will meet before dawn."

38

CLAIM TO TRUNK

PARIS TO BIEVRES - APRIL 1719

A comedy of errors inevitably provides excellent
opportunities for a wise man.

Francis de Brangelton to Henrietta d'Arringnon – 1694

"Is it time?" Raoul groaned when the yellow light
of a candle shone into his eyes. He staggered out of bed to make
his way to the washstand and splashed the water in his face.
"Are your certain your dearest will be here before dawn?"

"Yes," Antoine answered curtly.

"For certain, you have completely lost your mind." Raoul
rubbed his eyes. "Does she wear an armored corset under her
men's clothes?"

His brother did not condescend to answer.

"Should I ask her?" Raoul started to dress.

"Wear full body armor if you do. Hurry up if you care to
eat before we leave."

Henri and Charlotte promptly showed up in the bleak mist of pre-dawn. They arrived at the Musketeers' Headquarters when the first bright line of light appeared on the horizon and the men were loading the trunk onto the cart. Lieutenant de Clouet greeted Henri and Antoine, squinted at Charlotte, and shook his head.

"No." De Clouet pointed his finger at Charles. "He is not welcome," he said to Henri.

Charlotte marched toward de Clouet. "We have no spare time for any futile arguments. Forget your groundless objections, or I will cause no end of trouble for you."

He helplessly looked at Henri. "You are my second in command. Send him home."

"Why are you worried about d'Arringnon? I assure you that he will cause no trouble," Antoine promised and tossed Charlotte a Musketeer's cloak. "Put it on."

"What are you doing?" de Clouet asked in dismay.

"Giving our expedition official legitimacy," Antoine explained, "Attacking a Musketeer invites official attention, and our adversaries might think twice if they want to avoid publicity."

De Clouet closed his eyes and crossed himself before climbing onto the cart and taking the reins. Antoine introduced de Brault, whose startled stare was fixed on His Majesty's Musketeer Charles. Henri issued orders for the formation. Antoine and Charles guarded the rear, de Brault and a soldier drove the cart, de Clouet and three soldiers rode at the sides, and Henri and Raoul led the way.

"This is my mission. I am in charge here," de Clouet contented.

Henri gave him the scathing look of a seasoned officer. "I did not realize you desire to have d'Arringnon under your command."

De Clouet emitted a stoic sigh, and rode toward his place in the cavalcade.

Henri led the cavalcade across the Seine, outside and around the city limits. The sun had risen by the time they passed the turn to the Route de Fontainebleau. Henri called for a brief halt at the Route d'Orleans crossing to rest and water the horses, and they continued until Chatillon where they stopped for a meal.

"We may need a scout to ride ahead. If you suspect an ambush, fire a warning shot and gallop to the camp for reinforcements," Henri said to the soldiers after a brief consultation with Antoine. "Any volunteers for double pay?"

The trip progressed smoothly, but at the Bois de Verrieres, Henri motioned for the scout to ride ahead. The man kept an even pace between the trees and overgrown shrubs on the left side of the road and the wide-open fields stretching to the right. Raoul wondered why this precaution was necessary until he glimpsed a grove of trees on the right. Antoine inconspicuously eased his way toward him and Henri.

"What is wrong?" Raoul whispered.

"No one is traveling from that direction," Henri replied.

That was indeed strange. There were no peasants, no riders, no carts, and no carriages coming toward them. Behind, a couple of monks were walking, there was a lone rider, and a hay cart plodded along, but the stretch of road ahead was completely clear. On the left, the leaves of the forest foliage seemed too sparse to provide cover, and yet, Raoul suddenly had an impression that there was an odd movement beyond the soft rustle of the branches in the light breeze. Antoine's eyes thoughtfully swept the same area.

Ahead, the scout reached the grove and whistled as he rode into the alley flanked by the tall trees on both sides.

Antoine lowered his elbow to cover the pistol in his belt,

and Raoul followed his example. "Take my place next to Charles and remind him that in case of fighting, he is to break off, circle around through the fields behind the grove on the right, and ride for the camp. You stop anyone following him."

"Will stubborn mule Charles follow your orders?" Raoul asked. "He informed me that no one will dare to attack a Musketeer for the fear of investigation."

Before his brother even thought of an answer, a shot from a pistol shattered the air.

Henri motioned for the retinue to stop. "Watch the left side and the back," he ordered. De Clouet and two of the men cocked their pistols and rode back and forth along the cart. They watched for any movement behind the fresh greenery on their left. Charles moved to the right of the cart, toward the open fields. The birds chirped undisturbed.

Up ahead on the road, five riders abandoned their hiding place behind the bushes, and four more joined them from the opposite side. The riders advanced fast, in a column, but they could not steal the cart in that formation. The road was narrow and blocked, and half the riders held on for dear life, including the one in the lead, which explained why they were not galloping. Henri, Antoine, and Raoul had drawn swords and held cocked pistols, hiding them behind the horse's necks.

The attackers slowed to a walk.

"Stop. Dismount. Identify yourselves," Henri barked when only a dozen paces remained between the horses' muzzles.

The first man to abandon the cover raised his arm to stop the assault. He was an older man with a neatly trimmed gray moustache. His clothes were spotless, and his other hand customarily resting on the hilt of his sword.

"This trunk belongs to me," said a round man, his face red with the exertion of staying seated in the saddle. His clothing was unkempt, his slouching posture betrayed the fact that he was no soldier, but his voice seemed familiar. Raoul searched his memory.

"Who are you?" Henri asked. His tone was not lacking threat and intimidation.

The speaker hesitated in his answer and glanced at the other man. "This trunk belongs to us. To me," he repeated. There was a movement in the trees ahead on the left.

"Stay sharp!" de Clouet commanded. He and two soldiers fanned out from the cart and kept their pistols aimed at the disorganized column. Oddly, the attackers had no firearms.

"Who are you?" Henri addressed the man with the gray moustache.

The man regarded the Musketeer's cloak with a frown of concern and apprehension. "You are outnumbered," he addressed their self-proclaimed Musketeer.

"By how many?" Henri posed another inquiry.

The man, flabbergasted by the questions, hesitated in his response. His hand nervously gripped the hilt of his sword. Henri spurred his horse forward and punched the man in the stomach, but the man's experience allowed him to partially twist away and diminish the effect of Henri's fist. Henri's sudden lunge and the backing up of the man's horse caused confusion among the riders behind him. Henri rode through to ram his horse into one inept rider and knock him down while Antoine plunged in to finish off the leader with a strong punch to the jaw. General chaos erupted, and two inexperienced riders fell down when their horses bolted. Raoul knocked the terrified rotund man off his horse. Four more foes abandoned the foliage cover and galloped to the rescue of their comrades.

The Musketeer's cloak streaked across the fields on the right. One of the new assailants broke from his group and followed her. Raoul spurred his horse in pursuit, throwing his knife boot as soon as he could. The knife lodged in the man's shoulder. He tumbled off and Raoul wheeled his horse around.

Henri and de Clouet cut off the galloping reinforcements while Antoine and the soldiers faced the remnants of the column. De Brault, left alone in the cart, struggled to keep the agitated horses under control. Raoul came to his brother's help and slammed one man onto the ground before anyone even noticed him. The Musketeer's cloak appeared behind the enemy's line. Charlotte scratched the horses' flanks with a tip of her sword's as her mare flew at full gallop. The animals neighed in pain and reared in panic. Two men fell down in the confusion. Antoine and Raoul calmly and methodically dispatched the rest of the adversaries into unconsciousness. Henri and de Clouet were finished with their adversaries, and the soldiers started to round up the dazed opponents.

Raoul barely had time to dwell on the thought that there might be more enemies when Charlotte suddenly dismounted and held the bloodied sword to the neck of the rotund leader quivering on the ground. "How many of you?"

"Four.... Four... Fourteen," the man stuttered. His face turned pale as he watched the red droplets falling from the tip of the sword onto his clothes.

Antoine conducted the head count. "Thirteen." He dismounted, kicked the man so he flipped on his back, and replaced Charlotte's sword with his own. "How many?"

"Fourteen, as God is my witness!" The man fervently crossed himself in terror. "One man is in the grove. His horse was shot and he fell down," he whimpered.

Henri reached down to clamp his hand around a captive's throat. "How many?" He pulled the man up till his toes barely touched the ground.

"Fourteen!" the man wheezed.

Henri released him and swept his eyes around the attackers.

"Bring the last man here," Antoine ordered the man on the ground.

"Yes, yes, Monseigneur." The man scrambled to his knees and crossed himself before he ran forward in uneven strides. It did not even occur to him to ask for a horse. "Come here!" he screamed. "Monseigneur ordered so!"

Antoine kneeled over to check the condition of the man with gray moustache. He was certainly the leader.

The travel resumed on the road. An indignant courier stopped to lodge an official complaint with the self-appointed Musketeer. "Two thugs held up the traffic for at least an hour, I tell you. Disgraceful! Then a pistol discharged, in broad daylight. Appalling! And a man galloped by recklessly. Reprehensible! What happened to this cart?"

"Be assured, I will report this incident and appropriate measures will be implemented as necessary. No action is needed on your part. Move on," Charlotte briskly dismissed him.

De Brault moved the cart off the road, Henri, Antoine and Raoul tied up and lined up the prisoners behind it, de Clouet and de Brault rounded up the horses, and a military cadre materialized. De Rousard, dressed in civilian clothes, observed the peaceful landscape with evident satisfaction until he beheld Charlotte's borrowed uniform and her formal salute. "What is this madness?" His heated glare alternated between Henri and Antoine.

"No need for Captain d'Ornille to know," Henri replied. "And if he ever finds out, you can blame his favorite goddaughter."

"Yes, I am certain she will have an explanation to drive Captain to drink." On firmer ground, de Rousard complimented the professionalism of their scout and offered a dozen men to deliver the cargo while he and the remaining soldiers took care of the prisoners.

"Thank you. Why were you in Bievres?" Antoine asked.

"Captain d'Ornille officially sent me on a covert mission. We don't want a scratch on Lord Nelson's precious hide, do we?"

"No," Antoine replied. "You can blame me for this assignment, de Rousard. I warned Captain d'Ornille about the Lord's clandestine excursion. Did you escort him to the garrison?"

"No. He arrived with the Marquis de Ternille, and we don't want a scratch on his hide either. Note that, de Flancourt." De Rousard switched his attention to Charlotte. "Take off that cloak! There is no official involvement of the Musketeers in this enterprise!"

Antoine helped Charlotte obey the command.

"Did those adventurous aristocrats ride here by themselves?" Henri asked.

De Rousard spat in disgust. "Of course not. Lord Nelson is accompanied by Lord Stevenson. Since it's a clandestine affair, de la Norte also showed up, along with his valet. De Ternille brought only two servants and a cretin in his service named Prassal, who bleated an unsolicited conjecture that this attack could have been orchestrated by the mythical Marshall cousins," de Rousard scoffed.

Raoul caught fleeting glances among between Antoine, Henri, and Charlotte. Was one of the Marshall cousins named Charles?

Consciousness slowly returned to Honore de Courbet. He opened his eyes and studied the emerald-green blades of new grass. He attempted to move, but his hands and feet were secured with tight knots. He turned his head to a pair of boots at his eye level, and looked beyond, to the route ahead. All his men were bound up, and the amount of men guarding the trunk had seemed to double. He closed his eyes till the dizziness subsided, and when his head cleared, he wished for unconsciousness again as he began to comprehend the scale of the disaster befallen onto him. He had made so many mistakes. His strategy to split his force into three groups had been hasty and raw, just like his desperate decision to attack after the scout's warning shot. He should have disbanded his troops when he noticed the Musketeer.

"Is he awake yet?" A booted foot nudged Honore's side. The foot belonged to a young man with a noble bearing and unmistakable air of authority. His boots were custom-made in the military style, the scabbard of his sword was practical and sturdy, and the pistol in his belt was tucked within easy reach.

Honore slowly sat up. The reinforced guard formation around the cart included men in military uniforms, and all Honore's men were lined up. Honore became aware of mercenary-courtier scrutiny.

"Stand up," the young man ordered.

Honore staggered to his feet. He recognized the square face, the brown-and-green doublet, and the expensive lace trim at the throat and cuffs. This well-dressed mercenary had knocked Honore out.

Honore caught a moment to glance at the corporal. "Senlis," the corporal mouthed. Honore's heart sunk. The men who had repelled the attack in Senlis bested him now.

The man in plain civilian clothes, but with a demeanor proclaiming him to be an officer of long standing, led Honore and the column of prisoners onto the road. The commander never allowed anyone to exchange a single word, but he set a reasonable pace to march after St. Elias' relics. By the time the sun had set among the ominous dark clouds, Honore prayed for a bolt of lightning to smite him for his deceit, ambition, and cowardice. A sense of peace and acceptance of fate finally settled on Honore during the march. He trudged into the shame gates of purgatory. He no longer cared if he was recognized, and he no longer cared if St. Elias' relics were on the way to the Comte de Chambreau or anyone else.

39

DELIVERY AT BIEVRES

BIEVRES - APRIL 1719

*There are seven reasons why people lie: fear, greed, envy,
pride, foolishness, desperation, and love.*

Laurent de la Fleure to Henrietta d'Arringnon – 1694

FROM A DISTANCE, CHARLOTTE GASPED IN DISBELIEF AT
the reception committee waiting by the entrance to the garrison. No mistake here, the man in full Captain's regalia was
Captain de Varbes himself.

Antoine leaned over. "May I introduce, truthfully this time,
my brother Raoul? That cutthroat is Charles d'Arringnon
today. He freely uses Raoul's name, much to my brother's
displeasure and despite his vehement objections. I sincerely
apologize, Captain de Varbes, for withholding the truth from
you last September, but it was not my secret to disclose."

The Captain scratched his head. His eyes flickered to

Henri, then to Charlotte. He smirked in understanding. "No hard feelings, de Flancourt. Our guests are impatiently waiting for you in the pavilion with a French Royal Standard flying over it." He waved them on.

De Clouet and de Brault entered the tent first. Henri supervised the unloading of the trunk and followed it inside. The guards hesitated to admit more people, but Charlotte pushed her way through and the de la Fleure brothers rounded off the delegation.

A large, bright lantern was hanging from the massive post in the middle. Five men were clustered around a folding table with a crystal decanter of refreshing spirits. Lord Nelson's face was glowing with both drink and anticipation. Lord Stevenson was asleep in the chair. Upon Charlotte's entrance and crisp military salute, horrified amazement flashed on de Ternille's face. De Chambreau slumped his shoulders in resignation. De la Norte gasped. Antoine's spine stiffened and he motioned for Raoul to remain by the entrance. The soldiers set the trunk down and filed out and de Clouet followed his men.

Antoine conducted formal introductions.

Duke Collingstone eyed Henri. "Another de Brangelton?"

"Compared to Charles, I am a sane man." Henri glowed with innocence.

"Shall we behold the paintings?" His Grace caressed the top of the trunk and gestured to de Chambreau. "Comte, do the honors and cut the seals."

De Chambreau fumbled with the knife but eventually pried the lid loose. The Duke reached inside the trunk, pulled the cloth off the top, and froze in horror. He slowly raised his eyes and exploded into oaths able to shake the Earth. De Chambreau gasped and staggered back, his face drained of color. His mouth opened, but no sound escaped. De Brault choked and grasped the pole for support. De la Norte's face paled. De Ternille's face twisted in shock. Henri's glance was of puzzled interest. Charlotte eased herself to the side of the trunk, and Raoul peeked over her head. Antoine's hand clasped her shoulder.

"Knights of St. John," he whispered into her ear. Inside the trunk sat a small casket covered with imposing purple, red, and gold seals. A skull and a bone were clearly visible through the glass panels on top.

"What is that? Where are my paintings?!" the Duke demanded from de Chambreau.

"They should have been inside this trunk!" His choked voice was coarse. "I saw the paintings myself! I do not know what happened!" De Chambreau turned on his nephew.

"I don't know!" De Brault dropped on one knee and feverishly crossed himself. "We brought the trunk directly from the Musketeer's Headquarters."

"From where?!" Duke Collingstone loudly exhaled, snatched the decanter of brandy, and smashed it down on the contents of the trunk. De Brault shrieked. Antoine pushed Charlotte out of the way and clasped de Brault's shoulder to prevent him from throwing himself between His Grace and the relics. Henri kicked the lid closed. The glass bottle shattered on hard wood and the contents spilled over the sides, falling onto the floor and splashing brandy on His Grace's breeches. In his frustration, the Duke pounded on the trunk with his fist, seized a chair, and hit it on the closed lid. He accidentally clipped the lantern and knocked it down. The metal frame bounced off the trunk, but the glass panels broke and a cluster of red flames sprung up on the straw-covered ground. Lord Stevenson sheltered His Shocked Grace from the fire. Glass goblets shattered to sparkling pieces when Henri tore the heavy linen cloth off the table and tossed it over the burning straw. De la Norte picked up the metal jar of water and poured the contents over the escaped embers. Raoul assured the guards at the door that there was no need for alarm. De Ternille dissolved into the canvas fabric of the pavilion. Duke Collingstone, oblivious to everything, kicked the opposite side of the trunk. His hat fell down and caught on fire, and Charlotte stomped on it. The Duke picked up an empty water bucket and pounded the lid of the trunk with enough force to indent the surface of the bucket. Splinters flew; his eyes bulged, and he indulged his rage until the misshapen bucket hit him in the arm. Only then did he drop the misshapen form to the ground. "What the bloody hell is the meaning of this, de Chambreau?"

"Your Grace," de Chambreau whimpered. "I myself sealed the pictures inside the trunk at the warehouse in Le Havre."

"How dare you deceive me!" the Duke spat at de Chambreau.

"I knew nothing of this!" The Comte crossed himself.

"How do you explain these bloody bones?" Duke Collingstone was dangerously close to violence again. Any moment, he might remember the blade on his side.

Antoine slid behind His Furious Grace, ready to subdue any bloody impulses, while Henri slipped behind Lord Stevenson.

Charlotte pushed back her hat. "May I ask you a question, my lord?" she asked calmly.

His breathing was heavy and his face was distorted in anger, but the entrenched habits of courtly manners resurfaced in her presence. "Pardon my vulgar display of bad temper, dear lady." He bowed.

Charlotte smiled. "No harm done," she reassured him. "I understand there was a mistake? What was it that the Comte de Flancourt, my brother, and I were supposed to deliver?"

Her timing was impeccable. Duke Collingstone, not quite

recovered from his fury, did not censor his answer. "Bloody Florentine paintings!" he screamed. " Pardon my coarse language, Mlle. de Brangelton."

"What were the paintings of, my lord?" Charlotte innocently asked and exchanged amused glances with Antoine and Henri. Would His Proper Grace discuss Johnson's portraits with her?

"I bought, or at least I was led to believe that I bought," he said, emphasizing his disappointment with a bitter glance toward de Chambreau, "exquisite art by the old masters. A battle of the Crusades, St. Mark and the Lion...What else, de Chambreau?"

"The Holy Family and the Magi, St. George and the Dragon, a seascape of a storm and a sea serpent," the Comte readily supplied. "And a Satyr guarding a Greek temple."

"An interesting collection," Charlotte murmured.

De Brault stared at her with silent trepidation, de Ternille slowly exhaled, and de la Norte was absorbed in his own thoughts.

"Lord Nelson is here not to inspect the contents of this obscure trunk." Antoine's modulated tone was perfectly noncommittal. "Lord Nelson arrived here because the Marquis de Ternille had kindly arranged for him and Lord Stevenson the unconventional privilege of inspecting a French garrison. Isn't so, my lord?"

His Sobered-Up Grace expressed his agreement.

"That unconventional hospitality will send me back to London," de Ternille hissed.

Antoine's shrug spoke volumes. Henri's and Raoul's eyes gleamed in appreciation. Charlotte felt begrudging admiration for her Comte's deviousness.

"I have enjoyed my visit in the garrison long enough," Duke

Collingstone reckoned. "Shall we head out to our accommodations in Bievres?" he asked de Ternille.

"Yes, of course." With a venomous glance at Antoine, the Marquis followed Lord Nelson and Lord Stevenson. Raoul generously held the entrance panel open for them, and, upon a nod from Antoine, stealthily followed them outside.

Bitter silence settled in the pavilion. Antoine watched de Chambreau. The man was in obvious distress. His face was ashen, cold sweat glistened on his forehead, and his nephew was in a trance. De la Norte stood still as a statue, his eyes glued to the top of Charlotte's head. Antoine had a nice view of her profile. He knew that slight movement of her lips meant that she was plotting their next action. Antoine arranged the overturned chairs, Henri wiped the stains and ashes off the trunk, and de la Norte straightened the table.

"What happened?" De Chambreau uttered in a hollow voice. "What was it in the trunk?"

"That's what I would like to know as well," Antoine said with the edge. The possession of relics, authorized or not, was a matter of Catholic religion. If anyone, like the Jacobites in Scotland for example, ever traced it to the Anglican Duke Collingstone, a diplomatic scandal of unimaginable magnitude and the Duke's disgrace would be the best outcome. A war between England, France, and Portugal would be the worst.

"The casket belongs to the Knights of St. John," de la Norte stated quietly.

The Comte de Chambreau gasped. "So those attacks were by the Knights! We must return–"

"Yes, of course." Charlotte did not wait for him to finish the sentence. "If this trunk indeed belongs to them, it must be returned."

Antoine grasped at her ingenious implication. "Indeed, there was no strategy to the attacks. The Knights of St. John would have employed military tactics."

"What are you saying?" De Chambreau slumped in the chair.

"Besides, I would expect them to claim their property in a civil manner, and to contact the Comte de Chambreau before resorting to force." Antoine glanced at de la Norte, whose eyes remained fixed on Charlotte's hat. Antoine motioned for de Chambreau to follow him, and they exited the pavilion. In the alley between the pavilion and the gate, Raoul supervised preparations for the departure of the subdued English Lords and the distressed French nobleman. Antoine led the way to a large oak tree in the middle of the wide open space; the massive trunk shielded them from most of the garrison's population. He looked up. If anyone had had time to hide in the branches, the birds' singing and chirping would drown their voices.

"Do you have idea whose trunk is it?" Antoine balanced his tone between threat and boredom.

"No." De Chambreau shook his head. "I have no business with the Knights of St. John. I have a painter on retainer. He found the Florentine paintings in 1716, on their way from the New World. These pictures were stored at Rabatin's warehouse at Le Havre. De Bourzat inspected them first and confirmed they were genuine. I myself saw these paintings last year."

"Why did you leave these pictures in the warehouse?"

De Chambreau nervously rubbed his hands. "I was on my way to London when I made the purchase. I meant to retrieve them on the way back." He wiped his forehead with a handkerchief.

"While in London, I heard about Duke Collingstone's interest in some, er, misplaced paintings. I became suspicious of the circumstances surrounding my purchase. I was careful, even if there were no guarantees that the paintings were the same. It took time to meticulously compare and match the descriptions. You certainly understand how arduous it is to arrange a deal with His Grace."

"Who sold you these pictures?"

"Comte de Flancourt, I was pledged to secrecy," he pleaded.

"Comte de Chambreau, as the matters stand now, you are implicated in the kidnapping of cargo probably belonging to the Knights of St. John, as well as leading His Grace Duke Collingstone on a wild goose chase. Would you like to deal with the Knights of St. John and search for the missing Florentine paintings by yourself?"

"No, no, no." De Chambreau clenched his hands together. "But I gave my word not to disclose Captain– my seller's name. He insisted on secrecy."

"I see." Antoine waited until de Chambreau's knuckles were white. "I will guess the name. If I am wrong, you will tell me so. If I guess correctly, you say and do nothing."

The Comte crossed himself.

"Captain Mathew Johnson of the *Golden Sails*," Antoine gambled and won.

Guy de Brault showed no inclination to follow his uncle, and Bertrand de la Norte exhibited no intention to leave. Henri utilized the top of the trunk as a comfortable bench, and Charlotte contemplated the situation. Today had been a whirlwind of unpleasant surprises - the attack by a Knight of St. John, the

Florentine paintings gone missing, and the trunk with St. Elias' relics had been dropped at their feet.

"I have a room reserved at Bievres for tonight," de la Norte said. "Mlle. Charlotte, you and your brother are welcome to take it."

"Thank you, but I prefer to be here when the prisoners arrive," Henri replied. "Charlotte and I have stayed at military garrisons before."

De la Norte's reluctant nod was tingled with concern and disappointment.

De Brault woke from his trance and scratched his head. "Have you heard about the Marshall cousins?"

"Along with tales of Cupid, werewolves, and mermaids," Henri answered. After all, the question had been asked of everyone present and probably the pigeon strutting at the entrance.

The obvious implication was lost on de Brault. "They blew up Marseille Harbor to take the Duke's Florentine paintings and the portraits of Duke's mistresses."

"Florentine paintings," Charlotte mocked, "of Duke's mistresses? Or were these portraits of the Marshall cousins' mistresses?"

De Brault winced. De la Norte visibly startled.

"Did they also steal the Great Mogul Diamond a century ago?" Charlotte pressed her advantage. "How many Marshall cousins are there? How many generations?" She spread her arms. "I have only heard two names."

"Maybe they are Knights of St. John?" de Brault soldiered on.

"Maybe they are whores of Marseille?" Henri retorted. "Just as likely of a theory as any other."

Bertrand de la Norte cringed.

"Speaking of paintings and whores." Henri drummed his

fingers on the trunk. "What is the connection between the Florentine paintings and the erotic private portraits?"

De Brault's face reddened. He desperately pulled on his collar in a pathetic appeal to Charlotte.

She beckoned to de la Norte, and they exited the pavilion.

Charlotte led de la Norte around the pavilion, toward a large oak tree where de Chambreau was babbling to Antoine's unperturbed face. A large flock of sparrows pecking at the dirt on the ground and scattered at their approach. "May I ask what is your business here, M. Bertrand?"

His face flushed, and he nervously played with his ring. "You were exposed to danger because of these pictures!" His eyes lit up in anger. "I promise, I will find out who is behind this attack."

Nightmarish visions of de la Norte meddling in Antoine's affairs and the aftermath arose in Charlotte's mind. "M. Bertrand. My brother is committed to delivering the Florentine paintings to Duke Collingstone. Please, promise that you will not act without consulting Henri," Charlotte insisted.

He swallowed and nodded, but a frown remained.

She felt that another reason for de la Norte's indignation was lurking under the surface. "I will always stand by my brother, Monsieur. If you endanger him, you endanger me."

"No! I would never! You mean the world to me." He bit his tongue. "I apologize. I have no right."

"M. Bertrand," Charlotte interrupted before the conversation deteriorated into irrelevant nonsense. "We have a problem on our hands, and I am in the middle of it. Again, may I ask why are you here?"

"It's a sensitive matter, Mlle. Charlotte." He twisted his ring again. "Will you keep it a secret?"

"I can make no such promise, M. Bertrand," Charlotte warned him.

He was visibly torn between his desire to discourage her and the knowledge he could not disclose. "Will you tell me first, Mlle. Charlotte, how you became involved in this affair?"

"I blundered in this business because I took a silly wager." Maybe she could extract more information from him, but Charlotte wished neither to mislead him nor to be obligated to him, and she would not stoop to rekindling his tender feelings toward her.

He collected his thoughts. "In 1712, my father purchased the Florentine paintings for Duke Collingstone. These paintings disappeared in Marseille Harbor, along with the portraits. My father sent me here to make certain that the Florentine paintings were restored to their rightful owner. My father would like to find out how de Chambreau came into possession of these Florentine paintings." There was a trace of guilt and odd tension. Was he trying to obtain information from her?

"How do the portraits fit with these paintings?"

He averted his eyes. "They were placed in the same trunk for delivery to Duke Collingstone. I cannot disclose more, Mlle. Charlotte. I gave my word."

"I respect that, M. Bertrand."

He swallowed. "Mlle. Charlotte. Do you know the man from the Three Diamonds?"

So he knew of Prassal's (and, by extension, de Ternille's) involvement. "Never met him before, but I was amused when he mentioned the mythical Marshall cousins."

"Mlle. Charlotte!" He inhaled. "Will you please abandon the search for the portraits?" he pleaded. "I cannot endure the thought of endangering you."

"Is it a warning, M. Bertrand?"

He wrestled with an array of conflicting emotions before he made his decision. "I will tell you almost everything I know, Mlle. Charlotte." He carefully weighed his words. "The portraits were stolen from Duke Collingstone in London and displayed in Vienna. Within a year, they were stolen again and resurfaced in Venice. They disappeared from Venice in 1712, but there were rumors they resurfaced for sale. These portraits must not appear in public. I apologize, Mlle. Charlotte, but this is all I can tell you without violating the trust and confidence of others. Please, I beg you again, leave this business alone!"

Charlotte shook her head. "Not unless there is a compelling reason."

"I will pray to God there is no peril for you!" de la Norte cried out. "I will appeal to your brother. It is inexcusably reckless to involve you." He unconsciously glanced at Antoine's motionless figure under the tree.

"Will you please inform my brother that de Flancourt and I will return to the pavilion after speaking with Captain de Varbes?" She hurried away without waiting for an answer.

De Brault had more imagination than common sense. "Maybe these portraits belong to different Knights of St John? Assuming these men had a pact to have portraits of their mistresses–"

"Or maybe these portraits belong to chiefs of Indian tribes in the New World," Henri dismissed yet another ridiculous theory. "Next time you meet a Knight of St. John, inquire how many of his brethren commission portraits of their mistresses."

"I am not a cretin to ask that," de Brault protested. "That's what I am saying, if they don't want their, you know, activities widely known."

Mercifully, before de Brault could finish his thought, de Chambreau returned to the pavilion. He had the countenance of a man who had just seen a ghost. His conversation with Antoine must have been quite illuminating.

"Comte, do you believe that the Knights of St. John are willing to toss out those sealed bones in exchange for the portraits of voluptuous women?"

"What?" Both uncle and nephew yelped.

"No!" De Chambreau crossed himself. "That is the most preposterous and sacrilegious speculation I have ever heard!"

"I agree," Henri said. "But your nephew is convinced that it is so."

De Chambreau ranted at de Brault until de la Norte came back. Brief and stiff exchanges led Henri to detect mistrust and resentment between de la Norte and de Chambreau.

"Why are you here, de la Norte?" Henri asked.

He startled. "I rode here for recreation." He avoided de Chambreau's eyes.

"Comte de Chambreau, why are you here?" Henri pounced.

De Chambreau's face drained of color again. "I have not thought about it yet," he admitted.

"For Duke Collingstone's benefit, do we all agree that the Comte de Chambreau and M. de la Norte met here to transfer ownership of the Florentine paintings?" Henri expanded Antoine's version of events and paused upon de Chambreau's loud intake of air. "What is the problem, Comte?"

"We don't have the paintings!"

"We'll pretend we do. De Flancourt, Charles, and I will search for them."

"What happens if you don't find them?"

"Who will care? That's a private business between you and de la Norte."

"But what about this trunk?"

"De Flancourt and I will make inquiries and discreetly restore it to the ownership of the Knights of St. John."

De Chambreau bobbed his head in assent.

De la Norte's hands shook as he nervously twisted his ring. "De Brangelton, you don't mean to continue this affair with your sister's involvement! There was an attack. Can't you leave this matter to de Flancourt?" He implored.

"Isn't there a dispute between the Knights of Saint John and the Portuguese Knights of Christ about St. Elias' relics?" de Chambreau blurted out.

"What?" De la Norte's voice cracked an octave higher.

"De Flancourt, Charles, and I will investigate these rumors," Henri stayed on the course.

"Maybe the Marshall cousins are Portuguese Knights of Christ?" de Brault piped in.

"Don't be a simpleton!" Henri's response was seconded by both de Chambreau and de la Norte.

A quarter of an hour later, Antoine and Charlotte showed up. Raoul followed them with the welcome news that English visitors left the garrison, much to Captain de Varbes' elation.

"About time." Henri flung the lid of the trunk open.

The golden glow from the overhead lantern generously illuminated the contents of the casket. The skull sneered through the glass panels. De Brault gasped and feverishly crossed himself. De Chambreau moaned and crossed himself. De la Norte loudly exhaled and crossed himself. Henri, along with Raoul, Antoine, and Charlotte, felt compelled to cross themselves with equal fervor.

"Here are the seals of the Knights of St. John and the Pope," Antoine stated. "And a seal from the Church of Byzantium."

De la Norte craned his neck to inspect the papers under the glass. "Yes."

"What is that smell?" Charlotte asked.

"Hashish," Henri and Antoine said at the same time. De la Norte shuddered. De Chambreau backed off. De Brault gaped. Raoul reached inside the trunk and lifted a piece of packing canvas to reveal a roll of shimmering fabric underneath it.

Henri positioned himself between the entrance and the trunk before nodding to Raoul to stand shoulder-to-shoulder with him. "Stand guard by the door and allow no one inside," Henri commanded de Brault.

"I cannot see," de Brault complained.

"Watch the entrance," Henri barked at him.

Charlotte took a blanket and a bed sheet from the stand in the corner and spread both over the ashes on the muddy floor. Antoine carefully dislodged the bundle, and de la Norte took the other side of the roll. They lowered it on the ground and unrolled a length of shimmering, smooth, pale blue silk. Nothing was hidden inside.

De Chambreau helped to roll it up. "What are we looking for?" he asked.

"Papers, seals, contraband, anything to identify ownership." Antoine removed a small package, unwrapped a small oil painting in a golden frame with pearls, and handed it to Charlotte.

For the next hour, silence reigned. Henri and Raoul rummaged through the seams of large Indian bedcovers embroidered with elephants, crocodiles, tigers, oxen, peacocks, and flowers. Antoine, de la Norte, and de Chambreau inspected Persian rugs and rolls of silk. On the table, Charlotte assembled a small fortune consisting of the framed painting, a gold bowl, a salt and pepper set encrusted with rubies and pearls, two exquisite white and blue porcelain vases from the Orient, a crystal decanter with six matching Venetian glasses with gold trim, and an onyx and ivory chess set in a rosewood box with silver hinges. Only the sealed casket with St. Elias' relics remained inside the trunk, but no identification papers were found.

De Chambreau and de la Norte departed to their lodgings at Bievres. Raoul and de Brault accompanied them with the purpose of procuring an acceptable dinner with which to treat Captain de Varbes and his senior officers. Henri and Antoine re-sealed the trunk, tied the ropes around it, and sealed the tight marine knots with wax. For the night, the trunk was tightly wrapped in chains and secured to the center post of the pavilion. Charlotte checked their sleeping accommodations. Captain de Varbes provided a tent positioned by the outside fence. The tent was set at an angle to provide a small sheltered area between the tent and the fence. Apparently, clandestine accommodations were more common than any civilian knew. The tent could serve as a living space for two people, but four could sleep in relative comfort. As darkness fell, Raoul and de Brault returned with a generous and excellent dinner of spicy mutton stew, cabbage-filled pies, bread, an entire crate of wine, and a box of dates and walnuts.

Aside from a leisurely dinner, there was nothing else to do. At the rate de Rousard's march was progressing, the prisoners would not reach the garrison till early in the morning.

"I appreciate the advantage of you bringing along your dearest," Raoul loudly whispered to his brother on the way to their tent. "The population of this garrison well exceeds housing capacity, and I anticipated spending the night in the open."

"We can arrange that for you," Henri offered.

At their tent, Charlotte discovered that a soft mist of light had leaked through the canvas into the private space behind it, which made it easy for Charlotte to make herself comfortable for the night. De Varbes generously provided them with four sleeping pallets, neatly arranged in a row. Henri stretched along the farthest. He saved Charlotte the space next to him. Antoine sat on her other side, and Raoul smirked behind him. "I understand I met Captain de Varbes last September. What have I accomplished to distinguish myself in his eyes?"

"Nothing," Charlotte hissed before Antoine had a chance to possibly bring up their cozy accommodations that night. She could vividly picture Antoine in the room at Lonjumeau.

"That usually means you don't want to talk about it." Raoul yawned and lay down. "Antoine?"

Charlotte picked up Antoine's hat and leaned forward to hit Raoul with it before realizing she was leaning on Antoine. She drew herself back and lost her balance. He steadied her, and she ended up sitting on his pallet. Charlotte hastily scuttled back. "Be quiet, little brother!"

Raoul picked up his own hat, reached over his brother, and slapped her with it. Without thinking, Charlotte seized his wrist. He sharply rolled over, pulling her back to Antoine's pallet. She released her hold on Raoul's wrist and toppled over Antoine again. He lost no time catching her in his arms.

"I am sleeping here." Henri raised his head. "What are you doing?"

"Nothing," Raoul mocked while Charlotte untangled herself from Antoine's embrace and moved as far as possible without inviting any comments from either one of them.

"I am not speaking to any one of you." She settled on her pallet and pulled the hat over her face.

Raoul whispered to his brother. Antoine snarled back, Raoul snickered, and everyone fell silent.

No reason to be uptight. It seemed that none of de Varbes'

men had recognized Charlotte, and besides, why would they remember who spent the night when and where?

"You are not going to sleep in your hat all your life," Antoine interrupted her efforts to clear her mind. Behind him, Raoul stirred and she did not dare to respond.

INQUIRIES

BIEVRES - MAY 1719

Unexpected discoveries often pave the way for tremendous opportunities.

Francis de Brangelton to Paul d'Ornille – 1705

THE COOL DAMP AIR OF EARLY DAWN SEEPED THROUGH Raoul's clothes and mercilessly woke him up. He pulled up the cloak tightly around himself, and almost fell asleep again, but the darkness retreated and gray light basked the still forms of his companions. Antoine blissfully slept with his arm draped across Charlotte's shoulders. She moved her leg in her sleep and accidentally kicked her brother. Henri made an unintelligible sound, but continued to slumber. Raoul turned on his back and focused on the troubling feeling of forgetfulness. A vague memory tagged at his mind. He sat up. No, his recollection was important. It could not wait. He leaned across Antoine and Charlotte and poked Henri in the ribs with the tip of the scabbard. "Wake up," he quietly hissed.

Henri slowly brought himself to a sitting position. Charlotte moved in her sleep, and Antoine's arm tightened around her. Raoul picked up his weapons, boots, his cloak and hat, and crawled outside into the wet mist of the dawn light.

Henri noiselessly followed him between the rows of tents toward the empty long tables and benches. "What is it?" Henri sat down to put his boots on.

Raoul quickly told him what had transpired in the room at the Rose and Arrow Tavern years ago. "The man who pretended to be leading the gang yesterday is the same man who delivered the trunk to the Rose and Arrow." He pushed Henri off the bench and used a handkerchief to dry the cold dew from his feet.

Henri cut short his stream of expletives about his sister's lack of reason. "Tell Antoine." He disappeared among the tents.

Raoul found a place to freshen up, returned to the night's accommodations, and carefully peeked inside. His brother and Charlotte kept each other blessedly warm and were still idyllically asleep.

"When I lay my weary head upon sweet Charlotte's breast," Raoul sang. He had altered the lyrics, but even this tone-deaf couple should recognize the tune.

Antoine grunted and she muttered, but neither of them moved.

"Wildcat, do you remember the trunk at the Rose and Arrow?" Raoul asked.

Charlotte's eyelids flittered for a moment before she tossed Antoine's arm off her waist and jumped from her prone position into a full upright standing position, a feat worthy of a professional acrobat. The top of her head jabbed into the canvas and the whole tent would have collapsed if Raoul had not secured a post and Antoine had not fully awakened to roll over and to grab another post.

"The Rose and Arrow?" Antoine exclaimed from the ground. "What trunk?"

"Does the false leader of this inept cadre look and sound familiar?" Raoul asked Charlotte.

Her eyes glowed in the dim light. "Same man! What about the other man with a pistol?" She trailed off, picked up her hat, and slapped it on her head. "That must have been de Courbet!"

"What pistol?!" Antoine's shout drowned out Raoul's "Who is de Courbet?" question.

"I will warn Henri." Charlotte forgot to put on her boots or to button up her doublet. "Where is he?"

"I will find him. You tell Antoine about the pig. I mean, about the trunk. Dress up. You are indecent." Raoul dropped the entry flaps of the tent and hurried away. The drum roll and bugle sounded the signal to rise and the garrison sprung to life.

The dawn light brought a sense of gloom to Rene Prassal. His nerves had shattered when he heard about the attack. When the trunk was brought over, there was fire and shouting in Duke Collingstone's tent, and the fright settled. The Marquis de Ternille left the garrison for the comfort of the inn at Bievres, but Rene was ordered to stay behind and glean information about the attackers. The mercenaries who had brought the trunk stayed at the garrison as well, and, to add to his confusion and discomfort, Rene found out that the tall man leading this cadre was the young Chevalier de Brangelton himself. The Marquis might be besotted with Mlle. de Brangelton, but her brother was no friend of his, which was no concern to the Marquis, just as Rene's comfort was not important. He barely slept on the hard ground, he shivered from cold under the grimy blanket, and there was a commotion in the middle of the night when the line of prisoners was brought in. Rene stretched his stiff back. The recognizable, tall, and broad-shouldered figure of de Brangelton loomed in the prisoners' area. Rene had never met him face-to-face, but maybe if he were to present himself on the Marquis de Ternille's behalf, de Brangelton would dismiss him from this establishment. Rene headed into that direction, and froze in shock upon recognizing Durrant. He and two other prisoners were isolated from the rest and each other. Durrant jerked his head to attract Rene's attention. Rene's heart was beating like a drum, and his knees almost gave in when he found himself face-to-face with a specter of Marseille, Andrew Marshall himself.

"No," Rene crossed himself. It could not be. It was just a devilish coincidence. Andrew Marshall would have matured to manhood in those five years, but this man, if he was Andrew Marshall, had not aged at all. Rene wiped the sweat off his forehead and forced himself to look away. He slowly turned around to slip away and barely suppressed a scream. He had indeed turned to face the real Andrew Marshall. There could be no mistake this time. Rene's hand found a rail to support himself and he had barely started to breathe again when his vision blurred upon the sighting of the young cutthroat from the Three Diamonds. His opaque eyes momentarily narrowed at Rene, but no emotion showed and he followed Andrew Marshall toward the prisoners. Rene staggered back in horror, but a hand grasped his collar and he was lifted up to balance on his toes which barely touched the ground.

"Prassal. Do you indeed wish the Marshall cousins found?" The voice behind him was low and menacing.

"No!" Rene croaked. "Not at all! I don't know what you are talking about!"

"That's better." His feet were allowed back on the ground and a slap to the side of his head made him twist around to follow the ringing in his ears. "What did you bray about today's attack?"

Rene's vision was blurred when he looked up. His hands and knees trembled. His heart was ready to jump out of his body. "Nothing! Nothing at all! It was a jest! Forgive me!" He crossed himself with shaking hands.

"Indeed." The hard black eyes seemed to pierce through him. "You are a goddamned stupid bastard. If the Marshall cousins expose your double-dealings, you will either hang or row in the galleys."

No, Rene thought, *it could not be,* but the resemblance was undeniable. There could be no mistake. Rene staggered backwards and grappled at the post to steady himself. The blood was thundering in his ears, and he slowly slid down to the ground. No one would believe him if he were to expose Henri de Brangelton as Harold Marshall.

"Listen carefully, Prassal." In a single motion, de Brangelton pulled him up. "You shall stop all activities of searching for the Marshall cousins. If you receive any command from your master, or anyone else, even remotely connected to the Marshall cousins, you shall immediately inform either me or the Comte de Flancourt before you even think of taking any other action. You shall squawk nothing to your master. Is this understood?"

"Yes, Monsieur," Rene said in a shaking voice.

"Do remember that if you desire to live a long life." De Brangelton motioned for him to follow.

Rene shuffled along until de Brangelton stopped him and pointed to Durrant. "You two know each other?"

Honore de Courbet and his men were delivered to a military garrison, where he was placed into a solitary prison cell. The space held a pallet, a pile of straw, and a barred slit in the wall which passed for a window; this place of confinement was intended for officers. He had been given preferential treatment. For the rest of the night, he remained awake from mental exhaustion despite physical fatigue. Honore nodded off in nightmarish slumber before the dawn, only to be awakened by the beat of drums, each measure pounding a jolt of pain into his heavy head. He forced himself to rise and peeked outside. In the pre-dawn mist, he caught a glimpse of a slim figure swaggering toward the prison. Honore heard a brief exchange between the high-voiced newcomer and the guards. The young man's tone was uncompromising. The guards' answers were limited to single syllables. The door opened, and the guards unceremoniously hauled Honore up to restrain him while the newcomer bound his wrists with nautical knots. The young man wore his hat low. It completely shielded his face, but Honore caught a glimpse of the smooth chin. The young man was probably barely out of boyhood.

"Move your carcass." The boy briskly turned and sauntered away without any doubt his command would be obeyed. The guards shoved Honore along to march between the rows of tents toward the large one with a Royal Standard flying over it. Next to it, under a large tree, stood a makeshift table with plates of bread, cheese, strawberries, and a large pewter pitcher with a lid. The mercenary-courtier was drinking a steaming mixture from a simple cup. *Had they brought chocolate with them?* Honore thought irrelevantly. He had not eaten since yesterday, but he was accustomed to fasting.

The mercenary-courtier eyed Honore with a mixture of

disdain, arrogance, and boredom before dismissing the soldiers from within hearing distance. His command was obeyed with a promptness and precision reserved for officers. The boy took the chair next to him, plopped his feet on the table, and bit into a strawberry. With the other hand, he idly tossed a knife into the air. Only his arm moved; his body remained completely motionless. Honore found himself unnerved by the hypnotic movement of the knife's even trajectory.

"What was the purpose of the attack?" The mercenary-courtier's voice was perfectly modulated to convey both boredom and threat.

Honore tore his eyes from the knife. "I beg your pardon, Monsieur, but I am not at liberty to disclose my employer's business," he said humbly.

The man showed no emotion. "Who is your employer?"

"I am bound to silence, Monsieur, by everything that is sacred in this and the next world."

"And in the Mediterranean?" the man eyed him with disdain.

Honore felt blood draining from his face.

The boy picked up a slice of cheese with his knife. "His brethren know well how to make a man talk."

Honore kept his eyes on the ground.

"An assault on His Majesty's Musketeer might be construed as treason," the man reckoned. "Attempting to kidnap sacred cargo belonging to the Portuguese Knights of Christ might be perceived as a major transgression, a cause for political scandal, and a sin."

"The Portuguese Knights of Christ?" Honore knew he had lost his ground when a sarcastic smile crossed his interrogator's face.

"Possibly." The indifferent expression returned. "That's

where the cargo is heading, unless you convince me otherwise. What is your real name, Monsieur?"

Honore had a sickening feeling that the man already knew. "Whose prisoner am I, Monsieur?"

"It depends on your cooperation." He took another sip from his cup.

Honore had no choice left. "Monsieur. You do understand the implications of entanglement into a dispute between the Knights of St. John and the Knights of Christ?"

"That dispute does not concern me."

The boy resumed toying with his knife. "You are not in a position to make threats, Monsieur." He raised his head.

Honore reeled back from the intense, glimmering, familiar eyes. "This is a very serious affair, Monsieur," he proclaimed to the mercenary-courtier.

"Spare me the lecture," the man countered sharply. "Do you want me to hand you over to Captain d'Ornille for attacking the escort led by his Musketeer? I will deliver the relics as I see appropriate." He picked up a knife to slice the cheese.

Honore held his head high. He might as well disclose his identity; the commander of the French military garrison might think twice about holding a Knight of St. John prisoner. "I am willing to cooperate with an honorable man, as I am certain you are, but I must know your name."

The man paired a slice of cheese with a chunk of bread and washed it down with his drink. He was not taunting Honore with food. Instead, he successfully conveyed the message that he not care. The boy used the knife's point to pick up a slice of cheese to nibble on, and took a few more delicate bites of the strawberry.

"What do you expect of me, Monsieur?" Honore asked.

The man carefully set his cup on the table. "The truth. Who are you? What are your plans for St. Elias' relics?"

"I am Honore de Courbet, Knight of St. John." Honore swept a formal bow as graciously as his tied hands allowed. "My purpose is to deliver St. Elias' relics to Bourges."

The man leisurely wiped his hands and pushed the platter aside. "By any chance, do you possess half a dozen paintings by old Florentine masters?"

"How did you know?" Honore was startled.

"Tell me what they are." He stood up.

"Joseph, Mary, and Christ; St. Mark; St. George; a battle of the Crusades; and two Classical scenes – satyr and sea serpent," Honore recited. Those images were etched in his mind. "Are you the owner?"

"No." The man walked around the table, easily untied the nautical knots of Honore's hands, and tossed the rope to the boy. "I am the Comte de Flancourt, at your service," he introduced himself. "Would you like to share the meal with us, M. de Courbet? We might be able to achieve an amiable agreement about the future of St. Elias' relics." He motioned to bring another plate set.

"Thank you." Honore rubbed his wrists with a pointed glance at the boy – or, rather at his hat.

The boy remained seated. "My alias is Charles d'Arringnon."

Honore dropped into the chair. He recognized the name, and the resemblance to her father.

At noon, a messenger brought a letter for Comte de Flancourt, to be delivered only into the Comte's own hands.

"What is it?" de Rousard asked.

"An invitation – summons – to accompany Lord Nelson to Paris." Antoine folded the letter. "Will you accompany de Brangelton and Charles to take the trunk back to the Musketeer's Headquarters?"

De Rousard also generously volunteered to arrange with Captain de Varbes to detain Durrant and his cohorts for another day. Shortly after, de Courbet departed in subdued solitude.

Antoine apprised Charlotte of the change in plans and rode to Bievres with Raoul, who had invited himself to accompany de Brault and, by extension, de Chambreau. De Ternille departed without waiting for Prassal. Lord Nelson invited Antoine to a meal of eggs and baked eel. By the time they set out on the road back to Paris in the late afternoon, the crowds of merchants, laborers, farmers, messengers, and noble travelers were the thickest of the day and travel was the most impeded. They had to reel off the road to allow an ornate coach to pass a slow donkey cart carrying wood and traveling in the opposite direction.

"I will never admit knowledge of the fact that these bloody bones belong to Knights of St. John." Lord Stevenson, upon a nod from Lord Nelson, returned to the subject of the trunk. "Do you have a theory how this debacle happened?"

"I am inclined to believe that we have suffered the aftermath of unnecessary caution." Antoine could not malign Rabatin or de Clouet or de Chambreau, but he had to devise a plausible theory which did not involve the Marshall cousins. "It is possible that the Knights of St. John purposely mislabeled the trunk to mislead the Portuguese."

The Lords exchanged apprehensive glances. "Is that argument still raging?"

"The latest I heard, it is winding down. The Knights moved the relics, and this action seems to confirm these rumors,"

Antoine improvised. "I cannot imagine how St. Elias' relics replaced the Florentine paintings."

"The Florentine paintings are the least of my concerns, de Flancourt." Lord Nelson waited for a passing group of courtiers to ride away, and backed his horse away even further from the road. "My immersion in the world of art produced private portraits." He succinctly described the charms and images of his former mistresses before disclosing the known history of the portraits so far. "But back to business. Two of these women are married to prominent members of the English Parliament, and one is related to the Bishop of Westminster Abbey. I cannot afford to allow these portraits to fall into the wrong hands. There are rumors of Spain instigating yet another Jacobite uprising, and Jacobites will use any means to discredit me and to shatter the peace between France and England again."

41

MEN AND WOMEN

PARIS- MAY 1719

*I am a brave man, but an innocent expression on de
Brangelton's face accompanied by a blank
expression on de la Fleure's face terrifies me.*

Paul d'Ornille to Henrietta d'Arringnon - 1694

Upon securing the trunk at the Musketeers'
Headquarters, Henri deposited his sister at home and returned
to his own lodgings with the overwhelming desire to drop in his
bed and stay there for hours, by himself. To his dismay, a
mound of notes from Cybille, Gabrielle, and Eloise was waiting
for him. What was a man to do? He chose to deal with his beautiful passions that afternoon instead of waiting till tomorrow,
and headed to Cybille's residence a block away from the Place
de Victories.

Cybille crossed her arms under her shapely breasts and

stomped her foot. "You are despicable!" she greeted Henri. "All this time, you have been lying to me. How dare you claim complete ignorance of your father's interest in the Company of the West!"

"Pardon me, love, I never lied," Henri corrected her.

"You never told me anything of value!"

"This is not the same as lying."

"Where have you been for the past week?"

"Love, why would I discuss business with you?" Henri no longer cared for pleasantries.

She gasped at his rudeness at first, but recovered. Her spine stiffened to a ramrod posture. "From now on, M. de Brangelton, when I ask you questions, I expect direct answers. I am tired of your evasions!"

"What would you like to know?"

"Where were you yesterday?!"

"I cannot divulge that, love."

The shocked disbelief gave way to ugly anger. She had a nerve to raise her arm in an attempt to slap him.

Henri caught her wrist. "Don't ever do that again, Madame." He released her at the same instant she jerked her hand away.

She stumbled back, tripped over the chair, and sat down with less poise than she would have ever intended. "I don't ever want to see you again!" she screamed.

"As you wish." Henri exited and rushed to the front door and into the street. "Good riddance," he grinned to himself as he rounded the corner. "I do not enjoy a tumble in bed when my mind must be alert." He crossed the Seine to pay his respects to Gabrielle.

Gabrielle studied her reflection in the mirror and purposely adjusted a stray lock of hair. "Do you truly love me?" she asked Henri.

"Yes, love." What favor was she was planning to ask for?

"At the hunt, you left without ever speaking to me. I have not seen you since then."

"Your husband participated in the hunt, love."

"Were you jealous?" She pouted her sensuous lips.

"Yes, I was jealous beyond reason." Henri handed her another hairpin.

"Oh, you should have showed your interest in me."

"Making him jealous would have been unwise." Henri wanted to stay on the subject of jealousy.

"On the contrary. He might have challenged you." She traced his jaw with a tip of her finger.

"I don't want to quarrel with your husband, love," Henri explained. Indeed, why would he provoke his own exile from Paris?

"You don't? Of course I would grieve for him if something tragic were to happen, but if he were not in the way, we could marry." She put her arms around his neck.

"Why would I..." Henri almost blurted out that he would never consider marrying her, but caught himself and continued with a more polite, "...wish for something tragic to happen to him?"

Gabrielle gasped. "I thought you loved me!"

"He is very kind and generous to you, love, and very tolerant of me," Henri said innocently.

"He suspects that I am unfaithful," she pouted.

"That is awful." Henri dropped his face into his hands to stifle the laughter at his own words. "But I understand, love. I bid you farewell."

"Just like that?"

"I do what a man of honor must do," Henri bowed over her hand to hide his amusement.

"Go away." She pulled her hand free and raised it in an attempt to slap him. "I don't ever want to see you again!"

"As you wish." Henri released her wrist and stalked out, shaking his head in disbelief. "Good riddance," he decided as soon as he rounded another corner. "I would never run my sword through anyone on her account." He crossed the Seine again and passed the Tuileries on his way to Eloise.

Eloise set down the unopened box of sweets. "How dare you ignore my messages!"

"I am elated to embrace you, love." Henri pulled her close. "I was away. I missed you."

She inhaled the air at his collar. "Do you have another woman in your life?" she asked suspiciously.

"No, love." As of this afternoon, that was the true state of his love affairs.

"How can I be certain?" She tossed her golden hair back.

"Upon my word, love, you are the only one," Henri reassured her, barely refraining from yawing.

"Why do I smell a woman's perfume on you?"

"Are you certain, love?" After visits to Gabrielle, Henri usually stopped at a smokehouse to neuter the aroma of her perfume, but today his visit was short and he had not expected her perfume to cling.

"Oh, you never loved me! You did not ever bother to shave and make yourself presentable!" Eloise managed a theatrical sob.

"It seems to me, Madame, you are attempting to quarrel."

Her hand went up in the air, a familiar gesture today. "Leave me alone!" she screamed when he caught her wrist. "I don't ever want to see you again!"

"As you wish," Henri readily repeated for the third time in three hours and left. "Good riddance," he congratulated himself again, a block away this time. "Never again will I involve myself with more than two passions at the same time."

He went home in an exuberant mood, and fell into a deep sleep as soon as his head touched the soft pillow.

The day after their return from Bievres, the brothers begun their rounds, as Raoul expected, with a visit directly to Wildcat's home. Upon discovering that Charlotte was out with her mother, the disappointed Antoine chose to participate in the leisurely activity of watching a tennis match or maybe participating in one, and the brothers proceeded to the Louvre. The viewing gallery was surprisingly crowded.

"Why is de Ternille approaching us?" Participating in a duel over the most insane woman in France did not appeal to Raoul at all. Although, if Antoine were to be exiled from Paris, the three of them could probably cajole his dearest to accompany him.

Antoine smoothly moved toward the back wall for more privacy. Raoul followed him.

"Comte. I understand you had journeyed to Orleans last September?" De Ternille wasted no time in pleasantries. He was either more courageous than Raoul had originally given him credit for, or less intelligent, or he must have really lost his head over Charlotte.

"Orleans is a lovely town," Antoine said blandly.

"Maybe we should chat about this lovely town in private, Comte," the Marquis snarled.

"I unconditionally trust my brother."

Raoul would not miss such a promising exchange, no matter what Captain d'Ornille and Lieutenant de Rousard expected. He could just blame it on Wildcat.

De Ternille glared at him, but continued. "Comte. You must be aware that your brief appearance in Orleans last September is common knowledge, along with the fact that Charles d'Arringnon traveled with you."

Antoine politely inclined his head in acknowledgement.

"You and I know who Charles d'Arringnon is," Marquis continued. "I suspect Mlle. de Brangelton would prefer to keep Charles' true identity unknown."

"Marquis. What gave you that idea?"

De Ternille blinked in surprise. "Don't you have any concern for Mlle. de Brangelton's reputation?"

"I am most concerned about Mlle. de Brangelton's happiness and well-being."

"In that case, Comte, I suggest that you leave Paris, and allow me to dissipate vicious rumors about a certain resemblance between Charles d'Arringnon and Mlle. de Brangelton."

"Since when do you feel compelled to meddle in Mlle. de Brangelton's affairs?" Antoine dropped the courtly veneer.

De Ternille matched his tone. "We are discussing Mlle. de Brangelton's reputation, aren't we?"

"Do not concern yourself with Mlle. de Brangelton," Antoine wisely chose to end the debate. No one around them had paid any attention to the tennis match. "To borrow her favorite statement, go to hell."

Raoul pondered if Antoine's other second should be Lieutenant de Rousard or Henri de Brangelton.

Marquis swallowed. "Hell is not large enough for both of us," he growled. "Let the truth be known." He spun on his heel and walked through the parting crowd to the exit.

The tennis match resumed, and the heads of the spectators swiveled back to the tennis court.

"Your dearest Mlle. will be enraged when he blabbers

about Orleans," Raoul predicted. "Do I want to witness her violent reaction when she finds out the role you played? Or should I hide miles away?"

"This will repay my dearest Mlle. for, uh, never mind."

"For being herself?" Raoul prompted.

42

END OF CONFUSION

PARIS - MAY 1719

*I suspect our daughter and her worthy young man
aspire to marry without ever admitting their love for
each other. They will probably argue all the way to
the altar.*

Francis de Brangelton to Henrietta de Brangelton -
March 1719

To commemorate Duke Collingstone's visit to Paris,
a ball was held in the Town Hall. During the carriage ride,
Charlotte took inventory of the reasons to dread this glorious
occasion. Henri was assigned to thwart M. Patrice from making
a fool of himself, mother was in formal attendance to Duchess
Helene, father had found an excuse to regretfully forgo the
occasion, and Charlotte was left to her own devices, or, more
accurately, to the company of her dear Comte and his intolerable brother. Raoul had become her worst nightmare. With a

gleam in his eyes, he threatened to *"arrange for my brother to meet you alone,"* and, knowing Raoul, he would proceed to do so at the first opportunity. When the aforementioned brother offered to escort her to the ball, Charlotte reprimanded him that his duty was to formally introduce his younger brother around. Antoine reciprocated by reminding her that she owed him and Henri for the riddance of de Ternille, and when she countered with *"I am not conducting my personal affairs in your presence,"* his clenched jaw made her regret that he was not escorting her; that would prevent him from engaging de Ternille in any disputes.

"According to the latest circulating gossips," Henri said with reluctance, "there is general curiosity about why Mlle. de Brangelton's absence from the social scene coincides with the Comte de Flancourt's absence."

Charlotte softly hit the back of her head against the padded wall behind her. "Did anyone realize that Mlle. de Brangelton's absence also coincides with her brother's absence?"

"Apparently not. Everyone assumed I was occupied with my passions." Henri fired off the explanation without any trace of guilt.

"And now my reputation suffers because of your womanizing!" Charlotte pounded on the seat with her fist. "Fine brother you are. I certainly hope my dear Comte has the decency to deny any personal involvement with me."

"Who would believe him?" Henri snapped.

"You are worse than Raoul!"

Upon entering the ballroom, Charlotte and Henri went separate ways. Charlotte wandered to the furthest window to take the measure of the large and diverse crowd, and uneasily perceived speculative and envious glances in her direction. Duke Collingstone's entourage included de Ternille, de la Norte, de Chambreau, and her dear Comte. Henri seemed stunned after a brief consultation with de Contraille. He motioned to Raoul and de Brault, and they sauntered toward the group surrounding Patrice de Seveigney. Charlotte barely recognized the man at Cecilia de Fabvre's side. De Rameau had traded his uniform for a formal gray suit with yellow trim, powdered his hair, and firmly planted himself by her side. Was it he and Cecilia who had noted the coincidence of her and Antoine's absence?

"Mlle. Charlotte, I must speak to you in private." De Contraille's distressed voice at her side startled her.

"M. Geoffrey, what are you worried about?"

He guided her toward the table with refreshments. "Your brother feels I ought to warn you that de Flancourt challenged the Marquis de Ternille." He held his breath.

"What?" Charlotte fixed an icy glare at the nearest half a dozen courtiers who heard her exclamation over the music being played by three musicians in the opposite corner of the room. "When?"

"This morning." He broke off at the sight of the Marquise de Fabvre's fingers tightening around de Rameau's forearm as she gasped in Duke Collingstone's general direction.

"What is my dear Comte doing now?" Charlotte belatedly realized that she had uttered the question aloud. The spectacle across the room included the Comte de Flancourt and the Marquise de Ternille breathing fire at each other, Lord Stevenson stepping between them, Duke Collingstone gaping at them, de Chambreau's face draining of color, and de la Norte's face turning crimson. Henri was in mid-step, but Patrice de Seveigney held him back with a hand on his shoulder. Charlotte braced herself and headed toward the source of disturbance with de Contraille trailing on her heels.

Raoul blocked her way. "Don't even think about interfering," he hissed in the sudden, brittle silence of the ballroom. She did not even notice when the music had stopped.

Charlotte walked directly into him without slowing down, swayed her body at the last split moment, and shoved de Contraille into her place. While the men tangled in their unexpected struggle to keep balance, she left them behind and the only sound in the ballroom was the clicking of her heels on the marble floor.

"I beg your pardon, Your Grace." Charlotte's curtsy to Duke Collingstone was accompanied by the resumed music. "May I steal the Comte de Flancourt from you?"

Once again, Henri's day started earlier than he would have liked. At sunrise, de Bonnard showed up at his residence to warn him about the latest wide-spread speculations about de Flancourt and Charlotte, and Henri felt obligated to warn his sister. At Town Hall, Henri was confronted with yet another tale by de Contraille of the Comte de Flancourt's chivalrous actions on Mlle. Charlotte's behalf. Henri sent the flustered de Contraille to warn Charlotte; she could deal with her dear Comte. Since when did that epithet apply to Antoine? Henri had barely exchanged greetings with Patrice de Seveigney when dangerous silence descended into the room. Charlotte had risen to the occasion and effectively chained the source of the disturbance to her side. Now Antoine was obligated to attend on her for the rest of the evening. Charlotte had marched her dear Comte toward the musicians, commanded him to sit down next to her, and immersed herself in a study of the nearest chandelier. Antoine had immersed himself in talking to her profile.

"I am not speaking to you," Charlotte mouthed. He continued his monologue until she vehemently reacted in a short torrent of words, glared at de Ternille, and embarked on an extended response to Antoine. He interjected an objection, and a heated argument erupted. Most lovers quarreled with less passion than those two. For the first time since their arrival to Paris, Henri scrutinized Antoine and Charlotte. He leaned against the wall as amazement, comprehension, and certainty dawned on him. There was no love lost between them upon their arrival to Paris. When had it changed? November? December? By January for certain. The robe Antoine gifted to Charlotte probably cost more than all his farewell vases! Henri tentatively identified his unease as embarrassment. How did he fail to understand Charlotte's eagerness to dispose of all her admirers and the motives of Antoine's duels on her behalf? Their conversation in Senlis alone had been a glaring declaration, and yet Henri disregarded it at the time. Had the lack of sleep muddled his mind?

"I will kill her if she does not marry him," Henri concluded.

Henri plied Patrice de Seveigney with drink until the man could barely stand up straight, and then he arranged for Raoul and de Brault to escort the semi-conscious aristocrat to his residence. Then Henri sought out his sister and her devoted accomplice. "Shall we leave now?"

"Yes," Antoine answered. "Would you like to know what Lord Nelson expects of us?" He gallantly helped Charlotte into the carriage and unceremoniously took the seat next to her. Henri sat across from the again-not-speaking-to-each-other couple, and they rode in ominous silence. Upon reaching their destination, Henri abandoned Antoine to assist his prickly flower in descending from the carriage and hurried inside to pour brandy into small goblets. The couple marched and Charlotte gulped the contents of the goblet before dropping into the armchair. Undeterred by her icy demeanor, Antoine planted himself on the armrest. Henri replaced his goblet with a larger one and refilled it.

Francis woke up early and quietly dressed. He descended the stairs and surveyed the peacefully slumbering Henri and Antoine. Had they managed to hide Antoine's latest action to distinguish himself as the violently-inclined admirer of Mlle. de Brangelton? Unlikely, since by early afternoon yesterday, everyone had been dissecting the morning scene at the tennis courts.

Upon an echoing knock at the front door, Henri and Antoine jumped off their respective settee and chair. Red Jacques peeked out of the window and gaped with amazement. "The Marquis de Ternille to see you, M. Francis," he announced.

"Why?" Henri yawned.

Antoine grabbed his sword.

Henri scooped up Antoine's clothes, shoes, and sword, and tossed all items to him. "Go to Charlotte's room. Father, will you hand him the key?" Henri's implication rendered Antoine incredulous to the point of almost dropping his belongings before he caught the key and sprinted upstairs two steps at the time. In a moment, he disappeared inside and locked the door behind him.

"A true moment of brilliance, my son. I am proud of you." Francis motioned to Jacques to admit their illustrious visitor.

"Comte de Tournelles, I apologize for disturbing you at such an impolitely early hour." The Marquis paused in observation of Henri, who made a large show of being preoccupied with the buttons of his doublet. "I was hoping to discuss the most important matter with you alone. Confidentially."

Henri acknowledging de Ternille with a curt nod and sauntered to the door.

The Marquis sat in the preferred chair and carefully arranged his body and clothes for ultimate comfort and display. "Comte de Tournelles. I believe you are well aware that I truly wish to marry Mlle. de Brangelton. I fervently hope you approve of the match."

"Is she aware of your intentions?"

"Yes, most certainly, she realizes my sincere feelings," he prevaricated. "Unfortunately, there has been a regrettable complication."

"And what is that?"

"May I be completely frank with you? Mlle. Charlotte and her brother are quite inseparable." De Ternille exhaled in resignation. "Alas, Comte de Flancourt is quite inseparable from them. I repeat, Comte de Tournelles, that I wish and intend, with all my heart, to marry Mlle. de Brangelton, despite the disturbing rumors of her affair with the Comte de Flancourt," he stated generously. "The same de Flancourt who threatened me. You understand, of course, that my position in society does not allow me to engage in the uncivilized matter of forbidden dueling."

"Of course." Francis genuinely appreciated the man's determination to fulfil his ambition by any safe and creative means. Blackmail, for example.

"Thus, Comte de Tournelles, encouraging de Flancourt to leave Paris will certainly serve our common interests," Marquis proposed. "In his absence, I could possibly convince Mlle. de Brangelton to marry me, before any vicious rumors cause enormous damage to her reputation."

"Marquis de Ternille," Francis said, choosing the civil route. "If my daughter chose to marry you, there would be no need for any subterfuge. I would raise no objections. You are a worldly and intelligent man, Marquis. Do you indeed desire for a willful, courageous, and devious wife whose heart belongs to another man?"

Antoine noiselessly closed Charlotte's bedroom door. He deposited his clothes and sword on the chair and placed his shoes under it. He was finally alone with Charlotte, despite her very skillful pretended ignorance and stubborn avoidance of all his attempts to discuss their personal affairs.

Charlotte's tousled hair covered her face, just as he remembered it from Lonjumeau, when he glanced at her in the morning and felt happy about the uneventful night. Antoine forced himself to look away. Her hat with the blue feather hung above the dressing mirror. On the table beneath it, containers of never-used rouge and hair powder sat on top of each other. An assortment of cream jars, decorative boxes with hair pins, ribbons, dress laces, brushes, and a dozen of perfume bottles crowded the space. Charlotte never used the exact same perfume twice. She played with mixing different ones. He unfolded the note tucked into the mirror frame. *"Charlotte de Brangelton, I believe the colors of this sword shoulder strap perfectly match your favorite travel hat. Antoine de Flancourt."*

The heavy blue and yellow drapes covered the windows as he remembered, but Charlotte had added sheer white curtains to admit light and to provide privacy. The linens were embroidered with floral patterns of blue, yellow, and red, and a modest amount of lace trimmed the pillows. A map of the world covered one wall and a woodcut of a horse brightened the space opposite from it. Besides the hat, Charlotte's special touches were man's boots by the bed, her knife within easy reach, and her sword and embroidered shoulder belt hanging on the bed post by her head.

Antoine's bare feet made no sound when he walked to the window to peek outside and saw Henri sauntering away. He glanced again at the dresser, and lost his ethical battle to curiosity about the notes carelessly thrown into a carved wooden bowl. He briefly glanced at de Vergne's sonnets, tossed back de Rameau's ledger of fencing round wagers, and skimmed the notes from de la Norte - polite and respectful, as expected. *"Wildcat,"* started the affectionate greeting from Raoul's long letter written in January, and most of his epistle was almost word-by-word a recital of the letter he had sent to Antoine, mainly describing fencing school and Troyes. *"I anticipate defeating you in a fencing round,"* it read. *"Do not even think about using de la Norte- the man has no common sense, I suppose? - as an excuse to avoid paying up when you lose. You must explain our wager to him. I do not want to cause any trouble for my brother. Now, about my singing -"*

The bedsheets rustled. Charlotte rolled over onto her back and her hair spilled on the pillow. She opened her dreamy eyes and leisurely stretched. Antoine gathered his remaining wits to wish her good morning, but Charlotte sat up and the blanket slid off her bare arms. Speech failed him. Charlotte hiked up the modest neckline of her sleeveless nightshift, rubbed her temples, swung her very shapely legs over the side of the bed and felt for the slippers. Her half-aware gaze swept around the room. Upon the sight of him, Charlotte frantically leapt out of bed. Her nightshift and blanket tangled up, and she would have tumbled down if Antoine had not caught her.

"Oh, no, you don't."

Antoine motioned for silence. "Your father has a visitor," he whispered.

"Hand me the dressing gown." Charlotte twisted out of his arms when he reached for it. He held the garment up for her. Charlotte seized it and managed to hold the dressing gown in front of her while thrusting one arm into the sleeve. She pulled the other sleeve over her other arm, and finished the ensemble by tying the belt with a mariner's knot. They softly treaded toward the door and leaned against it, but could hear nothing. Antoine brought a cup with watered wine to Charlotte. She drunk some, handed it back to him, and walked toward the window to peek out.

A loud knock at the door startled them. "Charlotte!" her mother called.

Charlotte stood motionless long enough for Antoine to cross the room and open the door.

The stunned Mme. Henrietta, dressed in men's clothing and armed with pistols, wordlessly surveyed the scene. Antoine's heart leapt at the realization that Mme. Henrietta, as well as M. Francis behind her, were leaving for their trip.

Charlotte faltered. "Mother! I have no idea what he is doing here."

"We will see you in a couple of weeks." M. Francis kissed his daughter's head, nodded to Antoine, took his wife by the elbow, and nudged her away.

"Francis! Explain to me what is happening in this house." Mme. Henrietta's voice faded as they descended the stairs and out of hearing distance.

Antoine was left alone with Charlotte on his own terms.

"Get out of my bedroom," she said.

Antoine slammed the door closed and locked it. "Charlotte..."

She pushed him away. "No, you don't."

"Charlotte!" Antoine wrapped his arms around her lithe body, perfectly molded to his.

"Don't even think about it!"

"Think about what?" Somewhere in the back of his mind, a

voice of reason reminded him that if Charlotte had decided to free herself, he would have a black eye by now.

"I shall not have an affair with you!" Charlotte shook him by the shoulders. "If you want me, you will have to marry me!"

Antoine was rendered speechless for a heartbeat by that blessed declaration. "Shall we marry tomorrow?"

Her dark blue eyes were brilliant. "You are not serious!"

"I am serious!" He caressed the smooth skin of her neck. "Damn serious."

"But -" Charlotte uttered.

He was in no condition to discuss anything. "Marry me, Charlotte de Brangelton." He kissed the corner of her mouth.

"And -"

"Say yes."

"Yes, Antoine de la Fleure, my dear Comte de Flancourt." Charlotte wrapped her arms around his neck. She was very reasonable when she chose to be.

EPILOGUE

PARIS – JUNE 1719

*Anything can be justified and explained, but not
necessarily accepted and corrected.*

Francis de Brangelton to Paul d'Ornille – 1690

FRANCIS' THREAT TO ASSIST ANTOINE IN RECONCILING THE
state of affairs between the young man and his beloved
produced the desired outcome. The couple finally ended their
juvenile stand off and rejoiced in perfect understanding. The
gossip about them (They traveled together in Orleans last
autumn! Does her brother even care?!) had entertained the
society of Paris until the young reprobates recalled their noble
responsibilities and obligations. The Comte Antoine de Flancourt and Chevalier Henri de Brangelton promptly acted on
the behalf of their fathers and requested (and received) a Royal
dispensation for the marriage of the Comte de Flancourt and
Mlle.de Brangelton. By the time Francis and Henrietta

returned and the Comte and Comtesse de Chatreaux arrived in Paris (for Marguerite became frustrated by the couple's ludicrous behavior as vividly depicted in Henrietta's letters), the gossips had dwindled to the admiration of Mlle. de Brangelton's betrothal jewelry. The Comte de Flancourt, in the best traditions of the de la Fleure family, had chosen a large cushion-cut diamond surrounded by emeralds and dark blue sapphires for his betrothed.

The Duke of Orleans generously permitted the couple to exchange the marriage vows at the sacred jewel of Sainte-Chapelle, and Francis proudly walked his daughter to the altar. The ceremony commenced, and his thoughts strayed. He always knew that eventually his girl would leave home and blend into another family, but he still felt a pang of sadness that it was happening so soon. Even if that family consisted of his and Henrietta's best friends, people who knew and loved Charlotte, and Antoine was the best-suited man for the girl. Francis pushed away the uninvited philosophical musings and reveled in the moment. True happiness was love of your spouse and pride in your children, and he wished that for the young couple.

The sun illuminated the stained glass windows, the diffused light flooding the interior with red, gold, blue, and green jeweled clouds and brightening the vivid colors of the wedding party. Charlotte looked exquisite in her new lapis-blue, English-style, close-fitting gown with jade-green trim and underskirt. Antoine wore the uniform of the de la Fleure family, a dark green jacket and breeches along with a checkered white and gold waistcoat. His father had chosen a dark green suit with gold trim, and Raoul proudly displayed a gray waistcoat to play off his Musketeer future. Marguerite looked fine in an olive-green gown, while Henrietta was young and handsome in her stylish maroon dress. Henri wore his favorite outfit with an excessive amount of braids and embroidery on the cuffs, lapels, pocket flaps, seams, and edges, all topped off with a black and gold waistcoat. Among all that glitter (even Henri's shoe buckles were gilded, and there was enough lace on the guests' cravats and flounces to make a full petticoat), Francis himself wore his best formal attire, black breeches and jacket with cherry-colored cuffs and lapels. The black and gold embroidery on his own waistcoat matched Henri's excesses.

Francis smiled at the misty-eyed Henrietta and Marguerite, glanced at the proud-looking Laurent de la Fleure and Paul d'Ornille, and winked at the grinning Henri and Raoul. He silently paid tribute to his and Henrietta's families in the New World. The future of mankind lay there, where the government was local and flexible to suit the denizens even when the semblance of order bordered on chaos. The world fate would be different if the power and glory of France hadn't been irrevocably destroyed by Louis XIV's religious intolerance. The absolute, unlimited, unchecked power of either the monarchy or the Church destroyed nations. The Venetian Republic shrunk when the Doges cut off the flow of any new ideas and influences. Russia rose when the Tsar brought in foreigners. The Spanish Empire collapsed when the Inquisition gained prominence. Now England, secured by her mighty Navy, vast overseas colonies, and rowdy Parliament, stood poised for worldwide dominance. Where would Fate guide Antoine and Charlotte if Louis XV were to start to imitate his predecessor?

For the near future, Henri had arranged for Charlotte and Antoine to spend a tranquil week in the village of Versailles. After that idyllic interlude, they planned to spend the summer in Lyon. Would they chase after the missing trunk full of lascivious portraits, or delegate that enterprise to Henri and Raoul?

Duke Collingstone attended the wedding with Her Grace Helene de Seveigney, the Dowager Duchess Montmurrant.

Francis briefly contemplated if His English Grace had acquired any suspicion about Blanchard's identity, but so far he seemed oblivious to any resemblance. Francis fractionally inclined his head to acknowledge the Regent who discreetly stayed in the back pew, and returned his attention to the ceremony. The intonations of Cardinal de la Fleury's speech indicated that he was concluding the long-winded sermon on the blessings and benefits of marriage.

Le Havre, France – September 1719

This mystery of the cargo exchange intrigued Francis. He, his brother Batiste Bradforde, and Daniel Rabatin had been partners for many years, ever since Rabatin set up the first storage space in the old abandoned dungeon. Their holdings included a large shorefront property along with a larger fortified building within the city limits, and two more within an hour's ride. The trunks destined for inland storage were recorded and claimed in the shore warehouse, and transported back and forth under armed guard, carefully selected by Francis and Batiste from soldiers of fortune formerly in the royal military or seafaring. Rabatin was a diligent and competent man, with an acute sense of danger and intrigue, and Francis trusted him not to switch the trunks on his own will, free or otherwise. Their system of keeping records was efficient but simple: Rates were based on the size of the goods, storage duration, and location; the identification system was highly confidential and impersonal. The first number was a code for the size and shape of the container, and the second number was for identification. For each and every transaction, Rabatin issued a document containing these numbers, a description of the container, the date of transaction, the location of the warehouse, and stamped warehouse identification seals. The same information was diligently recorded in the official books in the client's presence. No one, except Francis, Batiste, and Rabatin, knew that, after the client paid and left, a brief description of the client, and the name if known, was recorded in a secret ledger stored in a vault designed by Francis, built by Rabatin, and closed with a hidden mechanism provided by Batiste.

Francis shut the door of the back room. "I need to check the records starting in 1712, about cargo belonging to Captain Mathew Johnson of the *Golden Sails*."

"The name sounds familiar." Rabatin went to the secret vault, pushed the hidden lever, moved the uncovered mechanism, and retrieved the unofficial ledger. He carefully placed the ledger on top of the desk, unlocked the drawer, pulled the official records, and opened them next to the unofficial ledger.

"The Captain stored his property inland," he read off the page. "Brought two trunks in 1713. One measured four feet long and two feet wide. Another was five feet long and three feet wide."

"Tell me about the larger one."

"Johnson came back in 1716. Page one-twenty-seven." he supplied.

Francis took possession of the unofficial ledger. "With an artist, a short man, about forty years of age, with a gray-brown curly moustache," he read. "The trunk was returned to the warehouse. Six months later, the artist came back with a nobleman about thirty-five years of age, who had a protruding chin, powdered hair, brown eyes, slightly shorter than average height. That's when the ownership changed." He felt they were on the right path. "Look for another trunk of the same description. It would have been brought after 1712, most likely, to the inland warehouse."

"Yes, a trunk of the same shape and dimensions was brought in four months after Johnson's... page two-forty-one," Rabatin said. "The same trunk was retrieved in 1716. Two months later, the owner brought along a mercenary and ranted that his possessions were replaced!"

"I remember your letter." Francis did not bother to correct that mercenary was, in reality, a Knight of St. John. Was there even a difference? "Any idea how the valuable cargo inside this trunk could have been switched with Johnson's?"

It took Rabatin a few moments to understand the implication of this question. "Switched?" He gasped, the color draining from his face. "No, it is impossible, you know that! How could anyone switch the trunks' contents?"

"It happened."

"How?" Rabatin sank back in distress. "No, both trunks were sealed before the return to the warehouse. They had different numbers."

Francis flipped from page to page of the records, looking for two similar numbers. He reached for a blank sheet of paper, tore it in half, wrote the numbers on each, and held the pieces of paper at a distance. He stood up and moved away from the light. For certain, he knew the answer. "Were these trunks stored side by side?"

Rabatin rubbed his forehead. "Possibly."

"Probably," Francis corrected. "The size and style of these trunks is very common. Johnson deposited his trunk first. The other man brought his precious cargo in a few months later. Next, the contents of Johnson's trunk were verified and the trunk was re-sealed and stored. Now, Rabatin, tell me again, what are the chances that these trunks were located side by side?"

"High." His partner swallowed non-existent moisture in his mouth.

"When the unknown owner retrieved his trunk, he did not check the contents, did he?"

"No, that I remember clearly," Rabatin confirmed. "That proved my suspicion that the man wanted to keep the transaction a secret."

"Now, I am willing to wager that when Johnson's trunk was retrieved, no one checked its contents either."

Rabatin's hands shook. "Still, the trunks were clearly labeled."

"With numbers." Francis tossed both pieces of paper onto the table to test his theory. "Identical numbers, Rabatin."

"No, it's impossible! The numbers on these papers are identical."

"Look at these numbers closely."

Rabatin sat back down and picked up the pieces of paper. His eyes darted from one to another. "It's the same number on both... No!" Horrified at the coincidence, he choked on the exclamation, and slowly raised his eyes.

"Johnson's trunk was labeled 28-866, while the other was 28-886," Francis confirmed. "These numbers were misread and mistaken for another. Twice. Neither owner checked the contents of the trunks. Twice. What were the chances of that?"

Dear reader,

We hope you enjoyed reading *The Legend of Marshall Cousins*. Please take a moment to leave a review, even if it's a short one. Your opinion is important to us.

Discover more books by Z.A. Angell at https://www. nextchapter.pub/authors/za-angell-historical-fiction-author? rq=angell

Want to know when one of our books is free or discounted? Join the newsletter at http://eepurl.com/bqqB3H

Best regards,

Z.A. Angell and the Next Chapter Team

ABOUT THE AUTHOR

As long as Z.A. Angell can remember, she has always loved reading books with intricate plots, memorable characters, swashbuckling adventure, and lively dialogue. The books fueled her imagination; a myriad of her own literary creations inhabited her mind throughout the teen years.

These imaginary friends went into deep hibernation when she graduated from California State University, partied in Los Angeles, and embarked on the career in a corporate world. When the daily drudgery in a drab cubicle threatened to erode her soul, reading fiction became a virtual escape. Slowly but surely, her own literary characters reappeared in her mind and demanded attention. She had no choice but to pick up a proverbial pen and to start narrating their adventures. There was no return.

The Legacy of the Marshall Cousins is Z.A. Angell's first completed novel. She is currently working on the second book which takes place twenty years before the Marshall Cousins wrecked chaos in Marseille. She is fascinated with the historical time period of late 1600s to early 1700s. - That was the era of discoveries, opportunities, rapid changes in social norms and behaviors, and anything seemed possible. - That was the dawn of the modern world where people's dreams, hopes and motivations were similar to current times. The temptation to draw parallels through the centuries inspired her to write two short stories: currently published *Clare and Axel* and the upcoming *Clare in Marseille*.

Z.A. Angell, her husband, and their daughter live in Southern California. Away from writing, she enjoys hiking on local trails, hanging out at the beach, and, of course, reading. She also takes time to check out Marvel and Star Wars movies, and to listen to good old rock-and-roll music.

The Legacy Of The Marshall Cousins
ISBN: 978-4-86752-790-0

Published by
Next Chapter
1-60-20 Minami-Otsuka
170-0005 Toshima-Ku, Tokyo
+818035793528

6th August 2021

Lightning Source UK Ltd.
Milton Keynes UK
UKHW040650190722
406066UK00002B/390